# Charlotte Dent

## A NOVEL

Morgan Richter

Luft Books
www.luftbooks.com

This book is a work of fiction. Names, characters, places, and incidents either are products of the author's imagination or are used fictitiously. Any resemblance to actual events or locales or persons, living or dead, is entirely coincidental.

Copyright © 2014 Morgan Richter

Published in the United States by Luft Books.
www.luftbooks.com

IBSN 978-0-9909367-2-5

Cover art by Elsbeth Monnett

**PRAISE FOR *CHARLOTTE DENT*:**

"The unrelenting grimness of an aspiring actor's struggles, the stress of cattle-call auditions, the shabbiness of Equity-waiver blackbox theatre, the indulgences that come with big-budget moviemaking and the trauma of being mistreated by a prima donna director on a low-budget art film are all depicted with entertaining authenticity. From start to end, this is a crisp, fun treatment of Hollywood life."

—*Publishers Weekly* (review of an unpublished manuscript version written for judging purposes for the 2008 Amazon Breakthrough Novel Award)

## CHAPTER ONE

CHARLOTTE'S HEELS CLICKED on marble, professional and correct, as she navigated past the stone urns overloaded with white lilies and lemon leaves that flanked the entrance to the reception area. Always lilies, fresh every Monday, except throughout December when they were swapped for white poinsettias. The reception desk swept up from the floor in a high dark curve, a ship's bow rising from a dead gray sea. The firm's name in hammered silver letters lit with pinpoint lights hung on the storm-colored wall above Frieda's head. The font, the spindly letters that appeared on all the firm's stationary and publications, was trademarked by and named for the firm: Ausberger.

At the desk, Frieda's posture was impeccable, her eyes fixed on her monitor screen. She spoke into her headset in a modulated stream of words, a near-constant rhythm of repeated speech: "Ausberger Bender Bob. Thank you. Ausberger Bender Bob. Thank you." One hand hovered just above the switchboard, the pad of one finger pressing buttons in rapid succession. This was a cultivated skill, the ability to infuse her voice with the proper balance of warmth and professionalism while connecting callers to the appropriate party. Charlotte had manned the switchboard for one white-knuckled afternoon after Frieda had gone home with a bad case of food poisoning, and her nerves still hadn't recovered.

Easy to spot the celebrity in the trio of individuals seated on the charcoal suede armchairs, even if Charlotte hadn't known her on sight. Paragon Dufresne was a splotch of vivid color against all the muted grays, her strapless sundress the color of an ocean someplace Charlotte had never been. Saint-Tropez, maybe. Barbados. Crete. Pale hair, pulled off her face with a scarf, fell in an uninterrupted spill of a white sand beach over one shoulder. She was tiny and bronzed, primped and polished, her small face dominated by gigantic white sunglasses.

Charlotte walked over to the assembled group. "Good morning. Are you here to see Marti Bob?" Face hot, heartbeat erratic. Huh. Nervous. Intimidated, even, by this wisp of a girl, this pop star of indeterminate talent, maybe ten years her junior, better known for her romantic escapades than her body of work.

The man in the chair beside Paragon jumped to his feet. "That's right. I'm Josh." He thrust out a hand. Charlotte took it, hoping hers wasn't sweaty or sticky. "That's Paragon, and the other one's Charity."

Paragon's appeal was such Charlotte had barely noted the girl beside her. Cutoff jean shorts and flip-flops, ironed platinum hair. Thin and tan and plain, a low-wattage version of her more-famous older sister. Charity played with the phone in her lap and didn't look up at her dad's introduction.

Josh grinned, wide and natural. He seemed too young and energetic to be the father of teenagers. Shiny tanned face, yellow polo shirt, white shorts, whiter teeth. Too casual for a business appointment, all of them, but this was Los Angeles. He looked like a youth pastor at a church camp, or a charismatic cult leader. "Are you Marti's assistant?"

"That's right. I'm Charlotte. If you'll follow me, Marti will be with you in a minute."

"You bet. Girls?"

Expressionless behind her sunglasses, Paragon got to her feet and picked up her purse, a woven straw monstrosity best suited for toting magazines and bottles of suntan lotion to the beach. Charity didn't take her attention away from whatever captured her interest on her phone's tiny screen. Without looking up, she fell in line behind her sister.

Charlotte led the procession to the big conference room. She heard a brief scuffle behind her, followed by an explosive burst of giggles. "Dude, you farted."

Hard to tell which of the little darlings it was. "Did not. You liar. It was you." More giggles, jostling, possibly the sound of someone knuckle-punching someone on the arm.

"You did. I can smell it."

"It's not me. This place smells bad."

"Girls, come on." Josh's tone was indulgent even in a reprimand.

Charlotte took a discreet whiff. The office smelled like it always did, like copy machine toner and chemical air freshener.

Whispers behind her back, a chorus of hushed giggles. Charlotte felt her back muscles tensing as though she expected to be attacked. They weren't necessarily talking about her, mocking her, but they could be.

It was time to make an adjustment. She flexed her feet inside her shoes. Black pumps, some synthetic material made to look like shiny patent leather, cheap and scuffed yet not without style. They didn't make the same satisfying click on the gray carpet as they did on marble, but she focused on placing one foot in front of the other in measured paces, heel-toe, heel-toe. Get into character from the feet up. That was one of the first things she'd learned in a lifetime of drama classes. This situation called for summoning up an alternate version of Charlotte Dent, one better equipped to handle Paragon and her sister.

Moving up through her spine now. . . She relaxed her shoulders, let the tension at her neck uncoil. Her eyebrows lifted, her chin raised. At the next round of giggles from behind, she moved her head to the right, not turning all the way around, moving nothing beside her head and neck, letting them know she'd marked their antics and, like any self-respecting high-level assistant in a formal corporate environment would be, was Not Amused.

It worked. Hot dog. The giggles stilled. She faced front once again, eyebrows still high.

She held the door to the conference room open while the procession trooped in. "I'll make sure Marti knows you're here. Would anyone care for coffee or water?"

"Coffee's great, thanks, Charlotte." Josh grinned.

Aw. He'd remembered her name. One point for him. "Cream, sugar?"

"Do you have soy milk?" That was Paragon, and she seemed genuinely invested in the answer.

"Of course." The lobby shop carried soy milk, probably.

Paragon grinned, her smile almost as charming as her dad's, and Charlotte forgave her a bit for being so pretty and ill-mannered. Charity didn't look up from her phone.

When Charlotte left the conference room, Marti was pacing up and down the hallway, agitated. She was bright-eyed sparrow of a woman, spindly and small-boned and sharp. She frowned at Charlotte. "Is she in there? Have you gone downstairs yet?"

"I'm just on my way." It sounded defensive. Charlotte smiled to take away any bite.

"Pick up a box of tampons and leave them in my top desk drawer. I'll owe you one."

"No problem."

Marti patted her arm once and went into the conference room.

The little shop in the lobby was well-stocked for Charlotte's purposes. She picked up half a dozen muffins, a couple of crois-sants, a plastic container of mixed fruit: blackberries, shaved coconut, honeydew chunks and halved strawberries. Ah, there was Paragon's soy milk. She snagged Marti's tampons and paid for her bundle with her overused debit card, making sure to get a receipt.

Charlotte stashed the tampons in Marti's drawer and headed for the lunchroom with her bags of goodies. The coffee, in a graceful silver percolator, had finished brewing. She arranged everything on a tray—food, coffee, porcelain cups and matching tiny plates, the linen napkins with the company monogram that were kept in the locked cupboard above the sink—and headed for the conference room.

Marti was in with the Dufresne family. Charlotte tapped on the door once, then glanced through the side window to catch Marti's attention. Marti gestured for her to come in. She looked tense and humorless.

Josh broke off whatever he'd been saying to grin at her. "Cof-fee! Fantastic."

Charlotte set down the tray. Charity didn't look up, her atten-tion on her hands. She'd peeled off her nail polish, leaving flakes the color of dried blood on the table, like a pile of picked scabs. Paragon, sunglasses still on, stared out the window at the tall, shiny buildings of Century City, Fox and MGM and CAA, all whispering promises of success and fulfillment of wishes.

Music broke in, a loud snippet of a pop song, a breathy voice gasping unintelligible lyrics. Paragon frowned, pulled out her phone, glanced at the display, and stuck it back in her purse. The ringtone continued for a few seconds longer before stopping. The song was familiar, something currently in heavy rotation on radio stations Charlotte didn't listen to. One of Paragon's own songs, maybe.

Charlotte set the soy milk down in front of Paragon. Paragon smiled at her. "Oh, thanks."

Charlotte smiled back and left, annoyed at feeling star-struck again.

Marti wouldn't need her until the meeting was over, so she headed back to her desk. Typed up a letter for Dale, did some photocopying. Waited.

Commotion in the reception area, the Dufresne girls yapping like Pomeranians, Marti and Josh exchanging pleasantries. The meeting was over. She went to the conference room.

One of the croissants had been eaten. That was Josh, she was willing to bet. In front of Charity's seat, next to the pile of nail polish peelings, stood the lonely bottom halves of four muffins, their crowns missing. Three half-full coffee cups, one of them Marti's. Paragon's cup was unused, the soy milk unopened, the fruit plate untouched.

This end of the hall was quiet. Dale's and Ken's office doors were open, their computer screens dark. Out to lunch, probably, maybe somewhere in nearby Beverly Hills where they could linger over porterhouse steaks and *pommes frites* while discussing cases.

Marti popped her head into Dale's office. "The guys go to lunch already?"

"I think so. I didn't see them leave," Charlotte said.

"Damn them. I told them I'd be done by one." Marti frowned. "Is the conference room cleaned up?"

"Yes. Do you need anything else, or can I take my lunch now?"

"Go ahead," Marti said. She looked tired and irritated. At moments like this, when Marti seemed human, it was easy to feel bad for her. It couldn't be easy, viewing each day as an endless series of minute negotiations, analyzing every action for possible slights. Charlotte did plenty of that herself, and she was an amateur compared to Marti. "Dan just called and said he's on his way in, so you won't need to cover my phone this afternoon."

She laughed, a thin, uneven sound unsupported by genuine feeling. She leaned against the small stretch of wall between Dale's and Ken's offices and folded her arms across her chest. With mild horror, Charlotte realized she was settling in for a chat. Girl talk. "He took the morning off for an audition. I knew I shouldn't have hired an actor."

"Did he say what the audition was for?" Good for Dan. She'd grill him about it later.

Marti examined the nails of one hand. "I don't know. A car commercial or something. He said it didn't go well."

"That's too bad," Charlotte said. A car commercial meant a big national campaign. The auditions were hard to come by, and the competition was always stiff, but landing one could've changed Dan's life.

"I'm sure his parents appreciate shelling out money for acting classes so he can star in commercials." Marti smiled, the thin bones of her face standing out tight. "I'm glad you're not into any of that business, Charlotte. You've got more sense than Dan."

Charlotte was still for a moment. Her skin was too thin today. Marti wasn't being snide. She didn't know. Marti never paid attention to her life outside the office, and why on earth should she?

It wasn't worth explaining. Charlotte smiled, noncommittal, and waited for Marti to head back to her own office. She left the letter she'd typed for Dale on his desk so he could sign it upon his return.

A flicker of movement at the window made her pause. She looked closer.

A bird was on the windowsill, a pigeon. Unusual to see one this high up. She approached the glass.

The pigeon seemed to register her movements on the other side of the window. Its head bobbed from side to side in bursts of frenetic motion. She could see the details of its feathers and the bright glint of its beadlike eyes.

It bobbed up and down, scooted a bit to the side on the thin windowsill. Careful not to startle it, she moved closer. She placed her palm against the glass just opposite it.

It could see her, and it wasn't afraid. It seemed to be trying to get inside, confounded by the illusion of the window. It hopped to the side and teetered. She stayed very still.

The pigeon hopped backward off the ledge and disappeared from sight. She glanced down to see if it had taken flight, but saw nothing. Maybe it was flying, swooping through the air, its brain no longer clinging to what had been its most important goal moments earlier.

Looking straight down from this height gave her vertigo, even with her forehead pressed against the thick glass and her hands braced against the sill. She left the office and went to lunch.

## Chapter Two

TRINKET WAS FEELING creative tonight. That couldn't be good. From the back of the class, Charlotte watched as Trinket plopped a sturdy file box on the stage and extracted oversize envelopes from it.

"Take one and pass them down. Boys take the white ones, girls get the yellow. Don't open them yet." Trinket padded across the room, bare feet sticking out of her wide-legged pants, eyes barely visible behind a bush of yellow-gray hair. "Wait until everyone's got one, then I'll tell you what we're going to be doing."

A tap on her shoulder. Charlotte turned and saw Bob. "Hey, Chuck. Are you going to Heaven tonight?"

She thought a bit and deduced, correctly, that Bob was referring to the nightclub on Las Palmas. "Should I be?"

"Alumni night. Networking. Half-price drinks. Free eats until nine. They have it every month. You should go."

How did Bob know about these things? "Are you going straight from here? Can you give me a ride?"

She didn't want to go. She wanted to take the bus home from class and go to bed early. But Bob had said the magic word—networking—and she was trying to do as much of that as possible. Even if it killed her.

"Sure, if you can find your own way home." Bob didn't offer a reason. Maybe he had late-night plans, maybe he didn't want the responsibility of playing chauffeur to get in the way of hooking up with someone at the club.

"No problem. Thanks." The envelopes reached the back of the room. They took theirs, making sure to get their gender-appropriate colors, and awaited further instruction from Trinket.

Trinket held her hands in front of her chest, palms and fingers touching. Spine ramrod straight, feet turned out, posed like a brass statue of Shiva. "In your hands is today's assignment. Each of you has a scene from a brand-new play from a contemporary playwright. Your part will be marked. First of all, you need to find your scene partner. Then you and your partner will have fifteen minutes to read through your scene and create your character. Remember all we've learned thus far about character study. Go."

Did drama class really need to be run like a game show? She opened her envelope. Already students were milling about, peeking onto others' script pages in search of their scene partner. She looked at her scene and saw she was playing someone named Harmony. Her lines were highlighted. Trinket must have spent the whole day highlighting lines and sticking script pages into envelopes. Harmony's scene was opposite someone named Addie. She looked around for her Addie.

Oh, hell. It was Melissa. Melissa had the matching scene, only with Addie's lines highlighted. Melissa was glossy and beautiful and lifeless, a low-wattage vortex that dragged her scene partners into the abyss with her. Charlotte had never worked with Melissa. She might be a lovely person, and Charlotte might be a rat for thinking so poorly of her. She smiled at Melissa and held up her script. "I think we're partners."

Melissa looked at her and shrugged and didn't say anything. She looked down at the scene, then up at Charlotte. "What are we supposed to be doing with this again?" she asked.

"Read through it. Figure out our characters, discuss them with each other. Perform it."

"Oh." Melissa looked back down at the pages for a long time. "Am I Harmony or. . . how's that pronounced?"

"Addie. I think that's you. See, your lines are highlighted."

"Oh." Melissa looked at her pages again, eyes fixed on the brief lines of character description at the top of the page. Charlotte read them, too: *Harmony is a beautiful, strong-willed sixteen-year-old impoverished Appalachian girl who has become pregnant by Thomas, the governor's son. In this scene, her God-fearing, tyrannical mother Addie throws her out of the house for what she perceives as a mortal sin.*

"So I'm supposed to be an old lady?" Melissa wrinkled her nose.

"You're the mother of a sixteen-year-old. You might not be exactly ancient."

Melissa thought about it for a moment. "I think I'd had have a better understanding of the other character, the girl. We should probably switch."

Because the Melissas of the world tended to get under her skin more than they should, Charlotte let her dangle. "The focus of the class is on developing characters. Good practice to play a character you're not comfortable with."

The look Melissa gave her was so humorless and filled with so much dislike Charlotte was sorry she'd bothered. She shrugged. "If you really want to switch, I don't care."

"Thanks." Melissa beamed at her, best friends forever, and handed her the script pages. "It makes more sense. I'm just a young girl. It's not like I'd ever be called on to play an old lady."

"Fair enough." It wasn't. Charlotte should forget about it and move on. In the long run, this attitude would stunt Melissa's future growth as an actor. In theory. In reality, the Melissas tended to do quite well for themselves, thank you very much. "Should we read?"

They did. The dialogue was bad on the page, leaden and obvious. That didn't mean anything; good performers could deliver clumsy lines with grace. Melissa was stumbling and stilted, her inflections wrong, her delivery that of a child mangling the Scriptures at a Nativity pageant.

Melissa stopped mid-sentence. She reached into her pocket and extracted her vibrating phone, then frowned at the display screen.

"It's my agent. I need to take this," she said. She moved to the door and stepped into the hallway, already talking.

Agent. Melissa had an agent. That didn't mean anything. It wasn't a quantifiable measure of success. It didn't mean Melissa was on the road to somewhere whereas Charlotte was doomed to a life of photocopying and fetching coffee.

Alone, Charlotte flipped through the scene and arranged her thoughts. Addie. Maybe forty, maybe just under. Appalachians. Alabama, maybe? The scene was written in heavy Southern dialect, which made it worse. Trinket loved accents. Loved, loved, loved them. Charlotte could do accents with research and practice, but improvising one would take concentration away from other aspects of her performance.

Addie. Charlotte had to find a way into Addie's head, just from these pages. Addie was furious with her knocked-up teen daughter, and maybe Charlotte could understand that. Maybe "furious" wasn't right. She was cold and hard, and her anger came from a place of righteousness, not emotion. Harmony had violated the law of the roof by sleeping around, even if it was with the governor's son. Maybe that made it worse. She'd gone and slept with someone who wasn't part of their social class. Class distinctions were something Charlotte understood.

Addie's life would center around the church. What would she be? Southern Baptist, maybe, something along those lines? Something inflexible, something that formed the core of Addie's life. If Addie had any vanity, it would lie in her never-spoken belief God favored her for her stoicism and adherence to the Bible, her quiet assurance of milk and honey at the end of the mortal trail.

Now was the time to feel her way into the character from the floor on up. Footwear wasn't much help; Charlotte wore ballet flats, whereas Addie's shoes would be solid and utilitarian. Her feet hurt, though, and Addie's would, too, all the time. Addie, her Addie, would be sturdy and unbowed. She took her strength from a higher power, and she'd want to stand tall.

Trinket took the stage and clapped her hands for attention. Melissa slipped in through the door just as Trinket started to speak. She glanced about the crowd, her eyes passing over Charlotte once before returning, as though she hadn't quite remembered who her scene partner was.

"Okay, I assume you've all had enough time to work this through with your partner." Trinket assumed a lot. "Take a look at the number written on the top of your pages. We're going to do this chronologically so you can get some idea of the play as we go along. The group marked with a one, we're going to begin with you. Come up onto the stage and show us what you can do."

Bob was in the first group, paired with a dreamy-eyed girl named Laurie or Lauren or Laura. They started in on their scene. Laurie/Lauren/Laura was Harmony in this incarnation; Bob, Charlotte guessed, was the rake of a governor's son. Bob was good with the material, natural and funny. Charlotte had been in a couple plays with him at school, and it was always the same. Witty and sharp, with enough energy and charm to muddle his way through. A fair amount of muddling was needed here; the dialogue wasn't good. Charlotte looked over at Trinket and saw her mouthing the lines along with the performers. Ah. Trinket was the playwright.

She and Melissa were in the fourth group. Charlotte had seen three Harmonys, but she was the first Addie. Good. There'd be no chance of her performance looking like a photocopy of earlier interpretations.

They performed. Melissa's reading was still awkward, and Charlotte wasn't quite there yet either, she was too much in her own head and not enough in Addie's. The scene was lifeless. She could hardly argue with Trinket's expression of dissatisfaction.

"More energy," Trinket said. "Try it again."

Melissa was smoother this time. Her dialect was big and round, a classic Southern belle, a juicy Georgia peach of a drawl. Not quite right from a geographical standpoint, but it sounded good. Melissa interpreted Trinket's request for energy as a command to ratchet the emotion up to histrionic: She was shouting now, wailing at Charlotte's Addie with full lungs. Maybe that was okay for Harmony, maybe Melissa's Harmony was more of a bratty teen than a headstrong young woman in a rough spot, but her Addie wouldn't yell back.

Addie was firm. Addie was strong. Addie was powerful, the full weight of God and the church and a blameless life on her side as she faced off against her sinner of a daughter, who was currently yelling and. . . crying?

Oh, for God's sake. Melissa was crying, or pretending to cry, by pressing back of the hand that wasn't carrying her script pages against her lips and shaking her head in a pretty facsimile of crying that hadn't been in vogue since the days of silent films. It was mannered and meaningless, and it jolted Charlotte back out of Addie and into her own skin just as Melissa sobbed out her final line.

Trinket applauded. Why was Trinket applauding? "Bravo. Much, much better." She walked closer. "Melissa, I felt your pain. That was wonderful. You really inhabited Harmony."

Melissa clapped her hands and jumped up and down in excitement. "Yay! Thank you! Thanks."

Trinket turned her attention to Charlotte. "Your energy could have been higher. Don't be afraid of volume. Remember, you're an angry mother. Still, big improvement."

Charlotte nodded. Hardly harsh criticism. She'd had worse every day in drama school. Trinket was never cruel. But Trinket confused volume with energy, Trinket mistook mannerisms for character. Trinket was a fraud and didn't know she was a fraud. And Trinket was churning out class after class of little frauds.

*Nothing here can help you. This can only hurt.* And yet dropping the class would be another step away, another sign she was reaching the conclusion this life was not for her. And there was nothing else for her, so what could she do?

She could go to Heaven with Bob and hope for a renewal of purpose.

## CHAPTER THREE

CONSIDERING HOW CRANKY and old she felt by the time she reached Heaven, it was a shock to be carded. The bouncer at the door asked for her ID—hers only, and Bob and Charlotte were the same age. He squinted at her DMV-issued California identification card; she half-expected him to raise a stink that it wasn't a driver's license, but he handed it back and let them inside without another word.

"It's because you look so young, Chuck," Bob said as soon as they were past the door. She couldn't hear him over the blasting sound system; only by looking at his lips could she make out what he was saying.

"Clean living," she shouted back. She shouldn't mind getting carded—if it wasn't apparent she was closing in fast on thirty, so much the better—but she suspected it wasn't so much a case of looking in the first bloom of youth as looking unsophisticated. Unformed. Out of place. The bouncer let her know she didn't belong.

Bob said something she couldn't hear and headed off in another direction, the crowd opening around him and swallowing him whole. And the only person she knew in the place had vanished.

She made her way to the bar, three-deep with well-dressed clubgoers. She'd had never been here before, but this was a trendy spot in Hollywood, and cocktails would be priced accordingly. Even with half-price drinks, she needed to be careful. One drink only, and she'd pay in cash, and she'd make sure to reserve enough for the bus home. When the bartender finally turned his harried attention to her, she ordered a glass of the house red. The free hors d'oeuvres Bob mentioned consisted of a tray on the bar lined with grease-stained doilies and a single sad triangle of cheese toast. Too bad. She was hungry.

She should network. That was what this was about, wasn't it? She didn't have any idea how to network. If she did, she'd be having a much better time of things.

There was a familiar face down at the end of the bar. Familiar as in personally known to her, and also familiar as in kind of famous, which was the networking double whammy. She angled her way through the crowd, careful not to jostle her wine glass, then reached over and tapped a young woman on the shoulder. "Rachel. Hi."

Rachel turned away from her male companion and looked at her. Her expression was blank.

"Charlotte Dent. From USC." She managed to not make it sound like a question. They knew each other, damn it. Rachel would remember her.

"Charlotte! Oh my God. It's good to see you!" Rachel looked like she meant it, too, like she was half-thinking of giving her a hug despite the bodies in the way. "How've you been? It's been forever."

"I'm good. You look fantastic." Having been welcomed, Charlotte deemed it acceptable to slide a little closer to the bar. "I saw you on *The Tonight Show* a few weeks ago. You were really great."

"Thanks." Rachel slid over to give her more room. She turned to the man seated beside her. Expensive haircut, expensive tie. "Charlotte, this is my husband, David. Charlotte and I were in drama school together."

David's cool hand clasped hers. "Charlotte. Great to meet you."

"We got married in March. In Malibu." Rachel turned a little pink. "David's also my agent."

"That's great. Congratulations."

Rachel smiled. She looked happy and in love. "Thanks. Wow, it's great running into you. What are the odds?"

"It's alumni night." Rachel looked blank. "The drama school alumni are meeting tonight. I guess it's a monthly thing."

"No kidding?" Rachel looked around, then exploded into giggles. "I thought a lot of people looked familiar."

Charlotte laughed along with her. They leaned their heads together so they wouldn't have to shout over the music. Rachel placed her hand on her wrist. There was something so convivial about their body language, like they were close friends instead of acquaintances who hadn't seen each other for the better part of a decade, that Charlotte felt a little melancholy.

"Have you seen *Eden's Folly*?" Rachel asked. Excited and proud, but a little embarrassed, like she didn't want Charlotte to think she was boasting.

"Only a little bit. I liked what I saw of it. It looks like you're having a lot of fun."

Rachel nodded. "It's great, it's fantastic. You have no idea. Since graduation, I'd been doing nothing but going on auditions and getting deeper into debt and feeling like a total loser, and then I had one good reading, and boom, everything changed. It's so awesome."

She was being disingenuous. There'd been other small successes along her path—commercials and guest spots on other shows, a juicy role in an online series, a bit part in a romantic comedy, a pattern of experience and achievements clearing the way to her recurring television role.

Rachel squeezed her arm. "Tell me. What have you been up to? Are you acting?"

"Here and there. I shot a pilot that didn't get picked up." It hadn't been during this most recent pilot season, nor the one before that, but Rachel didn't need to know specifics. "Mostly I'm going to auditions, taking classes. You know."

"Yeah, I do." Rachel drained her glass. Champagne. Festive. "I sure do. What classes are you taking?"

Charlotte shrugged. "It's at the Sunset Playhouse. Trinket Augustine."

"I know that name. Why do I know that name?"

"She used to be on a soap. I can't remember which one. And she's done a lot of theater in New York. She writes plays, too."

"Yeah, I think I know her." Rachel looked at her for a moment. "Are you working, or. . .?"

"I'm working. I'm a legal assistant in Century City."

"Wow." Rachel stared at her. "That sounds like a real job."

Charlotte knew what she meant, and it wasn't a good thing. A real job meant one which precluded the possibility of getting any acting jobs. Actors got real jobs when they couldn't afford to be actors any more. She'd been working at Ausberger for the better part of a year. She knew what it meant.

"They're good about letting me go on auditions." They probably would be, if she'd ever had any auditions to go on. "It's entertainment law. So it's sort of in the industry. Good for connections."

"Oh, that's good." Hard to tell if Rachel was just being polite. "Do you get to see a lot of celebrities?"

"Not really. Mostly they don't come to the office. Paragon Dufresne was in today, though."

"Paragon? Really? Did you get to see her?"

"Served her coffee and everything."

"That's pretty cool. How'd she look? I hear her skin's bad."

"She looked good. Pretty. She's very thin."

"What was she in for?"

"I don't know. She's a client. We handle all her routine legal affairs." Rachel looked a little disappointed, so she found herself continuing. "She uses one of her own songs as her ringtone."

Rachel wrinkled her nose. Her eyes sparkled. "Ohhh, that's awful."

"Isn't it?" She smiled, but she regretted spilling that bit of information. Point of sober fact, she didn't know for certain it was Paragon's own song, and it was a cheap shot to mock her for something that might not be true.

The conversation stilled. Her glass was empty. Now she was obligated to order another. She was saved by David, who leaned in and touched Rachel's shoulder.

"Hon, our reservation's in twenty minutes. Would you rather stay here? We might not get a table later."

Rachel looked at her, uncertain, and Charlotte was touched that she was considering canceling her plans, whatever they were, so she could stay and chat. But it was late, and it was a work night, and the chat had run its course. She set down her wine glass on the bar.

"I should get going, too. Rachel, it was so good seeing you."

Yes, it was the right move. Rachel looked relieved. "You too. We should really get together more often."

They should. This was what networking was all about. She should somehow maneuver her way around to asking Rachel about helping her find work. They should exchange numbers at the very least. She should hang out with Rachel more and meet more people who could help her career, or she should do any one of those million things she wasn't going to do, because Rachel was a nice person who didn't need someone leeching off her good fortune.

Rachel stood up from her stool to give her a kiss on the cheek and a hug, which was unexpected and lovely and uncomfortable all at once, bone against bone, no softness on either of them. David settled for a handshake, and Charlotte took her leave of the happy couple and melted into the crowd.

People danced and jostled to some song she hadn't heard since junior high. She wished she were the type of person who could join the dancers, throw up her arms up over her head and toss her hair back and lose herself in the crowd of bodies. But she wasn't, and it was time she was home.

A short walk up Las Palmas to Hollywood Boulevard, a quick scout for the nearest bus stop. Hollywood was busy tonight, always busy, bustling with tourists and club rats and panhandlers. Another woman stood at the stop, and she didn't look homeless, but she didn't look quite right, either. Charlotte had lived in Los Angeles long enough to spot mental illness at twenty paces, and something about this woman—stained velour track suit, bumpy red face, disheveled hair, bulging vinyl drawstring bag repaired with duct tape—was crazy. Charlotte hung back a few feet, in the shadows of a gated and shuttered storefront that sold replicas of Oscar statuettes and postcards of James Dean.

The woman muttered to herself, low and unintelligible, in the manner that used to attract more attention in the years before hands-free phones became commonplace. The woman didn't have a phone that Charlotte could see, so that added more fuel to the crazy

21

fire. Charlotte could make out words now, an angry racial epithet repeated over and over. Lovely.

The woman looked over at her for the first time. The skin across her nose and cheeks was mottled from sun damage, like a world map emblazoned across her face in white and angry pink. For a minute, it seemed okay; she looked confused, not hostile. Then: "I don't like you."

Nothing good ever came from engaging the mentally ill in verbal battle. Charlotte knew that, but she was tired and melancholy, and she just wanted to wait at the bus stop in peace. "That's okay. I don't like you either."

"Yeah, well, I wish you'd get stabbed and die."

Okay, then. She glanced down the street. No bus that she could see. She could walk to the next bus stop, or she could just walk home. It was dark and somewhat dangerous, but the route was familiar. It was also summer, and while the night wasn't especially cool, it was good being outside when the sun wasn't trying to kill her.

Charlotte started down Hollywood. She stared at the pink stars on the sidewalk, at the bronze names inscribed upon each one. She'd been here long enough to know these, above all, were a meaningless tribute, a way for the city of Hollywood to raise revenue from fan clubs. Didn't mean she didn't want one.

A car slowed. A young guy with messy college hair stuck his head out the window. There was another college kid beside him, possibly more in the back seat. "Hey!" he called over to her.

She paused, expecting to be asked directions. To the Sunset Strip, to the Hollywood Bowl, or maybe the Observatory. "Do you need a ride?" he asked.

"No. Thanks. I'm good," she said.

"You sure?" The young man seemed concerned. Stoned, maybe, and maybe kind of horny, but not a murderer. He and his friends would give her a ride, maybe offer some weed, maybe suggest they hit another club or two, but she'd get home safe in the end. Her naked body wouldn't be found wrapped in duct tape a week later in the Angeles National Forest. Still wasn't worth the chance.

"Yeah. Thanks. I'm just walking." Friendly smile, so he wouldn't think she was assuming he was a killer.

His friend in the driver's seat said something she couldn't hear. The car behind him honked once. With a shrug at Charlotte—her loss—he drove off.

She looked up at the sky. There were stars up there somewhere, but she could never see them inside the city, even on a clear night like this. Too many city lights. The sky went on forever, an abyss of black.

## Chapter Four

It was a Tuesday, and Charlotte was in the pit of despair. She was at her desk, actually, sipping at a cup of lukewarm chamomile tea and thinking hard about the stack of files that needed to be copied before Dale's deposition. She didn't want to copy the files. She didn't want to with such intensity she thought she might break out into hives. It had happened before. It was possible she was allergic to photocopying.

It was possible she was being a brat, throwing a snit fit because she had a job she didn't like much. There were worse fates than photocopying for a living. Many people had much worse jobs than this. She'd had worse jobs, in fact, in her not so distant past. She knew all this, and yet all the pep talks she could summon were having no effect. She still didn't want to do the photocopying.

Maybe if she goofed off online for a bit, she could unwind and get over herself enough to do her job. With an eye on Dale's closed office door, she opened up a browser and surfed through her usual battery of message boards and casting sites in search of upcoming auditions or leads on agents willing to take on new clients.

Pickings were slim. A commercial for anti-depression medication—that sounded right up her alley these days. No, it wasn't an open call—the contact information was available to agents only.

She moved on to another site, then another. Another. Clicking on links, straying from her original paths. She was probably twelve links in, on a message board she hadn't visited for over a year because it never seemed to have much current content, before she found something promising.

Auditions tonight, starting at six. A play, community theater, something called the Hollycould Players. The name was too twee by half, but a quick Google revealed they were legitimate. The auditions were at a theater up on the shabbier end of Sunset, just west of downtown. Okay, she could get there by six, if the buses were running on time. Didn't say what the play was, didn't have much information in the posting other than a list of character names and brief descriptions. She took a quick look to see if there was anything that could be right for her. Annemarie, nineteen and flighty, a social butterfly-in-training. Could she pass for nineteen? The bouncer at Heaven had thought so.

Tingle of anticipation. An audition. A goal. Something to distract her attention from the photocopying. First priority was to figure out what she was getting into. The name of the play might not be listed in the posting, but that didn't mean she couldn't sniff it out. The character names were distinctive, musty and English. Agatha, Annemarie, Fletcher, Rudyard, Wempie. Fed them into a search engine, sifted through the results.

She had it. *The Twilight Butler*, 1918, Dalton Winslow. Hadn't heard of him, but he would be Edwardian, a contemporary of Shaw, Ibsen, Wodehouse. Was the text of the play online?

No dice. She found reviews from other performances, though, and from these she scraped together something of an idea of the plot. An English drawing-room play, a drama about mistaken identity, some elements of a murder mystery. Sounded solid and respectable. The casting notice hadn't mentioned anything about accents, but it was prudent to assume she'd be called upon to be English. Received Pronunciation for Annemarie, who appeared to be a nitwit, but a wealthy and well-educated nitwit.

She always carried her headshots and theatrical résumé with her, in a vinyl envelope in her messenger bag. Her headshots were four years old, but they weren't bad, and her appearance hadn't changed much. Plus, she still had a good supply left; no sense wasting them by going in for another sitting.

She'd have to go straight from work. Her work clothes were okay, a navy skirt suit and a plain white button-down blouse. A little drab, but that couldn't be helped.

The day crawled onward. Once she'd finished her flurry of research, the insecurities flooded in. She really, really didn't want to do this. She could skip it and go straight home after work, change into comfortable clothes, read a book, get to bed early. Didn't sound so bad.

When had she last auditioned for something? Six months ago, maybe more? It had been for another play, a small stage in Venice, and she'd blown it. She hadn't found a rhythm, she'd been sweaty and graceless, and she didn't get a callback.

That was then. This was different. She went to catch the bus.

Good bus karma today. The theater doors were still locked when she arrived, about twenty minutes before six. It wasn't a great neighborhood, this end of Sunset. The industrial side of the film industry was on display; prop houses and post-production facilities were nestled alongside storefront liquor stores and shabby doughnut shops. There was a wooden bench beside the theater doors, but the closer she got to it, the more it smelled like old urine, so she stood in the speckled shade of a tree by the curb and waited.

A blonde woman, middle-aged and leathery, propped open the front door of the theater with a cinder block. She shielded her eyes against the sun with her hand and squinted at Charlotte. She frowned. "Here for the auditions?" she asked. A purple velvet halter top barely confined her extravagant bosom; her feet were bare, and her toenails sparkled with purple glitter. "You're early."

"I can wait outside until you're ready," Charlotte said.

"No, whatever, come in. You can't audition until the director gets here."

Charlotte followed her into the theater lobby. Faded green carpet, chairs with ripped vinyl seats, a display case featuring faded handbills. Smelled like fresh paint and dry rot.

She took a seat on one of the vinyl chairs. A moment later, two girls entered. They were maybe still in their teens, sleek and lithe with glossy manes of hair. More aspiring hopefuls arrived, maybe a few dozen in total. She scoped out the crowd. Young. Very young. A bunch of nervous kids. Male-to-female ratio of about one to four. Pretty typical.

Had this process ever been fun? Maybe a little, back when she was a kid auditioning for local plays in Idaho.

The blonde woman reemerged, hands full. "Hi, gang. Nice turnout," she said. "Welcome to Hollycould Players. I'm Holly." Charlotte's stomach churned a bit. "We're about ready to get started, if you all could sign in on the clipboard. If you've got your headshots with you—which you all really, really should—have them ready to hand to the director when it's your turn. And you need to fill these out as well."

She held up a stack of stiff white cards, then set them beside the sign-in sheet on a table near the entrance. The table was instantly mobbed. Charlotte hung back. They'd audition in the order they signed in, and while it would be nice to get this over with, there was no benefit to going first.

She picked up one of the cards. It asked for her name, her contact information, her rehearsal availability. It also asked whether she had a reliable form of transportation. She had good walking shoes and a working knowledge of the bus system, so she responded in the affirmative. It was a lie, sort of, but her lack of a car would be a big mark against her. It might even knock her out of consideration.

Holly had put out the sides, too, in small stacks arranged by character. Charlotte picked up Annemarie's scene and glanced through it.

"Crud. How late am I?" Charlotte looked up at a new arrival. A woman, late thirties, tall and fair and willowy, wearing a floral wrap dress in wispy crepe.

"Don't worry. We're still signing in," Charlotte said.

"Good. I haven't blown it. Have they collected headshots?"

"We're supposed to hand them over when we go in."

The woman looked so familiar, sounded so familiar. . . Charlotte glanced over her shoulder while she signed in and snuck a peek at her name.

Erica Fallow. Of course. When the woman looked up at her, Charlotte blushed.

"I'm sorry. I thought that was you. I just wanted to make sure."

"Yeah, it's me." Erica smiled, embarrassed and pleased and wary all at once, the instinctual reaction of the famous when confronted with the public.

"Sorry. I don't want to bother you. I just really liked *Mad World*, that's all. I was addicted to it in college."

"Thanks. That's nice to hear." Erica's smile deepened, turned a bit more genuine, as though she had sussed Charlotte out and deemed her harmless.

They were still standing at the table in the middle of the room. Charlotte wished they were somewhere else, so she wouldn't look like a star-struck fangirl in front of all these other actors. "I stopped watching after the third season. It wasn't the same after you left."

Erica laughed. "That's what I think, too, but I'm biased." She picked up one of the information cards. "Are we supposed to fill these out?"

"Yes." There was no way she was going to ask why Erica was auditioning for unpaid community theater. Something of her curiosity must have shown in her face, though, because Erica turned a little pink.

"I like theater," she said. It was a little defensive. "I never got a chance to do much of it. I started working in television pretty much right after high school. So now that things have cooled down, career-wise. . ." She shrugged. "This could be fun. It's nice to have the freedom to go on auditions like this, you know?"

Charlotte didn't know. She'd give a great deal for the freedom not to have to go on auditions like this. "Might be a nice change of pace."

"Yeah." The topic exhausted, Erica looked around the room. Probably trying to gracefully extricate herself from the conversation. It was a pleasant surprise when she turned back to Charlotte. "Should we sit down?" she asked.

They settled into the ugly vinyl chairs. "If you get cast, can you take the part?" Charlotte asked. "Could you take an unpaid role?"

Erica made a noise that sounded like a snort. "Not a problem. I'm not SAG anymore. Not AFTRA, not Equity. I haven't been

29

working, and I let my dues lapse." She looked at the sides she'd picked up. "You know anything about the play?"

"1918. English parlor drama," Charlotte said. "Heavy on the mothballs. How are you at accents?"

"Fantastic," Erica said. "Or passable, at least." She looked up. "You suppose that's the director?"

Charlotte looked at the man entering the lobby from the stage and supposed it was. He was dark and rail-thin, with the intense look of a humanities professor or, indeed, a community theater director. He walked over to Holly and spoke a few quiet words.

"Hey, everyone? We're ready to start." Holly gestured at the man with the exaggerated motions of a game-show hostess. "This is Kyle. He's going to be directing this monstrosity, so if you want to kiss some ass, his would be the one."

"Who's she?" Erica asked, very low.

"That's Holly," Charlotte said. "Hollycould Players, right?"

"Ah." There was a wealth of information in that single syllable.

Holly picked up the clipboard and frowned at it. "We're going to go ahead and take the guys first, since there are so few of you," she said to the group. "Jeff Jones, you're up."

One of the few males got to his feet and trailed Kyle and Holly into the inner sanctum. Charlotte looked around the room, calculating. "Eight guys for six male parts. Thirty women for two female parts. Does this seem fair to you?"

"Silly girl. Acting's not supposed to be fair." Erica looked at her. "I don't know your name," she said.

"Charlotte."

"Charlotte. I'm Erica." They shook hands.

Silence fell. Charlotte remembered she was anxious. Erica looked down at her lines; Charlotte watched the door to the stage.

Jeff Jones returned from his audition. "Jeff Fisher?" he said.

A mop-haired kid raised his hand. "They said for you to go in next," the first Jeff said. The kid went in, came out in a moment, called out the next name. The auditions were only taking a couple minutes apiece. Good. She'd be out of here soon.

They finished the men and started in on the women. When the summons came for Peregrine Swanson, Charlotte turned to Erica.

"I'm going to be next," Charlotte said. She'd noted Peregrine's name above hers when she'd signed in and had felt a brief and fervent wish she had a cool name like Peregrine, too.

"You'll be great," Erica said. She looked at her. "If you take your hair down, you'll look less sporty," she said.

Sporty wasn't what she should aim for with Annemarie-from-1918, was it? She keep her hair in a ponytail pretty much full time during the summer; she had a lot of hair, and it got hot in the sun. She yanked out the rubber band and fluffed her mane. "Is that okay?"

Erica nodded. "Better," she said.

Peregrine came out just then. She was, Charlotte was delighted to note, a tribute to her name, brooding and beaked. "Charlotte Dent?"

Charlotte stood, making sure she had her sides and her head-shot and her information card in her hand. "Here goes," she said.

"Break a leg." Erica waved three fingers at her. Charlotte smiled and went into the theater.

It was a hot black box, a perfect square of stifling misery, a squeaky rotating fan providing the only moving air. A low ceiling lined with lights, three sets of risers surrounding a low stage. Walls draped with cheap black fabric, the cement floor painted black, scuffed and marked from sets and chairs and shoes. Holly sat on a folding chair on the stage, in front of the backdrop for the theater's most recent production, a plywood flat painted like a child's idea of a forest. Green-topped trees with thick brown trunks against a blue sky dotted with cotton-ball clouds. The huge yellow sun had a smiley face on it. It was ironic, Charlotte was sure of it. Pretty sure, at least.

Kyle sat on the lowest step of the center set of risers. He didn't smile. "Hi. Charlotte?"

"Yes. Good afternoon." Charlotte held up her headshot. "Do you want this?"

He held out a hand for it. Stared at the picture, flipped it over, stared at her credits. They'd stand up to scrutiny here, at least. "Are you ready to read?"

"You bet." She was perky. It was always a good idea to be perky at auditions, even if it didn't come naturally. She walked over to the stage area and smiled at Holly. "Hi."

Holly looked bored, but she was polite. "Hi. You've got the right scene? You're reading Annemarie, right?"

Kyle picked up his steno pad. "I'm asking everyone to give the accent a shot. You good with that?"

"No problem." Ready for anything. Big grin.

"You need a minute to prepare?"

She took a lightning-fast inventory. Annemarie: English and flighty and pretty. "I'm good. Let's do this."

Holly gave her the opening cue. Holly was Rudyard. Holly wasn't bothering with an accent. Wasn't bothering to act, really. That was okay. Charlotte was ready: "But you really mustn't think, my dear, that I have *quite* the proprietary interest in this. . ."

The accent wasn't right. "Proprietary" came out wrong, one syllable too many. It would come, it sometimes took her a couple sentences to slide into it properly, but that was a bad start.

Charlotte went through the motions of the character, feeling Annemarie's movements and grace, her affected laugh, her mannerisms. It was okay, but she wasn't submerged in it. She was Charlotte-as-Annemarie, and right now, Charlotte needed to be absent from the scene.

They finished. She remained standing. Kyle looked at the pad in his lap. He wasn't writing or moving. Had he nodded off? He looked up.

"Can you try that one more time from the top?" he asked. He sounded annoyed. No, maybe that wasn't accurate—he'd sounded the same way earlier in the lobby with Holly, so maybe this was just his default personality.

"No problem," she said. "Is there anything you want me to do differently this time?"

He was quiet for a long moment. "Not really," he said. "Just do it again."

They launched into the scene once more. Better this time. The accent was right, if nothing else. She finished and looked at Kyle.

He didn't say anything. Long after the silence had grown awkward, he shifted in his chair. "Okay. Thanks." He flipped over her information card and scanned it. "I'll be making decisions by the end of the week."

No callbacks, then. Probably the small turnout didn't warrant it. "Great. Thanks a lot. It was nice to meet you."

Now was the point when she needed to do something to make herself stick in his memory. She could make some comment about how much she liked the play, maybe. No, that was dumb and doomed to backfire, seeing as she'd only heard of the play today. She was no good at small talk. Best to leave quietly.

She waved goodbye to Holly. She should shake hands with Kyle, maybe, but he was engrossed in his notebook again, and she was a little scared of approaching him.

"Send in Katrina Harold on your way out, okay?" he asked.

And that was that. She left.

Erica's face was bright and expectant. "How did it go? Was it scary? Kyle looked like he might be scary."

"It went fine. He seems okay. Not very talkative."

"You were good?"

"I was okay." Maybe, upon reflection, she'd upgrade her assessment to good, but right now she felt confident only in a strong okay. She hadn't missed a cue, or stumbled over her lines, or mispronounced her dialogue, or accidentally spat on Holly. She'd been prepared, she'd had a good grasp on the character and the material. She'd probably been bland, and that would probably cost her the role.

"You look upset," Erica said.

Charlotte shook her head. "I'm not. Just post-audition letdown, I think." She looked around. "I'm going to take off. It was really great meeting you." She paused. "I hope you do well. Not just here. Everywhere."

"You, too," Erica said, and seemed to mean it. She looked like she wanted to say something further, but didn't. Charlotte thought she might know what she was feeling, because she was struck by it too, that almost primitive urge to connect with another friendly human being with whom she might share a few interests, maybe go for a cup of coffee or see a movie together. Maybe she wasn't alone in her lack of close friends. Maybe this was an experience shared by others in Los Angeles.

But Erica didn't say anything, and Charlotte wouldn't say anything, so there was nothing else to do but walk out of the theater into the dazzling sun outside.

## CHAPTER FIVE

CHARLOTTE DIDN'T EXPECT to hear anything further. Calling all the rejects would be time-consuming and thankless, and people in L.A. avoided doing things that fell into either category. It was therefore a shock when she checked her messages as she was about to leave for lunch the next day and found she had one from Kyle. It was even more of a shock the news was positive.

"Charlotte Dent, this is Kyle Matthias from the Hollycould Players." Somehow it was a relief he used her full name, so there could be no mistaking who he was trying to reach. "You auditioned for me yesterday? Anyway, if you're interested, I'd like to offer you the part of Agatha in *Twilight Butler.*"

He's said Agatha, not Annemarie. Agatha was the other female role, the elderly governess who got murdered midway through the first act. Even as she listened to the rest of Kyle's message, her brain reordered itself around this new information, ditching all her thoughts about Annemarie and preparing a new dossier. What she'd gleaned about Agatha from her fast investigation of the play was an impression of a grim, spectral creature, humorless and brooding. Could be interesting.

The message continued. "We're having a read-through tonight, and I know it's short notice, but it's important to be there. You can buy the play at Samuel French."

Not before tonight's rehearsal, she couldn't. The message ended, still lacking a few key bits of information. It was probably safe to presume the rehearsal would be held at the same theater, but she didn't know what time, and Kyle hadn't left his number.

She'd assume the rehearsal started at six, same as the audition. If she was wrong, it wouldn't get things off to a great start, but there wasn't much she could do about it, and fretting about it just took attention away from the important thing: She just got the part, thus breaking a long, unhappy dry spell. Agatha wasn't Annemarie, but she was all hers, and she was a lovely consolation prize.

She wanted to celebrate. Tell someone, at least. There was no one to tell. She could call her parents, but her mom would be at work, and her dad would be asleep or in no state to talk.

Dale came over to her desk just then, arms laden with files. "You look worried," he said.

"Do I? I'm not." She cleared her throat. "I just got cast in a play."

"Did you? Congratulations." Dale looked surprised, but pleased. "I didn't realize you acted."

A stab of exasperation. Silly of her. No sense getting frustrated when people didn't know things she hadn't told them. "Yeah. Yes. I do. I majored in drama in college."

"Well. You'll have to let us all know when it is," Dale said.

"Of course," she said, but Dale was already moving on, leaving her alone in her cubicle.

"That was pretty bad," Kyle said.

He was right. The read-through had few saving graces. It'd been halted and stilting, rife with mispronounced words and mutilated lines. Charlotte was good at dry readings, even while leaning over to look at Jeff's—one of the Jeffs; there were two—script, and she shared Kyle's frustration with the others.

Of a cast of eight, two hadn't shown. Holly read the missing parts.

Erica was Annemarie. This was a development Charlotte could support. Erica, seated beside her on the risers, rolled her eyes at Kyle's words.

Kyle was silent. Kyle was prone to long, awkward silent spells. He glanced at his watch once, then looked back at his actors and was silent some more.

"We have to be out of the theater by eight, so we don't have time to run through it again," he said eventually. He fell into silence again, then shrugged.

"I don't know. I don't know. We'll try again tomorrow night. Everybody, you really need to have your scripts by then, so make sure you pick them up before rehearsal tomorrow. Be professional." Only two cast members—one of the Jeffs and the obnoxious guy in the UCLA shorts and the dirty flip-flops, whose name Charlotte thought was Robbie—had brought scripts. It was a bad sign for future director-cast bonhomie that Kyle had been so vexed by this.

Kyle gathered up his script and notebook and engaged Holly in a quiet conversation. The letdown of a poor rehearsal washed over Charlotte. She'd have to ask Dale if she could leave work a bit early tomorrow to pick up her script. Otherwise, she'd be doomed to another day of displeasing Kyle.

Erica nudged her arm. "Want to take a run to Sam French to get our scripts?" she asked.

"Can't. They're closed already."

"We can go tomorrow before practice. Or do you work?"

Erica didn't have a day job, lucky girl. Charlotte shrugged. "Yeah, I work. I don't know when I can get over there."

"I'll go tomorrow. Want me to grab one for you while I'm there?"

"I don't have any cash on me."

Erica shook her head. "You can pay me whenever."

"Thanks. I really appreciate it."

Erica looked at Kyle, standing over on the stage area with Holly. "I wouldn't want you to get flogged for not having a script tomorrow."

Charlotte smiled, but said nothing. It was far too early in the rehearsal process to start trash-talking their director.

She walked with Erica out of the theater. It was bright out, though the sun was low on the horizon. Still plenty warm. A gust of wind caught them, and it was hot and dry, warmer even than the still air. The wind rattled the dry leaves of the fig tree, and just that noise made her nostalgic for fall and cooler weather.

"I'm around the block. Where are you parked?" Erica asked.

She shook her head. "I took the bus."

"Oh. Wow." Her answer confused Erica, she could see that. It forced her to change her assessment of Charlotte to allow for this new information. Charlotte lived in Los Angeles, and yet she took the bus, which meant she somehow wasn't normal, despite appearances. "Do you need a ride?"

Charlotte hesitated. The bus was a hassle, and it would be nice to talk to Erica some more. "Which way are you going?"

"I'm in the hills. Mount Olympus," Erica said.

That settled that. "I'm in the other direction. Near Hancock Park." Less Hancock Park, more some indeterminate area of mid-Wilshire that wasn't quite Koreatown, wasn't quite Miracle Mile.

Dropping the Hancock Park name was snobbery, springing forth out of a sense of inadequacy to the glamour of Mount Olympus. "It's an easy bus ride."

"If you're sure. . ." Erica looked worried, but not like she was going to insist on driving her, so Charlotte figured she'd rather not be taken up on her offer.

She headed to her bus stop, right outside the stoop of a liquor store. A young man, bearded and barefoot, sat on the steps of the shop, a bottle of tamarind soda in hand. He said something to her in Spanish. She didn't catch much of it outside of *chica*, but his grin seemed friendly, so she felt okay about smiling back and nodding, the international language of the well-intentioned and harmless.

## CHAPTER SIX

REHEARSALS SETTLED INTO a manageable pattern: the bus from work, the stuffy rat-trap of a theater, the mangled lines and Kyle's disapproving glares. It was good having a project to throw herself into. She stopped going to her acting class without guilt. She had rehearsals every weeknight, after all. So long, Trinket.

She studied Agatha, building a durable bond between herself and her character. She wasn't the best in the cast—that was probably Erica, though Jeff Fisher was strong—but she wasn't the worst, either. She fell somewhere squarely in the middle, probably. Seemed about right.

Erica stopped by around three on a Saturday. Charlotte wanted to invite her inside, but her apartment didn't have an air conditioner, and it reached thermonuclear temperatures in the late afternoon, so she met her at the gate instead.

Charlotte handed her a bottle. "It's a Pinot Grigio. I thought it would be nice on a hot day."

"Good call." Erica looked at the label and didn't register any visible distaste at the mass-market brand.

She was parked at the curb, an unwieldy silver behemoth, shiny and expensive. Gray leather interior, new car smell. Charlotte had to haul herself up into the passenger seat. "Nice car," she said.

"Thanks." Erica glanced over her shoulder and eased into the traffic on Olympic. "It's too much vehicle for me, really, and it sucks up the gas like nobody's business, but it makes me feel safe, you know? The last car I had was this little sporty thing, and I always felt like I was going to get crushed any minute." She glanced over at her. "You don't drive?"

"Nope." It took too long to figure out where the seatbelt was. The shoulder strap was attached to the ceiling far behind her.

"Can I ask why?"

"Can't afford it. I was unemployed for a long time, broken up with a lot of temp jobs that just covered rent."

Erica turned onto La Brea. Heading north, up toward the hills. "I haven't had a paid job for five years. I couldn't imagine living here without a car."

"It's not so bad. You'd get used to it." It wasn't bad and it was, all at once. "Why'd you leave *Mad World?* Can I ask that?"

"Sweeps." Erica smiled. "I got fired. Not because the producers didn't like my character, and not because of anything I did. It was sweeps, though, and they thought a major character death would spike the ratings. So I got picked." She craned her head to look in the rearview mirror. So many things drivers had to pay attention to, all to avoid killing themselves or others with their great, bulky, metal monsters.

"That sucks," Charlotte said. A legion of English teachers would disagree, but she'd always found "sucks" useful. It didn't drip of mawkish sentiment; it got her point across to Erica without making either of them uncomfortable.

"It does indeed." Erica grinned, though it didn't reach her eyes. "The worst part was, they were right. The ratings spiked after I left, and they stayed up. So they made the right call."

There wasn't much to be said to that, unless Charlotte wanted to trot out her all-purpose "sucks" rejoinder again, so she fell silent while Erica navigated her metal monstrosity through the weekend traffic. The sun was in her eyes, and she didn't have her sunglasses with her, but she was a little hesitant to flip down the sun visor to shield her eyes. It seemed wrong to tamper with someone else's vehicle, to roll down the windows or adjust the vents or recline the seats.

They stopped at a deli on Third to pick up provisions. Erica ordered a variety of foods: cold ceviche overflowing with raw shrimp and onion, grilled eggplant and yellow peppers dressed in olive oil, a compote of mangoes and raspberries garnished with fresh mint. She picked up a couple bottles of grapefruit soda in frosted bottles with an intricate Italian label and a box of lemon bars wrapped in wax paper. She paid for it all, waving aside Charlotte's offer to pitch in. Did Erica buy all of her food like this, eschewing grocery stores in favor of gourmet shops? Did Charlotte want to live like this? She looked at the tall jars of multicolored olives, the whole roasted chickens, the rustic loaves of fresh bread, the fragrant cheeses coated in wax shells. Yes. Yes, she did.

They drove up into the hill, up where the buses didn't run, on one of the rambling, twisty paths that roamed across the face of Mount Olympus. The road was ridiculous. Narrow and serpentine, only a single lane, bordered by a skinny dirt shoulder lined with parked cars. They didn't meet anyone going downhill, thankfully, even though it must happen all the time, and somehow the street must accommodate it.

Erica's house was set into the face of the hill, jammed in between two equally small and equally cute cottages. She parked on the crowded shoulder, mere centimeters away from the cars in front and back.

Charlotte got out, clutching her wine. She felt a sense of vertigo as she dropped from the passenger seat to the curb. "Wow. How do you manage that drive every day?" she asked.

"I'm used to it by now. It's only really bad if someone's throwing a party up here or something, if we get a bunch of people who aren't used to the way things work around here. I've had people try to park on my lawn." Erica got out her keys and unlocked her door. "Watch out for Rusty. He's harmless, but he barks."

The caution was unnecessary. Rusty was barking already. Rusty, at a guess, spent most of his life barking. He was a small Irish setter, copper-colored and beautiful and obnoxious. He ran up to Erica, paws skidding on shiny wood floors, yipping out a greeting. "Hi, Rusty," Charlotte said. She held out a hand at sniffing level.

Rusty had no interest in her hand. He focused on lavishing affection and admonishment in equal doses upon his owner. Erica nudged him out of her way with her bag of deli food. "Move, stinker. I'll be with you in a minute," she said. She set her bag down on the kitchen counter.

"Corkscrew's in the top drawer, glasses in the cupboard straight above. I'm going to take Rusty for his afternoon constitutional, if you want to get us started on the wine?"

"Sure." Charlotte fiddled with the corkscrew. Good thing Erica wasn't around to see her muddle her way through this. It was one of the ones shaped like a rabbit's head, and it took her far too long to find the trick to it. Mission accomplished, she poured out the wine and looked around.

She had an immediate case of house envy. The place wasn't large, with a small living room connected to the kitchen and beyond that a short hallway that led to what was probably two bedrooms. The back of the living room had French doors, which opened out onto a tiny rectangle of green surrounded by a low rock wall built into the side of the hill. There was a lemon tree and a border of what looked like jasmine bushes, and a white wooden bench. She could imagine sitting on that bench, out there in the shade, maybe with a cup of coffee early in the morning when everything was wet with dew.

She was struck by the crisp cleanliness of the house. The walls were white and looked recently painted; the floors were dark and shiny. Brown suede couch, dark wood coffee table. Floor-to-ceiling bookcases that held mostly scripts and a few recent novels.

Erica and Rusty returned from their stroll. Erica ushered Rusty out through the French doors into the backyard, where he bounded around while yipping away to his furry heart's delight.

Charlotte handed her a wine glass and raised her own. "Cheers."

They clinked and swilled. The wine tasted okay to Charlotte, but her palate wasn't sophisticated. Erica didn't grimace or spit it back into her glass, so she guessed it passed muster.

The containers from the deli were attractive enough to serve straight from them, but Erica transferred the contents to a set of white porcelain serving dishes bordered with painted red flowers. Charlotte had been in Erica's kitchen two minutes, and already she knew all of Erica's utensils and plates and pots would be tasteful and chic. This was the type of existence she knew she should scorn—the trappings of neo-yuppies, a sense of taste accumulated through visits to higher-end mall stores and mail-order catalogues—but she aspired to this. To eat off of those tiny white cheese plates daily, sitting on that suede couch, feet up on the coffee table. . . it seemed like unbelievable luxury.

They settled in with the food. The ceviche was glorious, salty and tart with plenty of fresh lime juice and cilantro.

Erica ruined the moment by talking shop. "So, the play's a sinking ship, you know."

Charlotte took a swallow of her wine. It tasted better after the smoky eggplant, crisp and dry like a good green apple. "It's early. It'll go better when we're all off book."

"If that day ever comes," Erica said. "Kevin can't read, and he doesn't understand anything he's saying anyway."

"He might be okay," Charlotte said. "He's done other plays, right? If he gets his lines down, he'll be pretty good. There's kind of a sympathetic quality to him, don't you think?" It was that quality— a blend of sweetness and confusion—that, combined with the small pool of male auditionees, must've been the basis for Kyle's decision to cast him. It was also the quality that made her feel an urge to defend him, even though Erica was clearly right.

"Could be. In better hands, he could be fine. But Kyle doesn't know what he's doing."

Charlotte didn't want to have this conversation. "You really think so?"

Erica shrugged and took a drink, most of her face masked by her oversized goblet. "Yeah. He's a dud. Holly says this is the first play he's directed. He'd worked tech on a couple of past shows she's put on, lights and sounds and stuff, so she's giving him his big chance here." Erica refilled her glass, looked at Charlotte's still-full one, and set down the bottle. "It's a dead end, this play. All we can do is our best, right?"

"Right." Charlotte looked around the living room. "This is a really great house," she said.

Erica smiled. "It's nice, isn't it? I bought it as soon as we got renewed for a second season. By then, I figured it was safe to start making big purchases." She leaned back against the back of the sofa and propped her feet up on the coffee table, slim legs crossed at the ankles. "Payments are a little out of hand, though. I really need to start working again, really working, not wasting my time on some crappy little play."

"I'm working and wasting my time on some crappy little play all at once. It's possible to do both," Charlotte said.

"You are, aren't you? I don't know how you do it." Erica stared out into the backyard. "I don't think I could have any job other than acting. I mean, I really couldn't. You work in an office, right? And it's every day, nine to five, year round, right?"

Eight to five. Charlotte didn't correct her. "Don't remind me," she said.

"I need a job." Erica drew her lips into a line. She was a universe away all of a sudden. "If I can't get paid acting work, I need a job. But I don't know where to start." She shook her head. "I haven't even gone to college. What am I going to do, answer phones for a living? Make copies?"

Charlotte had graduated from college, and much of her life involved answering phones and making copies. It wasn't the end of the world—most of the time, it wasn't the end of the world—but from Erica's position, it could seem like it. "You'll be okay," she said.

Erica snorted and refilled her glass. She gestured around the room. "I should sell this place. Sell it before they take it away from me."

"Do you think that's going to happen?" Charlotte asked.

"Naah. Something will come through. Something always does." Erica tilted her head over the edge of the couch and stared at the ceiling. She startled Charlotte by straightening up abruptly and turning toward her. "Hey, do you want to move in with me?"

Charlotte looked at her, confused. Erica continued. "I can clear all my stuff out of the yoga room, it's supposed to be a bedroom anyway. We can split the mortgage payment, I'm sure it wouldn't be that much more than your rent. It would be fun."

Charlotte was silent. Her immediate, forceful reaction was negative. She liked Erica. They'd probably get along; Charlotte got along with most people. Living with Erica would give her a built-in social life, which was something she was missing. And the house was great, the backyard was paradise, and yippy little Rusty was sort of adorable.

But she'd have to surrender her solitude. Erica was in debt, she'd strongly implied, and yet there was that monstrous new vehicle parked out front. Erica didn't work and possibly would never work. It was enough of a chasm to make living together unfathomable. Still, she couldn't say any of that to Erica, so she moved on to the next item on her list of excuses. "I couldn't live up here without a car."

"Yeah, I guess that's right. You could get one," Erica said. "You can get them for really cheap."

A flicker of annoyance, sharp but fleeting. "There's insurance, and gas and everything. I couldn't do it."

"Okay. You're probably right." As Charlotte knew it would, playing the no-car card put an end to the discussion.

They moved on to lighter topics, fluffier topics. They drank serviceable wine and ate excellent food until the shady backyard grew dark and it was time to be going. This was always the bad part, the part that made her feel useless and immature, this business of needing a ride home, like she was a child being dropped off by a friend's mother after a Brownies meeting.

They were talked out. The outside air was prickling and stifling, and the sun was low. This was the time of day she liked least, when the sun was always in her eyes and everything was in silhouette, when the stark contrast between bright and dark seemed to penetrate through her eyelids into her brain. In the passenger seat, Charlotte leaned back and closed her eyes for the drive down the hill.

She opened them only when Erica spoke. "Are those the tar pits?"

"Yeah. Haven't you been to them?"

"I've driven past but never stopped. Can you go right up to them?" Erica craned her neck over to look.

"There's a fence, so you can't go wading or anything, but you can get close. Do you want to see them?"

Erica parked on the street on Wilshire, right next to the Screen Actors Guild building. "Is that where SAG is? I never knew that, either," Erica said.

Charlotte had known that from her first month living in L.A., going to the theater school at USC, filled with excitement and grand ambitions. Twelve years later, and she still didn't have a SAG card.

They leaned against the railing and looked down at the tar, at the sculpted tableaux of the mother mastodon drowning in the tar while her mate and her child looked on. "So that's just it? Tar?" Erica asked.

"Historical tar," Charlotte said. "Tar of great paleontological significance. But yeah, tar." She stared at the bubbles that rose and burst on the surface.

"And all these animals just wandered in and drowned, huh? Like quicksand."

"It doesn't drag you down. You just get stuck. You'd die of exposure before you drowned." She looked down at the patch of grass they were standing on. "Look. It's getting us already."

Black tar oozed up through the banks of the pits, staining their shoes. Erica made a noise of disgust and backed away. "God. Yuck," she said. "This place smells. Let's go."

She was right. Hot tar on a hot summer day was never pleasant. The air smelled sick with chemicals and noxious vapors. So it wasn't like Erica didn't have a point, but still, she could be more impressed with the tar pits.

Then again, looking at the set of Erica's jaw as she stared at the drowning mastodon, Charlotte thought maybe it wasn't a matter of being unimpressed after all.

## CHAPTER SEVEN

THEY CLOSED OUT August with nightly rehearsals. They'd learned their lines, more or less. They'd hashed out the blocking and straightened out the trouble spots in their fake accents. They'd sweated, making the small, stuffy room rank with their collected body funk. The sets were cut and assembled, though unpainted. And yet. . . if Charlotte were Trinket, she'd purse her lips and tell everyone their performances needed to gel. The play was inert: not bad enough to be campy, not good enough to be worth the thirty bucks Holly and Kyle were charging for tickets.

At least it was fall. It didn't feel like fall, and wouldn't until at least October, and even then things wouldn't get cold, but Charlotte's soul revived at the falling leaves and the cooler air that moved inland in the evenings.

Tonight was hopeless. Charlotte felt unfocused, and Robbie was sour and obnoxious, and Kevin had finally learned most of his lines, but his delivery was wrong, his enunciation off, like he had no idea what his words meant. Erica was gloomy, and her clashes with Kyle were beginning to have an edge.

They ran through act two again, which meant Charlotte didn't have anything to do but sit and watch from the risers. Kyle sat a few rows in front of her, narrow shoulders hunched inward, a volcano waiting to erupt.

"Let's do that again. Robbie, you're still waiting too long before your lines. Erica, get your energy up. You're dragging everything down."

"That's bullshit," Erica said. Charlotte winced. It *was* bullshit—Erica's performance had been fine—but Kyle was in a mood to pick a fight, and it looked like Erica was in a mood to give him one.

"I'm sorry. What?" Kyle asked.

Holly sat onstage, subbing for Jeff Jones, who hadn't shown up to rehearsal. She looked openly entertained by the growing tension in the room. Charlotte hated her for that, just a bit.

"It's bullshit. You always tell me I have low energy when you can't think of anything else to say. If I'm not doing anything wrong, why not tell me that?"

"You are doing something wrong. Your energy sucks, and you've got a shitty attitude, and it's bringing everything down."

"I've got a bad attitude because you've never said anything complimentary about any of us, and we're tired of it. If you think I have bad energy, why did you cast me in the first place?"

Kyle couldn't be the worst director Erica had ever had in all her years as a working actress, could he? Kyle might be a jerk, and he might not know what he was doing—more and more as the production continued, Charlotte grew certain his poor communication skills were not masking a brilliant creative maestro—but he was more or less tolerable.

"I hired you because you've got name recognition. You'll bring in audience members. You're too old for the part, but I thought you could handle it. It looks like I was wrong."

Erica was quiet for a moment. Then: "Go fuck yourself."

She didn't exactly flounce out of the theater, but it was close. The stage door slammed behind her.

Everyone was quiet for a moment. Robbie gave a low whistle and made some kind of comment under his breath. Charlotte could barely make out one word: "PMS."

Kyle broke the silence. "Okay," he said. He looked around. "Let's try it again. Charlotte, since you're not in this scene, you want to read Annemarie?"

Feeling disloyal to Erica, Charlotte picked up her script and went onstage.

When rehearsal was finally over, as she was standing at her bus stop, Kyle spotted her and frowned. Well, she *had* claimed she had a reliable form of transportation, hadn't she? She felt an absurd impulse to lie, maybe to claim that her car was in the shop, but thought better of it.

"You need a ride?" he asked.

"Thanks, I'm fine. I don't want you to go out of your way."

"You're mid-Wilshire, right? I'm at Park La Brea. Come on."

He probably wanted to ask her about Erica's meltdown in private. She followed him to his car.

To her surprise, he didn't say anything about Erica. The ride home was quiet at first. Then: "I've about had it with Kevin. He doesn't know his lines, and he's sucking the energy out of rehearsals."

Charlotte made a noncommittal sound in reply. Kyle continued: "And Robbie's attitude really stinks. He's not taking anything seriously. It's like he doesn't want to be there at all."

Robbie didn't want to be there. Of course he didn't. Neither did Charlotte, nor, she imagined, did Jeff or the other Jeff or Kevin or Holly or any of them. "I think we're all getting tired. We've been at this a while," she said cautiously.

"Three more weeks," Kyle said. He exhaled. "Can you do Annemarie? Be ready in three weeks?"

She looked at him, but he was watching the road. "Sure. Of course. You think Erica's not coming back?"

"Doesn't matter. She's out."

Would Erica be mad at her for taking her role? "Who'd play my part?"

"Maybe Holly could do it. If she doesn't want it, I'll call in someone who auditioned. It's not that important. Someone can learn it pretty fast. I'm more concerned with Annemarie."

"Okay." Charlotte looked out the windshield. "You need to get over to the next lane soon. You'll be turning right on Olympic." Another moment of silence. "Thanks."

Kyle changed lanes. "You want to go out sometime?"

Ten million replies presented themselves, all of them inadequate to the situation at hand. "The timing's not great right now," she said.

Damn it. That was an anemic response, not at all as unambiguously negative as she wanted it to be. She hoped that Kyle interpreted that as it was meant, a gentle suggestion to never bring up the subject again. He didn't respond, just looked straight ahead.


Charlotte waited until her lunch break the next day to call Erica. "You okay?"

"Yeah. I'm fine. What did Dickhead say?"

"Not much. You know what he's like." She cleared her throat. "He offered me your part."

"Oh, thank God." She could hear nothing but amusement in Erica's voice. "I thought he was going to give it to Holly, and then the production would be really screwed. Good for you."

"Thanks." She paused. "Hey, what happened last night?"

"Nothing. Bad day, and it was time to desert that sinking ship anyway. Wish I'd had the sense to kick him before I went."

Charlotte thought about telling her that Kyle had asked her out, but decided against it. "Good. I just wanted to make sure you were okay."

"I'm okay." Pause. "Hey, don't get offended if I don't go to performances or anything, but let's keep in touch, okay? You're a good person."

"Yeah. Definitely." They clicked off. Charlotte remained where she was, sitting on a concrete bench outside her office building, the remnants of her brown-bag lunch beside her, her skin hot and prickly beneath her suit jacket, and wondered if she'd ever hear from Erica again.


She was no longer Agatha. She was Annemarie. This required a new strategy.

She researched. She memorized. She experimented. Annemarie was simple, vibrant, flamboyant, silly. Annemarie was a delight to play.

Kyle brought in Peregrine to play Agatha, beaky brooding Peregrine, and she was a fantastic pick: intense and gloomy and yet somehow vibrant, bringing life to the role in ways Charlotte never had. So that was all for the best.

Charlotte was the female lead. Time to maximize possibilities. She printed up a bunch of postcards emblazoned with a modified version of her headshot, then addressed them to casting agents, added a quick message about the play with performance dates and a note that she would leave tickets at the door, should they care to attend. These postcards never did much good—agents received stacks of them each day—but this time maybe someone would take her up on her offer.

So everything was good. Except the play still sucked.

It wasn't gelling. It was hobbling along like a lame horse, dying a little more with each rehearsal. Kyle offered her rides home afterwards, and she always accepted, because she didn't know how to refuse without it seeming like an insult.

The cast dynamic had changed. Whereas before she'd had an easy relationship with her fellow cast members, things had cooled, now that she was Annemarie. No, she realized, it was because becoming Annemarie had coincided with her new camaraderie with Kyle, and none of the actors liked Kyle. Kyle was a bad director and an unpleasant person, and since he had singled her out for positive attention, it meant there was something not quite right about her.

A week before performances began, with the first dress rehearsal set for Monday, and Kyle dropped the bomb.

"We're not ready," he said after Friday's rehearsal. "We're going to have to move performances back." He looked at the ceiling, performing mental calculations. "Two weeks. If we push everything back by two weeks, we can do it."

Charlotte's fellow cast members looked worried and perturbed. Her stomach lurched, thinking of the cheerful postcards she'd sent with the performance dates on them.

"We can't," Holly said. "The theater is booked already. Hector says there's another company coming in here at the end of the month, and we have to be finished by then."

"We can work something out," Kyle said. "They can come in when we're done and rehearse after us."

Holly pursed her lips. "You get to talk to Hector yourself," she said.

"He's not going to make a big stink about this, is he?" Kyle said, the disgust clear in his voice.

At that moment Charlotte hated him. She looked at the floor to hide her expression.

After rehearsal, Kyle met with Hector, the theater's manager. Charlotte didn't want to be around for this discussion, so she waited on the stage while Kyle talked with him in the lobby.

In the tiny backstage area, there was a white concrete wall covered with scribbles in permanent marker, signatures and dates, the legacy of past performers in this theater. When rehearsals had first started, Charlotte had wondered if the cast would add their names up there when performances were done. They wouldn't. Even if they muddled through and somehow pulled off an okay show, they wouldn't. There'd be no cast party. Maybe they'd go for drinks after the final show, then they'd all take pains never to see each other again.

Kyle poked his head in the stage area. "Come on," he said.

They walked through the lobby. Hector waited by the door, ready to lock up behind them, looking flustered and unhappy. Kyle's face was red. Charlotte smiled at Hector and wished him a good night. He didn't answer, but he smiled back in reply. Kyle didn't look at either of them.

The drive home was miserable. Kyle glowered.

"He won't let us extend the schedule. He won't even let us come in after the other group finishes. It's just two weeks. He's being unreasonable about it."

"We can stick to the original schedule, can't we?"

"No, we can't. You guys aren't ready to perform."

Charlotte loved, loved the use of "you guys." It took any responsibility for their suckiness right out of Kyle's hands.

Kyle shifted gears in an angry motion. "I need a drink. You want dinner? Let's go get dinner somewhere."

"I can't." The lie was immediate, reflexive. "I just need to get home."

"Why?"

"I'm tired. It's been a long week," she said.

"What's your problem?" Cold and combative. "You act like you don't like me."

She stayed quiet. She needed to get better at confrontations. Maybe there was a class she could take for that.

"I mean, if you don't want to go out with me, just tell me, okay?"

She looked at him. "I don't want to go out with you."

She should soften that with some meaningless words: "I think you're a really great guy," maybe, or the old "I don't want to ruin our friendship" standard. She was too tired and too angry, so she let the statement stand by itself.

"What's the matter with you?" It was venomous. They were only a few blocks from her house, and that was good because she couldn't stay in this car much longer. "I gave you the lead role. You owe me dinner at least."

They were at a light. It was red. Good. One move to grab her purse, another to unbuckle her seatbelt, a third to grab the door handle. "Go to hell," she said.

She swung open the door and stepped out in the middle of stopped traffic. Slammed the door behind her. Stalked over to the curb. Legs trembled, just a bit.

Traffic started moving. She heard honks, maybe because Kyle hadn't moved when the light turned, but she didn't know for sure, because she refused to look back. She walked on, eyes straight ahead, heading for home, away from Kyle.

In the morning, she felt foolish and sick. Things were messed up, and while last night was Kyle's fault, mostly, the situation needed fixing. She'd put too much time into the play to quit, and anyway, if she left now, she'd screw over her cast mates, who didn't need to be punished for her problems with Kyle. She had go to practice and see what damage had been wrought.

When she arrived the theater after work, it was locked. Holly sat on the steps with Jeff Fisher and gave her a small wave. "Hector's not here to open up, I guess," she said. "No sign of Kyle, either."

"It's still early," Charlotte said. She took a seat on the stair beside her.

"What do you think about extending rehearsals?" Holly asked.

"I don't think Hector's going to let us," Charlotte said. "Their talk last night didn't go well."

"I told him it wouldn't," Holly said. She looked glum. "We're going to have to keep to the original schedule, aren't we?"

There was Hector now, parking at the curb. He got out and looked at the assembled party on the steps. "Sorry, kids," he said. "It's off."

Holly was the first to speak. "We can't rehearse tonight?"

Hector shrugged. "Tonight, every night, whatever. Kyle left me a message today. Said he was calling the whole thing off."

"He what?" Holly was very still.

"Said it wasn't ready to go. I said okay. I assumed he'd tell you guys."

Jeff shifted on the step. "You've got to be kidding us."

"Nope. Sorry, guys, I know you all put a lot of work into this." Hector shook his head. "Means I've tied up this place for the past month for nothing, and I'm not getting my cut of the box office out of it." He held up a hand at Holly's look of alarm. "Don't worry, Holly, it's not you, I know. I'm not going to look for reimbursement. Just. . ." He shook his head. "Don't work with Kyle again. The guy's damn unprofessional."

He moved past them and unlocked the theater. Charlotte remained on the steps with Jeff and Holly.

"Damn," Jeff said.

Holly turned to her. "Kyle didn't say anything to you? I know you two have gotten close." There was a hint of malice in the words, but Charlotte couldn't blame her much.

"He didn't say anything." She could have prevented this. If she hadn't blown up at Kyle, if she'd gone to dinner with him and spent an unpleasant hour calming him down and persuading him to keep to the original schedule, things would be fine.

"I feel like I've had the wind knocked out of me." Jeff looked around. "You think he means it? Maybe he'll change his mind."

"Do we need Kyle?" Charlotte asked. "I mean, we're almost there. Everything's in place. Can't we finish up without a director?"

Holly thought for a moment, then shook her head. "Nope. I'm calling it done. I'm sick of it. It's over. Sorry, gang."

Funny how little Charlotte felt like arguing the point.

Jeff Jones arrived now, on time for once, waving at the group. The rest would come too, and they'd all have to be told.

That'd be Holly's job. The play was over, botched, mangled beyond repair. It was time to move on. Charlotte stood up. "You'll call us if anything changes, right?" she asked Holly.

Holly nodded. There was an awkward moment as Charlotte stood there, uncertain of the correct farewell protocol for the situation. She settled on waving to both Jeffs and giving a nod of acknowledgment to Holly before walking off.

## Chapter Eight

SUNDAY WAS A day of miracles. First of all, it rained.

It started raining sometime late Saturday night. She woke to the unfamiliar and welcome noise of rain on the windows. She lay in bed motionless for a long while, trying not to get her hopes up, but no, it was rain.

Sunday morning she was up by six. The rain wouldn't last forever. The clouds would burn off by mid-morning, but she could get out and run while it was still coming down. She changed into a long-sleeved nylon jersey over shorts—just because it was wet didn't mean it would be cold—and jogged up to Wilshire, then headed west toward the ocean.

The rain was wonderful. Sputtering and intermittent, just enough to cool things down and get her plenty wet without hampering her run. A raindrop rolled down her nose and onto her lips, and it tasted of exhaust, but it was the first rain since March, and it was most welcome.

The run helped. The kinks in her system, the stress coiled at the base of her spine, the frustrations of the canceled play, all that melted away. She ran fast, steady and rhythmic. It hurt her lungs in the best possible way.

Hills through Westwood. She charged up them like a pro, not shifting her pace. Her brain overruled her body, not giving her calves a chance to complain about the pounding she was giving them. Not much traffic out: Los Angeles wasn't big on Sunday mornings.

There was more foot traffic here than in her own neighborhood. Westwood, with nearby UCLA, was a college town, and sometimes college kids kept early hours. Dog-walkers, fellow runners, kids with backpacks and books sitting on the covered patios of coffee shops. Good to see Charlotte wasn't the only one enjoying the inclement weather.

As she was waiting for the light to change at Gayley, a small car pulled to a stop on Wilshire beside her. A red convertible, top up. A window rolled down, and a man leaned across the passenger seat toward her. Someone wanting directions, probably, a tourist looking for the way to the Getty, or to campus, or to the beach.

The driver was a young man. Brown skin, white t-shirt, baseball cap. Jazz blasted from his car stereo. Charlotte hated jazz, but that was probably a character flaw on her part, so she wouldn't hold it against this stranger. He didn't have a map, she could see that from a glance into the front seat, and that made her wary. Maybe he was going to offer his phone number, or just a ride to the soaked girl running in the rain. He smiled, shy and goofy, and she was reassured.

"Hey, can I ask you something?" he called out.

She remained where she was, several paces away on the sidewalk, well out of grabbing range. "Sure," she said.

"Are you an actress?" He squinted up at her through the passenger window. Her first reaction was an internal groan, and then she realized he was asking the question like it mattered, not like it was part of his pick-up routine. It disturbed her that her first impulse was to answer no. She'd have to file that thought away and examine it at some later point.

"Yes," she said. Now that she was looking at him, he looked familiar, like maybe he was someone she went to USC with. Or maybe she'd seen his picture in the trades or on television somewhere.

"Can I'm talk to you for a second? I'm a director, my name's Ted Darling, I directed *Runaway Plane*, it came out last year, remember?" He fumbled in the pocket of his shorts. The light turned; traffic honked. He glanced in his rearview mirror, flustered, then turned back to her. "I don't think I have a business card on me, but I can show you my driver's license."

Which would mean nothing to her. His name sounded familiar, maybe, but she hadn't seen *Runaway Plane* and didn't know much about it, much less who directed it.

He got his wallet out, but didn't open it. He stared at it in confusion, as if he'd reached the same conclusion about the usefulness of his identification. "Look, can we go for coffee? I need to talk to you about something."

Split-second decision. "There's a place around the corner. Mount Java," she said, pointing down Gayley. "Want to meet me there?"

"Hop in," he said. The automatic lock popped up on the passenger side.

No way to that. He seemed harmless, but she wasn't stupid. She shook her head. "I'll get your seats wet. Meet you there."

She had a walk sign now. Without giving him time to reply, she shot him a quick wave—friendly, she hoped—and headed across the street toward the coffee place. He turned, she was glad to see. She thought she was glad to see. No, she had better not think anything yet, not until she knew more. She was going to meet with him, and she'd listen to what, if anything, he had to say.

She waited under the awning while he found a parking spot. No sense dripping on Mount Java's floors.

He held the door for her and grinned. He had a friendly face, which was saved from being handsome by too-prominent front teeth. "Want anything?"

"Drip coffee, if you're treating. I don't carry money while I'm running," she said.

The place was crowded, so she staked out a small table by the windows while he ordered. He sat across from her and arranged their drinks on napkins. He'd ordered something fancy and girly for himself, topped with a mountain of whipped cream and caramel and garnished with chocolate curls.

He smiled at her again. "I've seen you running on Wilshire every weekend for about the past year," he said. "Could've sworn I saw you walking a couple weeks ago. Up on Sunset, near Western?"

The theater was just east of Western. "That was probably me," she said. "I walk a lot."

He grinned and nodded and took a sip of his drink. Whipped cream got on his nose, as she could have predicted it would. He wiped at it while regarding her with that pleased, friendly stare.

Oh. "I'm Charlotte," she said. She stuck her hand out. It was cold and probably clammy and unpleasant, but Ted shook it anyway.

"Nice to meet you, Charlotte. Thanks for meeting with me. I hope I didn't weird you out by stopping you."

"You didn't." It was true; she dealt with her fair share of freaks on a regular basis, and she could tell Ted probably didn't qualify.

Ted cleared his throat. "So. You said you were an actress, right? Have I seen you in anything?"

"Not a thing." She smiled and made sure her tone was extra bright. She was on, she needed to be on, even though she was wet and cold and her hamstrings hurt, and her jersey top was probably clinging to her more than it should in this public place. She was blithe and merry, willfully ignoring her sopping hair and bright red face. "I've done a lot of local work." Using a liberal definition of "a lot." She shot down her internal critic and forged on. "I was just in a play up on Sunset, in fact. We got canceled yesterday, so I'm wide open." She smiled and peeled off the plastic lid of her coffee to let it cool. Wet steam rose up. She closed her hands around the cup and let them soak up the residual heat. She was growing chilled. Any minute now her knees would start knocking together. Maybe her teeth would chatter. She turned up her smile another notch.

"I completed the theater program at USC. So I've been out here mostly doing stage work since graduation."

He was quiet for a moment, contemplating his grandiose beverage. He picked up a chocolate curl between two fingers and ate it. When he looked at her, it was like he'd come to some decision. "See, I'm prepping this film now. *Queen of Angels*. Based on the comic book? You heard of it?"

She shook her head. "I'm not sure."

"Should be pretty cool. It's this weird, dark little culty graphic novel. Kind of about the end of the world in L.A. And we start production next month in Vancouver." He shrugged. "We're finishing up the casting right now, and there's this cool little part that I think you'd be great for."

She was quiet for a moment. Ecstatic, but quiet, and cautious. This sounded good. This sounded awesome. "Wow. What's the part?" she asked. Interested but calm.

"You'd be a killer robot." His eyes crinkled when he grinned. "A kick-ass killer robot. Not much in the way of lines, but you'd get to do that grim look like when you're running through the hills."

"I can do grim." She smiled. "I excel at grim, as a matter of fact."

"You know, I have no doubt you do." Ted grinned back, and she didn't know whether it was the psychosomatic effects of her feigned enthusiasm, but she was enjoying this meeting. "You know any martial arts or anything?"

She took a drink of her coffee to give her time to get her answer together. It was strong and good. She grinned again. She had grinned more in the past five minutes than she had all year. "Wouldn't it be awesome if I said I was a black belt?"

Ted laughed. She shook her head. "No martial arts. But I used to take gymnastics lessons"—too many years ago to be counting them here—"and my coordination is good. I learn things fast." She paused. "Does the killer robot have a lot of fight scenes?"

"Nothing but." Ted scooped up whipped cream on his index finger and nibbled it off. His drink really should've come with a spoon. "So does this sound like something you'd be into?"

"It sounds like something I'd be all over. It sounds great." No time for hesitancy here. If she had any cards, they all needed to be on the table.

"Cool." He thought. "It's not really my decision, you know. There's a bunch of suits at the studio who need to have their input."

Studio. He'd said studio, not production company. That meant a studio backing, big money, almost a guaranteed theatrical release. She tried not to get her hopes up: It also meant they'd want to cast name actors, even for the small parts. Ted might be the director, but that didn't mean they wanted him pulling random people off the street and sticking them in his film. "So what's the next step?" she asked.

"I don't know. I'll call you and let you know after I talk to my people, I guess. You got an agent?"

"Nope."

He thought a moment. "Headshot?"

"Sure. Not on me." She grinned. Taking this conversation casually, lightly, as though all the hopes of the past decade weren't culminating right here, was the only way to do this. If she stopped and thought about it, her heart would explode.

"Can you email it to me?" He extracted a pen from his shorts pocket and scribbled on a napkin. "That's my cell number, too, but email's probably the best way to catch me." He passed her the pen. "Let me have your info."

She was sold on him by this point. She scribbled down her cell number and her email address. Her work number, too, for good measure. She had to override the million automatic warnings her brain gave her about getting her hopes up and letting strangers into her life, because she felt sure of his intentions, and it would be stupid to let this pass her by. She wrote out her name, just so he'd remember who he'd been talking to. Maybe he'd find some other girl jogging home later on, maybe he'd think she'd make a good killer robot too. Maybe that random girl would scrawl her number on a napkin as well. Maybe he'd forget all about Charlotte by the time he got home.

He looked at her name. "Charlotte Dent." He looked at her. "Nice meeting you, Charlotte Dent. Here's hoping we can work together soon."

She raised her cup in a toast. He clicked his against hers, and she felt a rare moment of connection, the ephemeral sensation of two human beings moving toward the same goal. It felt good.

## CHAPTER NINE

TWENTY-SEVEN HOURS since having coffee, twenty-five hours after emailing her headshot to the address on the napkin, and Ted called.

It was astounding how far hopes could drop in a day, how a moment of sheer happiness could erode into doubt. She was astonished to hear Ted's voice.

"So I showed them your headshot and rez," he said. "Angie wants to know if you can stop by this afternoon."

Angie. He hadn't mentioned an Angie before. Should she know who Angie was? She'd investigated *Queen of Angels* immediately upon finishing her run, had researched Ted Darling and confirmed he was the same person she'd had coffee with, but she had no idea about Angie. "Sure," she said.

Not so fast. She was at work. She shouldn't even be answering her cell phone at her desk, but Dale was behind closed doors, no one was around, her phone had been ringing, and it had been too important not to pick it up. No. She could meet this afternoon, even if she had to fake an aneurysm to get out of the office.

"Great. I'm meeting her at two at the production company, so we can talk to Mike at the same time, would that work for you? Mike's office is in Beverly Hills." He gave the address. Just a short hop down Santa Monica. Good.

"Sure. Who's Angie?"

"Sorry. Should've mentioned. Angie Craig, she's with the studio, she's one of the EPs, you'll love her. She's been bulldozing this project through, and she's awesome. If Angie likes you, girl, you're home free."

"I'll be there. Is this going to be like an audition?"

"No, no, nothing like that. You won't have to read. Just a meet and greet. So they can link up a personality to the picture, you know."

That meant she'd have to make sure she had a personality for the meeting. Sometimes hers up and left when she got nervous.

The call ended. Dale stepped out of his office. "Can you print some documents for me? I just forwarded you the email."

The trip back to the mundane was jarring. "Yes, sure." She cleared her throat. "I've got an appointment at two. I don't know how long it will last."

It was unprofessional to spring it on him like that, last-minute, but the situation warranted it. "That should be fine. Try to make it back if you can." Dale paused on the way back to his office. "Job interview?" It was a joke, and it wasn't.

She laughed, just like she was supposed to. "No, nothing like that."

The production company was Clarion Films. Their offices inhabited a small suite in a two-story brick building on Little Santa Monica just north of Wilshire. Charlotte only had to wait a moment in the lobby before Ted came out to meet her.

"Hey! Charlotte!" He grinned his gorgeous, ungainly grin and threw open his arms. "Good to see you!"

"Hi, Ted." The open arms were not, apparently, going to evolve into a hug, but were merely an uncontrolled extension of Ted's high spirits. She held out a hand; Ted clasped it in both of his.

He looked her over. She'd been nervous about this part. The last time he'd seen her, she'd been soaked to the bone in skimpy jogging clothes. She looked different in her civilian duds. Maybe different enough to no longer fit his conceptualization of his killer robot. He grinned.

"You look great. You just came from work?"

"Yes." She followed him behind the reception desk, down a short hall. The Clarion offices were cheerful and bright. Lemon walls, bright aqua carpet, red furniture, like a kindergarten without the smell of paste and tempera paints.

"I've just been telling Angie about you. You'll love Angie. She's really psyched about this project. It's awesome." Ted led the way into a small conference room. "Hey, Angie, this is Charlotte."

Angie got up from her seat to shake her hand. Angie was a Valkyrie. Heavy-set for Los Angeles, with a build that would be described as athletic anywhere else in the country. Early forties, thick ginger hair that stopped at her shoulders, pale freckles, a snub nose anchoring a pleasant face. She looked both brainy and brawny, like she'd once captained the lacrosse team at Vassar. "Charlotte. Thanks for coming in on such short notice."

"My pleasure. Thanks for meeting me." Big smile. This was all about being upbeat and accommodating and happy to be here.

"Take a seat." Charlotte sat beside Ted. Angie sat across the table from her. "Mike was supposed to be here, but he got caught up in a meeting across town, so he'll just have to meet you later."

No clue who Mike was. Charlotte kept smiling.

"So I have your headshot," Angie said. "Looks like you've been doing mostly local stuff?"

"A lot of theater." She decided not to bring up her failed pilot. Old news, and it would be embarrassing if Angie pressed for details.

"Our start date is going to be October 22 at this point. That's looking pretty firm. All principal photography will be in Vancouver, except maybe some pickups locally later on. Is that going to be a problem?"

"Not at all." She cleared her throat. "How long do you think the shoot will last?" Exotic lingo, "shoot." Slid it into the conversation like a pro.

"Eight weeks, tops. We'll be wrapped by Christmas. We won't need you for the whole time, obviously, but we need you to be available."

Something in her soul soared at the way Angie was talking, like her involvement was a done deal. "Sounds great," she said.

"You know the role? Any questions about it?"

She thought for a minute. "Will there be any nudity?" It wasn't a sticking point, but it'd be good to know going in.

Angie shrugged. "I can't imagine there would be. Not in the drafts I've seen." She glanced at her watch. "Well, look, we're still bringing in people and nothing's set, but either Teddy or I'll be getting back to you pretty soon. Ted's got all your contact info? Ted? Good."

Ah. Still bringing in people. That was a more familiar path than this giddy whirlwind of success. So it wasn't a done deal at all. Nothing to do but wrap things up and hurry back to the office to finish copying files.

"I'll walk you out," Ted said to her.

"Really great meeting you, Charlotte." Angie stuck her hand out again and smiled as though she meant it.

"You, too." Should she do something else? Say something to leave an impression? Compliment Angie's shoes? This was the part at which she was pathetic, this business of sticking in people's memories. She shook hands and left with Ted.

Ted patted her on the arm. "I told you she was really cool. She liked you."

"Yeah?"

"Yeah. And if I like you and Angie likes you, it's pretty much set."

"I hope you're right." It sounded too personal, too much of a confession, too much genuine need and weakness right on the surface, but something about Ted's overt enthusiasm brought out a desire to lose all her layers of protection. "I really hope you're right. It'd be great to be in your film, Ted."

"You will be. Have faith. It's going to be awesome. You know we've got Taura Trejo committed to it? And John Hyde is playing Mephistopheles. The script is awesome, and I can't wait to start shooting." He sounded more like a giddy fanboy than a seasoned director, and that was both delightful and a little frightening.

"So I was thinking, you're probably going to want to have an agent when they get talking about contracts and stuff," he said.

"Yeah, ideally," she said. She searched her brain for the best way to point out that if getting an agent were simply a matter of wanting one, that hurdle would've been cleared way back at the beginning of the steeplechase.

"Here. Let me give you a number. His name's Rick Tooley." Ted waited while Charlotte got out her phone and entered the name into her address book. "No cracks about the name, he's heard all of them. He's with UTM. He represents a whole bunch of people, me included. He's a good guy. He'll hook you up."

Calling people out of the blue to ask favors. That was another thing she was poor at. As if reading her hesitation, Ted continued.

"I'll give him a call right now and talk to him about you, then you call him later this afternoon. He'll make things go a whole lot smoother for you." He shrugged. "Ten percent, you know, but he'll more than make up for it with you. You're a first-timer, so the studio's going to try to get you as cheaply as possible."

She knew the SAG minimums. As cheaply as possible was still more money than she was making, more money than she had ever made. Still, it would be good to have someone looking out for her interests. "I'll call him. Thanks, Ted."

He did hug her then, at the elevator, a quick gesture of uncontrollable excitement and affection. Once again, it dawned on her that she was missing human contact these days. There was something nice about a quick hug from someone who didn't know her that well, but thought she was pretty good stuff anyway.

Back at the office, safe in the file room with the door closed and the copy machine whirring, she called Rick Tooley.

An assistant answered the phone, male and brisk. "United Talent Management. Rick Tooley's desk."

"Hi. I'm Charlotte Dent. I think Ted Darling told Mr. Tooley I'd be calling?" "Mr. Tooley" was over-formal for Los Angeles, maybe even a little obsequious, but agents intimidated her, and UTM was one of the majors.

"One moment." Ah. She'd be put on hold while the assistant sent a text to Tooley announcing her call, then Tooley would text the agent back to take a message. She'd temped in an agency once for a long month; she knew this drill.

"Charlotte. Rick here." The smooth voice on the line almost made her drop the phone. "You there?"

"Yes. Sorry. I don't know if Ted had a chance to—"

"Yeah, he did. *Queen of Angels*, right? He said you were going to need someone to negotiate your deal with the studio."

"Yes, that's right. But this might be premature. I don't even know if I have the role yet." She was talking too fast, her words flooding on top of each other.

Rick sounded amused. "From what Ted was saying, sounds like pretty much a foregone conclusion. Just need to hammer out a contract, and that's that. You want me to handle it?"

"If you would, that'd be great. Thank you."

"Hell, don't thank me. This is easy money for me. It's not like I had to get you the audition or anything." There was a pause on the line. "They're going to offer scale. I can get you more than that, but I got to be honest with you, nobody knows you from Eve here, they're not going to come up that much."

"Honestly, it doesn't matter. Whatever you can do will be awesome. Thank you."

"You don't play poker much, do you? Probably a good idea I'm handling this for you. You got your SAG card yet?"

"Not yet."

"You want to get yourself one of those? You can waive it, you know, for your first Guild production, but if I were you, I'd get it over with. I'll get the studio to cover your initiation fees, how's that?"

"That'd be great. Thank you so much." She had a sense she'd thanked him too many times already this phone call. "What's the next step?"

"I'll call Angie, maybe talk to Mike." Ah, the mysterious Mike again. "See who I'm supposed to be talking to at the studios. See what kind of deal I can get you. Then I'll run it by you, and if it's okay, you get to sign about a bazillion papers. And that's pretty much everything."

"Sounds good. Great, actually," she said.

"I'll send over our agency agreement today. You can look it over, sign it, send it back. You at home?"

"Work," she said.

"Yeah? Where do you work?"

"Ausberger, Bender, Bob. It's a law firm—"

"In Century City. Sure. You work with Dale and Ken and whatshername, the new partner, Marnie?"

"Marti Bob. Yes."

"Yeah, we do a lot of business with Ausberger. Good company. Look, if you're on good terms with any of the suits, you get them to look over whatever you're signing first, okay? Tell them it's from me, they know me. Any time you can get yourself some free legal advice, you take it." He was quiet for a moment. "You know you're going to have to ditch the job for the film, right?"

"It's kind of a selling point," Charlotte said.

Rick laughed. "Okay, Charlotte. I'll courier over the agreement now. You can scan it and email it back to me once you've signed it, then drop the original in the mail, okay?"

"Okay. And. . . thanks." That made four times, but it seemed like he deserved it.

"No sweat." And Rick was gone, and the copy machine was silent, waiting to be loaded up with fresh originals.

## CHAPTER TEN

CHARLOTTE SPENT THE next two weeks waiting for her life to change. And then it did.

She'd become superstitious, convincing herself if she told anyone, she'd jinx it. So she kept silent during two consecutive weekend phone calls with her parents, which was hard, but if she told them and it fell through, their shattered expectations would be piled on top of hers.

But now, the courier from UTM had just dropped off an envelope at the office, and inside the envelope was her contract, with her start date on it and everything.

Rick Tooley had done his part. Her salary was more than SAG minimum, though not by much. She was guaranteed five weeks, possibly extending to the full eight, and it worked out to almost as much money as she had made all of last year. She inhaled, dizzy.

Dale was at his desk in his office. She got up, contract in hand, and knocked on the door frame.

"Do you have a minute?" she asked.

She closed the door and sat in his client chair. She held the contract in both hands.

"I just got cast in a film. And they sent over the contract. Do you think you could take a quick look at it to make sure everything's okay?"

"A film?" Dale held his hand out for the contract and put on his glasses. She handed it over. He glanced at the top. "Clarion? Is this that comic book thing they're working on, the one with the *Runaway Plane* director?"

"*Queen of Angels*. Ted Darling. Yes." She waited while Dale flipped through it.

"Featured role. Congratulations." He looked at her over the tops of his glasses. "I assume this means you'll be leaving us?"

"Yes. I'm sorry. I'll have to. The start date is in mid-October."

"We'll be sorry to lose you." Dale handed back the contract. "It's fine. Boilerplate. You're going to read it yourself before signing, right?"

"Of course."

"Got an agent?"

"Rick Tooley. UTM." Technically, Rick was only her agent for this project—she couldn't expect him to continue representing her beyond this—but it was good to have him in her corner for the time being.

"Oh, Rick. Good man. I've talked with him a couple of times. Good company, UTM. You'll be fine." He smiled at her. "Congratulations, Charlotte. When you get a moment, type up a letter of resignation, will you? Doesn't have to be today. Just something I can send over to HR."

"Sure." And that was that. Elation, relief, fresh worries about the unknown future, all hitting her at once. The legal assistant chapter of her life was coming to an overdue finish.

She read the contract at her desk, struggling to keep her brain from drifting off into speculation on how her life would be improved. She signed where indicated—Rick's assistant had placed sticky arrow tabs on the correct spots—and made a copy for her own safekeeping.

She could consider herself hired. Cast. An industry professional. Would there be an announcement in the trades? Maybe Rick would drop a hint to the *Hollywood Reporter* or *Variety* about the casting. Or maybe that was something a publicist did. Maybe she needed one of those.

Maybe she was getting ahead of herself. She had three weeks before filming started, and she still had a job making copies up until that time, and there was a lot of preparation that needed to be done.

She called her parents when she got home. Her dad answered. Tired and out of breath just from picking up the phone. "Hello?"

"Dad. It's Charlotte."

"Oh, Charlotte." He sounded confused. Probably the medication, though usually he was sharper in the early evening, when the pills he took in the morning had a chance to wear off. "How are you, Charlotte?"

"I'm fine. I have good news." She was using her bright voice, the one she used with her parents these days, the one infused with cheer and laughter. The one that made her sound like a kindergarten teacher on methamphetamines. "I got cast in a movie."

"That's terrific." He was quiet. Breathing heavily. "That's. . ."

There was a long pause. Maybe he'd finish his thought eventually, but she couldn't stand the dangling silence and the labored breathing any longer, so she started talking. "It's called *Queen of Angels*. It's based on a comic. I just have a really small part. I'm playing a robot." She laughed. "I'm one of the bad guys. It should be a lot of fun. We're filming in Vancouver."

"Vancouver. . ." He was drifting. "That's terrific. Really terrific."

"Yeah, I think it is." Silence. "Is mom around?"

"She's still at work. She'll probably call you tonight when she gets in."

"Great." She paused. "How are you?"

Heavy breathing. "Fine. Are you going to make it home for Christmas?"

"Yeah. I'll be done by then." Her throat was tight. "That's all I needed to say. And I love you."

"I love you, too." There was silence. "I'm proud of you, Charlotte."

She was going to cry if she didn't hang up soon. She severed the connection, leaving her parents' home in Idaho far, far behind.

Three weeks. Three weeks to prepare.

She kept the news about her film quiet, but everybody at work knew. Nobody was impressed, or at least they weren't showing it. Made sense. Everyone knew too much about the industry to be too enchanted by someone else's good fortune in it.

On her first Saturday after signing her contract, she made a detour to the big comic book store on Venice. Research purposes.

Had she ever been in a comic book store before? She didn't think so, at least not as an adult, and as with most new experiences, it left her a bit thrown at first. The interior was dark and disorienting after the dizzy brightness outside. It took her a while to suss out the layout.

*Queen of Angels* was published by Montezuma, that much she knew. She looked at the boxes of comics laid out on low tables, wondering where to begin.

"Can I help you find something?" The clerk, young and hairy.

"Do you have *Queen of Angels*?" she asked.

"If you're looking for individual issues, probably not. I think we've got the graphic novels in stock," he said. He led the way to the bookshelves across the room. He scanned the shelf, pulled down a volume, handed it to her. "That's the first one. It's a compilation of the first eight issues. That what you want?"

She glanced down at the cover. A lurid line drawing, a scantily-clad winged woman standing in front of a splatter of bright red blood. Lordy. "That's it. Thanks."

She followed him up to the counter and paid for it. He glanced at her. "They're making it into a movie, you know."

"Yeah." She cleared her throat, uncertain. She was official now, she could talk about this, couldn't she? "I'm actually. . . I'm in it." At his look, she clarified. "I just got cast in the film. I thought I should read up on it."

He stared at her for a moment. "No kidding. Who are you?"

"Ah. . . Jin. I'm Jin. That's the killer robot, right?"

"You're Jin? No shit, really? Wow." He stared at her. She could tell he was comparing his mental image of the character with her. There was no way it would be an exact match. Was she a disappointment? "That's really cool. Congratulations."

That was a nice response. Good. "Thanks."

"Have I seen you in anything else? What's your name?"

"Charlotte Dent, and no, you haven't. This is my first film."

"Lenny Carter." He stuck out his hand. "Nice to meet you. Look, you think I could ask you something?"

"Sure."

"I have this blog, Dead Man's Blurb, it's about comic books and entertainment and stuff. There's a lot of interest in the *Angels* movie—do you think I could interview you for it? It wouldn't take long."

Her immediate reaction was to say yes, and then it occurred to her she needed to be cautious. "You know what, I'd really like to, but I can't. I'm sorry. I don't think I'm allowed to discuss it until they tell me I can."

He shrugged. "Yeah, okay, no problem. I get that." He didn't sound like it was no problem. He sounded disgruntled. Damn it, she hated letting people down. "Good luck."

"Thanks." She took her bag with the comic—graphic novel—in it and left, feeling like she'd ruined what had been a promising encounter.

Sure enough, that evening, when she visited Dead Man's Blurb, her fears were realized:

*So as my regular readers know (both of you. Hey, if there's more of you out there it wouldn't kill you to drop me a line now and then and let my know how I'm doing okay? Its the little things that get me thru the day) Ive been following the press for the big-screen version of Ramirez' Queen of Angels. Everything's been very hushush so far but today I got my first scoop when I ran into Christie Dent, the girl who'll be playing Jin. And no you haven't heard of her before. I had a chance to talk to Miss Dent. She's cute (you know the type: very Miss LA, blond, short, skinny) but not the knockout I expected Jin to be (hey, Ramirez drew Jin without a bra for a reason, right?) Anyway like i said the Dent girl is O.K. but not what I pictured. And she might want to loose the 'tude. . . when I asked for an interview youdve thought Id just asked her to marry her or something. Honey, my advise to you is, get over yourself cuz you ain't nobody yet and with that attitude you wont ever be.*

Well. That was wonderful. Her cheeks were hot. Wow. Her first-ever bit of publicity. Wow. It kind of. . . kind of sucked, really.

So the barely-literate scribblings of some guy who felt snubbed because she wouldn't—couldn't—do him a favor had the power to affect her. She could feel this ruining her day, and that was stupid, beyond stupid. Because she wanted to be famous, or sort of famous at least, because there was no way she would put herself through all this otherwise, and at the first taste of public life she had no business feeling repelled.

It was time to go offline. She broke out her copy of *Queen of Angels* and settled in to see what she had gotten herself into.

The artwork was weird: spectral, skeletal ink drawings, blotchy like a Rorschach test, solid blocks of powerful colors. The story itself was evocative and grim, all about a post-apocalyptic Los Angeles inhabited by wraiths and mutants and wretches. It was heavily steeped in Mexican culture: Catholicism blended with Santeria, Day of the Dead and mystic images. If she'd been a film executive, she'd be cursing right now that someone had snagged the rights before her.

And there was Jin. Tiny hotpants, shirtless beneath an un-zipped jacket, boots up past her knees. Ah, yes. And Ted had seen her jogging in her wet jersey and shorts and had thought she'd make a fine Jin. Huh. Jin didn't do much other than shoot ridiculously large weapons and kick her way through brick walls and look fantastic while doing it, but she felt an absurd rush of pleasure that this character was hers, all hers.

Three weeks. Three weeks at this rate, and she'd whip herself up into a blind panic before she ever made it to Vancouver.

Erica called the day before her flight. She hadn't heard from her since she'd ditched the play.

"So I was thinking we should get together for cocktails or something," Erica said. "You can tell me how the play turned out."

"It didn't," Charlotte said. "Kyle canceled us before performances started."

"Rough. I'm sorry, Charlotte," Erica said. She didn't sound like she meant it.

"It's probably for the best. We were sucking anyway," she said. She paused, then stalled. "What's new with you?"

"Nothing much. I think I need to get a job." Erica laughed, tinny and strained through the receiver. "I mean, I really think I need to get a job. I was wondering if you had any suggestions. Maybe the place where you work, maybe they need someone part-time?"

"I don't work there anymore," Charlotte said. "Friday was my last day." It had been a good day. Ken and Dale and Marti got her a cake, and everyone seemed sad to see her go. "I got an acting job. Paid."

"No kidding? Theater?"

"A film, actually. It's called _Queen of Angels_. Ted Darling, the guy who directed _Runaway Plane_, he's doing it. I just have a tiny role, but I'm going up to Vancouver tomorrow to start filming."

"Charlotte, that's awesome. Congratulations. I'm really happy for you."

"Thank you."

There was a pause, then Erica cleared her throat. "We'll have to get together when you get back so you can tell me all about it. How long are you up there? A month?"

"Just about. Five weeks, I think. I don't really know. We should be done by Christmas."

"That's. . . awesome." Erica was quiet. "Look, I shouldn't keep you. You've got a million things to do, I'm sure."

"Yeah. Thanks, Erica." She wanted to add something about how Erica needed to hang in there and her luck would turn, too, but it would sound condescending, and she didn't know if it was true. In the end, she settled for just hanging up.

## CHAPTER ELEVEN

VANCOUVER. CLOUDY AND dark and pristine. Air so clean it burned her nostrils. Forests of tall pines, so green they looked black, gray mountains in the near distance, everywhere surrounded by water the color of rock. Charlotte fell in love with the city before she made it out of the airport.

She was met outside Customs by a girl with a dark ponytail and a baggy black parka. Rick had said someone would meet her; she hadn't known what that would mean, but apparently it meant a girl barely out of her teens carrying a hand-lettered sign reading "CHARLOTTE DENT." Ripped black canvas shoes, leggings bunched at the ankles, a tiny blue star tattoo at the corner of her left eye.

"Hi. I'm Charlotte," Charlotte said.

The girl glanced at her. She grinned. "Yes, you are." She thrust out a hand and shook. Metallic blue polish on bitten nails. "I'm Kerri. I'm one of the P.A.s." She looked at Charlotte's two suitcases. "That's everything?"

"That's all they let me bring on the plane," Charlotte said. In truth, she was over-packed for five weeks. She had to be on the set in costume most of the time, so she'd brought only the barest necessities for clothes. If she needed something in particular, she could always go out and buy it. And wasn't that a glorious, luxurious, gluttonous thought?

"Cool. Hang on a sec, I can get one of those hand trucks."

"I don't need it. They're light. I'm good. I'm balanced." A suitcase in each hand, and she was good to go.

Kerri grinned at her, as if she approved. "Let me take one of these at least. Here." She took control of one of the suitcases before Charlotte could argue. "I'm parked kinda far away. Hope you don't mind. I can bring the car around if you'd rather."

"Doesn't matter. I could use the walk." The flight had been only three hours, but she felt thick and slow. Besides, it was euphoric getting outside the airport at last and taking her first whiffs of that reviving Vancouver air. Los Angeles had been in the low eighties when she'd left this morning; here, it was probably thirty degrees cooler. It was wonderful. She was alive.

Kerri had a tiny car, something red and compact and probably not much younger than Kerri herself. Between them, they managed to maneuver the bags into the inadequate trunk space.

"How was your flight?" Kerri asked.

"Good. Uneventful. They put me in first class, which was kind of cool. I got a chance to read the script for the first time. It was just delivered to me last night."

"You're lucky," Kerri said. "They won't let me see it. Is it good?"

"Yeah, it's great. Should be a good movie." "Great" was stretching it. The script was okay. It was a disappointment after the gorgeous lyricism of the source material, but it wasn't bad. Plot lines had been simplified, characters were combined or deleted. At first read, it was clunky. Still, she wouldn't be able to see the full potential until the read-through. The creator of the comic, Freddie Martinez, was one of the three screenwriters credited on the title page, and that was a good thing, probably.

Jin had twelve lines in five scenes. She'd counted, twice.

"Have you ever been to Canada?" Kerri asked.

She shook her head. "Never. I grew up in Idaho, though, so I'm used to all the pine trees. It's really gorgeous." She looked at Kerri. "You're local? I mean, not with the L.A. crew?"

"I'm from here. I get a lot of work on film sets. Just freelance. They always need people to help out. And more of you come up here every year." There were reasons for that, reasons involving tax breaks and things she never found interesting, that made it cheaper to move an entire production up to Canada than to remain in Los Angeles.

Kerri glanced at her sideways. "You know, I don't know you. I'm sorry. Should I know other stuff you've done?"

"Nope. I've done nothing," she said. "This is my first film."

"Oh, good. See, I'm really bad with names, and a lot of times I watch movies without paying attention to the actors at all, so I didn't know if you'd think I was really stupid that I didn't know who you were." They drove into the city, merging on the freeway, approaching the towering glass spires of downtown Vancouver. "I picked up King Lear yesterday, and I couldn't remember anything he'd been in. I think I pissed him off. He was pretty cranky for the rest of the trip."

"King Lear?"

"The old English guy. I can't think of his name. He played King Lear in some film twenty years ago. He told me all about it. In great detail."

"You mean Sir John Hyde?" Hyde had played Richard II, not Lear.

Kerri nodded and shifted lanes. "That's him. He smoked all the way to the hotel, too. If my car smells like an ashtray, it's not my fault."

There was a heavy fog over the city as they approached, giving it a gray, ethereal look. Melancholy and beautiful and still, a million miles from Los Angeles.

"So a bunch of the others are already here. I've been taking people to fittings and stuff. Some of the actors—Taura Trejo, you know her? I met her last week." Kerri wrinkled her nose. Charlotte decided not to read anything into that just yet. "And that Ted guy, the director? He seems really nice."

"Ted's a good guy," Charlotte said. The last time she'd seen him, during her wardrobe fitting back in Los Angeles, he'd been just passing through on his way to a meeting, but he'd stopped to give her a quick hug and make sure everything was going well. Ted wouldn't be the kind of director to yell or throw things or make life miserable for anyone, and as far as she was concerned, for this, her first film experience ever, that was more important than being brilliant. Or even competent. Though hopefully he would be all of that, too.

The hotel was downtown, in a restored old building nestled between two graceful spires of steel and glass. It had a pale yellow brick façade and a cheerful red awning. A revolving door, all brass and glass, with a doorman in a smart green overcoat and cap. When Kerri pulled to the curb, her little car was surrounded at once: bellhops at the trunk retrieving her suitcases, a valet holding the door open and helping Kerri out. Everything was taken care of with a lightning-fast efficiency. Charlotte had a momentary fear she'd never see her suitcases again.

"Is everyone from the film staying here?" she asked.

Kerri shrugged. "Not really. Just a lot of the out-of-town crew and production staff, some of the talent, those who aren't local. We've got the ninth and tenth floors. Taura rented a house on the water, and I think Ted's got his own place, too. I haven't seen Doug Appleby yet; if he's arrived, he's not staying in the hotel. There's been some suits from the studio, too, but I don't think they're staying anywhere. They came up yesterday just for the day."

"That's a bit of a commute," Charlotte said.

Kerri grinned. "I know. They got here around ten, eleven in the morning, and then returned on an evening flight. I've been making lots of trips to the airport, believe me. I'll be glad when all of you are settled in."

Kerri handled all the arrangements at the check-in counter; Charlotte only had to sign where indicated and accept her card key. Kerri accompanied her up to her room. "I don't think you have one of the suites, it's just a single room, but this place is really nice, and the views are great," she said. She looked a little anxious. Maybe one of the other actors had given her a hard time about the size of the rooms.

The door was open, the bellhop already unloading her suitcases from his trolley when they arrived. The room was small but pretty, done up in greens and golds and pinks. The walls were covered with a muted striped fabric; the bedspread matched the walls.

"Is the room okay?" Kerri asked. She stuck her billfold back in her messenger bag. She'd tipped the bellhop while Charlotte was looking around the room; even though that was part of Kerri's job, to anticipate the needs of the talent whenever possible, it still made her feel a little useless.

"It's lovely. Thank you," Charlotte said. "And thanks for picking me up, too."

"No problem. I'm going to take off now. Here's my mobile number on my card in case you need anything, and that's the number for the production office. Someone will probably give you a call in a bit and let you know what's going on. As far as I know, nothing's happening today. There's a meeting tomorrow, but they'll tell you about it."

"Okay. Thanks."

Then Charlotte was alone at last, in this pretty hotel room in this pretty city. She went to the windows and pulled aside the stiff drapes to take a look at the view. She was on a high floor, so she could see far away: granite-colored water and hills and those tall, tall pines. Best of all, the window wasn't just a window, it was a sliding door that led out onto a tiny balcony with a single wire-frame chair and a skinny bistro table. She had a balcony of her very own.

She was restless and exhausted. Was she hungry? She didn't feel hungry, but she hadn't eaten since Los Angeles. She could order room service. Or she could venture out into the city and see what kind of food could be had in the immediate area. She could take a bath in the big claw-foot tub, using the complimentary miniature bottles of grapefruit-mint bath gel, then dry herself off on the thick white towels, then swaddle herself in the matching bathrobe. Were there slippers? There probably were.

Then she could sit out on her balcony in the crisp, damp air and wait for someone to call to tell her what she was supposed to be doing, then she could peruse the room-service menu, then she could explore the options on the flat screen television hidden inside the armoire. Didn't sound like a bad plan at all.

## CHAPTER TWELVE

THE MEETING KERRI referred to turned out to be the read-through, scheduled the next morning for the civilized and rational hour of ten o'clock. After a full night's rest in crisp white sheets, Charlotte breakfasted on her balcony: excellent French-pressed coffee, fresh fruit, and thick slices of toast with local jam. Huckle-berry.

When her phone rang, it was Kerri, informing her that her ride to the production facility was on the way.

Charlotte grabbed her script and went down to the lobby. A cluster of young men were seated in the overstuffed armchairs, talking amongst themselves. They looked like movie people. Jeans and canvas sneakers and windbreakers, slogan t-shirts over long sleeved shirts. Production staff probably. Screenwriters. She took a seat nearby and tried to look friendly and approachable, and hoped someone friendly would approach her.

It worked. A young man who looked scarcely out of his teens, in jeans and a baggy jersey for a sports team she didn't recognize, ambled over to her. "You with the film?"

"Yes. I'm Charlotte Dent."

"Trey Aaron." He stuck out his hand. "You talent?"

"Uh-huh. I'm playing Jin. You?"

"Yeah. I'm Escobar." Ah. She recognized his name from pre-liminary cast listing in the trades. He'd starred in some series for tweens, Disney Channel stuff, way out of her demographic, but at least he had verifiable credits, which was more than could be said for her. "You meet any of the guys yet?"

Trey led her over to the guys in the armchairs. "Hey, everyone, this is Charlotte. She's talent. Charlotte, these are the writers." Hey, she was good at this. "Bob and Freddie and. . . sorry, man, I forgot your name."

"Jerry. Nice to meet you, Charlotte." The overlooked man stuck out his hand without rising from his seat. She shook it, waved to the group in general, gave a series of hellos all around.

"Charlotte Dent, right? You're the girl Ted got for Jin?" That was Freddie. Tall and wiry and intense. He scrutinized her. "You look younger than your headshot," he said at last.

"It's an old picture," she said. Well. That was brilliant. "You're Freddie Ramirez, right?" she asked.

Freddie looked cautious. "Yeah?"

"You wrote the book, right? The comic, I mean?"

"Yeah. You read it?"

"I did. Just the first part, the first bound volume. It's great. I really enjoyed it."

The intense look lightened a bit. "Thanks," he said.

A man came through the revolving doors into the lobby and approached them. He had on a bright red windbreaker and held a walkie-talkie. "Van's ready outside, gang. Just you five, right?"

"What about Sir John? He's staying on my floor," Trey said.

The man shrugged. "Got a call that he couldn't make it. It's just you guys. All set?"

They were herded outside into a small waiting van that drove them four blocks to the makeshift production office. *Queen of Angels* had commandeered space in some local production company for the duration of the shoot. If this was going to be a usual routine, if they were going to be meeting here a lot, it'd be easier to walk. Only maybe they wouldn't let her do that, maybe there was some insurance prohibition about letting them do anything on their own.

They were shown into a conference room. Baskets on the table filled with bagels and croissants. Pink boxes of doughnuts, carafes of orange juice and hot coffee. It was a good thing she'd breakfasted earlier. She had a hard time resisting doughnuts, and she could see one with pink frosting and multicolored sprinkles calling out her name.

Ted sat at the head of the table, deep in conversation with Angie and a man clad in an expensive suit and a worried expression. Ted looked up and grinned. "Hey, guys. Hey, Charlotte. Glad you could make it."

Angie looked over at them. "First ones here. Thanks for being on time, guys. We really appreciate it."

Was it possible not to be on time? They'd been shepherded straight to this spot.

Trey and the writers dug into the bagels with gusto. She nursed a cup of orange juice. She wanted coffee, but she'd already had plenty at the hotel, and too much would either make her jittery and uptight or make her need to visit the ladies' room every twenty minutes. Either would be inconvenient during a run-through.

People arrived. No one she recognized. Low-level cast members like herself. Taura Trejo was the first big name to show up. She came with a bodyguard, whom she left at the door. Taura was gamine and lovely, with dark hair, huge eyes, and great skin. She clutched her paper cup of coffee and waggled her fingers at the group.

"Hi, everyone. Sorry I'm late. I overslept." She gestured to her pants. "I was in such a hurry, I just came here in my pajamas. I'm so lame." She laughed.

"No problem, Taura. We're just waiting on Doug," Ted said.

"I'm here, I'm here." Doug flopped into the only available chair. "I would have been here on time, but my stupid driver got confused by all the one-way streets and kept getting us further and further away. Asshole." He looked at the table. "Doughnuts. Who do they think's going to eat those?" He picked one up and waggled it at Taura. "Doughnut, Taura?"

Taura wrinkled her nose. "Ew. Get it away. That's gross."

Ted cleared his throat. "We should probably get started, folks. We've got a lot to do here." He motioned toward Angie and the worried man. "Most of you know Mike from Clarion, right, and Angie from the studio? They're going to be here with us today, and then off and on throughout filming, their schedules permitting."

"Hi, gang," Angie said. The worried man took his phone from his pocket, frowned at the screen, then put it back without saying a word.

"Sir John had to return to L.A. for an appointment last night, so he won't be here today. He was going to try to join us by speakerphone. . ." Ted turned to the man in the red jacket, who shook his head once. ". . .but it doesn't look like that's working out, so we're just going to have to go on without him."

"Do we have to call him Sir John?" Doug asked.

"It'd be nice if you did, yes. It's a form of respect," Angie said.

Doug belched. "Only if he calls me Sir Doug." He grinned at Taura, who shot him an exasperated look.

Angie looked blank for a moment, her gaze fixed on the wall on the reverse side of Doug's head, as though she could see straight through his cranium, then her expression shifted into focus again. "Ted, I think we're ready to start."

"Right. You all have your scripts? We're going to start at the beginning. Jerry and Bob, you want to read the parts for anyone who's not here? Freddie, you read the descriptions, okay?"

"We're going to be reading the entire script?" Taura asked.

"Yeah, that's the plan," Ted replied.

"But that'll take forever. That'll take longer than it would to watch the movie, right?"

"Two hours, yes," Angie said, her tone dry.

"It's gonna go fast, Taura. Come on. From the top. Freddie?"

Freddie started to read the opening description aloud. Charlotte closed her eyes and tried to picture it unfolding in her head.

Taura's delivery was wooden, but at least she could read. Trey was bubbly and fun. Doug stumbled over his lines. He was the bounty hunter, Gideon. Charlotte guessed the casting made sense, sort of: Doug was handsome and appealing in a mass-market way, but there was a frattish arrogance to him that put her off.

"We need to hide in the hills, Your Highness. We're not safe out in the open," Doug read. He whacked his script against the table. "Well, no kidding. They're shooting at us right now, right? No shit, it's not safe. This is really crappy, guys, I'm sorry."

The trio of writers sat with their mouths in tight lines, a mute Greek chorus of disapproval. Angie's lips twitched. She looked bemused, like maybe she was thinking of how Doug would look without his head.

"The line's fine, Doug." Ted shifted in his chair. "Let's keep going, everyone."

Thirty pages in, and Charlotte hadn't made an entrance yet. She was beginning to realize how very small her part was. How many days would she be needed on the set?

They took a break halfway through, which was a little ridiculous—didn't these people ever see a movie in a theater, or sit in a lecture hall or a long staff meeting?

In any case, she could get a breath of that clean Vancouver air and clear her head a bit before returning to the read-through. She gathered her script and rose from the table. Doug turned to her as if noticing her for the first time.

"You one of the P.A.s?" he asked.

"Nope. I'm in the film. I don't have any lines in the first act," she said.

"Dude. Why'd they make you come here, then? That kind of sucks."

"It's no problem. It's useful hearing the script read aloud, anyway."

Doug shrugged. "Whatever. Where do you show up?"

"I'm with Mephistopheles. I'm his bodyguard," she said.

"You local?"

"No. From L.A."

"So they're paying you to be here every day for just a couple lines, for the entire production? Why didn't they just cast someone from the area? They'd only have to pay them the days they actually worked. It'd be a lot cheaper."

"Except we liked Charlotte and wanted to cast her." Angie stood and joined the conversation. She slid an arm around her shoulders and gave her a quick hug. "Good to have you here, hon. Everything going okay?"

"Everything's great." Charlotte glanced at Angie, who was giving Doug a look that bore certain similarities to a glare. So Angie was coming to her defense. Nice to know she was wanted. To a certain extent, she was a warm body, filling a role any number of others could fill. It must be nice to be in Doug's shoes, or Taura's, where they could afford to be obnoxious, secure in their worth to the studio due to the enhanced value they would bring to the film. As important as playing Jin was to her, her involvement wasn't nearly as important to the studio. If she wasn't worth it, they could cut their losses and jettison her.

## CHAPTER THIRTEEN

THE NEXT DAY she was expected in wardrobe. Once again, she got a call in the morning. Once again, the van was waiting to take her to her destination.

The wardrobe trailer was parked outside on the lot surrounding the production facility. A friendly woman with a lot of red hair and clunky red suede shoes greeted her by name and ushered her inside. "Hi, Charlotte. Glad you could make it. Good to see you. Taura and I are just finishing up."

"Hi. Thanks. It's great to be here." Had she met this woman at the studio back in Los Angeles? She'd met so many people then, and she couldn't keep track of faces anymore, much less names.

Taura squinted in the mirror and adjusted her costume. Taura, as Gabrielle, the titular queen, had wings, charcoal feathers fastened to her bare arms via a structure meant to resemble exposed bone. Taura frowned.

"They're heavy. And the glue itches," she said. "And I thought they'd be pretty, like angel wings."

"They're more like bird wings. They'll look great on film," the redhead said. "Ted's already signed off on them. They're exactly what he wants."

"Yeah, but they're not what I want. They're ugly."

"They look really cool. Kind of goth," Charlotte said from the doorway. "You could wear them clubbing, and you'd fit right in."

Taura noticed her for the first time. She smiled. "You think so?" She had a nice smile. "Is it your fitting now? Sorry. I'm running behind." She looked at her in the mirror. "You were there yesterday, right? I don't know your name."

"I'm Charlotte. Nice to meet you."

"You really like these wings? They're horrible. You're lucky you don't have to deal with these."

"Charlotte has her own cross to bear," the wardrobe lady said. "No wings, but she'll have to spend more time in the makeup trailer than any of the rest of you."

"Why? Who are you playing?" Taura asked her.

For crying out loud. Taura had been at the read-through. "I'm Jin. The killer robot."

"Oh. Right. But you look human, right? How come you'll need so much time in makeup?"

"They'll have to do stuff to her skin to make it look like synthetic material. Makeup's going to want you after you're done here," the wardrobe lady said to Charlotte. "First, though, let's see how we've done with your costume."

She dragged out a wheeled rack of clothes and sorted through the hanging outfits. She pulled something off a hanger, something gold and shiny, and handed it to her. Ah, yes, these would be the hot pants, attached to a short, fitted spandex jacket.

Charlotte shimmied out of her street clothes as Taura removed her wings and shimmied into hers. Taura hung around to watch as she zipped herself into her wardrobe. Tight. Very, very tight. Unforgiving.

The wardrobe lady tugged at the collar of the jacket, pulled down on the hem to make it lie flat, yanked up the waistband of the tight spandex shorts. "Okay, that's about right," she said at last. "Knee boots. Size seven, right?"

She presented her with a pair of black suede boots with ridiculously high, skinny wedge heels. They came up past her knees, with a wide cuff that rolled down. Charlotte had to sit down to get them on, then had to grab onto the rack to stand back up. She wobbled. Precarious. Great merciful Zeus, was she actually expected to do physical activity in these?

She had a belt, too, wide black leather worn low across her hips. The outfit was pure fetish, and she couldn't honestly say she didn't like it.

The red-haired lady tugged at the costume some more. "We'll let out the seam in the sleeves a bit more. You've got more muscle than we thought." It might be a case of too much upper arm flab, but "muscle" sounded so much better.

She glanced at Charlotte. "Sorry about this," she said. Charlotte barely had time to wonder what she was sorry about before the lady reached out and cupped her breasts with both hands. "Yes. We're going to have to pad you out."

Charlotte could feel her face growing hot. Her breasts were small, granted, but she couldn't see why such fuss was made over blobby deposits of fatty tissue. Still, Jin's breasts, as depicted in Martinez's loving sketches, were plump and juicy and buoyant, whereas her own. . . weren't.

"We'll probably build padding right into the costume. That'll make it easier for all concerned." The wardrobe lady scrutinized her sub-par rack one more time. "They just have to look real, they don't need to feel real. And since this is what you'll be wearing the whole time, it'll be easy enough to make the size consistent from scene to scene."

"She only has one costume?" Taura said. "Lucky. I've got five. I've been here since eight this morning."

It was only ten now, so Charlotte wasn't quite sure what the drama was.

"Well, we're all done with you now, Taura," the wardrobe lady said, her voice full of good cheer. Charlotte recognized that tone. It was the voice she herself used whenever she was filled with bile and hatred and wanted to disguise it.

Taura rose from her chair. "I'm going back to my house. Do I have to do anything else today?"

"Not with wardrobe. I couldn't speak for anything else. Did they give you a call sheet?"

Taura shrugged. "Yeah, but I don't know where I put it. Tell them if they need me, they'll have to call me." She left the trailer.

The red-haired woman shook her head and tugged at her sleeves. "Two hours of her complaining. You'd think she was jerked out of bed at the crack of dawn to listen to her."

Charlotte smiled and let the woman tug and pin her costume into place. The woman stepped back and looked at her. "Okay, that's good. Can you get out of that thing while keeping all the pins in place? Try not to stick yourself. We'll make the last adjustments, and you should be all set. I think they want you in the makeup trailer."

She pulled her clothes back on. Her loose, comfortable, skin-concealing clothes. So wonderful. "Okay. Where is it?"

"There'll be a sign on the door. Ask for Marion, she's the lead makeup artist."

She found the proper trailer in the maze outside the sound-stage. She climbed up the steps and knocked on the side of the door frame. "Hi. I think I'm supposed to be here now?"

A woman in a black smock was talking to another woman. She looked up and beckoned her inside. "Hi, hon. Come in. You're Charlotte?"

"Yes. Are you Marion?"

"That's right. That's Gina over there, she's our hair artiste. Is Cassie all done with you?"

Cassie must be the red-haired wardrobe lady. Charlotte hoped. "Yes. She sent me over here."

The interior of the makeup trailer looked as a makeup trailer should. Six stations in front of lighted mirrors, open train cases jammed with cosmetics taking up every free inch of counter space. Marion escorted her over to one of the chairs and plopped her in front of a mirror. She scrutinized her reflection, took up a clump of her hair in one hand, stared at it.

"Ted thought we could go with a wig for you, but honestly, I think it'll be a lot better if we cut and dye your own hair. It'll save you time getting ready each day. Gina, what do you think?"

Gina came over and examined her head. "Yeah. The wigs they've sent over aren't great. Her hair's thick enough that it could probably hold the right shape. Charlotte, would you mind?"

Was this something she had any control over? She'd assumed they'd cut her hair to match Jin's hard, angular cut in the comics. She liked her hair fine as it was—longish, thickish, blondish—but had no qualms about changing it. "Go ahead. Chop it all," she said.

Gina laughed. She was older than Marion, brassy and cheerful. "The last time I cut an actress' hair off, she wouldn't stop crying. I thought I was torturing her." She pulled at her hair with a light touch. "Just so you know, it'll all come off at about chin-length. And we're going to go darker, dark brown, almost black. Still cool?"

"No problem."

Gina cut it dry, with only the aid of a comb and a spray bottle of water, and she cut in fast swipes, taking off great chunks of hair, pausing now and then to assess her handiwork. It was a severe, straight cut, with a heavy sheaf of bangs that fell in a straight line across the tops of her eyebrows. Gina stepped back.

"That's about right," she said. "Honey, I think we're going to dye you right now. It'll make your day a little longer, but Marion's got a lot to go over with you anyway, so I don't think you're getting out of here anytime soon anyway."

She'd never been a brunette before, and that was a shame, because the results of Gina's work were outstanding. It was darker than she had expected, and it made her skin look very pale and her eyes very large. The haircut brought out angles in her face she hadn't known existed.

Gina blew her hair dry and brushed it straight and sleek. "I think Ted's going to be happy with that. What do you think, Marion?"

"Looks great." Marion scrutinized her. "You want to take a break or anything? Once we start experimenting with body makeup on you, you're not going to get a chance to move around for a while."

"No, I'm good." It was true. This was a new Charlotte looking back at herself in the mirror, one she hardly recognized, and it felt great.

The body makeup took forever. Marion painted a thick layer of base on her skin, which gave it the look of shiny, hard, synthetic material. She experimented with painting small cracks and chips on it too. Face makeup was more of the same, plus contouring makeup added to give her face added angles and shadows. Brows were plucked into strong shapes, the fine pale hairs above her brow line and across the bridge of her nose waxed away. They gave her contacts, too, black floppy circles that fit over her existing contacts to make her irises look like huge dark pupils.

Ted came into the trailer as Marion was finishing up her work. "Wow," he said. "Freaky."

"What do you think?" Marion asked.

"Awesome. Exactly right. It's going to look just like that on film?" He touched the sticky, plasticky film on her forearm with the pad of his forefinger.

"Sure. It's a good effect, isn't it?"

"Sure is. Charlotte, you okay with all this?"

"Yes. It looks great. It's not too uncomfortable, either."

"How long did it take?" Ted asked.

"Just under three hours, and a lot of that was experimenting around. Shouldn't be more than two hours in the morning, and then a few touchups throughout the day," Marion said.

Ted looked at her from all angles. "Okay. I'm happy with it. Charlotte, I don't think we'll start shooting any of your scenes until early next week, maybe Monday or Tuesday. So you've got the rest of the afternoon free, and then tomorrow I want you to start training with Paul in the gym."

"Sure. Training?" she asked.

"Stunt work. Martial arts. Paul Yin, he's our fight choreographer, he's from Hong Kong, and he knows his stuff. He'll give you a crash course in everything you need to know."

Exciting and terrifying. She focused on the exciting. "Great. Sounds like fun."

"Okay, once you get all this crap off of you, try to find Kerri, she's hanging around here somewhere. She'll have a revised call sheet for you. Not that it applies to you right now, but it'll give you some idea what's going on." He nodded at Gina and Marion. "Thanks, ladies," he said and departed.

Removing the makeup was a gentler ordeal. Marion rubbed down her limbs with soft towels dipped in some kind of cream-based solution that smelled of alcohol.

She found Kerri, then was given a ride back to the hotel by a woman she'd never seen before, someone with a crew jacket and a clipboard and a walkie-talkie, who seemed to know who she was and what she would need before Charlotte had a chance to express it. Then she was back in her lovely hotel room, free for the afternoon and content.

## CHAPTER FOURTEEN

PAUL YIN MIGHT have been in his early thirties, or he might have been twenty years older than Charlotte. He had a lithe, wiry body with ropy arm muscles and unlined skin. Long hair tied back in a ponytail implied youth, but his grave demeanor suggested he'd been doing this all his life, and doing it very well.

It was just herself and Paul in an otherwise vacant room in a gym in downtown Vancouver. The floor was lined with mats, and she was dressed to move in sweat bottoms and a loose shirt.

Paul spoke perfect English, but he spoke only when he needed to impart information. He was a patient teacher who gave her ample time to practice the moves he taught her before moving on to the next segment. If her movie experience consisted of nothing more than getting paid to take karate lessons, it'd still be worth it.

Paul taught her the elements of a simple fight routine. The routine became tricky when broken down into individual motions, each movement a step in a complicated dance. The climax of the fight worried her, as it ended with Jin getting kicked through a plate glass window and falling several stories, where she'd smash to bits on the streets below.

"You won't have to fall," Paul explained. His consonants were clipped, vaguely British. "Or smash to pieces, of course. That will be CGI" —computer generated imagery. "I do need to teach you to crash through the window."

"That's the part that worries me," she said.

"Breakaway glass," Paul said. "If you strike it the right way, it's very safe."

"And if I strike it the wrong way?" she asked.

"Don't," Paul said. "You won't. It will be fine." He gestured around the gym. "This is a Hollywood film. It costs them too much money to let you hurt yourself."

In the scene in the movie, she'd be fighting Gideon. Doug. Shouldn't Doug be rehearsing this with her? Maybe he'd arrived on the set before her, maybe he'd already been through this. Maybe his skills were better than hers and he didn't need this week of training.

Five days of this, rehearsing with Paul from eight to noon, just the two of them. She had no idea what was happening with the rest of the film. She got her call sheet every morning, slipped under the door of her hotel room, but her name had yet to show up on it.

She was friendly with Trey Aaron, who had a room down the hall, but she'd barely met anyone else. Sir John Hyde had the room across from hers; she'd seen him only once, dressed in his bathrobe as he opened his door to pick up his morning paper. She'd said hello to him, all good will and friendliness, and he hadn't replied. Just went back into his room and bolted it shut.

She'd been without the internet for almost a full week. It was nice to take a break from the rest of the world. Friday morning, though, she wished she had web access, because she felt a compulsive urge to investigate Simon.

Simon showed up at the gym on Friday morning, dressed in sweats. Charlotte was there already; Paul hadn't arrived yet, so she'd been doing a few stretches to warm up. And here was this young thing, elegant and thin to the point of frailty, with an abundance of dark hair and the most prominent cheekbones she had ever seen in real life. He looked relieved to see a friendly face. He crossed over to her, padding across the floor mats.

"Hello, there," he said. An English accent. How marvelous. "I wonder if you could tell me where Paul Yin might be?"

"He should be here any minute," she said. "I'm waiting for him, too."

He looked at her. "Are you Charlotte Dent?"

"I am." He wouldn't be a crew member, would he? So lithe and pretty, he was an actor, of course he was an actor. But she had met all the cast, so who could he be, and how did he know her name?

"Ted told me I'd be rehearsing with you today." He smiled. He didn't have movie-star teeth; they were very white, but the bottom ones were scraggly. They were perfect in their imperfection. "I'm Simon Oliver."

The name meant nothing. She hadn't seen it associated with anything related to the production. She'd certainly never seen it on a call sheet.

He had his hand out, and she shook it. His hand was long and slim, cool and dry. Hers was sweaty. "Nice to meet you, Simon," she said. "You're in the cast, then?"

Oh, lovely. She was mimicking his accent, unintentionally throwing it back at him, and he'd assume she was mocking him. He didn't seem to notice. Just smiled that lovely smile. "Yes. I'm Gideon. I just started today."

Doug was Gideon, and that meant Simon, lovely Simon, was somehow mistaken. That was a shame, because she was already planning their wedding. She'd never thought much of weddings— the waste and excess and narcissism made her cringe—but she could see marrying Simon. It would take place in a castle somewhere, a craggy ruin on the coast near Dover, or maybe they wouldn't bother with a ceremony and just stay there for their honeymoon, huddled in goose-down comforters while winds howled and rain beat at the castle walls.

She must have looked confused, or crushed, or blank, or some combination of the above, because Simon hurried to speak, almost tripping over his words. "It's a last-minute thing. I just received word from my agent yesterday. Apparently the other actor—Doug Appleby, correct?—had some preexisting obligation that would conflict with the shooting, so he was released from his contract. And here I am," he said.

"Fantastic. That's great. Welcome aboard. I guess I'll be fighting you then, right?"

"I suppose so. I haven't had a chance to read the script all the way yet, but Ted Darling told me to come here and practice with you." He smiled. "You're the killer robot, yes?"

He had a dimple. Of course he did. He was adorable and beautiful all wrapped up in one delightful package. And he was here, and annoying Doug was gone.

Paul arrived. "Ah. You must be Simon." He looked Simon over from head to toe. "We'll start from the top. You'll be a bit behind; Charlotte has been working on this for the better part of a week."

Good. She'd look good in front of Simon, like she knew what she was doing, not like she'd been stumbling and tripping her way through the fight sequence for the past four days.

Simon moved well. He was tentative, restrained, but there was power behind his movements, and grace. Maybe he had a dance background, or some sport that required good reflexes and coordination. Tennis, maybe.

She knew nothing about him. She'd never heard his name before, she'd never seen him in anything. She didn't know his acting background, his age, whether he was straight or gay, single or married, whether he preferred cats or dogs, coffee or tea. She didn't know any of these things, and she wanted to know everything.

The routine required lots of close contact. With Simon in Paul's place, the touches took on whole new universes of meaning. At one point she tackled him, and for the briefest of moments she lay prone astride him. Their abdomens touched. It was a jolt even through their layers of clothing, and it left her stunned.

That was when she wished for a computer and a good internet connection. She wanted to investigate Simon, to find out everything she could about him, to visit his fan sites, if any existed, and if none did, to create one herself, to spread the word to an intelligent and responsive universe about the dark-eyed wonder who had come to Vancouver.

Physical attraction was a strange beast. When she was back in the womb of her hotel room and had a chance to think, the euphoria wore off. She knew nothing about Simon, other than he had a lovely smile and a lovely accent. Somehow that combination served to trigger all her underused hormones and create an unprecedented feeling of love or lust or both. It was a massive crush, of the kind she'd only had on celebrities before, and Simon was a real person. Or was he? There wasn't enough of Simon for her to love, not yet. He could be boring, or dumb, or spiteful, or offensive and awful.

Still, Simon's presence added a new dimension to the production. She'd be working with him, fighting with him, the elaborate stage combat choreography seeming more and more like a primitive mating ritual.

A paper slipped underneath her door startled her out of her reverie. The call sheet for tomorrow, Saturday. Ah, look, she was needed. Her first day on the set, the first time anyone involved with the production—Ted, Angie, anyone—would see her perform. If there was ever a time for her to get fired, this would be it.

Well, she was prepared. She knew her lines, all twelve of them. She'd done her research. She was ready. She was expected in wardrobe at five in the morning; it was time for her to get some rest. And if she went to sleep with thoughts of Simon in her head, so much the better.

The set was located in a cavernous soundstage, almost the size of an airplane hangar. The set didn't fill the space entirely, but it took up most of the back wall. Much of it wasn't anything at all, just a wall painted bright green to hold the place where the special effects would be added later via computer. The rest replicated the small splotch of government buildings in downtown Los Angeles: City Hall, the Chamber of Commerce, the Superior Court. . . She thought that was the Times building, but she wasn't sure. All of it familiar, all of it recreated in painstaking detail, but even at a distance, it didn't look real. It would look different on film, but right now, it didn't look like Los Angeles, post-apocalyptic or not. It looked like a partially remembered dream, where parts of the city intermingled with fragments of memories of different places to form patterns that made no sense in the light of day.

The crew bustled about, setting up cameras and coiling cables. The production assistants scurried here and there. She spotted Kerri in her bulky parka, grim and busy. They'd arrived on the set before her. They'd leave after she'd wrapped for the day. And they got paid a fraction of what she was earning.

Ted was on the set, deep in conversation with a young man in an exquisite dark suit. He looked up and spotted her. "Charlotte Dent! Get over here!" He grinned. "Take a look at you!"

"What do you think?" She held out her arms to her sides, showing off the wardrobe to full effect. She'd try to do a cute runway pirouette, but she wasn't the type who could pull off a cute pirouette without looking like an ass. Her hair was shellacked into place; the perpetual itch in her eyeballs reminded her the inky black contacts were in. It was getting easier to walk in the boots, though she wished she had thought to bring some moleskin or bandages. Her heels were sore already, and she'd have blisters by the end of the day.

"You look fantastic, Charlotte! You're amazing!" Ted's excitement and happiness was infectious. She thought she might very well be amazing at this moment. "What do you think?" he asked of the man next to him.

"Not too shabby," the man replied. She knew as soon as she heard him speak that this was Rick, her agent Rick, who up until now had only been a good-natured voice on the phone. "Hi, Charlotte. It's Rick." He extended a hand.

She took it. "I know. I recognized your voice," she said. "It's nice meeting you in person, finally."

"It is indeed. I'd hug you, but I don't want to mess up your makeup job. You look like you got a lot of things going on there." He smiled at her. He was dark and glossy, slick and handsome. Younger than she had pictured, around Ted's age. "How's this joker been treating you?" He nudged Ted in the ribs.

"Great. Everything's going really well."

"It's Charlotte's first scene today," Ted said.

"Really? Break a leg, you'll be great." Rick sounded as if he meant it. Everyone took it for granted she'd be fine. She hadn't auditioned or screen-tested, and her credits on her résumé, while legitimate, weren't extensive. For all they knew, she could blow.

A woman approached her elbow, someone she'd never seen before, with a headset and clipboard. Too old for a production assistant; production coordinator, maybe? Assistant director? She'd met too many people over the past few days. "Charlotte? Ted, is this a good time?"

"Hi, Nancy. It's fine. Charlotte, have you met Nancy yet? Nancy's my first A.D."

"No, I haven't," she said, and hoped it was true. "Nice to meet you."

"Sorry to interrupt, but Charlotte hasn't had her insurance physical yet. Before she goes in front of the camera, we'll have to get that taken care of."

"Shoot. That's right." There was something charming and goofy in the way Ted didn't use profanity. She was willing to bet Ted loved his mother very much. "I forgot about that."

An insurance physical sounded time-consuming. She thought of the two hours she'd already spent in makeup this morning. Would this hold up the production? Would they have to move on to a different scene just because of this? Maybe this wouldn't be her first day on camera after all.

"Doctor Howe's in the green room right now," Nancy said. "If you've got a moment, Charlotte, we can get this out of the way."

Ah. The production had a doctor on call. Of course they would. There was so much about this business she didn't know. "Sure thing," she said. She followed Nancy out of the stage area.

Doctor Howe was female and friendly. She smiled at her. "Hi, Charlotte. This is only going to take a minute." She looked at her costume. "Wow. That's quite an ensemble."

"It is, isn't it? Am I going to have to get out of wardrobe for this?"

"Not at all. This is just for the insurance carrier, so we can assure them we're not forcing anyone on death's door to work. Blood pressure first," she said.

It took a bit of doing to pull up the tight gold satin sleeve of the jacket enough so Doctor Howe could wrap the pressure cuff around her elbow. She pumped it up, then looked at the result. "A little low. Are you a runner?"

"Yep," Charlotte said.

"That'd account for it, then. That's very good, actually. You're probably in the best shape of everyone in the cast." She donned a stethoscope and checked her heartbeat. "Any preexisting conditions I should know about?"

"Nope."

"Allergies?"

"Mild hay fever every spring. Nothing else."

"Taking any medications?"

"No. None." She watched as Howe scribbled something down on her clipboard.

"Okay. We're done. I just need you to sign off on this." She passed the clipboard over to her and indicated where Charlotte should sign.

"That's it?" Charlotte asked.

"That's everything. The studio's covered its bases, the insurance company will be happy. Just don't drop dead on the set or there'll be hell to pay. You're doing some stunt work, aren't you?"

"I have a fight scene," Charlotte said.

Doctor Howe grinned. "I'll be on the set most days, so if you need anything—ice, aspirin, stinky analgesic balm—I'm the one to come to, okay?"

Nancy was waiting outside to take her back to the set, because there was every chance she would get lost walking across the hall to the soundstage. When she returned to the stage, Ted was deep in conversation with a silver-haired man wearing what looked like a heavy wool cloak over a business suit. Yes, a dark floor-length cloak, lined with royal blue silk, and he had shiny knee boots instead of more traditional footwear. This combination made her realize he was one of the actors. More than just one of the actors, in fact; this was Sir John Hyde. King Lear, as Kerri had dubbed him, and even if he'd never played the role, the moniker suited him.

She hung back, not wanting to intrude, but Ted saw her and beckoned her over. "Charlotte! Come here. I want you to meet Sir John. Sir John, this is Charlotte Dent. She'll be playing your bodyguard."

Sir John gave her a searching look, like he was assessing every inch of her appearance and by extension her personality and intelligence and found it all wanting. Strong nose, eyes like chips of slate. He extended a hand, and she wasn't sure whether she was expected to shake it or kiss it. "Miss Dent. A pleasure, I'm sure."

"It's an honor to meet you, Sir John. Your Richard II was the first filmed Shakespeare play I ever saw," she said.

Sir John grunted, though he didn't sound displeased. Done with her, he turned back to Ted. "Are we ready to begin?"

"In just a bit. They're finishing up the lights."

"Which means we might be standing around all bloody morning." Sir John didn't sound grumpy or argumentative, just like he was stating a fact. "I'll be in my trailer. Have someone fetch me when you're ready."

Ted nodded. "Sure, will do, no problem. It won't be long, I promise."

In twenty minutes, maybe less, the lights were fixed in place, Sir John was retrieved, and she was escorted to her place on the set.

It was the scene toward the end of the first act where Jin and Mephistopheles walked down the steps of the City Hall. The steps were there, plaster recreations of cracked marble, and the replica of City Hall behind them, but up close it didn't look right. She'd have to trust Ted and the post-production crew to work their magic on it later.

She had two lines in this scene, and she was anxious about forgetting them or messing them up, even though she knew them backwards and forwards, in and out of context in the script. Given enough time, she could make anagrams out of her bits of dialogue. First line: "But sir—," and then, it was to be hoped, Sir John would interrupt and not force her to improvise anything past that point. She was a robot, after all, so the "but sir" wouldn't be petulant or impatient, but factual and reasoned, and hopefully it wouldn't come out in a leaden monotone. She'd practiced, of course, in her hotel room during her free time, but it was hard to impart a wealth of believable character traits into a sentence fragment.

Second line: "Sir, I don't think that's wise." More to work with there, easy enough to keep in character on that. She had a bit of movement, too, a quick presentation of Jin's signature knives, a bit of flash and menace. Paul showed her how to grasp the knives and present them in a way that looked fierce and effective.

Cameras rolled. They used a clapboard to begin the scene, even though the sound would be digital. The clapboard was a relic: they didn't need it to synchronize the sound with the action.

Ted said, "Action!" Small spurt of adrenaline, and then the scene began.

She walked down the stairs, trailing behind Sir John. Going downstairs in the heeled boots was difficult since she had to navigate the artful broken chunks of fake marble, and she couldn't watch her feet.

The lights were bright and hot. Her makeup was going to melt before long. That would be a problem since she was wearing a lot of it, every inch of exposed skin covered in gunk. If she wasn't careful, it'd smudge onto her costume. People crowded around the set: the boom operator, the cameraman, the man at his feet whose sole purpose was to make sure the heavy cables stayed out of the path of the camera. Was he a gaffer or a grip or a best boy? She knew these things, knew the terms, but now she couldn't put them into their proper context.

She shouldn't be thinking about any of this, damn it. She should be focusing on staying in character, not wondering about the bobbing silhouettes at the edge of her vision. She heard her cue, and even with part of her brain preoccupied, she responded: "But sir—"

Sir John cut her off with his line, smooth and natural, and the scene continued. There. She'd delivered her first line in her first take of her first scene on the set of her first major motion picture.

Ted called "Cut!" They halted, retraced their steps up the stairs to the masking tape mark, and waited while Ted engaged in a quick conversation with the lighting crew. Her face melted. Sweat pooled in the corner of her eye, blurring her vision, making the oversized contacts sting.

Marion hurried up to her, sponge in hand, and dabbed her down, then finished up with a light dusting of powder. The cameras rolled again. "But sir—" one more time. Stop. Again. It took most of the morning before they even reached her second, longer line.

They were scheduled to shoot her scene until noon, break for lunch, then resume until three. If they finished it by then, she'd be done for the day while Ted and Sir John and the others started in on another segment. No Simon today; his name hadn't been on the call sheet, much to her disappointment. She'd been looking forward to seeing him in action. After today, three of her remaining scenes involved Simon, and one of them was their big fight scene. There'd be plenty of opportunities to find out more about him. She could be patient.

## CHAPTER FIFTEEN

MARION CROUCHED IN front of her chair and applied sticky goop to Charlotte's inner thighs with a little brush. Marion knew how to do her job, and there probably were reasons why she didn't use a bigger tool, but this would be so much faster if she used a sponge, or an airbrush. The makeup was getting to be tiresome. It was too early, and it was too cold in the trailer to have a good attitude about this. Exposed in her skimpy costume, she could see her breath.

They were on location today. The trailers were parked on the street in front of a convenience store somewhere in downtown Vancouver, remodeled for the day to look like one of the many Botanicas—Santeria supply stores—found in Spanish-speaking neighborhoods throughout Los Angeles.

She had a companion in the makeup trailer this morning. A local actress, Pansy O'Dell, who'd entered an hour earlier looking like a clean-scrubbed Canadian soccer mom with freckles and short strawberry-blonde hair, was in the process of being transformed into Esmerelda, a Santeria high priestess. Presumably Pansy was a versatile character actress, because otherwise this bit of casting confused her to no end.

"I thought Taura Trejo would be here," Pansy said. Gina adjusted a dark wig over Pansy's hair. Pansy squinted in the mirror at the result. "She's in this scene, isn't she? My son wanted to make sure I met her."

"I don't think she comes in until after lunch," Charlotte said.

"She wouldn't be here in any case, as in here, in this trailer." Marion's mouth twisted. "She's brought in her own makeup artist from L.A. to do her makeup for the rest of the shoot."

"Really?" That was Pansy. Charlotte kept quiet. From Marion's tone, this was going to be a Bad Taura story. There were plenty of Bad Taura stories circulating around the crew.

"She complained to the director that she didn't want me doing her makeup anymore. Apparently I was making her look, and I quote, whorish." Marion continued painting her thigh. The brush tickled. "Fine with me. I don't need her sour attitude every morning. The way that girl complains, you'd think it was this huge, horrible chore to be a movie star."

"That's too bad. She's so pretty, and she always seems like she'd be really nice." Pansy looked glum. "Charlotte, you've worked with her. Is she really that bad?"

"I've only met her a couple of times. She seems nice."

Marion and Pansy took the hint and moved on to a new subject. Good. Charlotte was determined to maintain her role as Switzerland for the duration of the production.

As soon as she left the trailer, one of the assistants ran up to her and draped an oversize jacket around her shoulders. "Photographers," he said in answer to her questioning look. "Ted spotted them in a parked van across the street. He doesn't want photos of the costumes to leak before the studio okays it."

"Ah." She looked over and spotted the van. She couldn't see anyone inside it. Maybe they were crouching under the dashboard. A cold, lonely existence, lurking outside film sets on a frozen morning. "Is Ted inside?" she asked, gesturing toward the convenience store.

"Yeah. Proceed with caution, though. He's in the middle of a fight with that lady from the studio."

Ted in a fight with Angie? Seemed incredible. She glanced inside.

Oh, happy day. Simon stood just inside the shop, elegant in a long wool cloak with some kind of cool, elaborate cowl neck. He turned to her and beamed. He was in makeup, too, heavily lined eyes with darkened lashes. Black leather pants. Good choice, whoever picked those out for him.

"Charlotte! My goodness. I almost didn't recognize you." He scoped her out from top to bottom. "You're wearing clothes under that, aren't you?"

The oversize jacket covered her costume, showing nothing but bare legs and boots. "Barely." She opened the coat and revealed her costume, feeling like a flasher. "You look fantastic."

"Thank you." Another smile. The smile alone took the chill off the day. "Something's going on, though I haven't figured out what yet. Ted mentioned something about not being able to shoot today."

He gestured over to the back of the store, where Ted and Angie were deep in conversation. Contrary to what the P.A. had claimed, they weren't fighting, really. It was more like a very intense, weighty discussion. Angie's voice wasn't raised, but her jaw was set. The cords in her neck stood out a little as she leaned in to Ted.

"What I want to know is why her agent is calling me like this is a done deal," Angie said. "Like it's not even open for discussion—she's going to fly out and look cute at her little premiere, and you and I can just go screw ourselves."

"I'm with you, Angie, I know. It was handled poorly, no question. But it's done, and we can work around it, so the best thing we can do is drop it and move on." Ted looked tired.

"Someone needs to sit that little girl down and have a talk with her about how easy she's got it here. Is she on her way?"

"Yeah, she got her makeup done already at her house, she'll be here just as soon as her driver finds the place. It's all good, Angie. Trust me." A grin, Ted's usual goofy grin, and Angie melted somewhat.

She rubbed at the back of her neck, then looked up and saw them for the first time. "Hey, Simon, Charlotte. Change of plans for today."

"Taura needs to be back in Los Angeles this evening, so we've got to get her shots out of the way first. It means we won't get to your scene until after lunch at the earliest, Charlotte," Ted said. "I'm sorry we couldn't catch you before you went into makeup."

"Okay. Should I just hang out?" It was just after six now.

"Yeah. I hate to ask you to do it, though. If you'd rather, you can get out of makeup and go back to the hotel and wait until we call you."

Getting into makeup once in a day was plenty. Maybe they'd finish with Taura early. "No, it's fine. As long as there's someplace I can go. . ." It was a valid concern. The convenience store they'd taken over was tiny, just this one room by the look of it, and it was much too cold to wait around outside.

"Do you want to wait in my trailer?" Simon asked.

"You wouldn't mind?"

"Not at all. I'm in the scene with Taura, so I won't be using it. It's not too interesting in there, but at least there's a heater." Simon looked wistful. It was cold inside the store, especially now that one of the crew guys had propped the door open with a sandbag.

"Thank you, Simon. You too, Charlotte," Ted said.

"You two are good sports about this. We appreciate it," Angie added.

Simon's trailer was a blank. A couch, a dining table built into the wall, a cooking range, a toilet, a television, an absence of personal touches. A good-quality leather duffle bag was propped on the couch. She wouldn't dare rifle through his possessions, but it was unzipped, and she could see it held only a gray wool sweater. His cell phone was on the kitchen counter, along with his hotel card key. The television was tuned to the CBC. No revelations there. There was a DVD player, but the tray was empty, so she couldn't see what his movie tastes were like. She knew as little about Simon as when she'd started.

It was hard getting comfortable, settling in on the small couch in a position which didn't wrinkle her costume or smudge her body makeup. She kept the baggy coat on, grateful for its protection. There was a heater built into the wall, but it looked sketchy— kerosene? It was chilly in here, but at least she was sheltered from the wind. She'd brought a book to the set with her. Good planning. She took it out and began to read.

She couldn't concentrate. She turned on the television and watched British Columbia's finest daytime programming. She broke down and turned on the heater, which coughed out a stinky burst of heated air.

She went stir-crazy, fast. It was Taura's fault. Pretty, selfish Taura, who nobody really liked, messing up everyone else's schedules so she could go to some party, either because she didn't care or because she liked having the power to disrupt lives on a whim.

Taura wasn't bad. She was young. She'd been famous, or sort of famous, for all of her adult life. She'd probably never had a stupid desk job where she had to file and answer phones, or a stupid retail job where she had to defer to customer wishes all day long, so she'd never learned how unimportant she was in the grand scheme of the universe. Maybe that was reason to hate her a little, but it was unfair to blame her for her current funk. So Charlotte had to kill some time on a movie set. Big deal.

Simon's phone rang. She jumped. She looked at the display screen: ALEX. Who was Alex? A friend, his agent, his brother? His boyfriend? Could be a girl's name, could be his girlfriend. His wife, even.

A knock on the door. Kerri stuck her head in. "Hey," she said. "I'm picking up lunch for Simon. Chinese. You want to order something too, or are you going to tough it out with craft services?"

"I don't know. Whatever they're serving is probably fine," she said.

Kerri wrinkled her nose. "I walked by when they were setting up. It's turkey and gravy. Didn't smell too good."

"Okay. If you don't mind. Just get me whatever Simon's having."

The nose wrinkle deepened. Kerri paired it with an icky face. "You won't like it. Simon's macrobiotic."

"Ah." She thought. "I don't really care. Something with a lot of vegetables."

"Will do." Kerri shot her a thumbs-up.

"Hey, what's Taura doing for lunch?" Charlotte asked.

"Don't know. Don't care. She sends her own assistant to get her food." Kerri grinned and scooted off.

Noon rolled around. Another knock on the door. She expected to see Kerri, but instead it was Simon, his arms full of white plastic bags.

"Hi. I believe I have your lunch here," he said. He held up one bag, frowned at it, then held up another. "Somewhere in here, Kerri assures me. Do you mind if I join you?"

"It's your trailer." She helped him settle his burden down on the small table. "I should be asking you if it's okay to eat here."

He smiled at her. Her heart went pitty-pat, just a little. She got to work opening cardboard cartons, sorting out their food. "How's the filming going?"

Simon considered. "Slow. It's not bad, but we haven't gotten as far along as I would have thought."

"So they probably won't be ready for me any time soon," she said. She pulled up a lid and glanced at the contents. Brown rice, chunks of tofu in a sticky brown sauce, and what looked like steamed kale. Unless Kerri had a cruel streak, that was Simon's.

"No, I don't believe so. Sorry," Simon said. "It might have been better if you'd gone back to the hotel after all."

"I don't mind." Another container. Steamed rice, some kind of shrimp and vegetables in a heavenly sauce that smelled of strong garlic and sesame oil. That would be hers. Good thing Jin didn't have much dialogue. She'd be breathing garlic on her costars all evening.

"Kerri mentioned you were macrobiotic," she said.

Simon nodded. He was using chopsticks, awkwardly and, because this was Simon, charmingly. He speared a chunk of tofu and nibbled at a corner of it. "For about three years now, yes."

"How's that going for you?" she asked.

Simon seemed surprised, or maybe a little confused at the question. "Fine. It's very healthy," he said. He was a little defensive about that. Maybe Kerri had given him a hard time. "It was hard giving up meat at first. Steak, I mean. I can have fish. I don't really like dairy products all that much, so that part I don't miss at all."

Maybe they couldn't be soul mates after all. There went her fantasy of her and Simon in the Alps, sharing a pot of fondue in a chalet miles from the nearest village. Still, it was a hurdle that could probably be overcome. Some people swore soy cheese tasted almost like the real thing.

"It's kind of weird, isn't it, the way everything is done for you on a set?" She wasn't sure where she was going with this, and neither was Simon, from his blank expression. "The way Kerri got our food. The way we get picked up from our hotel and taken to the set. The way someone tracks me down at the end of each day to get me to sign my timecard. We're not expected to do anything for ourselves at all."

"It is weird, isn't it?" Simon leaned forward a little. "You know what's awful, though, is that I love it. I don't think I'm supposed to admit it, but there it is." He smiled, sheepish, self-deprecating. Charming. "I'm an utter failure at doing anything for myself. When I'm in London, I'm incompetent at buying groceries, or paying my electric bill, or doing any of the things adults are expected to do on a regular basis."

She grinned. "In that case, this is the perfect job for you."

"I couldn't think of any other," he said. "You?"

"I've had other jobs. I didn't like them much. This is new to me."

Simon smiled. He didn't ask her about her other jobs, like she hadn't asked him about his life in London, even though she was bursting with questions. His answer implied he lived in London still. Did he have a place in Los Angeles? How did he come to get cast in this? Who was he, anyway?

An entire lunch spent with him, alone in the trailer, more intimate than if they'd been on a date, and she knew she'd come out of this knowing just as little about Simon as when she'd started.

## Chapter Sixteen

ALBERTA, THE OUTSKIRTS of Calgary. Inland, so it didn't seem as filled with water as Vancouver, didn't have the same palette of blues and grays. It was harsh and beautiful. Evergreen trees, tall and spindly. Hard ground, brown hills, a sky white with cold. Frost had come creeping sometime in the middle of the night, spreading across the grassy field in the center of the track too subtly for the eye to catch, until now, as morning threatened to break, the field turned silver-white. Ted had gone crazy about the frost for a while until he realized he wouldn't be filming the grass. On film, there'd be no way to tell it wasn't a warm California night.

She could see her breath. If she inhaled too deeply, the cold air made her cough.

Her legs were bare. She sat on the bleachers in the spectator stands and pulled the hem of the down jacket as far over her knees as it would reach and huddled into her body for warmth.

They'd flown here this morning—yesterday morning by now— even though it wasn't that far of a drive, one province over. Time concerns always outweighed budget concerns on a film set. It had been a private flight, a fifty-seat plane holding what members of cast and crew and staff were needed at this location.

This was a greyhound racetrack. She'd been under the impression that dog racing was illegal in Canada. The two middle-aged ladies who'd handed out leaflets by the entrance when they'd arrived disabused her of that notion. They couldn't have been nicer or less intimidating in their knitted balaclavas and sensible boots, even as they protested the decision to shoot here.

The racetrack was supposed to be the Los Angeles Coliseum. She couldn't see it, even with the extensive set redressing that had gone on for most of yesterday, but Ted could, and that was the important thing.

They'd shot her scene. Jin made a brief appearance here, vaulting over the railing while coming to the defense of Mephistopheles. She'd even hurled knives at Simon, in his guise as Gideon. Just a short routine Paul drilled into her, a number of simple steps linked together, then broken into component parts and put on film.

She wished she could change into warm clothes. She wished she could go back to the motel and take a long, hot bath. If her room had a bathtub. She hadn't had time to check. She'd been at the motel only long enough to drop off her bags before being driven to this location yesterday afternoon. She calculated the day's pay, time and a half overtime after eight hours, and felt a little less sorry for herself.

Her legs were growing numb, and her ankle hurt from landing on it after vaulting over the railing, take after take, a dull ache somewhere deep near the bone. The cold made it worse.

Taura and Simon filmed their scene down on the track. They looked good together, a matched set. Taura wore her wings, the charcoal feathers extending from her arms; if she still thought they were ugly, she'd been silent on the subject. She'd been good all day, it pained Charlotte to admit, keeping her complaints to a minimum in the cold air and long hours.

Simon said something, and Taura laughed and placed her hand on his upper arm. Damn it, she was flirting with him.

Ted called "Action!" Ted, who seemed impervious to the cold weather, was filled with the same high energy and excitement and good spirits he'd demonstrated when they'd commenced filming. How long had they been shooting here? Her brain was too tired and slow to work it out. She wasn't wearing a watch—when she'd last checked the time, it'd been four in the morning.

Watching Simon. In character, he moved in close to Taura. Even from a distance, his eyes were dark and glittery. Her breath caught in her throat just a little looking at him.

"Come on." A hand clasped around Taura's wrist, and she could feel it as though Simon were clutching her own instead, pulling her to safety. He was a good actor, really good, all nuance and subtlety. She was jealous, in a way, because he was doing things she didn't know how to do, minute bits of characterization that he must've thought through beforehand. Or was this just talent, some ability he was born with, some instinct for making the right acting choices?

Or was she reading too much into his movements, misinterpreting her attraction to him and ascribing it to his ability?

Ah, the protesters were back outside the gates, bright and early. She could tell they were there by the sudden flurry of barks. The women brought dogs with them, greyhounds they'd rescued from slated destruction, to put a canine face on their cause. Ted hadn't complained about the barking yesterday, even when it threatened to interrupt shooting.

A sharp wind picked up. Needles of pain against her bare legs. She was going to freeze out in the open. Quietly, so as not to disturb the scene taking place on the track below, she got to her feet and retreated up the bleachers, then settled into the protective cement alcove that led to the lavatories. There wouldn't be any wind here, and she was still within earshot if Ted needed her. She sat on the cement and tried to warm up.

Footsteps. She looked up to see Sir John. Gray and imposing in his makeup, he had a pack of cigarettes in one hand. He looked at her in surprise.

"Ah," he said. "Sweet Charlotte. I see I'm not the only one with the idea to get away from that yapping puppy."

Right then, from the field below, Taura laughed at something, her voice pitched a shade too high. Charlotte shot a look at Sir John, but his face was implacable.

She got to her feet and winced. She'd forgotten her hurt ankle until she put pressure on it. "I was just getting out of the wind. I can leave if you want to be alone."

He barked out a sudden laugh that shocked her and made her hope it hadn't disturbed the filming below. "Good lord, girl, that's not the correct response at all. You're supposed to say, 'Go away, you old fruit, I found this place first, and don't even think of using it as a chimney stack.'"

She didn't know the right response to that, so she settled for smiling. Felt a little thin and tight. All the makeup plus the cold weather was doing horrible things to her skin. If she smiled too much, her cheeks might tear apart.

"You don't mind if I stay, then?" he asked.

"Not at all. Please," she said.

He held up his cigarettes, silently requesting permission. She nodded. He lit up, his fingers slow and clumsy with cold. "You're far too accommodating, you know. It won't do you any good in the long run."

"I'm afraid of complaining," she said.

"Whatever for? Complaining is one of the great joys of life. It separates us from the apes." He sat down on the pavement, long legs drawn up to his body, his cloak pulled around him for warmth, and settled in to enjoy his cigarette. She hovered for a moment, then sat beside him.

"It's my first film role," she said. "I have this fear that if I complain too much, they'll replace me."

He looked at her for a long moment, the lines of his face standing out. The cold turned his skin gray, and his makeup sat on it, too orange and obvious. A painted corpse laid out for viewing in a funeral home. "Well, that's silly of you. Of course they might replace you," he said at last. "They might replace you because you complain too much. Or they might replace you because they don't like your nose or the sound of your voice, or because the pretty starlet some studio head wants to fuck wants your role. It's out of your hands entirely. There's no sense at all in worrying about it."

Was that reassuring, or not? She tried to think of something to say.

Sir John continued. "I don't know why they persist in these all-night affairs on this sort of thing. I'm an old man. I need my beauty rest." He settled back against the wall. "And yet, invariably, at some point, there will be a shoot that lasts all night for some silly reason or other, at terrible cost to the studio, I imagine. Perhaps it makes a good sound bite in interviews later, I don't know. Shows commitment and dedication and all that rot. I can't think of any good reason for it otherwise."

"Ted has to work around the racetrack's schedule, doesn't he?" she asked.

"Go to many outdoor races in November, do you? In bloody Canada?" Sir John asked, brows arched. He scoffed, a small sound in the back of his throat. "No, this is a display. The numbers men will point to this night as an example of the supreme dedication required to bring this piece of dreck to the cinema."

"So you don't think the film's going to be any good?" she asked.

"Please don't tell me you do." Sir John looked at her. "You do, don't you? Of course you do. I had forgotten."

"Forgotten what?" she asked.

"I'd forgotten what it was like in the early days, when I was first making films. Something about the total immersion into one project gives you blinders. If you weren't attached to this in any way, and someone—say, a school chum looking for reassurance—had given you a copy of the script to read, what would your assessment be?"

She opened her mouth; Sir John shook his head. "You don't need to answer that, it's quite all right. It's natural, and probably quite good for the morale of the production. I'm an awful old man for bursting your bubble like this."

He stubbed out his cigarette on the ground beside him. An American brand, something mainstream, which disappointed her. Someone of Sir John's stature should be smoking something more exotic. A rare European brand, maybe, or something imported from Turkey or Morocco. "I'm a fine one to talk. I read the script and I took this role. Of course, I have it a bit easier than you. I have my name, you see. I show up here and read my lines and do my little part, and the reviewers will love me. See if I'm wrong: 'Hyde lends a distinguished eminence to the otherwise slapdash proceedings.' Some major paper will have that exact line in a review, or near enough to count."

A glance over at her. "You'll make out of this all right, if they notice you. Some reviewer will make a crude quip about your assets, because that line never grows tired, but you're young and pretty. You'll do fine. Mind you, I don't know whether you should."

"What do you mean?" A tad defensive.

"Maybe you're a fine actor, I don't really know. You seem quick, and you read well. But anyone who rates your performance in this film one way or another is either a fool or a liar."

It was true. She was in so few scenes, and it was hard to put any kind of stamp on her character.

"The bulk of reviewers are, of course, lonely, horny men. It makes all the difference in the world," Sir John said. He gestured to the field below, where Taura and Simon were going through another take of their endless scene. "The yapping puppy is no damn good, but they'll be kind to her. Condescending, yes, and maybe snide, but gentle. They'll talk about her natural grace and her beauty and leave it at that. It's our boy Simon, simple Simon, who'll be thrown to the wolves."

"He shouldn't be," she said. "He's really good."

Sir John laughed again. "And if more reviewers were star-struck young ladies, I imagine Simon would come out of this quite well." He shook his head. "As it is, he doesn't stand a chance. A pretty young actor playing the stalwart hero, with an underwritten script and a poorly defined character? They'll murder him, and there's not a thing he can do about it."

Sir John was probably right. It was a shame, because Simon was good, very good. She was biased, she forced herself to admit, primed to admire his talent in the same way she admired his hair and his eyes and his lovely smile.

Sir John smiled at her. "You're turning red. You're sweet on him, my girl, aren't you?"

"He's very attractive," she said in what she hoped was a neutral tone.

"Ah. Sweet Charlotte and Simple Simon. There are worse pairings, I suppose. Far worse."

She was saved from having to answer by a commotion on the field below. Done with the scene. It looked like they were taking a break. Good.

Kerri, clipboard in hand, bounded up the stairs. The long, cold night didn't seem to be doing her much harm. She glanced around, spotted them, and came trotting over.

"Hi, guys," she said. Charlotte resisted the temptation to glance at Sir John to see what he thought of being referred to under the umbrella address of "guys." "Ted says you're clear for the day."

"Oh, thank heavens," Sir John said. Kerri handed the clipboard over so she could sign off on her timecard. Seventeen hours on set today. Sir John didn't have a timecard. His pay scale was such things like timecards didn't apply to him.

It was high time she got out of makeup and wardrobe and into warm clothes and found someone to take her back to the motel. She turned to Sir John, feeling she ought to say some kind of parting words, but he was already heading down the steps.

The makeup trailer was outside the stadium. That was where she had to go first, to get all the goop taken off of her body. Wow, it was full daylight already. She hadn't noticed that with all the bright lights on the racetrack.

A dog barked, and she glanced over with a small stab of shame. She didn't want to stop to talk to the nice ladies handing out flyers. They were in the right, the production was in the wrong for shooting here, and talking with them would only bring her feelings of guilt to the surface.

The ladies weren't at their card table with their poster taped to it. STOP GREYHOUND CRUELTY NOW, it said, with photos. She didn't want to look too closely at the photos. Simon crouched beside the table, talking in a low voice to a greyhound the ladies had brought with them, a skittish, bony creature who looked up at her and gave a low woof.

Simon looked at her and smiled. "Hi. Maggie went to find the loo, so I'm keeping an eye on Chester." He turned to the dog. "Do you want to say hello to Charlotte, Chester?"

"Hi, Chester," Charlotte said. Chester woofed at her once more, not unfriendly but not encouraging her to stay, either. Like he wanted Simon all to himself. She knew that feeling.

"They kill them a lot of times, did you know that? Maggie told me," Simon said. "When they're no good at racing anymore, the owners will shoot them, or electrocute them, or abandon them. They make all this money off of them, and then when they're all used up, they just kill them. Can you believe that?" He looked aghast, honestly pained.

"I know," Charlotte said. "I guess they don't make very good pets."

"But they do. That's what Maggie was saying. They can be trained. They just need a little attention. That's part of what Maggie does. She places the cast-off greyhounds into good homes." He looked at her, and she knew what was in those beautiful eyes before he spoke. "Do you think I could adopt Chester? He seems to like me."

"I don't really know," she said. The killjoy, the voice of cruel reason, the depriver of all fun and whimsy, that was her. "I think it'd be difficult getting him across the border. I don't know the process, but it might be complicated."

Oh, God. She hated depriving Simon of anything. How had his parents ever managed to say no to their boy? She was willing to do almost anything to keep those pretty eyes bright and happy. His expression fell.

"Yes. . ." he said. "I suppose you're right. I don't know what I'd do with him. I don't even have a place to live in Los Angeles. And I don't think I could take him back to England with me."

"You definitely couldn't," she said. "There's a quarantine. It's okay. Chester's got Maggie to look after him. She'll make sure he finds a good home."

"I know," Simon said, but he didn't sound like he believed it.

She looked at him, in the light of the rising sun, the frost on the grass around him sparkling and dazzling, and wanted to promise him anything.

Simon loved animals, in his exuberant, naïve, all-encompassing way. That was a concrete something about Simon, Simple Simon, that she could add to her very short list of facts about him. Didn't it suggest at heart he was a very good person and therefore worthy of her infatuation?

She didn't know. He was English, he could act, he loved dogs. Even as she summarized it in her mind, it didn't seem like enough to build a relationship around.

## CHAPTER SEVENTEEN

BACK IN VANCOUVER. Good. Calgary was lovely but so very cold, and as it turned out, her motel room hadn't had a bathtub.

Her ankle was still sore. It wasn't swollen much, and she could walk on it without limping, so she figured it wasn't sprained. It was a low-grade irritation only, a nagging pain that made her feel a little sorry for herself on cold mornings.

Now she was on the set once more, indoors, warm and comfortable even in her hot pants.

Jin got thrown through the window today. Most of that would be her, Ted and Paul had told her, but they'd need a stunt double for parts of it. It'd be her really going through the glass, though. Terrifying.

It was supposed to be the Bonaventure Hotel, the curved glass structure that was an unmistakable part of the downtown Los Angeles skyline. Jin would be kicked back through one of the windows and hurtle twenty stories down to the pavement. She saw the set, once more underwhelming up close. A curved wall of glass in front of a bright green backdrop. Breakaway glass. If she hit it just right, square against her back, head tucked forward like Paul showed her, it would be no problem at all.

Still, no matter how many times Ted and Paul told her otherwise, getting thrown through a window sounded like it might be kind of hazardous.

Paul would be on set today to help her with all of this, her fight scene with Simon and her dramatic plunge. The thought of wrestling with Simon was enough to give her butterflies.

She looked around. A crew member she didn't think she'd met before grinned and waved at her, so she went over to him.

"Do you know if Paul Yin's around?" she asked.

The man blinked, surprised. Then he laughed. "Sorry, Christina. I thought you were Margo there for a moment."

Charlotte was too busy trying to puzzle out if she knew Margo to correct him on her name. The guy continued. "Yeah, I think Paul and Margo are just in the hallway, getting some practice in."

"Okay, thanks." Was she terrible with names, or were there too many people on this film to keep track of?

She looked into the hallway. She had to stop and gape, because Paul was fighting Jin.

Jin. Her doppelganger, down to the hot pants and the fine makeup cracks drawn across her skin. Only this Jin was a better Jin than she herself was. She moved better, faster, more fluidly. Her kicks had more snap. She had bigger thigh muscles; Charlotte could see the sharp definition through her thin gold shorts. She looked lethal, like a real killer robot.

Paul saw her and stopped the routine with a quick word to Jin, then nodded at her. Jin turned and smiled. It was only then Charlotte realized she was staring at her stunt double.

She walked over to Paul and Jin. "Hi. You look amazing," she said. "Wow. I had a moment of total confusion there." She extended her hand. "I'm Charlotte."

"I'm Margo." When Margo talked, the resemblance faded. Her mouth didn't move like Charlotte's; her skin bunched and wrinkled in different ways. But with the same dark helmet of hair, the same outsized pupils, the same layer of heavy makeup, it was close enough.

"So I guess you're going to be doing all the difficult stuff, huh?" Charlotte said.

"You're doing most of it. Paul's just teaching me some of your fight with Gideon, in case it's needed."

Ah. So Paul was worried about her roundhouse. He was right to be worried; even after all the hours of one-on-one training, her kick was feeble. So if Margo had to step in and do it, it would be for the good of the movie. Didn't mean her pride didn't smart, though.

Margo looked uncertain, like she was interpreting her silence as a sign of disapproval. Charlotte hurried to fill the void with words. "Do you do a lot of work like this?"

"I've done a lot of television shows. This is my first movie," Margo said. "The rest of the time, I teach Tae Kwon Do at the rec center downtown."

"Cool. What belt do you have?" Charlotte asked. Tae Kwon Do had belts, didn't it? It better, or she'd just made herself look like an idiot.

"Black. I just tested for my second degree."

"Wow. I don't know why they didn't just cast you instead," Charlotte said. It was true. Margo was local, and thus cheaper. And she looked indistinguishable from Charlotte in wardrobe.

Margo shook her head. "I can't act," she said.

"They hired me without seeing me act," Charlotte said.

Margo laughed, but she looked startled, as though it had just now occurred to her how interchangeable she and Charlotte really were.

Paul looked from her to Margo, bemused. It was probably good Charlotte couldn't read his mind. "I talked to Ted. I believe the plan is to shoot the window scene first," Paul said. "Are you ready?"

"Sure," Charlotte said.

"If you're not sure you can do it, remember Margo's here. She'd be able to fill in."

A dichotic moment there. She wanted to pass the responsibility off to Margo, and at the same time she wanted to be irreplaceable. She couldn't have both, and it was far more important to be necessary. "No, I'll be fine. If you think I can do it, I can do it."

"Okay, then." Paul smiled. He didn't say he thought she could do it, but he'd say something if he thought she couldn't.

They practiced first. She was on a harness, a sturdy tangle of straps which would be digitally erased from the film. She was yanked back across the set, as though reeling from Gideon's kick, right into the wall. For the sake of rehearsal, the glass wall was moved out of the way. She slammed into a foam-padded plywood backdrop at a low speed.

"Tuck your head down further," Ted said, after consulting with Paul. "You're going to want your head and neck as much out of the way as possible when you hit the glass. Let your shoulders take the impact."

"Okay," she said. It wasn't too painful, getting slammed into the wall, but she'd be sore tonight from all the jostling.

"Ready to do it for real?"

"Yep." It sounded weak, so she supplemented it with a jaunty thumbs-up. Her ankle started to hurt again, which made her a little grumpy. This was no time to be cranky; she had a long, long day to get through.

"Okay. You're on your mark? Great." The usual shuffle of activity while Ted confirmed everyone was in place and the cameras were rolling.

"Action." Ted spoke it softly instead of yelling. It was easier on the nerves; it made each take seem like less of an event.

Only this take was an event. She braced herself. The harness jerked her backwards.

Flying through the air. Just like she should. No acting involved here, just a matter of making sure her body was where it should be. She wished she had taken more movement classes, more dance, because she was feeling a little stiff and graceless—

Smash.

- Back against the glass, shoulder blades both hitting at the same time, just as they should. She sailed through the window. Breakaway glass tinkling around her. Done.

She hit the ground wrong in her eagerness to get down, landed on one foot instead of both, and her ankle sent up a spasm of pain at that, but it was okay because Ted had already hollered, "Cut!"

Someone rushed up to unbuckle her from the harness, another of the multitudes of nameless crew members. It felt weird to walk, like her legs belonged to someone else.

"Charlotte, you doing okay there?" Ted hollered over to her.

"Yeah. I'm good," she called back.

"Okay. I think we got it. Let's just check the playback."

Too many people were clustered around the little monitor. She didn't want to join them, because she'd have to fight for space, and she was feeling a strange lack of curiosity about seeing her epic flight. It was done, and hopefully it was good, but everything else was bad, because her ankle was messed up all to hell.

Ted consulted with Franz, the director of photography. They pointed at the monitor, their faces solemn. Something was wrong. She'd screwed up. They'd have to do it again. Did they have another glass wall? Maybe they'd have to build another one first.

Ted looked up at last. He grinned. "Okay. We're good," he said. "Let's get this glass cleared away and set up for the next shot."

She started to move out of the way. She needed to sit down. Quietly, without drawing attention to herself.

"Charlotte? Is everything all right?" Hey, that was Simon. She hadn't even realized he was on the set yet. In full makeup and wardrobe, his eyes extra-pretty with all that eyeliner. Their fight scene today, that was right. Was it something he was looking forward to? Would he be uncomfortable or flattered if he knew how important this scene was to her?

She hadn't answered his question. He looked concerned. Adorably concerned. Brow wrinkled in distress. He had forehead lines, slight but noticeable, which probably put him around her age, maybe older. She wished she knew his age. She wished she knew everything.

"I'm okay," she said. "I just landed on my ankle wrong. It's not bad." That statement would have seemed more convincing if she hadn't burst into tears in the middle of it.

"Oh, gosh." Simon raised his hands as if to grab her by the shoulders, then stopped. He turned. "Ted!"

Simon shouting was such an anomaly that the hubbub of the sound stage quieted down at once. Ted looked up. "What is it?"

"Charlotte's hurt." She wished she could've stopped him from saying that, yelling it across the stage, because that meant she could no longer hide it. Action would be taken. Decisions would be made.

Ted hurried over. "How're we doing, Charlotte?" he asked. His face had gone almost gray with worry. Delays and expenses and concern for her well-being were all imprinted on his expression.

"I'm okay. I'm fine," she said. "I just think I landed wrong on my ankle."

"Sit down. Someone get a chair," Ted said.

Someone brought a wooden crate over, and Simon took her by the arm and helped her to sit.

Doctor Howe knelt in front of her. Had she been on the set all along, watching the stunt, or had someone gone to fetch her? "Which leg is it?"

"This one." Charlotte pointed to her right ankle. "I think I just wrenched it or something. It's not bad."

Doctor Howe took hold of her ankle, and she felt light-headed with the pain. She jerked her leg away, involuntarily. Doctor Howe looked up at her reaction and didn't say anything. She sat back.

"Could be broken," she said at last. "Get someone to take you to the clinic. I think you should get an x-ray of this."

Ted, to his credit, didn't flinch. "Okay. Charlotte, hon, Kerri can drive you."

"Okay." She took a deep breath. "I'd better get out of wardrobe first."

"Makeup, too, unless you want to scare them all in the waiting room." Ted smiled, but he had to be thinking along the same lines. Getting in and out of her makeup was no small affair. She might not be able to return to the set today.

"I'm sorry," she said.

"You got nothing to be sorry about. You did great. It looked great. Just get yourself taken care of, okay?" Ted patted her on the shoulder and stepped back. "Okay, folks, we're taking a break for a bit while I figure out what can be done today."

"Need any help standing?" Kerri asked.

"No. I've got it. It's really not that bad." She wished there weren't all these people around. She was no longer crying, but she probably looked streaky and distraught. She smiled at Kerri and got to her feet. It didn't feel good when she put her foot down, but it wasn't terrible, either.

Simon hovered around, like he wanted to be helpful but had no idea how. As Kerri and Charlotte made their slow way toward the wardrobe trailer, he faded into the background and disappeared.

Four and a half hours later, she was back on the set, back in makeup, back in her costume, the only difference a black Velcro cast affixed around her ankle and foot.

She could walk on it. No pain, thanks to the Demerol the doctor had given her. He'd provided her with crutches as well; she left them in Kerri's car above Kerri's protests that the doctor had told her to use them, not discard them as soon as she was out of his office.

"It's not too bad," Charlotte told Ted. "It could be worse."

"It's a stress fracture," Kerri said. Charlotte wished she hadn't. "Fracture" was a scary word.

"It's just a repetition injury," Charlotte said. "The doctor thought I probably cracked the bone earlier, and cracked it a bit more today. It'll be fine."

"Well, that's. . . good." Ted sounded dubious. "It's okay for you to keep filming?"

"Yep." That wasn't a lie. The doctor hadn't seen any problems with normal activity, as long as she kept off it when she could.

"The cast might be a problem," Ted said.

"Nope. It comes off." She knelt down and whisked it off to demonstrate. "See?"

"You're probably supposed to keep that on, right?" Ted said.

"Only if I want it to heal." She was being a little flippant. Might be the drugs. She felt pretty good, and she wanted to work. "Honestly, it's fine, as long as I wear it when I'm not shooting. Did we get far behind?"

"Actually, not too bad. Don't worry about it. We've been able to shoot some of Jin and Gideon's fight anyway, with Margo."

"Were you? That's great." It was awful, just awful.

Margo came up then. Still in makeup, still looking like her. "Hi, Charlotte. How's the leg?" She looked worried, and Charlotte knew why.

"It's fine. It feels a lot better now." Charlotte swallowed. "Thanks so much for filling in for me today. I really appreciate it."

Margo's expression lightened. "You're welcome. It was no problem. It was a lot of fun."

Rolling around with Simon. Yes, it would be. Margo had a great day, and they hadn't lost a day of filming due to her. What's more, Charlotte would be given credit for Margo's hard work onscreen. There was no reason for her to feel snitty about this. No reason at all. She smiled. "Well, where are we?"

"You sure you're up to working today?" Ted said. "Margo can finish up here, and then we can get insert shots of you another day."

"You know what, I feel great. I'm ready to do this." Big smile. Always a trooper.

"That's my girl." Ted grinned. "Okay. Margo, stay on hand just in case. Charlotte, you gotta let us know if we're pushing you too hard or if your leg starts to hurt, right?"

"You bet." Small chance of that. Her leg wouldn't start to hurt until the drugs wore off, and right now she felt good, very good. Ready to kick Simon's ass on screen. Ready to prove she was irreplaceable. Even if evidence pointed to the contrary.

She never got a chance to do her roundhouse. She didn't know whether that was bad or good.

Margo had done that. Had done all of the tricky stuff, it seemed, leaving her with an afternoon of posing and snarling. Everyone was solicitous of her injury, and far too much was being made about her continuing to work with a cracked bone.

A few days off, one more day of filming, one quick final scene. It was only mid-morning when Ted looked at the playback of her last shot and pronounced it good.

"Charlotte Dent, finished with the movie!" That was Nancy, the first assistant director, yelling it for all to hear. Charlotte was startled to be included in this tradition. There was a round of general applause, a few whistles. She was the first key player—if she could be considered such—to have wrapped her scenes.

Ted hugged her. "Congratulations, Charlie. You've been awesome." He'd been calling her Charlie for the last few days. She hoped it wouldn't stick.

"Thanks." She was smearing body makeup all over his clothes. No matter; she'd never have to wear this makeup again. "Thanks a lot. This has been a great experience."

Taura was the next to come up and hug her. It seemed genuine, even though Charlotte had to fumble to find a place to put her arms around the wings. "Don't leave me," Taura said, laughing. "I'm going to be the only girl on this set."

Charlotte thought that would suit Taura just fine, but it was nice of her to pretend otherwise. "Thanks. You've been great."

The cast and crew surrounded her. Sir John wasn't on set that day; she'd leave without saying goodbye. She wondered if she'd ever see him again. At the premiere, surely. She'd be invited to the premiere, wouldn't she? It was so hard to gauge her position in the pecking order of this production.

Simon kissed her on the forehead. It was brotherly, but it gave her a thrill all the same. "Take care of yourself," he said.

"Thanks. You too." She wanted to hug him, but the urge would be too strong to cling to him, and anyway, Simon seemed untouchable, like he'd snap in two if he were hugged.

Two weeks of filming remained for the rest of the cast, but she was done. Nothing was left but to pack up her suitcases, confirm with Kerri that she was booked on a flight to Los Angeles the next morning, and spend one final night in her pretty little hotel room with the pretty little balcony in this pretty little city.

## CHAPTER EIGHTEEN

HER APARTMENT, VACANT for six weeks, smelled of feet and must. Her fridge was empty, her plants were dead.

She picked up her mail from the post office. She paid her bills.

It was December. Three weeks left in the year. She was unemployed. Her bank account was flush. She had nothing to do, no promises to keep.

Her parents weren't expecting her until the week of Christmas. Bored and lonely in Los Angeles, she bumped up her departure date by a couple of weeks. Los Angeles to Moscow, Idaho.

At Moscow's tiny airport, she boarded the shuttle bus bound for the university. If she'd told her parents to expect her, her mother would have taken time off work to meet her flight. After the shoot, where her every move was controlled by the production, there was something luxurious about knowing that nobody in the world knew where she was at the moment.

The shuttle let her off at the entrance to the University of Idaho, just up the road from the paper mill. She could smell the sulfur in the air, faint but unmistakable. If she lived here, she wouldn't notice it. By the time she returned to Los Angeles, the odor would be trapped in her coat, her luggage, her hair.

Her bag in hand, she started walking. It was cold and icy, the sidewalk covered with frozen slush and ice. Her black wool coat was inadequate in this weather.

Her leg hurt. She'd never used the crutches and hadn't brought them with her, but the Velcro cast was still on her ankle. It hadn't bothered her much in Los Angeles, but here in the cold, as her feet grew numb, the bone began to ache, deep in her leg.

A wreath of jingle bells on the door to the mill announced her entry, but there was no one in the foyer to hear it. She hovered for a moment, uncertain, then crossed through the door into the factory beyond.

The deadening racket of heavy machinery. She looked at the gigantic apparatus taking up most of the room. Vats of pulp slurry, continuously stirred. The smell in here was strong. Men in work boots and plaid shirts and heavy gloves thronged around the machinery. She kept along the wall, head down. The commotion jangled her nerves, the relentless hammering and scraping of gears. It was a relief to duck into her mom's office and put some barrier between herself and that noise.

Her mom was at her desk in her office, which wasn't much more than a cubicle of glass separating her from the industrial floor. Charlotte felt a rush of reassurance just at the sight of her. Solid and practical, hair short and unfussy, gray streaks untouched, a beacon of competency. She looked up, and Charlotte saw the confusion in her face. It was the hair, still short and dark from the shoot, and she wasn't supposed to be here, in this office, in this state.

"Hi, mom," Charlotte said. "Merry Christmas."

A moment of silence. This wasn't a family for surprises; for a moment she regretted whatever impulse had led her to this place unannounced. Then her face lightened, and she rose from her desk.

"Oh, my gosh!" She opened her arms, and Charlotte let herself be enveloped. Her mom's heavy fleece pullover smelled of sulfur.

Her mom pulled back so she could look at her. "You've changed your hair."

"They had to do it for the film."

"You're all done?"

"I'm done. I didn't have anything to do in Los Angeles, so I decided to come here right away."

"Have you seen your father yet? He's going to be thrilled."

"No, I came straight here from the airport."

"Well." One syllable, filled with pride and pleasure, and she was no longer sorry. "If you can wait, I can run you home during my lunch break."

"That'd be great." She looked around. "Busy here?"

"About the same." Her mom was the day shift supervisor here, had been ever since they'd moved here from Boise eight years ago.

A knock at the window. Her mom gestured, and a stout woman wearing glasses with red plastic frames peeked her head in the door. Her sweater was appliquéd with a gigantic sprig of holly. "Gwen? Everything okay in here?"

"Hi, Sharon. This is my daughter, Charlotte. She just arrived from Los Angeles."

"Oh, this is the actress, right?" Sharon edged her way into the room. "Your mom tells me you were just in some kind of movie?"

"That's right. I just finished filming up in Canada." She smiled. Sharon examined her, and Charlotte couldn't tell what she was thinking, if she matched up to whatever stories her mom had told.

"Isn't that exciting?" Sharon smiled. She hovered in the door, papers in hand, not wanting to intrude on the mother-daughter reunion but almost trembling with some necessity. Charlotte cleared her throat.

"I should let you get back to work," she said. "I'll wait in the foyer until your break. Nice meeting you, Sharon."

She sat on the couch in the lobby and reread the paperback she'd read on the plane until her mom was free to drive her back to the house.

The car was new since she'd last been out, last Christmas. It was white. Old. Had some wear and tear on it. Still, the engine didn't make any knocking sounds when her mom started it, so that was a step in the right direction. "I like the car," she said at last.

"It's nice, isn't it? It's been pretty good for your father and me."

"Is dad getting out much?" Charlotte asked.

Her mom was busy adjusting the rearview mirror. "Well, no. I pretty much just take him to the doctor and back."

Charlotte was quiet. "How's he doing?" she said at last.

"About like he's supposed to." There wasn't much traffic on the road. Farm country: fields white and frozen.

"Is he going to have to go into a home?" she asked. Best to have this conversation now and not have it hang over the rest of her visit.

"Oh, no." Her mom sounded shocked. "It's not that far along. It'd be nice to have someone look in on him during the day while I'm at work, but that's a little beyond our means at the moment."

"That's good," she said. Conversation stilled until they got home.

A rental house, white and small. Seven Christmases spent here and she still doubted she could pick her parents' home out of a lineup of photos of similar small, white, two-story homes. Wooden porch and a bare driveway, her mother's garden, frozen in the backyard, brown and stiff and dead.

Dad was awake and sitting up in an easy chair. That was encouraging; she'd worried that he might be almost permanently bedridden by now. She'd been lax about researching MS since her dad's diagnosis four years ago. Her dad would get worse, and then he would die.

"Look who's here." Her mom's voice was a shade too bright and chipper. Was she always unnatural around her spouse, still, or was Charlotte's presence affecting her? "She just strolled into my office this afternoon."

"Charlotte." It was an effort for her father to raise his head and look at her. "It's good to see you. We weren't sure you'd be able to get. . ." He paused. "Home."

"I told you we'd be finished in time," Charlotte said. "I got done a little early." She was doing it too, the forced cheer. He must be sick of all the unnatural behavior around him.

"Well, I'm just going to leave you two here. I have to get back to work," mom said. She sounded relieved at the prospect. Charlotte didn't wonder. Caring for her father had to be more of a strain than she was showing.

After her mom left, her dad turned to her. He looked okay. Older, sure, maybe more gray than last year, but his color was good, his eyes alert. "How was Canada?" he asked.

"It was gorgeous. I didn't want to leave." She thought for a moment. "The film was fun. Everyone was really nice."

"Is it going to be a good movie?"

She thought of Sir John's words on that frozen Alberta night, then pushed them aside. "I think so. It's not art, but it'll be entertaining."

"I always thought movies should be entertaining. So many times directors think they need to be meaningful, but sometimes I just want to be entertained."

"I got to meet Sir John Hyde. And there was an actor in the film, playing the lead, who I really liked. Simon. He's English."

Her father's gaze, which had drifted, grew sharper. "Young?"

"My age, probably. Really nice guy. And he's very good looking. Beautiful."

Her dad regarded her. There didn't seem to be much wrong with his mental faculties, because he was staring through her, and she knew he was divining the meaning behind her words and reaching conclusions that were probably correct. "Do you like him?"

"He probably has a girlfriend. Or a boyfriend. I don't know."

"You should have dated more," her dad said. She stared at him, confused, until he elaborated. "I think we raised you pretty well. But if we were to do things over, I think we would have told you to date more."

She laughed, still confused. "I don't know that that's something you would have had much control over."

Her dad shook his head, indicating his wish to move on to another topic.

He was asleep in his chair by the time her mom arrived home. She heard the car pull into the cold gravel driveway outside and heard the car door slam, but long minutes passed, and her mom hadn't come into the house.

She looked out the window. She toed her shoes on, threw on her jacket, and crept out the front door so as not to wake her dad.

Her mom stood in her garden. It had been ploughed up and tilled under, the soil frozen into mounds and ridges. In the spring it had been a riot of tulips. She'd sent photos, dozens of them, all of the multicolored harvest, none of herself or her spouse.

Charlotte approached her where she stood, silhouetted against a moonless sky. The ground was dark and hard beneath her feet. "Mom?"

She turned, only slightly, so Charlotte could just catch her profile. Was she crying? Her features were plunged in darkness, so she couldn't be sure.

"It's not much to look at right now," she said. Cheerful "You should have seen it earlier."

"I saw photos."

Her mom looked at her and smiled. No sign of tears, so maybe Charlotte was feeling melodramatic this evening. "I expect you think your folks are falling apart."

"Not at all. You guys look great," Charlotte said. The melancholy passed and they moved back into safe, established patterns of conversation.

They'd go in and have dinner now. She'd tell them lively stories about the movie; her mom would talk a little about work and a lot about her garden. In a few weeks, they'd have their Christmas celebration, going through all the routines of the past twenty-nine years for at least one more time. It would be a good visit, and she'd be sorry to leave. And then she'd go back to Los Angeles and resume her other life, leaving Idaho far away.

## Chapter Nineteen

THE POST-PRODUCTION FACILITY was housed in a green glass structure far out on Olympic in that nebulous area where West Los Angeles turned into Santa Monica. Charlotte had meant to drive there, really she had—her new (used) car was seeing precious little use, and the only way she'd ever get better at driving was with practice—but the wide open road still terrified her, the act of sitting behind the wheel alongside thousands of other drivers still too daunting. It was easier to hop on the bus.

With a lingering sense of personal failure, she made her way to the recording booth. Angie greeted her.

"Charlotte, you look great!" She swept her up in a hug.

"Hi, Angie. How've you been?"

Angie shrugged. "Great. Great. The film's looking great—Ted and I were just in the editing bay earlier, watching what Ronnie's patched together, and already it's really shaping up. It's terrific." Meaningless words—Angie was from the studio, after all, and what else was she going to say?— but her enthusiasm seemed genuine. "We missed you during reshoots, hon. Vancouver wasn't the same without you."

There'd been reshoots? Charlotte glanced around. "Is it just me here today?"

"No, the talent will be in and out throughout the day. Ted's in with Simon right now. They should be finishing up soon."

"Oh, Simon's here?"

"You sound a little eager there," Angie said. She glanced at the closed door to the recording booth and lowered her voice. "He looks good, you'll be happy to hear. If I were in your position, I'd go for him myself."

"He's beautiful, isn't he?" Charlotte could feel herself blushing at the confession. "I don't really know him all that well, but he seems nice, doesn't he?"

"Oh, God, he's a darling. So polite and charming I wonder how he can stand it. Probably goes home and kicks puppies every night."

The door opened, and there was Simon, all eyes and hair and cheekbones. "Charlotte!"

A handshake. His hand, dainty and slim and cold. "It's good to see you. I almost didn't recognize you." He gestured. "The hair."

She touched her hair. "Oh. I went back to my original color after we were done filming."

"I had no idea you were a blonde." Simon examined her. Did he prefer blondes, or was he even now wishing she'd kept Jin's dark helmet of hair? "It looks quite nice," he said at last, then cleared his throat. "Are you next?"

"Yes, I think so. Is Ted in there?"

"He's talking to the sound man. Go on in." Impossible to gauge Simon's level of interest. He was delighted to see her, but in a general sense, because life delighted Simon, or at least he orchestrated his public façade to give that precise appearance, and he would have appeared equally delighted to see Angie, or Tim, or the sound guy, or the brown-haired receptionist who was even now sneaking covert glances at him. The world competed with her for his affections, and her odds of winning were remote. Nothing to do but leave him with Angie and enter the studio on her own.

Ted only wanted her to redo two of her lines—two of twelve, redoing seventeen percent of her dialogue—but in the way filmmaking had of dragging out even the simplest task, it took far longer than it should. She was surprised when she reentered the lobby to find Simon still there, engaged in earnest conversation with Angie.

Simon looked up. "That didn't take long, did it," he said.

"I'd better see how Ted's doing," Angie said. She shot her a glance which looked like it might be meaningful before giving Simon a quick squeeze on the arm and departing.

"Have you had lunch?" Charlotte asked Simon before letting herself think too much about it. "I was thinking of grabbing something to eat."

Simon looked startled. She opened her mouth again to give him a way out, but before she could, he spoke. "That would be nice. Thank you."

Hot damn. He'd said yes. Outstanding. "I didn't bring my car, so we should probably find somewhere around here, or. . ."

"I can drive," Simon said. "We can go anywhere." *Anywhere.* "If you need to be dropped off somewhere later, I can do that too."

"That would be great. Thanks." She couldn't think of anything else to say, couldn't dazzle him with her wits, could only smile at him as they walked toward the parking structure.

They picked a sushi restaurant on Pico neither of them had been to before. A tiny storefront place, red curtains printed with wood-block images of fish. She'd suggested it because it looked clean and inviting and not too aggressively intimate. They dug into soba noodles with shrimp in clear broth, split a plate of tuna sashimi, ate octopus rolls made with brown rice. It was all washed down with some brand of Thai beer that came in a stubby bottle with a black label, spidery Thai writing in thin gold letters.

"It has formaldehyde in it," Simon said. He wasn't so macrobiotic he was above a couple of drinks. Good to know. He twirled his empty bottle on the table. "They have it in London. I haven't seen it here, though. I thought there might be laws against importing it."

"Formaldehyde? Really?"

"That's what Alex always says. My flatmate. He knows this sort of thing."

Alex. The name on Simon's phone in his trailer back in Vancouver. His flatmate. Platonic friend, or something more? None of her research into Simon had given her any insight into his orientation. No known girlfriends or wives. "Do you live in London?"

"Yes. I'm thinking of moving out here permanently, though. If I can." He smiled. "I might buy a house. I hear it's easier to establish residency that way."

She thought for a moment, casting her mind about in search of ways to root for information about Simon. "I saw *House of Medici*," she said. "It's wonderful. I ended up buying the entire series."

"Oh, thank you." Delighted smile. "I'm so glad you liked it. I didn't think anyone had heard of it over here."

She hadn't heard of it before she started researching Simon, this culty little UK series in which Simon had starred. He was phenomenal: charismatic and vibrant and endearing all at once. "It took a while to track it down, but it was worth it. And that film on Keats you did for the BBC, I saw that too. You were amazing." She was as much as announcing her interest in him, wasn't she?

"I'm so glad you saw that. Thank you." He smiled. She smiled back. She was having a wonderful time, sitting in this cozy restaurant with a bowl of tasty noodles, smiling at Simon and feeling warm and happy from her formaldehyde-laced beer. It took her a minute to realize she should probably say something, and longer to realize she had nothing to say.

"I heard you had reshoots in Vancouver," she said at last.

Simon nodded, mouth full of seaweed and tuna, which he swallowed down with a drink of his beer. "Yes. We did. It went quite well. Very smooth."

"That's great," she said. "Have you seen any of the film?"

"What they've edited together, you mean? No. Ted says it looks quite good." He looked at her. "What have you been up to?"

"Auditions, mostly," she said. For the first time, it wasn't a lie. Upon her return from Idaho, she'd had a message from Rick wondering if she was up to starting work again. The easy assumption he would continue to be her agent was flattering. "Two for guest spots on sitcoms, the rest for commercials. None of it came to anything." She shrugged. "I was able to take a long break for the holidays. I visited my parents."

"Where do you parents live?" Simon asked.

"Northern Idaho." She was going to say "Moscow," but that would confuse the issue.

"Did you have a good time?" he asked.

She was going to reply with the usual pleasantries, but something about his interest and his sympathy spurred her to talk. "Yes and no," she said. "My dad was diagnosed with MS a couple years ago, so he's not in great health."

"I don't know what that is," Simon said.

"Multiple Sclerosis. It's a degenerative nerve disease. It's progressive. He spends a lot of time in bed now, and he's on a lot of medication."

"I'm so sorry. Is it something that can be cured?"

"No." She wasn't good at talking about this. She had never talked about this, actually, to anyone except her parents. She hadn't known how to, without seeming like she was seeking out sympathy or pity. And maybe that was what she was doing here, trying to gain Simon's sympathy, and she was using her father's debilitating illness to do it. She'd start crying if she thought about it any longer.

"Sorry. It's kind of a mood killer of a topic, isn't it?" she said.

Simon shook his head and didn't say anything, but he looked anguished. He was nice. So damn nice.

"Do you want to go to the beach?" he said. "If you don't have other plans, I mean. I've been meaning to get to the ocean for a while, and I thought this might be a nice day."

"The beach would be great," she said. "I'd like that." She hadn't been to the ocean in months, maybe a year. Strange how something so vital to the character of Los Angeles could go unnoticed, but she hadn't thought of going for a long time. Maybe because it was always crowded and bright, with the wide open expanses of sand and the sun high above conspiring to make her feel small and exposed. But walking on the beach with Simon would be different.

It was. It was a cool day, for one, and that made all the difference in the world. Now, in the last gasp of winter before the onset of spring, the sky was gray, and the beach was deserted. The carnival rides on the Santa Monica Pier, few and feeble, were still.

They walked on the sand, but just a little; Simon was wearing good shoes, shiny black leather, and he couldn't unbend enough to go barefoot.

They shopped. Simon was more of a shopper than a beach-goer. Upscale boutiques, on the Promenade and off, they browsed at them all. Simon spent a long time in stores, examining things, buying things: sunglasses and shoes, ninety-dollar T-shirts, thirty-dollar bottles of shampoo.

Furniture store. French provincial, antique and secondhand, beds with iron finials and dressers with chipped white paint. She surprised herself by falling in love with a bookcase. Heavy wood with a dark stained finish. Beveled edges and glass doors with iron knobs. It was expensive, sort of. She could afford it.

"It's good quality," Simon said, running his hands along the top. It seemed likely he would know. "Do you have a lot of books?"

She nodded. "Do you deliver?" she asked the floor salesman, and when he said they did, she knew she was going to override the portion of her brain cautioning her against spending money.

Dinner at a tapas bar off the Promenade. They split tiny plates of spiced food. Easy enough to order around meat and dairy to accommodate Simon's diet. They shared a bottle of wine, drinking out of chunky glass tumblers.

He drove her home. Dark, silent streets, the Los Angeles of the movies of her youth, glittering lights and a starless sky and darkened clubs that whispered of decadence. She leaned back into the leather passenger seat and stared out the window. Was this what Los Angeles was like for people with cars and money and no social phobias?

He pulled up to the curb in front of her apartment building. She spoke before she lost the nerve. "Do you want to come in for a minute?" Pause. "I could show you where I want to put that bookshelf."

On the drive home, when she was rehearsing it in her head, that seemed like it might not be a bad excuse to lure him inside. Out loud, it thudded.

"I'd love to. Thank you." Simon parked.

Her apartment would be clean enough, wouldn't it? Her morning coffee cup, probably half-filled, still on the table, some clutter of mail and magazines, but nothing incriminating. She'd taken out the garbage this morning, so there'd be no stink of decaying broccoli or discarded cans of tuna.

She flicked on the light. Relieved the place was clean, dismayed at how drab it looked. Simon entered behind her. He looked around. Did her possessions bear up under scrutiny? "You have a lot of books," he said at last.

Again with the books. It was said in a tone of wonder, and she knew from that alone he wasn't much of a reader. Time to quash her snobbery about non-readers; she'd been in the world enough to know it wasn't a sign of a lack of intellectual curiosity. People who didn't read much could be interesting people with livelier and smarter brains than hers.

"I thought maybe against that far wall. I could move all of these books onto the new shelf and get rid of this old one."

Simon nodded with every appearance of rapt interest. "Yes, I think that would work rather well."

"Do you want water or anything? I've got a bottle of wine."

She didn't want him to slip away, didn't want to risk never seeing him again. Did she really want him to stay? Stay the night? No. Too fast, and she was stuck too far in her recluse ways to be comfortable with the idea. Her sheets needed to be washed.

Relief and disappointment when he shook his head. "I should get going." He didn't specify why, which meant there was no reason. "Thank you, though. I had a lovely time."

He probably told his dentist the same thing. "So did I. It was good seeing you again."

He hesitated near the door. "Since neither of us are working now, maybe we can do something during the daytime? I've never been to the Getty."

"I love the Getty," she said. "Any time you want to go, I'd love to show you around."

"Tomorrow, maybe? If you're free?"

This meant something. This meant something. "Sure. That'd be great."

"I'll call you." An exchange of phone numbers, a solid plan made for their second excursion, and Simon went on his way.

## CHAPTER TWENTY

THE MARINE LAYER hung over the Getty. It was almost noon, and if it hadn't burned off yet, the day wouldn't heat up too much.

It was perfect weather as far as Charlotte was concerned. The air was just crisp and chilly enough to keep the crowds down. Then again, it was the middle of the week, and most people had to work. Not her. She was with Simon, all privileges hers.

Her museum-browsing tastes differed from Simon's. He liked to linger, to stare at paintings for an eternity. He didn't comment much on anything, apart from asking about her likes and dislikes; he didn't venture his own opinions. It was difficult to tell what, if anything, went on in that pretty head—was he forming conclusions, or analyzing his emotional responses, or just staring vacantly? Was this part of his own art somehow, some key to his ability to turn out those startling, nuanced performances, and if so, should she be taking notes?

She grew cranky. Breakfast had been too long ago, and her blood sugar must be low if she was getting irritated with Simon. After they'd exhausted the Dutch masters, she touched his arm. Lightly, because it seemed he might crumble under too much pressure.

"It's almost lunchtime," she said. "Should we grab something to eat?"

He looked surprised at the idea and reluctant at being brought out of his art-induced stupor. "Is there someplace nearby?"

"There's a café right here," she said. "Will that work?"

An eternity of frustration while Simon perused the posted menu before concluding yes, it would indeed work. They grabbed trays and joined the line.

A tall blonde stood in line in front of them, flanked by her friends. They were similarly tall and blonde, but all focus was on her. A backless satin halter, jeans, sandals with high wedge heels. Very thin and tan, hair long and straight. Sunglasses on.

"After my reading, Pierre told me I was the best he'd seen all day. He said I had star quality." The girl shrugged. "And it's like, yeah, he just wanted to get into my pants, but also I saw the competition in the waiting room, and I wasn't exactly worried. Bunch of little geeky drama school wallflowers."

Simon was listening to the blonde, Charlotte could tell. His expression hadn't changed, and he wasn't looking in her direction, but somehow she knew this random blonde with her star quality had Simon's complete attention.

The blonde looked over the array of wrapped sandwiches, wrinkled her nose, continued down the line with her empty tray. "Anyway, they had to give the part to some skanky little friend of the producer's, but Pierre said he's totally going to call me for his next film. He said he might write a part specially for me." She shook out her hair, flicked it back off her shoulders.

It was wrong to hate her. She might have many redeeming qualities. She might have a sick father whom she loved dearly. But Charlotte did hate her then, because it seemed altogether possible this Pierre, whoever he was, would indeed call her, and write a part for her, and maybe make her into a household name, because maybe she did have a star quality or some level of charisma Charlotte lacked, because Charlotte would swear Simon's attention had been fixed on her for the entire time they'd stood in this interminable line.

"Do you want to split the hummus platter? I'm not that hungry," Simon said.

It took her a minute to process the question. "Sure. Good idea."

They picked up a bottle of wine, too, which was a marvelous idea. Wine and museums were a magnificent combination.

Simon somehow made it to the patio door in time to hold it open for the blonde girl and her equal-yet-lesser blonde companions. She turned to thank him, and Charlotte could see the moment when she noticed him for the first time, when she had a purely visceral reaction to Simon in the flesh. Was it recognition, or sexual attraction, or just the simple identification of someone else with that intangible quality she possessed?

They sat outside. Simon placed his phone on the table next to a device Charlotte couldn't identify at first. An inhaler.

He smiled, bashful. "Asthma," he said. "I thought I was done with it when I turned twelve. Ever since I've been in Los Angeles, though, it comes back on occasion. I believe I may be allergic to this city." He poured out the wine and raised his cup in a toast. "To a lovely afternoon," he said.

They clicked, plastic to plastic. The girl and her friends settled in at a nearby table, right in her line of sight. The girl kept glancing over at their table, an empty tray in front of her, sipping at her bottle of water while her friends ate.

"I think you have an admirer," Charlotte said to Simon. Was that snide? Was it foolish as well, to alert Simon to the attentions of this very attractive stranger?

He barely turned his head. "Miss Star Quality, is it? Do you think she knows me?"

"I think she just thinks you're cute," she said.

"Does she?" Disaffected in the extreme. Her spirits rose.

"She's very pretty," she said. Why was she doing this? She couldn't seem to stop herself.

"I suppose. She looks like every second girl in this city." Simon sipped at his wine and appeared to be thinking. "She'd be tedious to live with, I think. Two minutes standing in line with her, and I don't feel I need to know anything more about her." He looked at her. "Whereas you have a universe going on beneath the surface. I can't imagine ever knowing too much about you."

Wow. That was. . . that was flirtatious, wasn't it? It was a compliment, that was for sure. She should thank him or something. Before she could get her thoughts together, Simon continued.

"Anyway, she wouldn't like me. I'm too much of a geeky drama school wallflower, myself," Simon said.

"Me too." They grinned at each other. A tingle of recognition, connection.

"Wallflowers make some of the very best actors, you know. I've never figured out why this should be so, but in my experience it's been true." Simon swirled a pita triangle in hummus, barely nibbled on a corner. No wonder he was so small. "You think we'd all be too shy to get up on a stage, but it doesn't seem to work that way."

"Shyness and stage fright are unrelated phobias," Charlotte said. "Just because you've got one doesn't mean you're any more inclined to have the other."

Simon cocked his head to the side and considered that. "I've never really thought about it that way, but I suppose you're right."

"Of course, shyness hurts in other ways. I get uptight if I have to call someone to ask about an audition or something. So that gets in the way."

"That's why I have my agent handle that part of it." Simon set the rest of his triangle down and took a drink of wine. "This is exciting, isn't it? In just a few months, you and I will have a film in theaters. Everything could change forever, if it's a hit."

She flinched to hear it out loud like that. Superstition, like Simon had just placed a hex on the film. What was wrong with her? A pattern of rejection had hard-coded her brain to expect the worst possible result from everything. She had made it through filming, and it had been a good experience. Why couldn't she accept the possibility of good things happening to her? "I hope you're right," she said.

"I want to be famous," Simon said. He grinned, and Charlotte knew what he'd looked like as a child. "I think it would be marvelous."

"I'd say you've got a pretty good chance of it," she said. All of a sudden, she felt. . . odd. Wistful, and envious, and maybe a little scared. The sun emerged from beneath the marine layer, bathing their table in white light, and Simon suddenly seemed defenseless, like he'd wither and burn if he stayed in it too long.

Later, as they stood at one of the many observation points and stared out at the panoramic view of the city, the downtown skyscrapers shrouded in a brown haze of smog, Simon slid his hand over to hers where it rested on the railing. Her knees went a bit weak whenever she glanced down at the sharp drop below; it was good to clutch the railing for support. Simon clasped her hand, once. He cleared his throat.

"I think Angie might be trying to fix us up," he said. His voice sounded strained. "Back at the post facility, she mentioned I might want to ask you out sometime."

She stared at the view. "Angie might have had reason to think I'd be interested in such an invitation," she said.

Simon was still for a moment, then he moved his hand from hers and rested it lightly on the small of her back. They stared out over the view.

Simon and Charlotte became a couple that spring, a gradual process marked by its lack of drama. They dined, they shopped, they watched movies and visited museums.

They slept together. In this, surely she should have found evidence of some deeper connection, but instead it was a tangle of neuroses. She was too pale, her skin too dry and uneven, too marked with red lines from the waistband of her jeans and the straps of her bra. Traces of eczema on her upper arms, silver-white stretch marks on her hip bones. Her breasts were too small and too pointy; the flaws clothes covered couldn't hide here. Simon was pale too, his skin almost translucent, and he was so thin she could count his vertebrae, but he was beautiful and exotic.

He was a conscientious lover, gentle and patient, but passionless, too. She was guilty of the same. It was a shame, she reflected after their first coupling, lying in what should be a post-coital glow but was more of a fuzzy shimmer, that two inhibited individuals couldn't find it in themselves to unbend a little during this most personal of acts. Then she looked at the man asleep beside her, long limbs and blue-white skin and thick curls, and revised her opinion: She'd just had the best night of her life.

This all took place at his temporary residence in one of the super-chic hotels on the Sunset Strip. No kitchen facilities: impossible to imagine Simon cooking. Expertly decorated in masculine grays and blacks, chrome and leather and glass, but not by Simon; it might or might not be to his taste, but it wasn't his choice and was therefore unrevealing.

It was getting close to summer, and for once she didn't regard this with dread. This summer would be different. This summer, she had an air-conditioned car and a hot English boyfriend with an air-conditioned hotel room, and most importantly, she had a major motion picture set to open in theaters in just over a month. She was debt-free with a little left over, and checks still kept coming in, bits and pieces of film-related payments.

Rick called one afternoon while Simon was out on an audition: "Heads up, some nice kid from *Jejune* magazine's going to be calling you in a bit to interview you about the flick. I told her you'd be thrilled."

"I would be, in fact. That's great, Rick. Thank you."

"Thank Angie. They wanted to interview Taura, but Miss Persnickety wanted it to be a cover story, they said they couldn't guarantee it, so she backed out. Angie said some nice things about you to their editor, so here you are. It's not going to be much, half a page maybe, just a few minutes of your time. Photo session later this week or next; they haven't booked the space yet."

"Okay. No problem. Anything on the audition front?"

"Got a call in about getting you in to read for something over at Fox. I'll let you know. Once the film's in theaters and casting directors have the chance to see you in something, it'll be easier to sell you."

"Okay. Thanks. I really appreciate all this."

"I know. You tell me that every time. Just be your usual appreciative self in the interview, and if you get the chance, be sure to say plenty of nice things about me then, okay?" Rick clicked off before she had a chance to grill him about what was expected of her for the interview.

She needn't have worried. The girl from *Jejune*—Kimberly, her name was, and from her voice, she sounded young and scared—called about twenty minutes later.

"So the lady from the studio—Angie, right?—told me that this is your first film?" Kimberly said, after fumbling introductions had been made and pleasantries exchanged.

"Yes. I've been acting locally for a while, but this is my first professional job." She hesitated. It was difficult to talk about herself, but what was the point of an interview if not to boast about accomplishments? "Ted—that's the director, Ted Darling—saw me when I was out jogging one morning, and stopped and asked if I'd be interested in a part in his film."

"Wow. That's really cool. I mean, that's like a Marilyn Monroe story, isn't it?"

Kimberly probably meant Lana Turner. Close enough. "I don't think Marilyn ever played a killer robot, though."

"Angie said you broke your leg during filming?"

Kimberly didn't have the hang of asking questions yet. Charlotte hadn't mastered the art of answering them, so they made a fine pair. "Sort of. It was just a stress fracture."

"What's that? Is that like a sprain?"

"It's a cracked bone. So, yes, technically, I broke my leg, but it really wasn't as bad as all that. We were shooting a scene where my character gets thrown through a window, and I guess I just landed wrong."

"But Angie said you kept working even with it broken, right?"

Wow. Angie really had been selling her for this interview, hadn't she? "I had a doctor look at it. Then I went back to the set and finished shooting for the day."

A long pause, which worried her until she realized Kimberly was just flipping through her notes, trying to find her next question. "Okay. Are you doing any other films now?"

"Nope." Cheerful. "I'm reading scripts and going on auditions. That's about it."

"Okay." Another long pause. "I think that's all I have." She sounded uncertain.

"If you think of anything else you want to ask me, you can always call me again," Charlotte said.

"Really? You wouldn't mind?" She sounded so startled Charlotte thought maybe she wasn't supposed to offer that. Maybe real actors didn't volunteer their time quite so readily.

"Sure. No problem. Good talking to you, Kimberly."

"You too, Catherine. . . Charlotte. Sorry. Charlotte." Kim hung up in a flurry of embarrassment. Charlotte was somehow charmed. They'd both muddled through that, feeling their way through a new experience, and God only knew what the final interview would look like, but it was in the past now.

When the new issue of *Jejune* came out, Charlotte bought a copy, resisting the urge to tell the bored checkout girl she was featured inside it.

Hardly worth much fuss—the article, photo included, took up a third of a page. The photo was a little strange. They'd picked out her clothes, a peach crepe blouse that was pretty enough but nothing she'd wear on her own. Her face looked unfamiliar, her skin smooth and unlined. There was no surge of recognition when she stared at the photo. It was a picture of a pretty girl with a generic smile and a burst of blonde hair.

The interview was a few short lines, a Q&A following a brief introduction. Discovered while jogging, no acting experience, broke her leg and went back to shooting on the same day. This Charlotte Dent sure was a plucky little thing, wasn't she? This Charlotte Dent was also, apparently, twenty-four. She stared at that number for a long time, then called Rick.

"How old am I?" she asked without preamble.

Rick chuckled, low and guilty. "Yeah, I thought I might hear from you on that. If you're going to be mad, blame Angie. Since this is your first film, she suggested it might be better for your career in the long run if we shaved a few years off. You upset?"

She thought about it. "No, it's not a big deal."

"Celebrate your recaptured youth. Nobody's going to question you on it. You still look like a kid." Having imparted the highest possible compliment to her, Rick hung up, leaving her to stare at the magazine in silence.

## Chapter Twenty-One

"Is it what you thought it would be?" Charlotte asked.

Simon was quiet, looking up at the buildings, his lips parted. She couldn't tell if he'd heard her.

"It is and it isn't," he said at last. "It's not much like London, is it?"

"I wouldn't know," she said. She knew London from books and films, just like she knew New York from books and films, but being here in Manhattan was different from reading about it, and no, she had to agree with Simon, it wasn't much like London.

"It's newer, I suppose."

Strange comment. Compared to Los Angeles, New York seemed Biblical. Compared to Simon's neck of the woods, perhaps not.

The surly young man who'd picked them up at the hotel and taken them in the elegant town car through midtown traffic held open the door to the studio. A syndicated daytime talk show, but she wasn't sure which one. She wasn't keeping very good track of Simon's itinerary on this gauntlet of promotion.

A tall lady in a suit met them in the lobby. High red heels and a headset. Manicured hand extended to Simon. "Simon? I'm Jessie. You're here for Randi, right?"

Simon shook Jessie's hand. "Yes, that's right. This is Charlotte," he said.

A flicker of a glance over her. Was it dismissive, or was she feeling sensitive? Charlotte had dressed comfortably, jeans and flats because they were easy to walk in, and nobody was going to be pointing any cameras at her today, but while the jeans were okay, the flats were a miscalculation. Every woman she'd seen thus far, the ladies in the restaurant they'd dined in last night to celebrate their visit, the staff of the local morning show Simon had just taped, teetered through the city on elegant spikes.

"Nice to meet you," Jessie said. "Are you staying for the taping?"

She was trying to figure out where Charlotte fell in the hierarchy. Agent, assistant, PR person, family member, girlfriend?

"I wouldn't miss it," she said with her best smile. "It should be interesting."

Simon, bless him, took the opportunity to rest his hand on her lower back and smile down at her. In that moment, the nature of their relationship clicked for Jessie, and her manner changed, just a bit.

"I'll show you to your dressing room. You need coffee or anything? I'll see if Randi's around. She usually tries to talk to the guests before the show."

Did she know who Randi was? She wasn't up on her daytime television. It was a new show, she thought, not more than a season or two old, and Randi was either that girl who'd won the reality show, or the former prosecutor, or maybe neither. For the next three days, Simon was booked solid with appearances in the middle ground, shows Charlotte had barely heard of. Was that a bad sign, or was it usual? Was the studio promoting the movie enough? Her view was so skewed, so insular—all she ever heard, from Ted and Angie, usually filtered through Simon, was the studio loved it, it

178

looked great, it was a surefire hit. As much as she liked Ted and Angie, their opinions in this were not necessarily to be trusted.

She was exiled to the green room during taping. Not that she was alone. Jill was in the green room, too. Of course she was. Jill worked in the studio's east coast offices. Publicity, or maybe marketing—Charlotte had a hard time figuring out the differences between the two departments. Jill talked on her cell, slumped on the sofa, her shoes propped up on the low table close to the tray of mini muffins and the fruit plate. She glanced at her and returned to her call. "I don't give a rat's ass what you think I said yesterday. I'm telling you today, that's not going to happen. We've got a tight schedule, and you're giving me the runaround, and I don't have to listen to you." She clicked off and looked at her. "Is Simon here? He's late."

He wasn't. The hired car had picked them up on time and dropped them off on time. "He's here. They took him to ward-robe."

"Just so he knows—just so you both know, this isn't a vaca-tion. He's here to work. We're only covering expenses for him, not his guests, okay? Make sure he knows that, because I don't want to have to explain it later."

Jesus. Jill hadn't been quite this prickly to Simon when they'd met with her yesterday—Simon was Talent and therefore unassail-able. Was she trying to be offensive? Charlotte considered and concluded that yes, she was. She was deliberately trying to put Charlotte in her place as a hanger-on: Charlotte might be in the movie, but here she was nothing more than Simon's fling.

Jill looked around the room. "Is there anyone here who can get me some decaf?"

Who was she talking to? Apart from Charlotte, the only other occupant of the room was a middle-aged lady with a red pantsuit and a good deal of stiff blonde hair. She sat in an armchair by herself, knitting; the knitting alone was a sign she didn't work here and thus would not be interested in fetching Jill coffee. Maybe Jill thought that could be Charlotte's job. Maybe Jill was dead wrong.

The television was tuned to a live feed from the studio floor. An empty set right now, a faux-cheery living room. Fake potted palms, cursive letters spelling out "Randi" on the back wall. They could watch the taping from here. Just the three of them. That'd be cozy.

"Damn it," Jill said, then got to her feet and stormed out of the room in search of her decaf. The blonde woman looked up and smiled at her. She didn't roll her eyes, but something in her expression made Charlotte realize she was looking at a kindred spirit.

"Hi. I'm Charlotte," she said.

"Mary Beth. I'm Murray Grossman's wife." She set aside her knitting long enough to shake her hand. At Charlotte's confused expression, she continued. "The relationship expert? He wrote *Bedroom Ways*?"

"Oh, of course," Charlotte said. It sounded familiar, or sort of familiar, like something she maybe had heard something about at some point in passing. "Is he a guest on the show?"

"He's on every Wednesday," Mary Beth said, with a touch of surprise she hadn't known this.

"That's great," she said with an enthusiasm summoned from some unknown depths. "That must be really interesting."

"Are you a friend of Jill's?" Mary Beth asked.

"No." Pretty adamant about that. "My friend, Simon, is a guest today. He's promoting his movie. *Queen of Angels*." Too much effort to describe it as "their" movie.

"That's wonderful. How exciting for him." Mary Beth held up the knitting in her lap. "It always takes longer than I think it will. That's why I bring my knitting. Murray keeps telling me I don't have to go to every taping, but I think it's so important to be supportive of our loved ones, don't you?"

Jill reentered then, a storm cloud of moody entitlement, so Charlotte didn't answer. She settled into one of the couches and picked up a magazine, wishing she had thought to bring a book. She'd have to remember that in the future.

Randi, it turned out, was neither the retired prosecutor nor the reality show winner. If Charlotte had to guess, she was a former beauty queen, or pin-up model, or something along those lines. Tall and chesty, probably in her early forties, though her skin had that ultra-smooth, hyper-stretched look that made it impossible to tell for sure. Her smile was plastic, but she seemed nice. Charlotte couldn't find any reason to bear her ill will, even though she took a bit longer than necessary to grope Simon when he first came onstage.

Simon looked good. Dark suit, no tie, pale blue shirt with the collar open. Hair messy. Pretty and charming. Alas, he was a little annoying. Charlotte couldn't figure out what was irking her about his performance—and it was a performance, that was clear—but for the first time ever, she found herself not liking him much.

"We decided to shoot it up in Canada, of course, because we could save a great deal of money that way, even though the film is supposed to be set in Los Angeles." Simon recounted the whole story of the production, very animated, eyes bright and shiny. "We" decided? How much say did Simon have in that, anyway? He made it sound kind of silly and trivial, and certainly it was, but there was something unkind about making it into an amusing anecdote on syndicated television.

What was wrong with her, picking Simon's innocent missteps apart? Adrenaline was making him unnatural and manic; she shouldn't criticize.

"You're adorable, you know that?" Randi said. "Is there a special someone in your life?"

"There is, in fact." Just the way he said that made her forgive him anything.

"Can you tell us anything further?"

"I can't, really, it's too new," he said.

Jill turned to Charlotte. "You should give him hell for not mentioning your name," she said. Charlotte felt a stab of contempt. She had secretly wished Simon would mention her name, and mention that she was his costar as well. But it was the wrong thing to wish, obviously, since Jill thought it was the correct course of action.

When Simon's segment was over, she fled the prison of the green room and met him in his dressing room. "Did you watch it? How was I? Was I okay?" he asked right away.

"You were wonderful," she said, and tried to mean it.

After the car dropped them off at the hotel, they had the afternoon free. Simon wanted to shop. He wanted to take a cab, but gave in to her wish to experiment with the subway system.

They bought Metro cards from the dispenser inside the station. Simon looked pale and peaked. For crying out loud, hadn't he ever taken the Tube in London? Was he so unfamiliar with public transportation that this was causing him to freak out? More to the point, was it wrong for her to feel triumph at proving herself so much more resourceful here?

The subway system wasn't how she'd pictured it. Nothing at all like Los Angeles' new and mostly empty subway; this was old. Tile walls and ancient wooden beams, a smell of hot rust and old garbage. Everything was dark and hot and old. Boxy cars, primeval creatures that rattled and rumbled and screamed their way up to the platform.

A short hop to Fifth Avenue—they could have walked, but Simon was wearing shiny dress shoes that looked uncomfortable— and they emerged from underground right near the rows of clean shops. Simon revived above ground, his color coming back at the sight of designer labels and high-priced goods, in his element once more.

Simon loved to shop. Charlotte liked to browse, but something about the racks of coats that cost more than her rent and the rows of stiletto heels that made walking impossible made her melancholy. But Simon was happy here, and it was always fun to watch Simon when he was happy.

He bought a dress shirt, the color of sun-faded stones. Chestnut-colored leather shoes with intricate tooled details, a gray cashmere sweater. Charlotte watched as he accumulated items, handing them off to the shop girl to be delivered to the hotel. She touched a shoulder bag with two fingers, careful not to leave sticky hand oils on it. Coffee-brown, a roomy satchel with a fold-over flap that buckled.

Simon stood at her shoulder. "If you want it, I can get it for you," he said.

It was twelve hundred dollars. An absurd sum, almost obscene, and it was a lovely bag, but not worth that, even if she had all the money in the world at her disposal. It was horrifying that Simon could—would—offer so easily to make it hers. "Oh, no. Thanks. I was just looking at it," she said.

"Are you sure? If there's something else you'd rather have. . ."

"I don't need anything." She kissed him on the cheek. He smelled good, fresh lemons and thyme. "Are you about finished here?"

All the same, it wasn't that much of a surprise, after they returned to the hotel following an intimidating lunch at an elegant bistro, to find the purse nestled in one of the glossy shopping bags delivered in their absence.

"I hope you don't mind," Simon said. He was eyeing her like he expected her to burst into a rage at his actions, and just that alone made her want to shower him with reassurances. "Your face lit up so much when you saw it."

"It's beautiful. Thank you. I love it." Because that was the only possible response.

## Chapter Twenty-Two

SIMON WAS ONLY famous among a culty little group of fans online, but to them he was a star.

Charlotte found three websites devoted to him. Two just had a bunch of pictures, transcripts of a couple interviews Simon had done for UK newspapers and magazines, some scant biographical information, most of which she already knew. Simon was thirty, he'd grown up in Portsmouth, he had a younger sister.

The third site was of greater interest, because it had message boards.

The boards had been active for maybe two years. For two years, this cluster of women—men too, for all she knew, but something about the hormone-soaked proclamations and the smiley-faced emoticons dotting every post spoke of women—had been discussing Simon in great detail. In this way, their relationship with Simon was more legitimate than hers; she'd only known of his existence since late last year.

Did Simon know about this? Was he pleased, or embarrassed, or what? More sites like this would be sure to spring up after the movie premiered. Would he consider this a good thing?

The message boards analyzed and dissected and ruminated over Simon's various talk show appearances during the blitz of *Queen of Angels* publicity. Of particular interest were his mysterious references to a girlfriend. As the girlfriend in question, shielded in her anonymity, she wanted to see their reactions.

So much for anonymity. Under the post headed, "GIRL-FRIEND!????!":

*Her names charlote dent*, she read with a mixture of fascination and alarm. *She's in the movie. Shes an actress. There's a picture of her here.*

Charlotte followed the link to a site where media sources could purchase photos. There were a number of thumbnail-sized water-marked photos from the set of *Queen of Angels*. Ah, that was that cold, cold Vancouver morning when they'd shot at the convenience store. They'd been told there were photographers about. That was the day she'd hung out in Simon's trailer and lunched with him. That was a good day.

One photo of her. It was fantastic. She wore somebody's coat thrown over her costume. Legs bare from the tops of her boots to mid-thigh, her haircut severe, her makeup heavy. A profile shot, squinting in the distance. She looked fierce and mean. God, she hoped she looked like that in the film. She made a note to use that photo as her Christmas card. Maybe she could Photoshop a Santa hat onto her head.

Back to the comments: *i know who she is. shes a model. shes the one in that gross ad with the perfume bottle shaped like a dick.*

Well, that was a stumper. It was an odd feeling to have people boldly and wrongly stating facts about her life. Model?

A post from someone named Joegirl: *She looks like a bitch. I'm sorry, she just does, and I'm sorry if that offends any of you, but that's just my opinion. Her eyes are too squinty and she looks mean.* Great. The ones who could spell were the nastiest ones. *You know she's just using him. She probably slept with the director to get the part, and now she's going to leech off Simon's fame.*

There probably wasn't any point in reading any more of this. Nevertheless, she continued:

*You don't know what you're talking about. I worked on Queen of Angels, and Charlotte and Simon were the nicest people on the whole set!* That was from KillerK. Presuming KillerK was telling the truth, who would she be? Kerri? Kerri would say nice things about her, wouldn't she? *She's totally cool unlike SOME actresses I could mention. She was really friendly to everyone, and she's really pretty, too, so you should probably keep your mouth shut if you don't know what's going on. You're just jealous, that's all.*

Aw. It was nice to have someone come to her defense like that. Her cheeks felt a little hot from the earlier attack. Nothing out of the ordinary, nothing too bad. The more popular she became—or, maybe more to the point, the more popular Simon became—the more she'd have to get used to this.

Her doorbell startled her out of her thoughts. Simon, probably. She hadn't given him a key yet. Should she make him a set of keys? Were they at the stage yet? What was the protocol? She got up and let him inside.

Simon looked bedraggled. "Hi, love," he said. He kissed her on her neck once and stepped inside, then kicked off his shoes.

"How was the class?" she asked. On the advice of his agent, Simon had gone to see some hotshot acting coach. She couldn't imagine he needed the additional training, but maybe it was a good way to get his name out there.

"Dreadful," Simon said. He flopped himself down on her loveseat. "The man kept yelling at me to show more emotion. He kept telling me he didn't feel my anger. What is it with Americans and anger?" Simon leaned his head against the back of the couch and stared up at the ceiling. "Finally, he threw his water bottle at me. It was empty," he added.

"Did you get angry then?" she asked.

"I did, in fact. I walked out." He looked at her. "Is that what most acting coaches are like over here? Is that what they think the process is all about? Hurling objects and pitching idiotic little fits?"

"Pretty much, yes," she said. "Do you want a drink?"

"God, yes. Thank you."

She went to the kitchen to pour the wine. When she returned to the living room, Simon had risen from the couch and was staring at her laptop screen. "What's this?" he asked.

"*Sweet Sexy Simon,*" she said. At his look, she nodded to the screen. "Have you ever seen this? It's a fan site for you."

She placed his wine glass at his elbow. He didn't look at it, his attention captured by the message board. "Really? That's bizarre. Who are these people?"

"Your fan base. This has been around for a couple of years. There's a whole message board devoted to you."

"How odd." He frowned. "How'd you find this?"

"I Googled you."

"I've done that before. All I found were a lot of Simon Olivers who weren't me." He frowned at the screen, his brows drawing together until they touched.

"You have to sort through a lot of links until you get what you're looking for. It becomes pretty easy the more you do it," she said. Simon looked rapt, like he wasn't even aware of her presence anymore, and she had a weird sinking feeling she had just opened Pandora's box.

"They're talking about you, aren't they?"

"Yep. It's because you mentioned me on the talk show. They're wondering who I am."

"They're not very nice." He pursed his lips. "In fact, they're downright rude."

"I know. It's not a big deal." They should move on from this, because it looked like Simon was getting upset, and it was a sucker's game to get upset about anything on a message board. "There are other threads where they talk about other stuff they've seen you in. They're pretty excited about *Queen of Angels.*" She took the mouse from him and clicked back on the browser, off the offending thread and onto the main board.

"Why do they do this?" Simon asked. He watched the screen as she clicked onto a thread about *Queen of Angels.* Should be innocuous enough, she hoped. "Why don't they just write to me instead? Nobody ever writes to me."

"Don't feel left out. Nobody ever writes to anyone anymore. This is much easier. They can meet people with similar interests. It's harmless enough. They just like you, a lot."

Simon didn't answer. She cleared her throat. "There's a couple other sites for you. Here." She opened up the browser history and clicked on one of the more innocuous photo-laden sites, hoping it would distract him.

Simon blinked. "How'd you find that?" he said.

"Brower history. See? These are all the sites I've visited today. Look, here's another fan site. This one has transcripts of interviews with you," she said.

"Go back to that other one, please. The one with the message boards."

So much for her attempt at distraction. She clicked back. "Don't take any of this too seriously, okay? They're just a bunch of girls who think you're cute. They get a bit silly about you, but it's harmless."

Simon wasn't listening. He was reading, his attention fully focused on the screen. He was in that mode again, like he'd been while looking at the art at the Getty, where the rest of the world was no longer real to him. After a while, she picked up her wine glass and retired into her bedroom to read while Simon got this out of his system.

Maybe an hour later, she heard an electronic squeal. Simon had closed the lid of her laptop without shutting it down first. She winced. A technophobe to the core, Simon was incapable of treating electronics with the respect they deserved. He came into the bedroom and sat down on the bed beside her.

"All done?" she asked.

He shook his head. "They don't seem to like me very much," he said at last.

"Are you kidding? They love you."

"They don't know me. They form a lot of conclusions about me that aren't right, and they treat them like facts. They don't like that I'm in Los Angeles. They don't like me appearing in a Hollywood movie. They think I'm selling out, or just doing it for the money or because you wanted me to." He looked at her. "I didn't even know you before I got cast in this! And I've always wanted to do Hollywood movies, always. I don't think it's beneath me, and they seem to be quite upset with me about this."

His color was high. She sat up and snaked her arm about his waist. "They're not upset with you. It's just the way message boards are. Everyone gets emotional and stupid about little tiny stuff that doesn't matter. They just feel like they know you because they relate to your characters so much. It's a good thing, really." She squeezed him once. "You're just going to get more and more of that the more famous you get, you know. I'm sorry. I shouldn't have showed that to you."

"No, it was. . . enlightening." He looked at her. "Sorry I got a little absorbed in that. Fascinating stuff, the internet, isn't it?"

"So they tell me," she said.

## CHAPTER TWENTY-THREE

THE PREMIERE WAS on Thursday, in advance of next Wednesday's opening. The day was lost to preparations. Charlotte had planned on going dress shopping by herself, but that idea had been kyboshed by Angie, who informed her the studio would provide wardrobe for Simon and her. It was an unexpected gesture; she couldn't be sure, but she thought it was one of appreciation for how cooperative they'd been through the whole process. Unlike Taura, who'd backed out of the entire New York publicity tour, which had probably caused the studio some consternation. Taura, after all, was a bigger draw than Simon, and her lack of participation could affect their box office.

Hair, makeup, wardrobe, all jammed into Simon's cramped hotel room. Preparing for the premiere was like shooting the film itself, only with an impromptu pedicure and foot massage thrown into the mix.

Her dress was selected for her by someone whose fashion sense trumped her own. It was a bright cranberry silk column with a long mauve ruffle that spilled over one shoulder. She wasn't crazy about the one-shoulder look—the dress reminded her of a toga, and that couldn't be good—but everyone told her how fabulous it looked on her, so she didn't fight it. Gold sandals, dangly earrings, a tiny and impractical clutch bag of mauve snakeskin.

Her hair was twisted into a great mass and secured with too many hidden pins. Makeup eradicated the texture of her skin and added shadows and dimension and sparkle where none previously existed. She looked, in the end, as little like herself as she had while costumed as Jin. An unnatural creature, unearthly, but ever so pretty.

Simon was luckier by virtue of being a man: black suit, white shirt, no tie. She was frankly jealous as she tripped delicately beside him toward the limo. The driver held the door open for them. Just a kid, really, in ill-fitting livery; he looked disappointed his charges for the evening were no one special.

Eliza sat in the back of the limo, nursing something in a plastic cup with a wedge of lime. "Hi, kids," she said. She leaned over and kissed Simon on the cheek, then rubbed at the fresh lipstick mark with two fingers. "You both look edible. I'm so jealous."

Eliza was Simon's publicist, and she would be accompanying them this evening. Eliza wore a plain yet expensive pantsuit; her hair was elegantly coiffed. "Charlotte, sweetie, I brought a big purse if you need me to hold your phone or your keys or anything."

"Thanks. I'm good." Charlotte had left her phone and keys in Simon's hotel room; her clutch contained only her license and credit card, and, almost as superstition, bus fare. Simon passed over his phone and his inhaler; Eliza tucked them into her purse.

"Maureen's already there. She says people are beginning to arrive—celebrities, I mean, not real people—so we've timed this perfectly." Charlotte had no idea who Maureen was, but she smiled and nodded.

"Of course you did. Thank you, Eliza." Simon leaned over and kissed Eliza's temple, then turned his attention to the minibar. "Champagne, Charlotte?"

"We won't have time." The distance from Simon's hotel on the Strip to the theater on Hollywood Boulevard was negligible.

Simon continued his exploration. Charlotte peered over his shoulder. Individually-sized bottles of champagne, vodka, Pellegrino, Campari, Red Bull.

This block of Hollywood was closed for the premiere. The limo driver showed some kind of credential to a uniformed guard, and they were allowed to drive past the makeshift roadblock and pull in front of the Chinese Theater. Nice that the premiere was here; there were better theaters in Los Angeles, but somehow this seemed the most authentic.

Eliza talked on her phone: "Yeah, we're here. I see it. Spread the word that we're here, okay? Give them as much prepping as you can. I don't want the local reporters fumbling to remember Simon's name."

Simon caught her eye and grinned. He held out his hand. "Ready?" His hand, as always, was cool and dry, though the rest of him was suffused with excitement. His curls quivered.

Red carpet and flashbulbs. Eliza hopped out of the limo first and navigated the crowd, stopping beside the first news camera to exchange a quick word with a woman with a microphone.

"Simon!" They shouted for him, photographers and reporters, urgent in their requests. Simon froze. He looked gray, like he'd stopped breathing; Charlotte worried about his asthma, then realized he was just discombobulated by the newness of the experience. She took hold of his elbow and wished she could think of some way to help him through this.

Eliza was quicker. She slid along Simon's other side and grasped his arm. "Nina Perez, Channel Five morning show. Come on."

Simon fielded Nina's questions. How did he feel tonight? Did he think the movie would be a hit? Soft, upbeat lobs that Simon lobbed back with soft, upbeat responses. Not sure whether she was in the camera shot, Charlotte kept her position on Simon's arm, smiling and trying to look delighted and attentive. Eliza faded to the background, moving down the line, paving the way for their next stop.

And so it continued, a process so time-consuming she began to worry they'd miss the start of their own film. No one paid much attention to her, which was for the best; the one time a reporter had turned the microphone toward her and asked what she was wearing, she had struggled to remember the name of the designer, which she was quite sure she mispronounced.

They were past the reporters. Good. Behind the press line, several feet removed from the red carpet, was a barrier with people behind it: fans of the comic book, fans of Taura, maybe fans of Simon, maybe some tourists or passersby who wanted to see what the commotion was about. Someone shouted "Simon!", and Simon turned to look, but there was no way to get closer. He settled for smiling and waving in the general direction of the shout.

Here, right by the doors, was an unexpected challenge: more photographers. They were expected to pause and pose.

At least one of them was. The paparazzo out front waved her away, shouting, "Just him!" Simon looked stricken at this, but Charlotte backed up to give him his moment.

One of the photographers tapped her on her shoulder. She turned, expecting to be asked to move out of his way. "Hi, honey, what's your name?"

"Charlotte Dent," she said. He scribbled it on a clipboard.

"Dent, as in. . . dent?" he asked.

"D-e-n-t, yes." She glanced down at the clipboard. He grinned.

"Photo agency. It helps if we spell the names correctly. You're Simon's girlfriend?"

"I'm in the film," she said, a little too firmly. It sounded like she was denying she was Simon's girlfriend.

He looked up at her. "Oh, yeah? You're an actress?"

"Yes." She didn't elaborate, because it was too hard to talk with all the noise and distractions.

He didn't look as though he believed her, but he raised his camera anyway. "Smile, Charlotte. You're beautiful."

Simon glanced over at them. He looked a little peeved. Was he not content with having only ninety percent of the attention this evening? She forgot her pettiness, though, when he came over to her side and took her arm and gave her a quick kiss on the neck. Flashbulbs popped. Or flashed, at least; they didn't really pop anymore, did they? In any case, the moment was immortalized, and she felt better.

It was calmer and quieter inside the theater. Eliza led them to their seats, which were roped off with masking tape. Third row, Eliza on the aisle, Simon and Charlotte beside her. Taura came in just as they were getting settled, on the arm of a much older man. Agent? Boyfriend? Husband? Father? She looked good, in a short bronze dress with knee-high boots. Hair long and messy; more casual than Charlotte, more natural. Charlotte and Simon got to their feet to let Taura and her escort slide into the seats beside them.

"Oh my God, can you believe this?" Simon got a quick hug from Taura, a quick press of her cheek against his. Taura leaned across his lap and repeated the treatment with Charlotte. The gesture seemed natural and unaffected, and once again Charlotte found herself revising her opinion of Taura. "The crowd out there is insane! It took us forever to get in here. You guys look awesome. Do you know Greg?" Taura's words tumbled out, one after the other, her thoughts blending into a giddy verbal mix. If she was surprised to see them together, she didn't show it. Maybe their relationship wasn't something Taura cared about one way or another.

Greg and Simon shook hands. Greg and Charlotte shook hands. They settled back and waited for the hubbub to subside and the film to start.

This was nerve-wracking. She hadn't realized how agonizing this part would be. Simon was clutching her hand; she didn't know how long ago he had taken it, her mind was so preoccupied with the film.

Her opinion fluctuated from scene to scene: Some parts were disappointing, some better than they had read on the page. Simon's American accent grated on her ears, but that was because she'd grown so used to his natural voice. He looked good, fierce and steely and handsome on screen. Her stomach grew a little tight. After this, more people would notice him, more than the little cluster of women who dwelled on his message board.

There she was. There she was. Jin, all legs and eye makeup and fast moves. The makeup looked unnatural and sleek and futuristic. She looked like a robot. She sounded. . . a little off, actually, she wasn't crazy about her voice. She sounded a little flat, a little lacking in resonance.

Her fight scene. She clutched Simon's hand a little tighter. Fast, staccato cuts. Loud, so loud, every punch and grunt amplified in the theater. It looked fantastic. This wasn't even her, she realized with a jolt, most of this was Margo, but she couldn't tell who was who. It all looked seamless and fluid. It all looked like her, and here she was getting full credit for it, while Margo was up in Vancouver teaching Tae Kwon Do at the local recreation center. And there Jin smashed through the window, silver glass flying all around her, and that made her heart stop a little. A steep tumble, smashed into bits on the pavement below, and that was neither her nor Margo, that was all computer imagery, but it looked great.

Taura was stiff, and Sir John was a little hammy, though she felt treasonous for even thinking such a thing, and the whole thing seemed silly if she examined it too closely, but it was fun, it was entertaining, and she felt an enormous surge of affection toward the finished product, toward the cast and crew and production staff, toward the five weeks in Vancouver, toward the slim, elegant, soon-to-be matinee idol clutching her hand. This was good.

There were congratulations in the lobby. Simon got hugged by strangers. She was included in the bonhomie by virtue of her proximity to Simon; without Jin's severe hairstyle, without those blasted gold hot pants, nobody recognized her.

Ted and Sir John stood on the other side of the lobby, sur-rounded by people, but Eliza steered Simon and Charlotte toward the door. She held up her phone. "The driver's waiting in the alley. Come on, let's get you to the party before traffic really gets bad."

The post-premiere party was at a restaurant on Las Palmas, a handful of blocks away, and it was absurd to drive there. Then again, her feet hurt in her borrowed gold sandals, so it was probably good she didn't have to traipse down Hollywood Boulevard.

She'd never been to this restaurant before, so she had no idea how the place looked under normal circumstances. It was decorated tonight with pieces from the set—or replicas of pieces of the set—to make it look like the destroyed version of City Hall. She hiked up her dress to step over faux-marble rubble to get inside.

Simon slid his arm around her waist. He was quiet. Not that he ever was a chatterbox, but she realized they hadn't had a chance to talk about the film with each other, about their shared experience of seeing their work for the first time. All of a sudden, she wished they could ditch the party and go back to his hotel room. They could order up a bottle of champagne from room service and compare notes.

"How are you holding up?" she asked.

He smiled, but he looked distant. "I'm doing fine."

"You sure?"

He pursed his lips. "I didn't like my accent."

Ah. Performance neuroses. She should have known. He'd been onscreen for so much of the movie, several times the amount of screen time she'd had, and of course he'd be picking apart his performance the whole time. "I thought your accent was lovely," she said. "You sounded very American. You were great."

"Thank you. As were you." He kissed her neck again. "Shall I get us something to drink?"

It was a night for champagne, followed by miniature hamburgers served on silver trays. Fried ravioli, fried samosas, jumbo shrimp, sautéed onions and feta wrapped in little parcels of phyllo dough; if there was a theme to the food (post-apocalyptic?), she wasn't following it. They weren't eating much—Simon because he never ate much, Charlotte because her nerves were still a jumble, her brain still processing the flood of images from the movie and trying to reach coherent conclusions as to whether she liked it.

Lots of hugs. Hugs from Angie, from Trey, whom she hadn't seen since Vancouver. A theatrical glower and a mock salute from across the room from Sir John. Everyone told them they were marvelous, the film was marvelous, the evening was marvelous. And it was, sort of, but her feet hurt and she wanted to go home. It was something of a relief when Simon touched her arm and leaned down and asked if she was ready to take off.

They found Eliza, who summoned the car for them and kissed them goodbye, assuring them she'd call a cab for herself later on. She must lead a strange life, existing on the fringes of glamour and yet being so much more competent than her celebrity charges.

They couldn't leave without collecting their goodie bags. She was more excited about these than she should be. Nylon satchels bulging with free goods. The products didn't come without strings, of course; her name and prestige, such as it was, would be forever associated with these items in some small tangential way. She opened hers up and looked inside as she trotted beside Simon to the parking lot. A digital camera. A tablet, sleek and compact. A glossy press kit about the film, designer sunglasses, a jumble of high-end cosmetics.

"Simon!" She spotted the girls before Simon did, the two young women—teenaged or college-aged—hovering by the front door. The night had grown cool—Charlotte was cold in her thin dress—and the girls, in jeans and halter tops, were clutching onto each other for warmth, or out of excitement, or some combination of both. "Simon! Can we talk to you?"

Simon came over. Smiling and obliging, without any trace of the tension that had dogged him throughout the party. "Hi, ladies."

"We've been waiting all night for you to come out," one of them said. Young, curly-haired, extremely pretty, cheeks high with color.

"Sorry. We were inside at the party," he said. Charlotte liked the way he talked to them, like he was having a conversation with a couple of friends, not a couple of fans who'd spent an evening angling for a chance to see him.

"We're huge fans," the other one said. "We loved you on *House of Medici.*"

"Really? Thanks so much. I didn't think that aired over here." He was being disingenuous—he knew from Charlotte that the entire series was available on DVD in the States—but he was doing it well, sounding genuinely surprised and delighted.

"Maureen found out online about the premiere being today, so we were waiting outside the theater," the first girl said. She was out of breath. "And we didn't get to see you there, so we heard someone mention that the party was here, so we came over here and waited outside, just in case. I hope that's okay?"

"It's great. I'm glad you came. You're Maureen, right?" Simon extended his hand to the other girl. She took it and clasped it once without shaking it. "And you are. . .?"

"I'm Charlotte," the first girl said.

"Really? Charlotte, meet Charlotte." Simon brought her forward with an arm around her waist. Charlotte shook hands with the girls.

"Nice to meet you," Charlotte said. The girls—Charlotte and Maureen—scoped her out. Openly curious about the kind of girl—woman—Simon would bring to such an event. Maybe a little envious, but not hostile.

"I was going to take pictures," Maureen said, holding her phone up. "But I forgot to charge my phone, so the battery died."

"We were going to try to find a drugstore and see if we could buy a disposable camera, but we didn't want to miss you in case you came out while we were gone," the other Charlotte added.

And there was the answer, simple and obvious. Charlotte opened up her goodie bag. "Hang on a sec," she said. She rummaged through the contents, pulled out the digital camera, checked it out. Pre-loaded with batteries and a memory card, of course, so the celebrity guests could start snapping immediately. Which was exactly what she was going to do. "Charlotte, Maureen, get in closer to Simon."

Simon smiled at her, an arm around each of his fans. The girls clung to him and grinned up at him. The flash went off. The photo looked good. Very sweet, all innocent crushes and fulfilled wishes.

She handed the camera to Maureen, because she was closest. "Here." And just to be fair, she handed the satchel to the other Charlotte. They could fight over the contents later. "It's mostly promo stuff."

Okay, she was buying their allegiance. Transparently. Because she didn't want to be the despised girlfriend, the enemy, the scourge of the message boards. It was an excessive gesture, maybe, maybe even a little lofty and condescending in its largesse, and part of her really did want to keep the loot all to herself, but she felt a little lighter and better to be rid of it.

Later, in the limo, alone together for the first time since leaving the hotel, Simon pulled her against him and kissed the top of her head. "Thank you," he said. She nestled in under his arm and allowed herself to be held.

## CHAPTER TWENTY-FOUR

SIX DAYS LATER, up before the sun, Simon still asleep in her bed. Their sleeping schedules didn't match. Charlotte had gone to bed last night when Simon was wide awake and ready for action; he'd suggested something about going to a bar, which she'd had nixed. Now it was early morning, and she was awake and restless, and Simon would be out for another couple of hours at least.

She crept out to her laptop in the living room. No need to be this quiet, because Simon didn't wake before ten unless someone was paying him to, but this required secrecy.

Online. Reviews. The movie opened in theaters today; the first reviews had started trickling into online news sources late yesterday afternoon. They'd be out in full force this morning. They weren't good, and Simon must never see them, but she felt compelled to read as many as she could.

She wasn't mentioned. A Google News search for her name resulted in exactly zero results. Well, that wasn't a surprise, was it? Jin and her twelve lines—ten in the final cut—and her five scenes hadn't made much of an impression.

But Simon. . . God. Sir John had been right, back on that cold lonely greyhound track in Calgary: Simon got it the worst. He was wooden, he was dull, he was sullen, he was lifeless, he couldn't act. There were a few knocks at Taura, but nothing like the vitriol ladled upon Simon. Simon didn't know how to use a computer and thus

203

wouldn't seek out the reviews on his own. His people—Eliza and his agent, Gregory—would sugarcoat it for him. Charlotte would keep it a secret. He'd never know she'd read all these reviews. She shouldn't read them, because they made the small of her back grow cold with fresh perspiration, but she had to know. Everything.

She powered down, flicked off the lamp, padded back to the bedroom, crawled into bed. Simon stirred—he always slept a little lighter when he stayed over at her place, not his sleep of the dead whenever they were at his hotel—and muttered something that sounded like a question. But he wasn't awake, so she didn't answer.

They let Erica pick the restaurant, because Erica had lived in Los Angeles longer than either of them, and because Erica was the kind of person who always knew how to choose a good place. It was a tiny, elegant bistro Charlotte had never heard of, somewhere south on Westwood Boulevard, and it seemed as good a place as any to celebrate opening weekend.

Charlotte had the risotto with snow peas and asparagus. She'd had forgotten she disliked risotto. "Dislike" was too strong, actually; it was fine, just unexceptional. Like eating a bowl of rice that somehow managed to be both undercooked and mushy. Simon ordered the tuna tartare with root vegetable chips. He was eating very little: scooping up chunks of marinated tuna on a crisp wafer of fried yam, nibbling at the edges, setting it back down on his plate. It was driving her crazy. Had they reached the point in their relationship where little things were going to drive her mad? Was he similarly irritated with things she did? She'd had so little experience with adult relationships, it was difficult to tell what was normal.

Erica had a steak. Bone in, served with a small tureen of green peppercorn sauce and a side of scalloped potatoes with a crackling brown crust, chewy with melted cheeses. It looked good. It smelled good. Hard to tell if Erica was enjoying it much; she didn't seem to be paying much attention to her plate. Her brows were drawn together, her expression distant.

Simon cleared his throat. "Charlotte tells me you used to be on a television show."

"Years ago. *Mad World.*"

"I don't believe I'm familiar with it. It must not have aired in the UK."

"Yeah, it did. ITV. Sundays." Erica shrugged. "I don't think it was that popular there."

"I must have missed it."

Erica set down her wine glass on the table with enough force to make them both look up. "I've been thinking of getting my real estate license." She cleared her throat. "There's an extension course. Adult school. Two nights a week, and they coach you specifically on the DRE exam."

"You'd probably be really good at that," Charlotte said. "You're good with people." She didn't know if that was true or not, but it seemed like the thing to say.

"Yeah. And it's not like I'd need any special skills." Erica shrugged. "Better than working in some office."

"Don't you still want to act?" Simon asked.

Erica looked at Simon. Erica didn't look at Simon the way Charlotte did, or the way people on the set had, like Simon was some rare and exquisite creature whose very presence brightened their lives. She looked at him like she'd rather be having a quiet dinner with a friend without having to put up with her friend's irritating boyfriend. "Of course. But I also need income right now. I don't see why I can't do both."

"Yes, but real estate is not like tending bar or waiting tables. It's more of a career, isn't it?"

"Maybe. But it's what I need to do right now. Acting isn't working out all that well for me."

"I think it's important to follow your dreams. If you want to act, that's what you should focus on doing. Otherwise you're never going to be happy." He'd said it before, and it irked Charlotte just a little, every time.

It irked Erica, too. Simon irked Erica, just in general. Charlotte could see it in the lines around her mouth that appeared whenever Simon said anything, like Erica was restraining herself from issuing a blistering retort. "Yeah, but that's not really helpful in the face of my mortgage payments, is it?"

Simon frowned and looked chastened. Erica exhaled. "I don't want to lose my house. I don't want to be foreclosed out onto the street. I've been following my dreams for a very long time, and it's not working out so well for me."

Simon looked at his plate. Erica looked around the restaurant. Charlotte looked at Erica's steak. She should've ordered the steak. Next time she'd know better.

"Is that what's-his-name? From the play? The annoying one?"

Charlotte looked up and turned around to follow Erica's stare. Kyle? Was Kyle in the restaurant? The rising surge of tension quelled when she saw it was only Robbie, of the UCLA shorts and the odious personality. He was now dressed in immaculate waiter whites, with a black apron tied about his waist. "Robbie. Yeah, that's him."

"Crap. He's seen us." Robbie had seen Erica, at least, and recognized her. He crossed over to their table.

"Hey, Erica. I thought that was you." He looked over and saw Charlotte. "Hey, both of you. Cool. What brings you guys here?"

Erica waved her wine glass at Charlotte. "Her movie opens this weekend, so we're celebrating."

"You're in a movie?" He didn't need to sound quite so incredulous.

"*Queen of Angels*." Simon was looking a little sulky, so Charlotte reached over and patted his hand. "Simon's in it, too. Simon, this is Robbie. The three of us were in a play together."

Robbie gaped at her. "*Queen of Angels*? I just saw that last night at the Arclight. Are you kidding me? You're in that?" Robbie turned to Simon at last. "Oh, right, you're that guy." He looked back at Charlotte. He frowned. "I don't remember you in it."

"You probably don't recognize her with clothes on," Erica said.

Charlotte smiled to hide a brief flash of annoyance. The comment seemed a little on the bitchy side, but she might be feeling overly sensitive. "I wasn't in it very much. I was Jin." She paused. "The killer robot." One of these days she'd find a way to say it that didn't make her cringe.

"No way. That was you?" He looked at her. "No way," he said again. His eyes dropped to her chest.

"I had a different haircut." He glanced up at her in confusion, like he had no idea why she was talking about her hair.

Erica snorted and took another drink of her wine.

"How'd you get that part? That's like a real part." He looked at her again, shocked she could have such a stroke of luck. "You must have a good agent. Who are you with?"

She paused, then decided to tell him. "UTM."

"Wow. UTM, huh? No kidding? Who's your agent?"

"Don't tell him." Erica looked at her over the rim of her glass. "Don't tell him anything. Because he'll either call your agent and say he's a friend of yours, or he'll ask you to put in a good word for him. Either way, you don't owe him anything."

Robbie looked wary, like he wasn't sure if she was serious or not. "Hey, I wasn't asking you."

"What's her name?" Erica gestured with her chin at Charlotte. "You've used my name in this conversation, but you haven't mentioned hers. If you don't remember her name, you don't get to ask her for favors."

"She doesn't need you to make her decisions for her."

"Maybe she does. Because Charlotte—that's her name, FYI, Charlotte—is a nice person and she'd probably let you use her name, maybe even give you a recommendation, and you've done jack to deserve it. You're not her friend. So why don't you go back to waiting tables and let us eat in peace?"

Simon and Charlotte were frozen. Robbie opened his mouth, closed it, walked off.

Charlotte looked at Erica. Simon looked at Erica. Erica set her wine glass very carefully down on the table. "Excuse me." She rose to her feet, placed her napkin on her chair, and walked off in the direction of the ladies' room.

Simon and Charlotte exchanged glances. Charlotte stood up and followed Erica.

The ladies' room was tiny and plush. Just beyond the door, there was a small seating area with a single lounge chair covered in rose-colored silk and an open door beyond that leading to a single stall and sink. Erica sat in the chair, her elbow propped on the arm rest, her chin in her hand. She looked up at Charlotte's entrance and didn't say anything.

There was no other place to sit, so Charlotte stood in front of the door and hoped no one would open it. "Everything okay?"

"Yeah. Sorry. Bad day."

"You were a little rough on Robbie. Not that he's not a tool."

"Yeah." Erica exhaled deeply. "See, I wanted to ask you for the name of your agent. I wanted to see if you'd put in a good word for me. I guess I was pissed Robbie got there first." She considered. "Scratch that. I guess I don't want to turn into Robbie. So pathetic and grasping and desperate."

"You can ask me for a favor. It doesn't mean you're pathetic. It means we're friends." Charlotte leaned against the door. "You want to talk with my agent, I can give him a call."

"No. Skip it. Thanks, but it's not worth it."

Charlotte examined Erica for a moment. "You don't like Simon, do you?"

Erica straightened up. "I like Simon. He seems very nice. We could probably have a great conversation about shoes or something. Not sure that's enough to build a relationship on, but he seems okay, and you seem happy enough." She shrugged. "There's just not much substance to him. I guess that bothers me a little."

"You don't really know him all that well," Charlotte said. "If you talked with him more, you might find there's more to him."

"True. And I might be talking out of my ass here, and I might just be cranky for a bunch of different reasons that don't have much to do with Simon, but I've run into his type too many times before. He's pretty and sweet and insubstantial. Like, I don't know, cupcake frosting or butterflies or something. And he seems to like you just fine, but. . . it's almost like you two don't really care all that much about each other. I just don't see you two having much in common." She looked up at her. "There's nothing insubstantial about you, Charlotte. I don't want you to settle because you think Simon's the type of guy you should be dating."

Most people wouldn't necessarily consider dating Simon settling. Maybe Erica's standards were higher than her own. Or, more likely, just different than hers. "He's a little distracted tonight. It's his first big movie, and this is opening weekend. A lot is riding on it. Usually he's more outgoing."

Erica nodded, but she didn't seem to be listening. "Real estate." She exhaled heavily. "It's your opening weekend, and I'm thinking of selling real estate. I don't want to sell houses. I just want to act, and I can't seem to do that anymore." She rolled her head back, like she was working a kink out of her neck. "I don't know. Just feeling a little run-down and cranky tonight. I apologize. It's a little hard for me to be around people who are having good things happening to them. The two of you are radiating all kinds of success and happiness, and it's not your fault, but it's really pissing me off."

"I'm sorry."

"Like I said, not your fault. It's my problem, not yours, and if I were a bigger person, I'd suck it up and be happy for you." Erica almost smiled. "So I don't want to be a bigger person right now. Tomorrow I'll be happy for you. Or maybe if I have another couple glasses of wine, I'll be happy for you tonight."

Charlotte nodded. "Are you coming back to the table?" she asked.

"You go on ahead. Give me a minute to get my happy face on."

Charlotte left and closed the door behind her. She stood in the narrow alcove by the entrance to the restrooms for a moment and looked out into the dining room where Simon sat by himself at the table, so small and so exquisite and so very far away.

Out of habit, she was up early the next morning. Feeling like she was doing something shady, she fired up her laptop. Went online. Doing this dance again, feeding her poisonous addiction while Simon slept. She shouldn't do this, because it was unhealthy, and it was unlikely the latest wave of reviews would be kinder than the last.

She had trouble starting up. Her laptop had been shut down improperly the last time it'd been used. That must be Simon. Huh. It must mean he'd been using it last night after they'd returned from the restaurant, after she'd gone to sleep. Maybe he'd wanted to visit his message boards. Or maybe he'd just wanted to surf porn, since his girlfriend had sacked out at an early hour.

Her laptop up and running, she went online. Was it a betrayal of trust to check the browser history to see what Simon had been doing yesterday?

Nothing new there, nothing unfamiliar. Maybe he hadn't been online after all. Just the sites she'd visited yesterday morning, all the movie reviews. . .

Damn. Had Simon been looking at the reviews? She'd shown him how to access the browser history, after all. Two things at work here, if he had: one, he'd read all those terrible, negative, inflammatory reviews of his performance, and two, he knew she'd read them as well and hadn't mentioned anything to him.

Damn it, damn it, damn it. She glanced at the door to the bedroom, where Simon lay sleeping within. She shouldn't mention it to him, should she, if he didn't say anything about it? Or was it better to broach the subject gently, get it out in the open?

No. Neither Simon nor Charlotte were much for getting things out in the open. Simon would prefer not to be ambushed by this, and she'd prefer not instigating an awkward conversation. She could easily be mistaken. It was better to be quiet.

She shut down her laptop and went to the kitchen to make coffee, feeling uneasy.

If the reviews weren't kind, the box office was. Second-best opening weekend of the year. The big summer tentpole movies were still a couple weeks away—Charlotte didn't think anyone considered *Queen of Angels* a tentpole—and so that record would be broken soon, but it was a good sign. Maybe it was better than the studio had expected, though it was hard to tell. Everything was spun to death; numbers were manipulated and crunched and placed into all kinds of different contexts until she couldn't tell what was positive and what wasn't. She didn't know what Ted really thought. His reviews, like Simon's, had been harsh; per the reviewers, Ted's directing was amateurish, inept, paint-by-number.

Simon had been quiet since the premiere, as though he still hadn't been able to form an opinion about the overall experience. He seemed sadder somehow, and maybe it wasn't connected to the reviews or even to the film itself. Maybe it had more to do with the opening of the film in an abstract sense, his first starring role in a major Hollywood picture marking the end of one lifestyle for him and the beginning of another. Or maybe it meant no such thing. Maybe after the glow of the opening week wore off, he'd be back in the same situation as before, struggling to find a breakthrough part that would introduce him to American film audiences.

Maybe Charlotte was in the same situation. Maybe she'd never have another paid acting job again. Maybe this was her chance, and if she hadn't blown it, maybe she'd failed to seize it and run with it and turn it into something bigger.

But right now, she enjoyed her moment. She half-expected to start hearing from old acquaintances who'd dropped off her radar, friends from drama school, old co-workers. If her schoolmates had seen the film, they kept quiet, but Aunt Emily called, her mother's sister in Cheyenne, to tell her how thrilled she was to see her on the screen.

"Your mother told me you weren't in it very much," Emily said. Did that mean her mom had seen the film—she'd mentioned something about waiting for it to come out on DVD, since dad was in no shape to go to the theater—or was she just regurgitating what Charlotte had told her about the role? "But I gotta tell you, Charlotte, every second you were on the screen, you had my undivided attention. The boy at the concession stand told me you were his favorite character."

"Aw. That's sweet." It was. It was probably said after her aunt had let the boy know Jin was a beloved niece, but it was kind of him to make the effort to say what her aunt wanted to hear.

"Oh! And I saw that picture of you in *Celebrity Style*," her aunt said.

"There's a picture of me?"

"At the premiere. You looked beautiful, Charlotte, but I wish I could see your pretty smile. You looked almost angry."

When was this? What picture? "I haven't seen it. I'll have to look for it."

"Well, you look just fantastic. Though I really think you should eat more. I know you actresses need to worry about your figures, but you looked awfully thin to me."

Good to know. Compared to some of the actresses at the premiere, she'd felt like a hickory-smoked slab of beef. If Wyoming worried she was too skinny, she was probably about right for California.

As soon as she was off the phone, she drove to the grocery store—funny how jumping into a car for even these small errands was becoming second nature—and picked up a copy of *Celebrity Style*. Safe in her apartment, she flipped through pages of photos. Celebrities at fancy events, mostly pretty young women in bright dresses. Ah, there was the spread for the *Queen of Angels* premiere. Simon in his nice suit. It was a good picture of him; he'd be pleased.

Charlotte Dent. The photo on the opposite page, the small photo in the corner, was captioned Charlotte Dent. She stared at it, trying to make sense, because the photo wasn't of her. It was a young woman, caught from behind, head turned to look over her shoulder at the camera. Blonde and skinny, in a scarlet sheath that wasn't that much different from the cranberry-and-mauve thingy she'd borrowed. She looked like Charlotte—or rather, she didn't look unlike Charlotte—but it wasn't her. This woman, whoever she was, was emaciated, her shoulder blades jutting out on either sides of her spaghetti straps. She looked taller than Charlotte, and angry, her expression somewhere between a seductive pout and a glower. And, apparently, she was Charlotte Dent.

Nothing to do but laugh it off and wonder how her aunt could misidentify her own niece. Well, it was a small photo, and if a national magazine claimed this woman was Charlotte, who was Aunt Emily to argue? She'd have to show it to Simon when he came over in the evening. They could have a good laugh at it.

In the meantime, though, was there any way to identify this woman? Online. The photo services were the first place to start.

*Queen of Angels* premiere, Chinese Theater. Scrolled down the page, looked at thumbnails of images. Charlotte Dent. There she was, correctly identified, in her cranberry dress, both on Simon's arm and by herself. They weren't great photos—she needed to figure out how to pose, how to hold her arms, where to place her feet, how to smile without looking tense or exasperated—but at least they were of her.

And now. . . Catherine Gates. The scarlet woman was Catherine Gates. The name meant nothing to her. There were other photos of her; she looked severe and contemptuous in all. But her face looked like Charlotte's face—small nose and mouth, pointed chin, nonspecifically pretty.

Time to investigate Catherine Gates. A fan site came up immediately. Catherine Gates, whoever she was, was more famous than Charlotte Dent. Which, really, wasn't difficult to achieve. Okay, she was a model. There was a fragrance ad Charlotte had seen a thousand times before, a wispy, pouty blonde who could be Charlotte's over-privileged and underfed sister lying on her back in a field in a diaphanous nightgown, a phallic-looking perfume bottle propped between her long thighs.

There were worse people to be confused with than a semi-famous model. So be it. And maybe one day she'd reach a level of fame where photographers would never confuse her with anybody.

## CHAPTER TWENTY-FIVE

CHARLOTTE WENT TO Vegas on her thirtieth birthday. That it was her birthday was incidental; she hadn't mentioned it to anyone, because she wasn't sure how old she was supposed to be. Simon knew her real age, and she should have mentioned the significance of the day to him at least, but lately Simon had been. . . different.

It was the week after opening, and the film had dropped to the seventh position at the box office. This seemed like a big drop to her, but no one else seemed to think this was anything out of the ordinary. The huge publicity blitz was over, but this weekend the cast was booked to appear at some huge annual science fiction convention. Or comic book convention, or something—she wasn't sure what, and nobody ever told her anything she didn't need to know.

Either Sir John had turned it down or, more likely, the organizers knew better than to ask him, because he wasn't appearing. Simon was, and Trey, and Freddie and the other screenwriters. Ted wasn't going to show. Charlotte had no reason to think it was because of the bad reviews he'd been getting, but she sort of did think that, that his enthusiasm for the film had been so damaged he wanted nothing more than to stay out of sight until it was out of theaters.

Taura was supposed to attend. Oh, Taura. She'd backed out at the last possible moment, conveying the word through her agent that she wasn't feeling well. It might be true. Whatever the story, she was out. Charlotte was in.

They'd taken a private plane. Thirty seats, half of them full, mostly with people she didn't know. Low-level studio executives, a cluster of young women in expensive suits who kept their sunglasses on the entire flight and didn't talk to anyone.

Instant shock upon emerging into the heat and sunlight. It was bright, a thousand times brighter than Los Angeles, and the desert heat came in waves off the asphalt. Simon, in his crisp white button-down shirt, seemed to wither. She glanced over at him, so pale he seemed like a mirage, and felt frightened for him, so far out of his natural habitat.

A van from the airport took them the handful of blocks to their hotel on the strip. Not one of the glitzy, gimmicky theme casinos, she was sad to note, but a nonspecifically elegant chain hotel, which was playing host to the convention. Simon and Charlotte had different rooms on different floors. Simon's room was a suite with separate sitting room and bedroom. Hers wasn't. She moved her bags into Simon's room. The hotel was cool, almost cold, and from Simon's windows the outside didn't look nearly so bright and bleak. Then she realized the windows were tinted to disguise the glare off the desert.

They went straight to the panel after freshening up. The convention took place in a huge meeting space on the hotel's second floor. Even here, it was impossible to escape the cacophony of bells and buzzers and sirens from the casino floor below. The panel was in a small ballroom at the back; they had to cross through the exhibition space to reach it.

Chaos. It was overwhelming, but interesting. She'd never been to a science fiction convention before. It was less geeky and more capitalistic than she'd imagined. Not much in the way of cosplay, just dozens of booths selling crap: comics, books, video games, toys, T-shirts, memorabilia of all kinds.

Suzanne guided them through the crowd. Suzanne was from the studio, and while Charlotte didn't know her title, she appeared to be the official talent liaison.

A large man in a t-shirt emblazoned with the convention logo guarded the door to the ballroom. Suzanne approached him. "Hi. We're with *Queen of Angels*. Can you point Jake out to me?"

The man pointed inside the otherwise empty ballroom at a man sitting in a folding chair. Suzanne led her charges across the room, a woman on a mission, right up to Jake. "Jake? Suzanne Courtney. We talked on the phone."

Jake fiddled with the phone in his lap. Texting someone, or browsing through his stored photos, or just pressing buttons at random. He looked up, but didn't get to his feet.

He was a behemoth of a man, overlapping the folding chair on both sides. Late fifties, black sport coat over a black t-shirt, black hair oiled back. Expensive watch, expensive shoes.

"Just so you know. . ." he began, and just from his tone, Charlotte didn't like him. "I've already had two guys today ask me for their money back because Taura Trejo backed out of this."

"I'm sorry to hear that." Suzanne smiled her nice smile. "Your promotional materials did state that all special guests were subject to change, right?"

Jake waved a large hand, dismissing this. "Yeah, yeah, we got all that. That's not what I'm talking about. I just want you to know, this isn't the deal we struck before, and don't think I don't know that. You promised me Taura Trejo, and you're passing off substitutes nobody's ever heard of."

Oh. That would be Charlotte. She could feel her face burn. Simon, beside her, was silent. If he was embarrassed on her behalf, or offended, or roused to any kind of emotion, he didn't show it. He looked blank, like only half of him was present.

Back to Suzanne. Calm and friendly. "Jake, we've been through this before. You agreed to the substitution and we've worked out all the details already."

"Yeah, I know, I know, but I'm losing money on this, and you people are coming out ahead. That's all I'm saying." Jake sighed and stuffed his phone into his jacket pocket. "They're getting ready to open up the doors and let people get seated in about twenty minutes. Your kids all right with that?"

Suzanne turned to us. "How are we doing, kids?"

"I'm all set," Charlotte said, because no one else seemed willing to jump in and say anything. "This should be fun."

Parts of it were fun. Parts of it were hell, sitting on the panel in front of a half-full ballroom of science fiction fanatics. The crowd might be made up of fans, but that didn't mean they were an easy audience.

The writers, Freddie particularly, got the bulk of the questions: Why was the plotline with the samurai trimmed? What was the significance of setting the climax at City Hall instead of Union Station? Why were Malachi and Zachary combined into one character? As Charlotte had only read the first part of the series, most of the discussion was lost on her.

A question for her, from a girl in a red hooded sweatshirt and lots of little braids. Before she spoke, Charlotte found herself hoping she wouldn't turn out to be one of the message board girls who was so pro-Simon and thus anti-Charlotte. Instead: "Did you really break your leg while filming?"

Aw. She was a reader of *Jejune*, apparently. "Yeah. I broke my ankle doing that plunge through the window at the end. They were able to put a cast on it and I could keep working." The tale grew in the telling, didn't it? She couldn't be sure, but she thought Simon shifted in his chair beside her, like he disapproved of her version of events.

The girl sat down, beaming at her, and she felt an absurd pleasure at having made someone's day just through that quick exchange of information.

The next question was directed at Simon, and it wasn't a question. A young man, early twenties, college kid in emo glasses and a black T-shirt: "I just want to say you suck, man. You're the worst actor I've ever seen, and I hope you never do another movie again."

Silence. Shocked laughter from the kid's circle of cohorts, a few boos from different parts of the room. Charlotte glanced over at Simon. He didn't look surprised, just resigned. Sick and weary. He leaned over to the microphone. "Thank you. Can we move on to the next question, please?"

Whatever fun or interest she was taking in this was over. Simon was miserable, she was nauseous with anger, and she wanted this to be over. She wanted to lean forward and speak into the microphone and come to Simon's defense. She wanted to, but she couldn't. It'd come out wrong—she'd come across as a hysterical, overprotective girlfriend, which she was, and it would escalate, whereas if they moved on now, they could all pretend to forget it. So she let it pass, feeling traitorous and cowardly.

Autograph session afterward. She'd looked forward to this, but now it was dead to her. This was held in their own booth on the exhibition floor. People lined up and handed over memorabilia to be signed. Everyone had the same photo of her as Jin, a still she hadn't remembered posing for. Someone here must be selling them, eight-by-ten color glossies, all legs and breasts and eyeliner. Plenty of teen boys presented it to her to sign; she must be a disappointment to them in person. Charlotte signed. Name only, they'd been coached in advance, unless they asked for personalization. Most would be selling them online anyway.

Simon signed beside her. There were plenty of young women in the line, and again she felt a stab of nerves. Some of them probably knew she was dating Simon; some of them probably hated her for that. Maybe they'd say something nasty to her. Maybe someone would say something further nasty to Simon; she glanced over at him and saw, with a lurch of her stomach, that he was signing a poster for one of the friends of the asshole who'd mocked him.

The guy moved on to her and proffered the poster for her to add her signature as well. She shook her head. "No. Not you."

"What?"

"I'm not signing anything for you. Goodbye."

"What the hell? Why?"

"You know why." Her voice was cold and flat. Funny, because everything else about her prickled with excitement and fury.

"Hey, look, it wasn't me—"

"I don't care. Tell your friend he's an asshole and I'm not signing."

Simon looked over at her. "Charlotte. . ." She didn't look at him.

The kid was already gone, rolling up his poster and storming off. She didn't feel any better about it. She felt cold and terrible.

Simon didn't mention it later, which wasn't surprising, because if he did, they'd have to talk about what happened in the ballroom, and she didn't see that happening any time soon. They were supposed to go to dinner with icky Jake, the six of them from the production plus Suzanne, but Simon wouldn't go.

"I'm not feeling well," he told her in the suite, where they were supposed to be changing for dinner. "Let's not go."

She didn't want to go. She wanted to stay here and fix Simon's enormous, incapacitating sadness. They could order some kind of ridiculous, excessive dessert from room service and celebrate her birthday. "I think we kind of have to go."

"That man Jake was rude to you. Don't go."

"I don't want to go. But it's expected of us." A flash on Taura, spoiled silly little Taura, backing out of her obligations.

"Then you'll have to go without me." Simon flopped onto the bed and turned onto his side, away from her.

"Simon—"

He sat up and looked at her. "Let's get out of here. Let's go out to dinner by ourselves, or let's catch the next flight out of here tonight. Or we can rent a car. We could go to the Grand Canyon. I've always wanted to go to the Grand Canyon."

For a giddy moment, she wanted to. It was hard to refuse Simon anything, anything at all. "We can't. We have to do this. It's part of the job. They don't expect much of us."

"They expect everything from me. Maybe they don't expect much from you."

Okay. He being a brat now, and she wasn't in the right mood. "I'll give everyone your apologies," she said.

Dinner was ghastly. The restaurant was elegant, the food exquisite, the service impeccable. Charlotte had grilled tilapia with roasted root vegetables and not enough wine to make Jake seem charming. He sat beside her and talked to her, forgiving her for not being Taura as long as she proved herself a good listener. She never quite grasped what he was—event coordinator? Head honcho in whatever organization arranged this convention each year?—and she couldn't care enough to do much more than smile and nod at the right places. Simon's absence was barely remarked upon; he'd been so withdrawn already this trip no one seemed to remember he'd been with them in the first place.

The only interesting tidbit came later, over coffee and apricot crème brulee. Trey leaned over to her. "Did you hear about Angie?"

"Hear what?" Charlotte asked.

"One of the girls from the studio on the plane was talking about it. I guess Angie got fired today. It's in the trades."

"Fired? For what?" Couldn't be for the film, could it? After their great opening?

Trey shrugged. "Overstepping her boundaries. Power plays. You know she got Doug fired, right, had him replaced with Simon because she thought Doug was a douchebag?"

She hadn't known, but she'd suspected it. And she agreed with the reasoning because, yes, Doug was a douchebag. "Was that it?"

Trey shrugged. "I guess there was more stuff like that. She'd play favorites a lot. Stepped on some toes. Too bad. She was a nice lady."

It was too bad, but she could almost see it. Angie did play favorites, and she hadn't minded because she'd been on her good side. For that matter, Angie had helped bring her together with Simon. And now Angie was gone, and now Simon was drawing away from her.

When dinner was over, she returned to their room. Silently, because the lights were off and Simon was in bed. He wasn't asleep, she knew that just by looking him, but he was pretending to be, so she should pretend she didn't know he was ignoring her. She undressed quietly and crawled into bed.

They flew back the next day. The studio plane was only half-full this time, the gaggle of executives staying behind to drink or gamble or take in shows or shop or whatever. Less than twenty-four hours in Vegas, and she hadn't set foot on a casino floor.

Simon ignored her on the flight back. He stared out the window during the short hop to L.A. It wasn't just that he was silent; she could deal with that. He seemed irritated with her, like she was a burden he didn't need during an already stressful week.

Well, hell. She'd about had it with him, too. He wasn't much fun to be with, and her pool of sympathy for his pain at bad reviews and nasty people was bottoming out.

There was a car waiting for them at LAX. "Are we going to my apartment or your hotel?" she asked.

Simon thought for a bit. "I think I'd just like to go to the hotel for a while. I could use some more sleep."

Meaning she wasn't invited. "Fine," she said. It sounded bitchy, which she regretted.

Simon didn't call that day, or the next. A full week passed before she broke down and called him: "Hey." A pause. "I just wanted to check how you were doing."

"Not too great, actually." He fell silent. She tried to imagine where he was. Alone in his hotel room? It was easy enough to think he'd been holed up in there for the entire week, nursing his wounds.

"Anything I can do for you?" Her tone was off. Her voice sounded tinny to her ears.

"No. Thank you. No." A pause, and she knew what his next words would be before he said them. "I think I just need some time to myself for a bit."

"Okay." She'd just been dumped, and all she could come up with was "okay." "Give me a call if you need anything."

"I will." There was another long silence. "Thanks, Charlotte," and Simon was gone.

## Chapter Twenty-Six

SHE'D BLOWN IT. She should have made more of an attempt to figure out what was eating at Simon, should have tried to heal the damage inflicted by bad reviews and nasty fans. And yet part of her was having trouble figuring this out. Was Simon really so fragile and self-absorbed he couldn't put things in their proper perspective and see it wasn't a catastrophe?

But did she really know what he was like? Three months to-gether and she didn't know much more about him other than he liked buying shoes and didn't eat dairy. She loved him, she really did, and yet she couldn't deny that when Simon said those terrible, polite words ending their relationship, her first reaction had been relief.

She mourned the loss of Simon, quietly and deeply, but it seemed a blessing to return to the selfish pleasures of single life. She could get to bed at a stupidly early hour, if she chose. She could drop the mask of perpetual kindness proximity to Simon made her adopt. She felt like herself again.

She moved into a new apartment, smaller and more expensive than her current one, but new and different. It was in her old neighborhood, but located on the right side of Wilshire this time, the north side, where rents were higher and tenants younger and hipper. A cute building, fresh beige paint with clean white trim, divided into six units, each with a separate outside entrance. It had a courtyard with a fountain and trimmed hedges and bushes of white roses, and it had been this as much as the hardwood floors in her unit that made her decide to take it.

She called Simon once when she was all settled in, under the excuse of giving him her new address. No signal from his old cell number. She called the front desk of his hotel and found he was no longer a guest. He was gone.

She called Erica and it was déjà vu: a disconnected number. Was this how relationships always ended among actors?

She drove up to Erica's house. She'd worried about the twisty, narrow streets of Mount Olympus, but her compact car handled it with ease.

The house was empty. Abandoned. No curtains on the front windows, no furniture visible in the living room. Erica, too, was gone.

Had the bank foreclosed? Had Erica taken yappy little Rusty and left town? Had she found work somewhere, either an acting job or a real-person job? Had she given up on Hollywood forever?

Charlotte needed to work again. It was a good day when Rick called to tell her Harris Holt was interesting in meeting her for lunch at Fredericks, if she was available, and she'd better be, because opportunities like this didn't fall out of the sky every day.

"I'm available," she said. "Don't worry, I'm absolutely available. Harris Holt? That's pretty cool."

"Yeah, it's for his new big thing, the Lana Turner biopic. He wrote the script, too. It's been floating around for a while. Couple guys in my office read it, say it's going to be huge."

"Great. That's awesome. Thank you, Rick."

"This time, you really got no reason to thank me, just passing along the message. I got the call from his people earlier today, they asked for you specifically. I didn't suggest you at all."

"That's weird. You suppose he's a closet *Queen of Angels* fan?"

"You'll have to ask him at lunch. Two o'clock. Fredericks. You know where that is?"

"I'll find it." Hard to prevent herself from thanking Rick again, but she managed.

Fredericks turned out to be located east of Alameda in downtown, south of the cluster of government buildings. She decided parking downtown would be too traumatic, so she took the bus. She wondered why the neighborhood gave her such a strong sense of déjà vu, then realized these were the buildings recreated in loving post-apocalyptic detail for the sets of *Queen of Angels*.

The interior of Fredericks was inky black after the brightness of outside. The hostess spoke to her before Charlotte even realized she was there. "One for lunch?"

"I'm meeting someone." Her eyes were slow to adjust to the darkness. A long bar, dining tables beyond, silhouettes and noise. "Harris Holt?"

"Right this way." She trailed behind the hostess, taking in more and more detail. Booths in oxblood leather, framed vintage newspapers on the walls. A moneyed crowd, middle-aged men in expensive suits drinking martinis.

She was led to a booth at the back. Holt was waiting. He didn't rise to meet her. "Charlotte. Hi. Glad you could make it on such short notice." He looked her up and down. She hoped she passed his inspection. Her most flattering dress, the purse Simon bought her, shoes with the highest heels she could wear on public transportation.

She slid into the booth across from him. "Thank you for inviting me," she said.

A waiter approached. Slicked-back hair, an immaculate apron wrapped about his waist. "Can I get you started with something to drink?"

"Lemonade," Holt said without looking at him. To Charlotte, he said, "Can't have alcohol. Doctor's orders."

That cleared up her brief quandary about whether to drink or not. "Lemonade too, please."

"You should have a martini," Holt said. "Or a Scotch. Scotch goes well with steak."

"Just lemonade, please," she said, and smiled her best smile at the waiter.

"You don't drink?" Holt asked. Incredulity in his voice, which was probably unwarranted from someone medically obliged to abstain.

"I drink. Just not right now." She smiled. He didn't smile back. He looked like he considered her a little untrustworthy.

The waiter nodded and started to walk off. "Hey!" Holt said, pitched a little too loud. The waiter turned. "We're ready to order now."

Were they? The waiter hovered, pen in hand. "Very good. Miss?"

A quick glance down at the menu. "I'd like the London Broil, please," she said. Fredericks was a steakhouse, a real, old-time, testosterone-laden steakhouse, and the menu was built around big slabs of red meat.

"Don't have the London Broil," Holt said. "That's an amateur's dish." He looked at her, tiny eyes in a bearded face. "She'll have the filet mignon. Rare. Porterhouse for me. Barely dead. Shrimp cocktail to start, creamed spinach as an extra." He passed the waiter the menus without looking at him.

Okay. He could win that battle. She liked filet mignon, and might even have ordered it had she not been squeamish about the price. Hating herself just a little, she didn't protest, just smiled as the waiter nodded and withdrew.

"I read an article on you," Holt said. "It said you broke your leg during your last movie, but kept on filming?"

Was Holt a reader of *Jejune*? The mind boggled. So the old chestnut about her leg was still generating interest. If she wasn't careful, this could come back and bite her in the ass.

"That's right, I did," she said. That wasn't being careful. That wasn't careful at all.

He shrugged. "Didn't see the movie. *City of Angels*? *Queen of Angels*? I don't waste my time on mass-market trash."

She thought carefully before answering. What she needed to do, instead of becoming prickly about everything he said, was to find some common ground with him. Otherwise, he'd leave this meeting thinking of her as an uptight prig, and that wouldn't serve her purpose.

"I really enjoyed it," she said. "Visually, it was gorgeous. It has some great moments in it."

Holt waved this away. "My point is, I haven't seen you in anything. I don't know if you can act your way out of your ass. And you know what? It really doesn't matter. Because even if you're the shittiest little starlet in town, I can draw a good performance out of you."

Charlotte was not the shittiest little starlet in town, she was pretty sure, and even though his statement had been hypothetical, it was hard not to feel offended. Was he trying to rile her up? If so, what response would he want? Should she defend herself, or let his words disappear into the dark corners of the restaurant?

He wasn't trying to rile her, she didn't think. He was just a prick, and this was just his way of dealing with people, and probably nothing she could say or do at this meeting would change his view—of herself, of actresses, of humanity—so she might as well sit back and enjoy the lovely filet mignon the waiter placed in front of her.

Oh, lord, the steak was good. Butter-soft, wrapped in smoky bacon, heaven. It came with a pile of onions fried in the drippings, plus the creamiest mound of mashed potatoes ever, a whipped cloud of buttery goodness. The food was so good she could feel it in her thighs.

"So you know what struck me about that article?" Holt spoke through a mouthful of creamed spinach.

That she was scrappy, resilient, dedicated. . . She waited for him to answer his own question.

"That you were desperate. Such a goddamned need to please everyone and not get your ass canned that you did the scene with a broken leg. I thought that was a metaphor for Hollywood, the way girls in this town will do anything, screw anyone, to become famous."

"I'm not sure my stress fracture measures up to all that," she said. Good, her voice sounded light.

He shook his head. "Don't get pissy. I didn't say *you'd* screwed around to get roles. I'm trying to make a point about how Hollywood sucks starlets like you in and spits them out."

Oh. That made it so much better. She waited.

"I'm doing a new film on Lana Turner. You know who that was?"

"Of course."

"Prove it." Challenging, staring at her over the bread basket.

It took her a second to compile information in her brain into a précis. "The Sweater Girl. An actress in the forties. She was discovered at Schwab's Drugstore." There was more to the story, a life of scandal. She'd murdered her lover. . . no, that had been her daughter. She wasn't on firm ground with those facts, so she left them out.

"That's apocryphal. She wasn't really." Holt sounded cranky, upset she'd known this. He'd wanted to show her up. Bastard. "Anyway, we've got Paragon Dufresne cast as Lana—you know Paragon?"

"I didn't realize she could act." Was that bitchy?

"She'll be able to when I get through with her." Holt looked lascivious. Ick. "I'm looking to cast a small supporting part, one of Lana's friends, a starlet"—Charlotte was beginning to hate that word—"who commits suicide after losing a part."

Ah. That was where she came in. "Sounds interesting."

"Again, I don't have any clue whether you can act." Holt sawed away at his steak. "But you seem like the kind of girl I need for this role."

"It sounds like the kind of thing I'd be interested in." Cool and businesslike. No need to give him any ideas about her level of desperation.

"Sure you would. I'll have my office get in touch with your agent. We're starting this month, so if you've got any plans, you'd better cancel them."

232

Had she just been hired? It sounded like she'd just been hired. Hot damn. Working with Holt wasn't going to be fun, but it'd be good experience and a solid credit to put on her résumé. Plus it might lead to better things. It was hard to see this as anything but positive, even though every atom of her being found Holt revolting.

## Chapter Twenty-Seven

SHE HAD THE part. Rick confirmed it.

"I've just been hammering out the details with Holt's people," he said. "You must've really impressed him."

"I don't think I did," Charlotte said. "I kind of had the impression he didn't like me much."

"Yeah? Somehow I doubt that. Apparently he said he couldn't picture anyone but you in that part."

"Hopefully that's a good thing," she said. "Did you get around to reading the script yet?"

"Haven't had time. I'm sure it's great. Hey, you okay with this? You don't sound too thrilled. Considering usually I have to get you to stop thanking me, I'm wondering what's going on. Holt give you a hard time?

"No, it was fine. We had a nice lunch." She paused. "I guess I'm just a little worried. It doesn't seem like he'd be the easiest person to work for."

"Well, no. Hell, no. That's his reputation, right? But he's an artist. Just look at his reviews. This is a fantastic opportunity for you, Charlotte. You'll do great."

"You're right. It'll be fine."

"Good news, too. The production company was talking about giving you scale. They didn't realize you had me in your hip pocket. Guess what I got for you?" He named a sum that made her turn cold with shock. It was, for her, for many, many people, big money. It wasn't celebrity money, or even name-actor money, but it was big money. "None of this timecard crap, either, not anymore. Lump payment, half up front, half upon completion of filming, not counting all those little extras you'll be picking up along the way."

The pressure she could feel between her shoulder blades started to lighten. "That's awesome, Rick. Thank you."

"See, that sounds more like the Charlotte I know." Rick sounded happier. "You going to be okay with the nudity?"

She paused. "Nobody's mentioned nudity."

"Huh. Seems like that's something Holt would have wanted to run by you. Yeah, there's a nude scene. Brief, I gather, just you in the bathtub, nobody else involved. It's your suicide scene, so it's not going to be gratuitous or anything."

She'd never quite puzzled out the distinction between gratuitous and non-gratuitous nudity. In theory, she was okay with either, circumstances pending. In actuality, it'd be no treat to be naked in front of Holt. And in front of an audience of hypothetical thousands, yes, but Holt worried her the most. "I'll have to see the script. I don't imagine it'll be a problem, though."

"Look, you want to come into the agency today to go over your contract in person, or should I just messenger it to you?"

"Messenger's fine. Whatever's easiest," she said. "Anything else I should know?"

"Just remember, if Holt's a dick, it doesn't affect you, right? You're not going to do anything to make him mad, he won't have any problems with you showing up to the set late or not knowing your lines or whatever, so don't worry about anything. Right?"

"Right, Rick." Rick clicked off, probably already dialing his next call.

She should celebrate. Call someone, go out, do something. She didn't have anyone to call. There was Bob from her old acting class, but she wasn't even sure she had his number. Erica was gone. Simon was. . . Simon.

She could research. That's what she should do, bear down and start knitting her protective blanket of knowledge. Research Lana Turner, old Hollywood, the time period—speech patterns and body language could be drawn from whatever she could learn here, and it was best to show up to this set as prepared as she could. Online. That was where she needed to be.

As long as she was online. . . A quick vanity Google. What was she looking for? Fan sites, cropping up after her handful of lines in her only movie? Reviews that favorably singled out her miniscule performance? She couldn't be that naïve, could she?

Message boards. Oh, this again. Message boards for Simon. Should it hurt more, thinking of Simon? There wasn't any pain, just a sick feeling she'd been stupid, though when she analyzed that emotion, she couldn't sort it out. Was she stupid for falling in love with Simon, or stupid for being oblivious to whatever was eating him up, or stupid for thinking it was going to work in the first place?

Message board thread: STILL WITH HER? She shouldn't read this. And yet she knew she would: *so i thought hed broken up wit that girl fm the movie but theres a pic fo them togheter in London resently. does anyone know if there still a couple i think they should break up caus shes just using him dont you agree.*

Huh? Oh, good, she'd included a link. Celebrity gossip site, a photo of Simon, dear still, walking with a small-featured blonde girl—not Charlotte, and not, she was glad to note, Catherine Gates, but the same essential type. London looked pretty. Rainy and overcast. The girl wore a long belted cardigan and brown pants rolled at the ankle. They weren't holding hands, but they looked close. So Simon was back in London? Was he dating this blonde girl, whoever she was?

Back to the message boards. Oh, Joegirl, there she was, posting again. Charlotte hadn't missed her. *I don't think that's her. They're definitely broken up, that's what I heard, and all I can say is, good riddance! I'm glad he finally came to his senses. She's so terrible in that movie, she just ruins it for me whenever she's on screen. I just want to punch her in her big dumb mouth. And she's not even pretty, her waist is kind of thick and she's squinty. She looks like a dumb bitch.*

Thank you, Joegirl. That was fun. She had to stop doing this, or at least she had to develop a masochistic streak before her next visit.

Her role wasn't important enough to warrant an invitation to the read-through for ULTP. That was what the script was called, Untitled Lana Turner Project, until such time as Holt could come up with a more marketable title. She had her copy of the script, and from that alone she was mighty glad she wasn't expected to sit in at the read-through. It was 223 pages long. That'd be a three hour film, roughly, unless Holt did some chopping.

It stank. She was sour toward it starting out, because Holt was the screenwriter as well as the director, and she really should try to improve her attitude for the sake of getting through the production, but she couldn't sit and read it without feeling a combination of scorn and revulsion.

The good: Holt knew how to tell a story, no getting around that. The narrative thread meandered, but eventually it stretched from point A to point B. The dialogue was tart and meaty; the action was visceral.

What she couldn't get past: Holt's worldview. His specific take on Los Angeles, and Hollywood, and the film industry in general, was so much at odds with her own experiences it seemed they couldn't exist in the same universe without canceling each other out. Did all his women need to be abuse victims, whores, nags, floozies? To be fair, the male characters were all blurry splotches of testosterone, beating and swearing and sweating and swaggering. Holt's view was mired in caricature, and she hated him for it.

Grace was okay, though. That was Grace Holiday, her character, the struggling actress who offs herself. She combed the historical material and found no reference to Grace; this, then, was a figment of Holt's imagination and not a real person. Grace was a bit of a sad sack, and desperate for fame and probably love and approval as well, but she could identify with that. She could find a way inside the character through that.

There was the nude scene, yep, in the bathtub while she slit her wrists. She wished, briefly, that her breasts were better, and then shoved that thought aside. Her breasts were her own, and they were fine, and more to the point, it was far too late in the process to change them.

Most difficult acting job of her life: showing up on the set each day with energy and enthusiasm for the production. It was a force of will to set aside all her negative thoughts and to not only pretend she was excited about this, but to believe it as well.

It had been a long day already, and she hadn't delivered a line yet. She was in costume. Bright yellow dress with a full skirt. Not a great color on her, but she wasn't the center of attention here, after all. Hair done up in a flip and sprayed into place. Ankle strap shoes and a padded bra beneath her cardigan, forming her breasts into high, stiff cones. It was right for Grace Holiday. The glamour would be left to Lana.

Paragon Dufresne. A year since Charlotte had first seen her, back in the law office, back when she used to have a desk job. Paragon didn't recognize her, of course, and Charlotte was damned if she'd refresh her memory of the meeting. Paragon made a lovely Lana, lush and winsome, her hair dyed glossy brown, and Charlotte kind of understood Holt's point about it not really mattering if Paragon could act.

Only Paragon couldn't. Paragon really, really couldn't act. There was no drama-school elitism in Charlotte's assessment. It was a sober fact. Paragon was a dud.

They filmed downtown, somewhere south of the gorgeous little steaks at Fredericks in some old Art Deco building that had seen better days, most of them eighty years ago. It was a coffee shop that had been converted into offices and then back to a coffee shop for the purposes of production.

Only not really. It was converted into a movie set of a movie set of a coffee shop, a scene from one of Lana's movies—she'd perused Lana's filmography, but Charlotte couldn't tell what one this was supposed to be, because Holt was playing fast and loose with Lana's past and it was hard to be sure what lined up with reality and what didn't.

They'd shot the same scene all morning. Paragon and Neil, the guy playing Artie Shaw, were in a passionate clinch on the countertop of the abandoned set. Neil's hands roamed under her lavender angora sweater. Paragon's hair was wild, her skirt was hiked up around her thighs. Her head was thrown back over the side of the counter in apparent passion. She looked the part. When she spoke, however, her limitations became apparent.

"Artie, don't stop." A monotone.

Time to stop evaluating Paragon's performance and concentrate on her own. That was her cue, and even though the cameras were rolling for Paragon, not her—they'd shoot her coverage later, probably after Paragon had left for the day—she wanted to give a good performance. "Lana, you're needed back on the set."

"Charlotte, don't you knock?" Paragon's—Lana's—eyes were wide with feigned shock.

She hadn't realized her error yet. On a different set, juxtaposing an actor's name with her character's name would be occasion for a little comic relief. Not on this set. Charlotte could feel the tension in her shoulders growing as she waited for Holt's outburst.

Paragon got there first. "Grace! I meant Grace! Sorry, sorry, everyone." She laughed. Laughing was a mistake.

"Cut!" Holt came forward. "Damn right you're sorry. You're a sorry excuse for an actress." He glared at Paragon. "Stupid cow. Get back there and do it again."

An anxious pause, and then Paragon slid off the counter and stomped off in the direction of her trailer. Charlotte couldn't blame her. If anyone called her a stupid cow, she'd stomp off, too.

Holt threw up his hands. "God damn it. Someone, get her."

Charlotte looked to Charity, the unlovely sister, Paragon's putative personal assistant. Charity sat on the sidelines, phone to her ear, ignoring the burst of chaos on the set.

"I'll get her," Charlotte said. An adrenaline surge had kicked in, and she wanted to move out of the situation fast. She was afraid of Holt and disgusted by him, and it wasn't a good idea to let him detect that.

The last trailer she'd been in was Simon's. Better not think about that now. She knocked on the door. "Paragon? Are you in there? It's Charlotte."

There was no answer. She opened the door and hovered on the steps, peering in. "Hey, Paragon, is it okay if I come in?"

Paragon's trailer was a flurry of girlishness, custom-kitted to what she supposed was Paragon's taste. Lots of lavender and pale yellow. Ruffled curtains and candles and throw pillows. Paragon lay facedown on the loveseat, sobbing into the chenille. This would really do a number on Lana's makeup job.

She stepped inside and closed the door. "Are you okay?" she asked.

"No." Muffled into a pillow. "He's an asshole."

He certainly was, and under other circumstances, she'd buy Paragon a drink and trade mean stories about him. "I know. But the sooner you get back to the set, the sooner you can get this over with."

"I'm never coming back. I'm quitting." It was said like a child proclaiming she was never going to return to school.

"If you quit, he wins." Actually, Paragon would win—she didn't need this movie, she had her whole music career to fall back on, and it would hurt Holt a great deal if she pulled out and let the movie collapse around him. It would also hurt Charlotte, though, and all the other people who would be out of a job if Paragon walked.

She sat down on the couch, tentative. She didn't want to invade Paragon's personal space. She wasn't sure she wanted her own personal space invaded by Paragon, either.

Paragon looked up from the pillow. Pretty even with her mascara smeared, not blotchy or puffy. "I can't go back there."

"You can. Just bluff your way through it. Don't let him know he's hurt your feelings."

"But he did!"

"I know, but there's no sense letting him know that. It's what he wants." Not sure that was true; Charlotte still couldn't figure out if Holt was a sadist or just oblivious to the feelings of anyone besides himself. Difficult to tell which was more dangerous. She stood up. "Come on, Paragon, let's go."

The brisk, kindergarten-teacher voice did the trick. Paragon sat up.

"I can't go outside like this," she said. Sullen. How old was Paragon? Twenty? Probably no one had ever told her to act like an adult, and probably she wasn't smart enough to figure out how to do it on her own.

A knock on the trailer door. Paragon didn't move, so Charlotte stood and opened it. It was John, the A.D., walkie-talkie in hand.

"Hi." He glanced past her into the trailer. "You guys ready to come back to the set? Harris wants to keep going."

"Yep. We were just on our way." John would understand why she was being so chipper. "Paragon?"

Paragon got to her feet and followed her out of the trailer. Charlotte fell into step beside John.

Back to the set. The makeup artist, Judy, set about repairing the damage to Paragon's face. Holt didn't pay them any attention. He was deep in conversation with one of the P.A.s, a young kid she hadn't met. Wasn't even sure of her name. Megan, she thought.

"They said they wouldn't have it done until tomorrow, there was nothing else I could do." The girl—Megan?—had a faint whine to her tone that Charlotte knew wouldn't go over well.

"That's bull. I've been driving that crappy rental car for two days now. Get on the phone and tell them they need to finish it tonight. And have them take it to my house. Or if they can't do that, go over there and drive it there yourself. I need my car waiting for me when I get home."

"I can't do that. They're already closed." Charlotte wished she could warn her not to whine. Holt would tear her apart.

"Why wasn't this taken care of this earlier? You've fucked up everything." Holt bristled, gross and scary.

Megan crumbled. She started to walk off. Holt held a plastic cup in his hand, some blended concoction of coffee and whipped cream and chocolate syrup. "Don't walk away from me when I'm talking to you, you little shit," he said. He smashed the plastic cup against the unmarked canvas of the kid's sweatshirt.

A mess of chocolate and coffee and ice. Everything stopped, and then Megan started running, an odd lopping gait, as though adrenaline and sudden humiliation had impaired her ability to move in a normal manner.

"And don't come back, fucker!" Holt yelled after her. It was unnecessary; of course Megan wouldn't come back. Charlotte hoped she'd report this to someone, or at the very least send an angry anonymous tip to some gossip blog. Not that it would help; everyone already knew what a creep Holt was, and yet people still clamored for the chance to work for him. Including her.

She wanted to run after the kid, get her cleaned up, take her out for a cup of coffee and let her know the world wasn't this awful most of the time. If she did that, though, she'd be tossing her job away.

It would be nice to be fired.

She stared at Holt. When Holt turned to her, there was a flicker of awareness in his eyes. For the first time, for one fleeting second, they were *en rapport*. They understood each other: She understood he was a wretch of a human being, and he understood she despised him.

She looked away first.

## CHAPTER TWENTY-EIGHT

AFTER THEY WERE done for the day, Paragon came up to her. "Later on, me and my friends are going to Hope," Paragon said. "You wanna come with?"

Not even remotely. Charlotte wanted to go home. She had heard of Hope, some bar or club or indeterminate night spot up on the Strip. She didn't know what "later" meant to Paragon—it was after ten already, and they had to work tomorrow.

Maybe it would be a fun adventure. Maybe she needed to have a drink or two and indulge in a little girl-talk with Paragon.

"Sure. That sounds like a good idea."

"Great!" Paragon smiled, and Charlotte found herself smiling back. "I'm going to go home and change first and I'll meet you there, okay?"

"Great." Now she was committed. When she got home, it was all she could do not to blow off Paragon and crawl into a hot bath and go to bed. Instead, she changed: short black skirt and matching blouse, because black was always appropriate. Did Paragon do this nightly? How did she have the energy?

There was a long line outside Hope. She took her place in it. It was wrong to wish she'd be turned away at the door so she could return home secure in the knowledge she'd given it an honest try.

"There you are! Come on!" Paragon clunked up the sidewalk in her knee boots, then grabbed her wrist and pulled her out of the line. Charlotte found herself on the receiving end of a hug and a quick kiss on the cheek. Paragon seemed slightly manic, like she'd been drinking or otherwise indulging already. She'd changed into a tiny backless turquoise dress with a wide belt.

They bypassed the line. Of course. A quick rush of glee. This was what she should have been doing when she was Paragon's age, going to glittery nightclubs and getting the VIP treatment instead of working dull desk jobs while waiting for her big break.

The doorman stepped aside and let them enter. They walked right into the club. No cover charge, no purse-search for contraband.

"I think Maxi is supposed to be here, and Brandi and Dini." Paragon shouted in her ear. Charlotte smiled and nodded, as though she had any idea who these people with names like trendy dolls were.

Paragon's posse had staked out a booth toward the back of the room. The club was nice, violet walls with brass lanterns, black lacquered tables. Paragon and Charlotte slid onto the narrow velvet bench.

"Hi, guys, this is Charlotte." Charity was there, deep in conversation with a girl with long blonde hair. They all had long blonde hair, except for Paragon, brunette at the moment. All were thin and tan. Dressed in skimpy dresses in candy colors, sipping candy-colored cocktails, tiny little-girl clutch purses and phones in rhinestone-covered casings on the table in front of them.

Charlotte ordered a cantaloupe martini, because anything that didn't look like it could be manufactured by Kool-Aid would seem out of place here. Sickly-sweet with a chemical aftertaste. She needed the drink, though, especially as soon as Paragon began holding court.

Paragon's childhood, all deluded bliss: "So then all of the other girls got jealous because I'd already sung the lead in the Christmas pageant, so they had their moms call the school and tell the choir teacher they didn't think I should sing the solo at the Spring Concert as well." That never happened. She barely knew Paragon and thus had no right assuming she was a liar, but she was willing to bet that never happened in any kind of universe.

Paragon set down her empty glass, picked up a full one. Hers, or one of her friends who was too much in awe to object? "Anyway, they're all still back in Kentucky getting all fat and working at, like, State Farm." She laughed. "It didn't matter how much they tried to sabotage her. My voice is a gift from God, and God made sure I could spread it across the world."

Paragon drank too much, treating the cocktails like soda pop. While she drank, she talked and talked.

Wasn't she married? She'd had her high-profile wedding in the spring, just before *Queen of Angels* had come out—Charlotte remembered the relentless tabloid coverage of the nuptials. Yes, there was the ring, a platinum band with five emerald-cut diamonds of increasing size. Where was the semi-famous reality-star husband?

One of Paragon's friends—was this Maxi? Brandi?—turned to her. "How do you know Paragon?" Interrogative, like she suspected Charlotte was an interloper. Good instincts, Maxi/Brandi.

"We work together." Made it sound like they were in the same office together or something. The thought of Paragon copying files was oddly appealing.

"Oh." It was gratifying to see Maxi/Brandi reassess her opinion of Charlotte based on this new bit of knowledge. "You're an actress?"

"Yes. What do you do?"

A scoff. "I'm the co-host of *Screen Styles* on The Gossip Channel. I've been there for like two years." Incredulity plain in her tone. She turned to the girl on the other side of her—Brandi? Dini?—to roll her eyes at Charlotte's ignorance. The girl wasn't paying any attention, so the effect was lost.

Nonetheless, Charlotte felt snubbed. So she didn't recognize some co-host of some show she'd never heard of on a channel only people with super-ultra-premium-deluxe satellite packages had access to. Hardly seemed to warrant a scoff.

Thumping beats of a new song produced a long, exuberant scream from Paragon. "Oh my God! I can't believe they're playing it!"

"It" was one of Paragon's songs. Charlotte knew that without having ever heard it before, and she could well believe they were playing it. Paragon's presence here wasn't going unnoticed by the club staff.

Paragon started whooping. When she climbed onto the table, her spike-heeled boots toppling drinks in her wake, Charlotte's flight instinct started to kick in. Even after as many drinks as Paragon had downed, she wouldn't think this was a good idea. There wasn't enough alcohol in the place to make her think this was a good idea.

Paragon started dancing, some anemic hot-girl dance where she kept her knees pressed together and closed her eyes and writhed and shimmied. She threw her arms up over her head. Her mini-dress crept up her thighs another few inches.

The crowd hooted and yelled. More than a few camera phones came out, capturing the moment for posterity. Charlotte had to fight the urge to tell Paragon to get down from there.

Paragon hopped off the table and headed out onto the dance floor, where she began to bump and grind with the first male bodies she saw, a trio of gelled and glossed young twerps in shiny open shirts.

Paragon leaned back against one of the boys, her ass gyrating up against his crotch. When Paragon started to rub her own crotch through the thin fabric of her skirt, Maxi got up and stalked over to the dance floor.

"God, Paragon. What about Kirk?"

Charlotte rose out of her seat and approached the action, though she didn't know why. This didn't concern her. This would be a splendid time to slink off and go home.

"Go 'way." Paragon didn't open her eyes. "You're just jealous." She opened her eyes and started laughing. "Yeah, you're just jealous, because I'm prettier and richer and famouser than you."

Did people really talk this way? Even drunk people?

Paragon burst out laughing and surged forward, flailing in the boy's grip, teetering and wobbling in her slick boots on the slick dance floor.

Paragon's perfect right breast popped out of her scoop neckline. A kid stuck his camera phone scant inches away.

"Put that away. Now," Charlotte told him. "Turn it off. Seriously." She couldn't make any threats—what was she going to do? Wrestle it away from him? Call his parents?—but she could bully him a little, at least.

He looked at her, surprised, like it hadn't occurred to him that maybe this wasn't a socially acceptable thing to do, and backed up. Now she had to get Paragon out of there.

Paragon noticed the breast and popped it back into her dress with a sheepish giggle. She sang along to her song, her voice high and breathy, botching the words.

"Come on, Paragon," Charlotte said, her voice bright and cheerful. "We're going to go someplace else."

Paragon didn't look at her. "I want to stay."

"They said they were getting ready to close soon. Let's go next door." Once she had Paragon out in the night air, it'd be easier to work on getting her home. Charlotte reached out and took Paragon's hand. "Come on. Let's go."

Paragon followed her. Charlotte stopped by their table and retrieved Paragon's clutch purse and cell phone from the mess of half-filled cocktail glasses and crumpled napkins. This was sticky, because Paragon blinked a bit and looked at her friends and said, "Wait, aren't they going with us?"

"Yeah, they're going to meet us there."

"Yeah, we'll be along soon, Paragon." Bless Maxi. She didn't sound convincing, but at least she was swift enough to pick up on Charlotte's intentions. Maxi caught Charlotte's eye and gave a quick nod of thanks or approval.

Charlotte kept her hand locked around Paragon's wrist, which she shifted to her waist as Paragon began to have trouble standing. Paragon laughed and laughed and clutched her. "Blinky lights," she said.

"Uh-huh." She tuned out Paragon's babbling and looked around for their waitress to see about settling their tab.

Their waitress shook her head when Charlotte found her. "Comped," she shouted over the music. "It's okay. But thanks." That seemed too bad, that the club would foot the bill for Paragon drinking all their alcohol and acting like a jackass. Charlotte handed her all the cash she had in her wallet as a tip, a messy bundle of bills, and hoped it would be sufficient.

Charity stood at the door, talking to some guy. Good. Charlotte could pass Paragon off to her sister.

Maybe not. Charity looked up, saw Paragon, and looked away. She was talking to the boy with the camera phone who'd been snapping photos of Paragon's breast. Maybe she was trying to get him to delete the photos. Charlotte could come up with a few equally possible alternate scenarios, but figuring out which seemed most likely required a more extensive knowledge of the Dufresne family dynamics than she had, or would ever want to have.

Paragon kicked up a fuss when Charlotte steered her toward her car. Damn. It would've been simpler if she'd been too drunk to realize what Charlotte was doing. "No! I want to take my own car."

"No, we're going to take mine." Bright and firm.

"I don't want to leave my car here."

"We'll come back for it." That was a lie. Hopefully in the morning Paragon would remember where she'd been and where her car was parked. Whether she did or not, whether it would be towed or stolen in the interim, Charlotte didn't much care. "Come on."

Paragon let herself be put into the passenger seat. Charlotte buckled her in. "Your car sucks."

"Thank you." It didn't. Her car was a little boring maybe, but it didn't suck. It was clean and in good condition. It was adequate for her purposes.

Charlotte pulled out and started heading west because she didn't want to make a left turn on Sunset. Driving was still a little harrowing. So many things to keep track of. "Paragon, where's your house?"

"Silver Lake." Crap. Wrong direction. "Hey, we're not going to my house, we're going to a better club! You said we were."

"Yeah. The other club wasn't any good, so we're just going home."

"How do you know that?"

"We wouldn't have a good time there. So I'm going to take you home."

"No!" Charlotte had a moment of panic as Paragon started to fumble with the door handle. "I don't want to go! Take me back to the club!"

"Where do you live in Silver Lake? Silver Lake Boulevard, or what?" It was an effort to keep her tone chipper yet unyielding.

"You're kidnapping me." Paragon released the door handle.

"No, I'm just taking you home." Flipping a U-Turn on Sunset. Not something she'd recommend. Hair raising. "Is it fastest to stay on Sunset?"

"You don't get out much, do you?" Paragon giggled. "I thought you might have a good time if you got out and hung around with me and my friends, but you're too much of a loser, aren't you?"

"Oh, for God's sake." Traffic on Sunset was murderous, as usual.

Another giggle. "You're jealous of me. It's because I have a star quality and you don't."

"There's no such thing as star quality, okay? You're a pretty girl with a good voice who's had a lot of luck and a lot of people trying to make good things happen to your career. You've been very lucky."

"God gave me star quality. It's my gift to the world."

"Let's leave God out of this, okay? God doesn't give a damn about you singing the lead in your school musical or your music getting playtime on the radio."

"You shouldn't say that. That's blasphemy. You're just jealous."

Silver Lake Boulevard. There was something to thank God for. "Right or left?"

"Right. I'm on Ivanhoe." Paragon scrunched up her face. "I think I'm going to be sick."

Great. She'd be cleaning up candy-colored vomit for the rest of the evening. "Try to hang in there. We're almost to your place."

Paragon gave her sullen directions to her house. It was modest in size, which surprised Charlotte, though it did have a fancy gate out front. "Okay. How do we get through the gate?"

"Push the button. Stupid." So slurred she could barely make it out. Paragon had been drinking hard alcohol all evening, and she was getting drunker and drunker. Good thing she was getting home safely. Charlotte tried to feel noble, or responsible, or something other than pissed off and downtrodden.

She rolled down the window, then leaned out and pushed the button mounted on the intercom by the gate. Male voice through the speaker: "Yo, what?"

Paragon leaned over her. "Jaime, it's me. I'm drunk. Open the fucking gate!"

Charlotte caught a strong whiff of ammonia when Paragon leaned. Either her perfume was particularly industrial in nature or... Damn it. Vomit would have been preferable. It smelled like a cat box in her car.

She drove up the short circular drive to the front door. A beefy guy in a dark suit—Jaime, presumably—came out and opened the

253

passenger door. "Okay, princess, time to get you inside." He took hold of Paragon's arm and helped her out. He looked at Charlotte. "Hey, thanks."

Charlotte shrugged. "Her car is still parked at Hope, whenever she starts wondering about that. Is her husband home?" she asked.

Jaime snorted. "That guy? He ain't never home."

Should that make her feel bad for Paragon or not? Right now, she was reserving all her pity for herself. She looked at the wet spot on the upholstery of the passenger seat where Paragon, beautiful, God-blessed Paragon, had pissed herself, then drove back out the gates, heading home at last.

## Chapter Twenty-Nine

THE CELL PHONE pictures hit the web the next morning. Charlotte found them on some trashy gossip site and viewed them over her morning coffee while summoning up the energy to get dressed and go to the set. Blurry and low-resolution—there was Paragon's breast, nipple nothing more than a dark smudge. Paragon looked drunk off her ass, but still kind of pretty. Half of Charlotte's posed pictures didn't turn out as well.

Oh, look, there she was. The little bugger had kept snapping even while she was chastising him, even while she led a drunk and argumentative Paragon off the dance floor. She looked pissed off and humorless, but competent. Not a bad photo of her, actually. Caption: "Club staff escorts Paragon out of Hope." Oh, she was club staff? Her black skirt and blouse did look a little waitressy, now that she thought about it.

She was almost done with hair and makeup by the time Paragon made it into the trailer. Paragon looked a little rough, but her skin looked good and her eyes were clear. She smiled and gave Charlotte a quick wave, bright and natural, before settling into the makeup chair. Resilient, or oblivious? Both were good survival traits.

Today they'd be filming Grace's suicide scene, her nude scene. Charlotte had avoided thinking about it. It was an ugly scene, in an ugly script, in an ugly production.

First there was a long morning to get through, a scene in which Grace had two lines, neither vital to the action. It was difficult to remain in character and not let herself get derailed by thoughts of what was to take place that afternoon.

A claw-foot bathtub filled with water. Grace would slit her wrists in the tub following a failed audition. Grace had a sense of the dramatic; there was nothing about this lifestyle worth killing oneself over.

The wardrobe lady gave Charlotte a bathrobe to wear on set. There were too many people around. Didn't they usually clear sets for nude scenes? If she asked, would Holt comply? She wouldn't ask, though. She wouldn't let Holt know this rattled her.

She dropped the robe. Climbed in the tub, far too aware of her body. Breasts were still unimpressive.

It was important not to be neurotic about this. This was a job, and she was a professional. She was Grace Holiday, struggling actress, who had just made the decision to abandon the struggle.

The set grew quiet. Holt called action.

She started crying. She'd worried she wouldn't be able to cry on cue, but there were no problems here. The discomfort of the here and now was enough. At Holt's direction, she dragged the prop razor across her wrists—she'd heard real suicides did it lengthwise, but Holt wanted her to slash across the width. Sticky, viscous fake blood from the punctured squibs hidden on her skin, too bright to be real. It didn't run off in the water, just stayed on her wrists like honey. She slashed and sobbed, and wished she could be anywhere else.

Holt yelled, "Cut!" He approached the tub.

She wiped at her eyes with the back of her hands, trying not to get any of the fake blood on her face. "How was that?" she asked. Cheerful and professional.

"We'll try it again. More crying this time," he said. He paused. "That was pretty good, though."

He was strangely gentle, like he had some awareness this was a distressing moment for her. She almost liked him.

She sat in the cooling water while her wrists were sponged off with alcohol and stared at her arms. A few small moles dotted the skin, a legacy of too much time outdoors. She could get them removed, now that she could afford it. The squibs were replaced; her makeup was retouched. Once more.

Crying was even easier now. She was cold. She was miserable. She sobbed. She'd never sobbed in public like this, her misery this transparent. Even after Holt called cut this time, she kept sobbing.

That was it. They got it; Holt was satisfied. That was good; she couldn't do this again. She didn't have it in her. She stayed in the tub and tried to get herself under control.

She needed her own trailer, a private space where she could either pull herself together or, if that proved impossible, fall to pieces. Instead, she left the set and, still in the robe, hid in the ladies' room and continued sobbing until it was all out of her system. Then she washed her face and headed for the wardrobe trailer to reclaim her street clothes and go home.

She was almost done with this damn movie. The meat of her role was in the proverbial can. Just a few more days remained of standing in the background and delivering the occasional line. She could handle that. She had survived the film. Holt couldn't get to her now.

A mid-morning call time, a light day scheduled. Nothing to fear. That didn't mean she was looking forward to it. She pulled into the parking structure downtown near the set and rolled down her window to talk to the security guard.

It was the one she'd seen every day of the shoot, a big man with a heavy mustache and sad eyes. He recognized her on sight, if not by name. He consulted his clipboard.

"What was that again, sweetie?" he asked.

"Charlotte Dent."

"You're not here," he said. "Are you sure you're supposed to be here today?"

"Yeah. I'm on the call sheet for today. They gave me this on Monday." She fished it out of her purse, unfolded it, and handed it to him.

"Okay, yeah, they must've changed the schedule since then. I got the new one right here. Doesn't look like you have to work today."

A bonus free day. A wonderful idea. "Can I go on the set and make sure?"

"Oh, yeah, sure, of course." Maybe he wasn't supposed to be so ready to allow interlopers on the set, but she probably seemed like a low risk.

Charlotte saw John first. He looked surprised and wary.

"Hi," he said. "Um. . . I don't think we need you today."

"Yeah, the guard at the gate told me I wasn't on the revised call sheet. Nobody told me."

"Yeah, sorry about that. Somebody really should have called you." John looked over his shoulder in the direction of the set. They were shooting in the lobby of an old downtown hotel today. Probably doing centuries of damage to the historic structure.

"It's okay. Things get lost in the shuffle." She paused, aware of an odd tension. "Anything I should know?"

John looked at her. Concerned, compassionate. Nice guy, John. "Look, Holt made some changes to the script."

"Uh-huh." She kept her face composed.

John shot a look around. "I'm not the one who should be telling you this. Someone really should have told you—"

"Yeah, they should have." She took a deep breath. "Did he cut me out of the film?"

"I think so, yeah. I don't really know. He doesn't tell me much of anything, but I have a copy of the revisions, and. . . Yeah."

She looked over at the set. Holt stood in a throng of people, talking to Neil and Paragon. "I need to talk to him."

"I can't let you. You're not even supposed to be on the set. You should just leave and call your agent and let this all get sorted out that way."

"Are you going to stop me?" She said it without any hint of challenge, just curiosity.

"No. Of course not. But look, it won't help anything—"

She walked toward Holt, John's protests receding behind her. Now that she was moving, the adrenaline started to surge, making her thighs feel unsteady and powerful all at once. She felt murderous. It felt pretty good, actually.

They were rolling. Murderous rage could wait for a bit; she wouldn't bust a take.

Paragon delivered two lines in her monotone. No lights on behind those lovely eyes, no awareness of what all those words in her script meant.

Then Holt yelled, "Cut." Then he saw her.

She spoke before he had time to say anything. "May I talk to you?" Calm and low.

"I'm in the middle of shooting," he said, his voice thick with annoyance. He wasn't looking at her, though; she knew from the way he turned away from her that the annoyance was an act. He was avoiding her because he knew he was caught doing something crappy.

"If you're going to fire me, have the grace to make sure somebody tells me," she said. It came out a hair too loud. Heads turned. The buzz of chatter on the set lowered.

"Somebody was supposed to call you. It's not my responsibility to keep track of stuff like that," he said.

"It damn well is your responsibility," she said. Ah, this was nice, that rush of righteous anger. She was fired, what the hell? She could bite Holt's head off right here and spit it across the elegant lobby, and he still couldn't fire her twice. "Of course it's your responsibility. It's part of your goddamned job." She wasn't at all sure it was, actually, but that sounded pretty good.

"I don't have time to discuss this right now."

"I don't care. You didn't make the time to call me and discuss this earlier, so we're going to discuss it now. If I'm fired, you owe me an explanation."

"Look, you weren't working out. I changed the script. I made a mistake in hiring you, and I wanted to correct that mistake before you messed up my entire movie." He turned away and waved a hand, dismissive. "Talk to somebody else. I don't have time."

John had been right; there was no point to this. One of the security guards ambled over to see what the raised voices were about. If Holt ordered her off the set, the guard would have no choice but to remove her, and that was a final indignity she'd rather be spared.

260

She walked to her car. She sat behind the wheel. She took a deep breath and assessed her condition.

Fired. Christ. She'd never been fired from anything in her life, and the blow to her confidence knocked the spirit out of her. Holt said she was screwing up his movie. No, that couldn't be the truth. Her performance was fine, maybe even pretty good, and even Holt had, in his way, complimented her on it. He didn't like her, and he knew she didn't like him, and maybe that made him want to get rid of her. Or maybe he thought the script was stronger without the character of Grace Holiday. Which. . . fair enough. His call.

Maybe it wasn't even Holt. Maybe someone at the studio objected to her. Maybe it was her nude scene, maybe her flat little breasts were deemed insufficiently sexy. Maybe it was something else entirely, something she'd never know.

She called Rick. Her hands shook; she hit several wrong buttons, had to stop, disconnect, take a deep breath, and try again.

He took her call right away. "Charlotte?"

"I got fired. Did you know I got fired?"

"Hold on, back up. Who said you were fired?"

"Nobody told me, that's the thing, I got to the set and I was no longer on the call sheet, and then Holt told me he wrote me out of the movie."

"Holt told you that?" Rick was quiet. "Okay, honey, listen, I don't know anything about that. I need to make a few calls, and then I'll get back to you. Are you at the set?"

"Yeah, I'm downtown." She sounded angry and shrill.

"Okay, you know where Los Habaneros is? Mexican place off Gower? Just get up to Sunset and start heading west, it'll be a big tacky place on the right. I'll meet you there. We can have some brunch and figure this out."

She didn't want brunch. She didn't want to talk to Rick, or anyone. "Okay," she said.

"Twenty minutes," Rick said, and clicked off.

Rick was already waiting when she arrived at the restaurant, seated in an enormous wicker chair on the back patio. There was a margarita, rocks, thick crust of salt, sitting at her place setting. Rick gestured for her to sit.

"You need that," he said, with a nod at the margarita. He was drinking bottled water himself. It wasn't quite eleven in the morning. Far too early to drink. She picked up the margarita, knocked the lime wedge into the glass, and took a long swallow. Rick was right.

The waiter materialized at her elbow. She picked up the menu, confused and unprepared.

"Have the special," Rick said. "You need salt and grease right now."

She had no idea what the special entailed, and she didn't want salt and grease, but a minute ago she would have sworn she didn't want a margarita, either. She nodded at the waiter.

"I'll stick with water," Rick said. He shrugged at Charlotte's look. "I have a lunch meeting right after this."

The waiter wandered off. She looked at Rick. "So. . .?"

"So Holt's an asshole, but we knew that already, right?" Rick shrugged. "Tina at the studio didn't know anything about this when I called her. She was horrified you found out this way. Holt didn't tell anyone anything, just made his own changes. She called him on the set just now."

"What'd he say about me?" Her voice was brittle.

"A bunch of bull. He said you were unprofessional, and don't even bother arguing that, because everyone knows it's crap. Tina'd

heard good things about you, and everyone knows what Holt's like."
He sipped his water. "So what's your side of it? I think Tina's half
afraid he tried to get you in bed, and he's being vindictive because
you turned him down, and now you're going to sue the studio for
harassment."

"He didn't. He didn't like me much at all." She shrugged. "I
don't know. Maybe he didn't like my breasts." The margarita was
going straight to her head.

Rick snorted. "I don't think that's the trouble here." He leaned
forward. "Don't feel too bad about any of this, okay? I'm sorry you
had to work with him in the first place."

"Am I going to get paid?" She'd already received her half up
front, but the other half. . .

"They'll probably argue against it, try to save themselves some
money, since you didn't finish your part."

"I came close," she said. "I just had a couple of little scenes
left."

Her eyes welled up. Her sunglasses rested on the table by her
plate; Rick nudged them over to her. "Here. Put those on."

There was no one else around to see them, and it wasn't like
the wait staff would know who she was or care that she was bawling
her eyes out over being fired, but showing a little public discretion
was probably a good habit to get into, if she wanted any kind of life
in the public eye. She put on the sunglasses and composed herself.

Food came. The special turned out to be a big plate of fried
eggs and beans and tortillas swimming in an oily red sauce. She
nibbled on a forkful of beans. Heaven.

"It's in my best interests to see you get paid, right?" he said. He
smiled. "Ten percent and all. I'll point out that you've done the
work. They can afford to pay, and it'll be worth it to them to keep a

good relationship with you." To keep a good relationship with Rick, more likely. "You going to be okay?"

"Yeah. I think so."

"You think you can take a break for a while? Maybe get out of town, go on a cruise, go to a spa or something? You look like you could use some rejuvenation."

"Is that agent-speak for telling me I look like crap?"

"Naah, you look fine. Maybe not your usual glowy self, that's all. A little blotchy at the moment. Ragged around the edges, who can blame you?" He looked at his watch. "Hey, I gotta get across town for her lunch, but I don't want to leave you in the lurch."

"Go. I'll be fine." She had the afternoon off, after all. Tomorrow off as well, and the day after that, all looming wide with no appointments. People got fired all the time; it wouldn't destroy her.

Rick grabbed the check and headed for the door. Charlotte nursed her margarita and felt herself return to life.

# CHAPTER THIRTY

SHE SHOULDN'T HAVE checked the message boards. Of course she shouldn't have.

The pit vipers knew she was fired. That was fast; it'd been less than a week. There'd been no word about it on the gossip sites. All she'd read about the film was the salacious tidbit that Paragon was so inept at learning her lines they'd started feeding her all her dialogue through an earpiece on the set. It was far-fetched, but she could almost believe it.

But the message board—Simon's message board, and why were Simon's fans still concerned with her?—was filled with news.

Oh, crap, there was Joegirl. Her nemesis, the anonymous Joegirl: *My coworker's friend works on the set. Yeah she got fired. Threw a fit about it, yelled and stormed off. Good riddance. He said she was really bad. Like she had some kind of scene in a bathtub where she was supposed to be upset and she was so over the top that everyone on set had a hard time keeping from laughing. So it's no surprise. I'm glad it happened after the way she treated Simon. Karma is a bitch, bitch.*

They were laughing at her on set? Should she believe that, any more than she should believe the report about Paragon?

*My coworker's friend.* . . Charlotte didn't have any idea who that could be. She'd thought the crew liked her well enough. But this might mean Joegirl was local, right? She wanted to post something

265

in her defense, but had just enough sense not to do that. But there might be other possibilities, if Joegirl was local.

She Googled "Joegirl". Sorted through too many results, whittled them down to a few likely contenders. Found a profile for a Joegirl on a social networking site. That sounded like her. Here was a blog post she'd written about *Queen of Angels*.

Yes. This was her: *Simon is WASTED in this movie!!!*, she'd written. *He looks as supersexy as always but he's doing an American accent which he should NEVER do!!! His real voice is much sexier, IMHO. The script is TERRIBLE—I don't know how movies this bad even get made—and the directing is just sort of blah. My friend Jessica and I laughed out loud at how crappy some of the sets were. I just did not think the actresses in it were good at ALL. Taura Trajo, she's pretty awful, but Charlotte Dent as the robot chick/whatever she was supposed to be (I wasn't paying close attention, to tell you the honest truth, because she was JUST SO BAD) was just really awful. It was like she couldn't even read her lines, much less ACT. As an actress myself, I know good acting when I see it, and Charlotte Dent is bad, bad, bad. I read somewhere that the director hired her because he saw her at a Lakers game. She had to be sleeping with him, because there's just no other way she could get cast.*

It continued in this vein for a while, with a discourse on her thick waist and her piggy nose. Maybe one of these days she'd develop a tough piggy skin to match.

Joegirl was an actress, though. Huh. She skipped to a non-defamatory part of the blog and read on.

Personal information. Oh, Joegirl. She should know better than that. Age: Twenty-four. Too old for this kind of crap, in other words. Location: Tarzana. Occupation: Actress, *"but I'm pouring coffee to pay the bills."* Pouring coffee. In Tarzana?

A comment on Joegirl's site had the answers. A posting from someone named Martin: *Christie! Love the site! Very imaginative! See you on the early shift at Joe!*

Thank you, Martin. Joegirl was Christie, and it only took a quick search to find out that, yes, there was a coffee shop called Joe in Tarzana.

Charlotte stopped and thought. Was she thinking of taking a jaunt to Tarzana? She was, wasn't she? What for? To confront Christie?

No. She wouldn't. She didn't think she would, anyway. That was a little bit psycho, even though Joegirl/Christie was a wee bit psycho herself. Far, far better to just ignore her for the rest of her life.

She mapped the route to Tarzana online. Printed the map. Took it with her to her car. Drove to the Valley, to Tarzana. To Joe. Tried not to think too hard on what she was doing.

A blanket of smog hung over the Valley. It was legitimately fall now, but no one could have guessed that from the temperature, or from the way the sun glowed through the poisonous white haze. The air made her nostrils prickle and her lungs itch, just from the short walk from her car to Joe.

Joe was a nice-looking place. Somewhat retro. Pointy roof, jaunty white lettering on a brown building. Red vinyl booths inside, like an old family restaurant retrofitted as a coffeehouse.

She approached the counter. Thank God for nametags, because she found herself standing in front of Christie.

If the nametag hadn't tipped her off, maybe Christie's reaction would have. Christie froze in the act of approaching the register. Her eyes widened a bit. "Hi," she said at last.

"Hi." A long moment passed. "Small latte, please."

Christie took a second too long to process the order, then rebounded. She nodded. "What kind of milk?"

"I don't care. Regular," Charlotte said.

Christie nodded and accepted her money and rang up the order. She had to know. She had to know there was no possible way, or at least it was very, very unlikely, that Charlotte would be at this place accidentally. Even now she was probably internally reviewing her message board posts, all her online activity, wondering what had tipped Charlotte off to her identity.

Christie was pretty. Hair a little indifferently styled, posture a little slouchy, her shirt and slacks under her apron a little frumpy, but even viewing her through critical and spiteful eyes, Charlotte had to admit she was pretty. Good bones, clear skin, thick hair. Charlotte would bet she wasn't a native, that she'd moved out here not too long ago with plans of becoming famous. She'd probably been the star of a few plays at her high school, had probably done well enough at her college theater program, and she'd misjudged the gap between that and the multiple layers of shiny polish she needed to make any kind of impact in Los Angeles. She looked about like Charlotte had when she'd come out here, so many years ago, unformed and arrogant and baffled by the way the world failed to conform to her ideas of how her career should unfold. Give her a few years; she'd learn.

Her co-worker fixed Charlotte's beverage while Christie rang up the next customer. At least she wouldn't have to worry about Christie spitting in the foamed milk. Not that this seemed likely; Christie looked deflated and odd, like she'd eaten something disagreeable but was too polite to mention her discomfort.

Charlotte wanted to tell her everything. That there was no need to hate her or envy her, because she'd been lucky and her luck had run out. That she hadn't crushed Simon's heart—Los Angeles did that for him, so he ran away to heal. That maybe Christie would someday become successful, or maybe she'd never have a lucky break like Charlotte had, but maybe that wouldn't be the worst thing ever.

When Christie handed her the latte, she didn't look her in the eye, and Charlotte didn't say anything.

She took it to a nearby table and drank it, feeling like a creep. Christie was probably feeling much the same way.

Maybe there was a moment of connection between them. Maybe Joegirl understood Charlotte didn't hate her. Maybe she'd stop hating her. Just in case, though, she'd stop looking at the message boards. If Joegirl posted about how Charlotte came into her workplace looking all piggy and how the workers all had a good laugh at her afterward, she thought her heart might break.

## CHAPTER THIRTY-ONE

BY THE TIME she got home, it was late afternoon. She threw her keys on the table, set her purse on the floor. Closed the front door.

Her apartment smelled bad, like undone laundry or something. A sour body smell. Huh. She walked to the kitchen.

She didn't have any clue anyone was behind her until she felt the stabbing pain under her left shoulder blade.

A tremendous pain. Almost more like a blow than a stab, but no, incredibly, she'd been stabbed. She swiveled her head and spotted a figure, a man, close-cropped hair and rank body odor. He yanked whatever he'd stabbed her with out of her back. Her skin and muscle resisted, and that was weirder and worse than the blade going in.

She thought she screamed. She might not have.

She stumbled forward. Fell against the kitchen counter, hit her chin on the edge of it, fell to the floor.

Another stab, to her lower back this time. Again like a punch, but not hard enough to puncture the skin. She scrambled forward and flipped around.

No one she knew. A complete stranger. Plaid shirt and dirty white pants. Holding. . . was that one of her steak knives? Thin blade, serrated edge, not very sharp. She would have sworn it couldn't do much damage.

He crouched down and stabbed at her again. She shrieked and tried to scramble back. He got her in the stomach. Not bad and not deep. If he was trying to kill her, he wasn't doing a very good job of it. He seemed so. . . off. No strength, not enough focus on the task at hand, no intensity.

He was close to her, so close. She grabbed for his throat. The neck was the most vulnerable part, wasn't it? That was what you were supposed to go for in an attack, if it was a worst-case scenario, which this certainly was.

Both hands around his neck, thumbs together across his Adam's apple, and pinched. Pressed in with her thumbs as hard as she could.

Inside his neck, something moved. He gurgled.

She grunted, some weird undignified animalistic noise. Her abdomen felt tight and sick, concerting all her strength and energy into squeezing his neck. He pulled back, gasping and spitting. He was stronger than her, obviously, and he'd able to break free. She couldn't let him do that, so she leaned forward and bit him on his shoulder, right below her hands, as hard as she could.

Her teeth sank through muscle and tendons.

He didn't react much. His reactions were so weird, and so wrong, all throughout this. He hadn't said a word, for one thing, hadn't made a noise, and wasn't that weird, trying to kill someone without saying anything? He wasn't moving as much as he should, wasn't fighting back, and she had the weird, awful, guilty sensation that she was maybe killing someone who maybe was letting her do it.

So real and vivid and awful, this moment. The colors were too bright. Blood swam in her head and swirled behind her eyes, and she was giddy from lack of oxygen, because she'd stopped breathing to concentrate on biting and squeezing, even though she didn't need to do that any more, because he was wasn't moving.

It took too long to release her grasp on him. Spasms of pain in her fingers and wrists when she unclenched her hands. Sick, sour blood in her mouth.

A dead man on her kitchen floor.

She couldn't stand on her own, but if she reached up and grabbed the counter, she could pull herself up. She looked down at the man. Eyes open in death. Maybe she should close them, but no, this was a crime scene, wasn't it?

Police. She had to call the police. Her cell phone was in her jeans pocket, but she couldn't get it out, her hands were too shaky. They hurt, too. She couldn't move her fingers without weird daggers of pain in her forearms. Her left thumb was all wrong. She'd use the landline in the living room.

Charlotte picked up the phone and listened to the dial tone. 911, right, only the emergency had passed, and anyway, she'd heard it was better to call the local police station than 911 in an emergency if you knew the number, that they'd be able to get there faster. She didn't know if that was true or not, and in any case she didn't know the number. She called 911.

"911 Emergency." Crisp female voice.

"Yeah, there's a dead man in my apartment. I just killed him." It was hard to talk. Hard to breathe. Why was it so hard to take a full breath? Was she hyperventilating?

"Are you sure he's dead, ma'am?"

"Pretty sure. I strangled him." Wow, that made her sound crazy. It was important to explain that she wasn't, so she kept talking. "He was in my apartment and he stabbed me. . ."

"You've been stabbed?"

272

"Yeah, in my back. And stomach. With a steak knife."

"Stay on the line, ma'am, paramedics and police are on their way. What's your address?"

The gate. The apartment complex had a locked gate in front of the courtyard. The police wouldn't be able to get in.

"Are you still there, ma'am?"

She had to open the gate. She tried to hang up the phone, but couldn't remember where the cradle was for the handset. She set the receiver down on the top of the bookshelf instead. It squawked, like the operator was still trying to talk to her, but she needed to get the gate open.

It was difficult to open her front door. She'd latched it shut. Why'd she do that? She couldn't wrap her hand around the latch. Her thumb wasn't working. Why wasn't it working? She switched hands and yanked it open, then emerged into the dazzling brightness of the sun outside. Couldn't see anything for a long moment, it was all too bright and white. Nobody was in the courtyard, which was good, because she'd just killed someone, and she probably looked like she was totally and completely out of her head.

Sirens in the distance. Good, that'd be for the man lying dead on her kitchen floor, whoever he was. She fumbled with the front gate, trying to get it open, just as someone approached from the other side. Someone dressed in black pants, black shirt. . . Must be a cop because he had a utility belt. Did they call them utility belts, or was she thinking of Batman?

He said something, probably to her, but she couldn't hear it, because all of a sudden he was far away. But she got the gate open, and then she was falling, and maybe he wasn't so far away after all, because even though he sounded like he was talking to her from the moon, he still managed to catch her before she hit the ground.

## Chapter Thirty-Two

A FOGGY PAIN in her head, a need for water so primal it cut through every other waking thought.

Charlotte blinked. Her vision blurred and her eyes burned. At first she thought it was related to her thirst, that her eyeballs were parched like her throat, then she realized she still had her contact lenses in. Felt like they should have come out hours ago. She lifted her hand to rub her eyes. Huh. Her left hand was in a Velcro cast, her thumb supported with an aluminum splint.

How did she get here, wherever this was? No, wait, she knew the answer to that question, and she knew she didn't want to think about it.

Hospital. Lying in a high bed shrouded with curtains; there was a television on somewhere in the room which made her think she wasn't the only occupant, but it hurt too much to figure out where her roommate was in relation to her.

She tilted her head to the side, just a bit. Her neck was stiff, and it felt like she pulled something in her shoulder when she moved. Her right side felt funny. Not painful, not really, but it was notable maybe for the absence of pain: it was where pain should be, and yet wasn't.

A plastic pitcher and a disposable cup rested on a small table to her right. If the pitcher contained water, it'd be a good day. She couldn't sit up—her muscles weren't listening to her brain—but she could reach for the pitcher. Water sloshed inside. Good news.

It'd be better if she could hold the cup in place while she poured, but that was beyond her. It was all she could do now to lift the pitcher one-handed and tilt it in the general direction of the cup. Some of the water splashed onto the table, but some got in the cup. Excellent.

The curtain was pulled back. She found herself looking up at a willowy woman in a plain blue smock. "Hey, there," the woman said. "Didn't realize you were up."

She tried to speak and only coughed. The woman took the cup out of her hand; Charlotte could have cried in frustration, until the woman held it to her lips, one hand lifting her neck, and helped her drink.

The water tasted sour. Maybe that was her mouth. "Thank you," Charlotte said. She glanced about the room. "I'm in a hospital."

"Yeah, you are." The woman smiled. "You're Charlotte, they tell me. I'm Doctor Gott."

"Doctor. . . God?"

"No relation." She glanced at the chart in her hands. "You passed out, more from shock than loss of blood. You've been gouged pretty badly, both in your back and your abdomen, but all we had to do was stitch you up. Broken thumb, too, so we set that. You're going to be fine. How are you feeling?"

Charlotte thought. "A little loopy. How long have I been here?"

"Ambulance brought you in maybe four hours ago. It's just past eight now." She looked at her, considering. "Police want to talk to you."

Police. Yeah, she supposed they would. Here it was, what she didn't want to think about.

Doctor Gott seemed to be waiting for an answer. Charlotte frowned. "Yeah, okay. Do I have to call them?"

"There's an officer posted right outside the door. I'll tell him you're ready to talk."

Posted outside her door. Huh. What did that mean? Was that for her safety, or was that to keep her from going anywhere? Maybe a little of both. She nodded. "Okay, sure."

"We'll get you some dinner first, how's that? Might help you think a little clearer. Anything else you need?"

"Is there some way I can take my contacts out?"

"I think that can be arranged." Doctor Gott smiled, looking both kind and competent. Charlotte wanted to ask if she was the one who stitched her up, because it seemed important to know, but she left the room before she could get her thoughts together.

Dinner was a shrink-wrapped sandwich: two slices of white bread, a slice of ham, a slice of sticky yellow cheese. A plastic cup of fruit cocktail, a carton of milk. She ate every bite, though she wasn't hungry. It was good to have something to focus on: unwrapping, chewing, swallowing. Her still-unseen roommate watched the local news. The sound of the television made her feel panicky, and she wished she could turn it off, or plug her ears, because she was very much afraid she'd hear her name mentioned.

The police officer turned out to be young and handsome, with big arms and a narrow waist. She couldn't be sure of anything, but she had the idea he was the one who'd arrived at the gate when she came out to open it.

"Detective Gutierrez, Wilshire Division," he said. He showed her his badge. She made a token attempt to look at it, because it seemed only polite, but she wasn't processing much.

He put his badge away, pulled the sole chair closer to the bed, and sat down. "You're Charlotte Dent?"

She nodded. "Yeah."

"Had kind of a rough day, Charlotte?"

She nodded again. "Yeah. That guy in my apartment. . ." She trailed off.

Gutierrez leaned a little closer. "What about the guy in your apartment, Charlotte?" Brisk, professional tone.

"Did I kill him?"

"You'd probably know that better than we would at this point, Charlotte. He was dead when I got there, if that's what you're asking. Did you do it?"

"Yeah. He was in my apartment when I got home, I didn't even know he was there until he attacked me." Her voice grew thin and high. She took a deep breath. "Who is. . . was. . . he?"

"You don't know?"

She shook her head. "I've never seen him before."

"You're absolutely sure of that?" He didn't sound like he didn't believe her, which was good. She was in no frame of mind to be arguing her case.

"Yeah. Never. I just got home and he stabbed me." Her eyes were wet. They stung.

Gutierrez waited a second for her to pull herself together. "We haven't identified him yet. No ID on him, none of your neighbors recognized him. Looks like he forced open your bedroom window and got in through there."

She digested this in silence. He continued.

"Got any enemies? Know of anyone who would want to hurt you?"

She shook her head. "No, no one at all."

"Your neighbors said you were an actress. You get any crazy stalkers or anything?"

Her neighbors knew she was an actress? She hadn't really met any of them yet, other than exchanging passing greetings. Weird to think they'd know her business. "I'm not famous or anything. No one knows who I am. It's not like I get fan mail." She started crying. Gee, she hoped this nice police officer wouldn't think she was bawling because she didn't get fan mail.

"Okay, Charlotte. Okay." He cleared his throat. "You got family in town, anyone?"

Her parents didn't know she was here. She had been stabbed, maybe could have died, and they didn't know. She shook her head.

He flipped his notebook closed. "We'll know more when we ID this guy. He might be some kind of druggie, maybe broke into your house looking for stuff to steal and you interrupted him."

She was silent. He shifted in his chair.

"We're going to need to get a statement from you, but that can hold until you're doing a little better. If you think of anything else, let us know, okay?" He left his card on her nightstand.

She nodded. Her nose started to run, and she couldn't wipe it because that would draw attention to how close she was to losing it. She looked down at the antiseptic white coverlet, at her pale arms. Her skin looked bad. Red bumps on white skin. Dry and old.

Gutierrez left without saying anything else, probably embarrassed by her tears. She settled back in the bed. Her unseen neighbor in the next bed changed the channel to a game show. From her perspective, she could only see a wrist clutching a remote, resting on the metal arm of the bed. The arm looked old and frail. Like her own.

They made her stay overnight. She would have raised a fuss, because it was no fun being in a hospital, but she didn't want to be out in the outside world, either.

Morning. She could go home today, if they let her. Somebody would come by and tell her when she could go, right? She had never been in a hospital before. What was the protocol?

From her bed, she could turn her head to the side and look out the window. An expanse of sky, bright white, with the outline of the sun trying to burn through the smog. The sky frightened her in some foolish and primal way. It looked too much like the sky in Queen of Angels, the post-apocalyptic haze over a ruined city.

The day dragged on. She didn't watch television, didn't read the newspapers on her nightstand, didn't talk to anyone beyond answering the cheery questions of the nurse who came in to check on her. She asked him when she could go home; the nurse said that wasn't something he handled, and that she'd have to wait for the doctor. Charlotte tried to sleep and couldn't. The sour smell of her attacker, the sensation of biting through skin and muscle, all that waited for her in the dark.

She was lonely. Horribly lonely. She missed Simon, so much the thought of him made her cry. She couldn't tell if she was missing him, actually, or just missing the idea of him. Probably the latter, though it didn't seem to make too much difference right now.

Footsteps in the hall. Rick at the door. Rick? Wearing an expensive suit and tie, carrying something she couldn't identify. A large red cardboard box.

He smiled when he saw her. "Hey. Up for visitors?"

"What are you doing here?" She struggled to sit up. "How'd you know I was here?" Oh, God, it had been in the news. She'd have to call her parents, before someone else told them.

He set the box down on her nightstand and settled himself into the bedside chair. "Nice police detective called the office this morning. SAG gave him my name. Just wanted to know if I had any thoughts as to why anyone would want to try to stab you to death, that's all." He shook his head. "And here I thought you were just ignoring my calls. Been kind of pissed at you, I lined up a meeting for you at Paramount this morning. Left a message and never heard back from you. Guess you had a good excuse, huh?" He glanced around the room, then back at her. "You doing okay?"

"Yeah. I'm fine."

"You don't know who it was?"

She shook her head. "Some random guy. The police think it might have been some druggie, just breaking into my place." Her voice grew high. She took a deep breath. "What's that?" she asked, nodding toward the box.

"This, little lady, is for you." The box was tied with a pink satin bow. Rick untied it, then pulled out a small tower of miniature cupcakes on a Lucite stand. "I thought food might be more welcome than flowers right now."

She glanced at them, pretty as gems, every one different and topped with colorful decorations. Glazed cherries, coconut, fresh raspberries. "Those look great. Thank you."

"Here." Rick plucked the one from the uppermost layer and handed it to her. Topped with cocoa powder and a fine layer of gold dust. "Tiramisu."

She didn't want it, wasn't feeling like she could eat anything, but she didn't want to be impolite, so she peeled back the wrapper and nibbled an edge. Cocoa and mascarpone dusted her cheeks. It was so good it made her feel lightheaded. She wolfed it down. Amazing to live in a world where anything could taste so wonderful and vibrant.

Rick watched her. "So they said you killed the guy."

"Yes." She set the empty wrapper on the table. She was betting that closest cupcake, the one with the cherries, was black forest. She loved black forest cake.

"Did you mean to?" Rick asked.

"Yes. I think so. He was trying to kill me."

"Good thing he didn't," Rick said. His tone was light. He looked at the ceiling, then faced her. "This hasn't been in the news yet, you know."

"Good," she said.

Rick shrugged. "If it was, maybe some good could come of this." At her look, he continued. "I've got friends at the *Times*, the local stations. They'd be sympathetic to you. It's a hell of a story, you know. It'd sure as hell get your name out there."

She looked at him. "No."

"It wouldn't be exploitative at all, just the honest facts. You'd get a lot of sympathy and support."

He was right, of course, and it was probably a sign of her lack of gumption that the idea was so repellent. "No."

"Okay. Your call." He looked around the room. "I should get back to the office. Anything you need here? Books or movies or anything? Xbox?"

"No, I'm good. I'm almost out of here. Thanks for the offer. And thanks for stopping by." She paused. "Rick. . ."

"Let me guess. Don't tell anyone about this. Wouldn't dream of it." He got to his feet. "Rest easy and mend up, okay? Give me a call when you're out of here and ready to start working again."

It would be a while. Rick looked like he knew that. She nodded and watched as he left.

## CHAPTER THIRTY-THREE

HER APARTMENT LOOKED dingy. She'd only lived here a few months, damn it. At least it was no longer a crime scene; the police had done all they needed. No blood; someone must've done some cleaning. What did her neighbors know about it? Had they talked about it, compared notes on what they knew about her? Did they think she'd brought it upon herself—a drug habit, a penchant for rough sex, some other seedy little secret?

The first night in her apartment after leaving the hospital was the worst. It was a hot evening; her apartment was stuffy and stale, but she didn't dare open the window. She had an air conditioner that she'd yet to use; when she tested it after moving in, it rattled ominously and gave off a smell of burning chemicals. Eventually, she broke down and turned it on.

Lying in bed, she thought she smelled a electrical fire. She thought she heard someone outside her bedroom window, she thought she saw a movement in the hallway outside her door. She was ashamed by how frightened and needy and helpless she felt, but she wanted someone with her. Again, she thought of Simon. She hugged a pillow to her chest and cried a little, weak and worthless and lonely.

She went grocery shopping in the morning. Driving in her car was okay, sealed inside a protective, air conditioned bubble. As soon as she stepped out onto the parking lot, waves of heat radiating off the asphalt hit her like a blow. She was too exposed under that bright white sky. She forced herself to walk across the hot pavement into the cold sanctuary of the supermarket, her heart pounding with unspecific dread.

She had to get out of Los Angeles.

Lieutenant Gutierrez took his iced tea with lots of sugar. Charlotte watched him stir his glass, the sugar swirling in patterns. It wouldn't dissolve in the icy liquid; by the time he got to the bottom, there'd be an inch of sugary sludge. Maybe that was the way he liked it.

She looked up from the photograph he'd passed over to her. "That's him, huh?"

"That's him." He set the glass down and looked at her. "Frank Gainsborough. Mild schizophrenic. Lived at a halfway house on Olympic, not far from here. The house reported him missing last week. One of their aides made a positive ID this morning."

She looked at the photograph. He looked harmless. Unsmiling, but nice. Pale blue eyes, short blond hair. "Why'd he break into my place? Was he trying to rob me?"

"Probably. Hard to say right now." Gutierrez looked old all of a sudden. "He had a record of breaking and entering, plus an old assault charge related to a burglary attempt. So there's a pattern there. I'd say yeah, it was just chance he picked this place, but the guy he shared a room with said he'd seen that movie you did. *Queen of Angels?* Guess he talked about it a bunch. So maybe there's a connection there. Could be a crazy fan. Probably isn't, probably random, but we'll look into it." He looked at her. "You're not unlisted, you know. Probably should be. He could've found your home address easily enough. He never contacted you? Sent you letters, anything like that?"

"Never." She looked at the table. It was worse, somehow, to think maybe it hadn't been random. That this man—Frank Gainsborough?—had maybe known who she was and hated her enough to stab her.

He cleared his throat. "Just as a heads up, the more people know about this, the more likely it is to make the news. Pretty actress gets stabbed, even if no one knows you, that's something the press might want to run with. It might not, you know, but I don't want you to get blindsided if the story breaks."

Then instead of the actress who worked on a broken leg, she'd be the actress who killed someone. That would be her niche. The thought was dirty, almost pornographic. She didn't say anything, just nodded.

"You doing okay about all this?"

She nodded. "Sure," she said. "What happens now?"

"We work on closing our file. You get on with your life." He almost smiled. "I saw that movie with my son, you know. Wouldn't have recognized you at all."

"What'd you think?"

He shrugged. "My son liked it. He's fourteen. You were his favorite character." Fourteen. That seemed to be her demographic. "Me, I thought it was too violent. I see enough of the real thing every day, I don't need to see it onscreen. I like comedies." He thought for a moment. "Lot of fight scenes in that. You know martial arts or something?"

"Most of that was a stunt double," she said. "I had a trainer on set who taught me some stuff, though."

"Good thing he did. Seems to have come in handy. Might've saved your life." He pushed his chair back. "Get your number unlisted as soon as you can, okay? And ask your landlord about getting bars on your windows. This neighborhood maybe isn't as good as you think it is." He stood. "Thanks for the tea, Charlotte. Take care of yourself."

She walked with him to the gate. "Am I still needed in this, or is it okay if I leave town for a while?"

"You can leave. Do me a favor, though, and give me a call first to let me know where you're going to be. Is it work?"

"No. Just thought I might need to take a break." Simon. London. "I might leave the country, would that be a problem?"

"That should be fine. Might do you some good." He smiled then. Lines around his eyes. "Might be the best thing in the world for you."

As soon as Gutierrez was gone, she went online. Simon was in London; he was doing a play, wasn't he? What play, what theater, where? It was her first, best chance of finding him.

So many results, none of them what she needed. Oh, message boards. She had never wanted to visit these again, and yet here she was, because they knew more about Simon than she did.

Joegirl. Charlotte saw the name and flashed upon an image of Christie, pretty Christie, filled with so much wrath toward her. What did Joegirl have to say?

*He's in a play in London at the Shaw Theatre,* Joegirl had posted. *It started last month. He's been getting good reviews for it. My brother's ex girlfriend lives in London and she saw it and said he's really AMAZING in it.*

Well, thank you, Joegirl. That was a remarkably useful bit of information. Did the Shaw have a website? Why yes, it did. And here it was: Simon Oliver in *The Twilight Butler*.

She felt a ripple up her spine, like she'd been electrocuted. She didn't believe in fate, or karma, or kismet, but it was even harder to believe this didn't mean something: Simon in that play, her old, botched play, right now. She could find him. She could visit him.

Should she, though? That was tougher. There was no reason to think he'd want to see her. More to the point, there was no reason she should want to see him, either, after the way he'd extricated himself from her life without explanation. Maybe that was the most pressing reason to see him. Maybe she deserved an explanation.

Maybe she was kidding herself. Maybe she just wanted to see him because she didn't have anyone else.

She booked a flight to London, leaving the following week. She felt sick and terrible immediately after purchasing the ticket. This was weird, this was wrong, this was kind of scary. But it was set in motion, and she was going to do this.

By the time she arrived at Heathrow, she felt sore and dehydrated and bleary. Her shoulder hurt, which made her wonder if she was pushing it, traveling so soon after her injury. She couldn't use the shoulder strap on her bag because of her stitches, or carry it with her left hand because of the splint on her thumb. An interminable time at Customs later, she stepped outside, groggy and dispirited, breathing in the heavy air.

London was dark and wet. She arrived in late morning, and it looked like twilight. The air was so full of moisture she couldn't tell if it was still raining or if it had recently stopped.

She checked into her hotel. Small. Drab. Expensive. She found the Shaw Theatre, which looked how a London theater should.

Stone and mortar, Victorian or earlier, the name of the play on a small marquee. This evening's show was sold out, but she purchased a single ticket from the box office for the following night.

The ticket was a valuable possession, more important right now than her passport or credit card. She tucked it away her purse, aware her heart was racing a little. It was no guarantee of anything. Simon might call in sick tomorrow and his understudy might do the part. But then again, she might see him, tomorrow.

She was really becoming a stalker these days, wasn't she? First she'd tracked down poor Joegirl; now she'd come halfway around the world, a lovestruck dupe in pursuit of the guy who'd broken up with her without a word of explanation.

Well, it was done. She was here, the ticket was bought. Nothing left to do but go back to her hotel room with the lopsided bed and the coverlet that smelled of other people and go to sleep.

## CHAPTER THIRTY-FOUR

LONDON MIGHT BE more fun with a friend, or a loved one. Charlotte would have to remember that for next time. Then again, London was a fabulous city for melancholy wanderings, which was how she spent her day. She sat by the Thames, she ambled down cobblestone streets, she looked into shops. She bought tea and a minted lamb pasty for lunch.

It rained, or misted, or fogged throughout the day. She had an umbrella, but she never got the hang of figuring out what was rain and what was just extra-soggy fog, so it stayed in the bottom of her purse. Her wool coat grew damp and heavy.

She arrived at the theater too early and loitered outside in the rain for too long. Her hands went numb; her nose ran. An anxious knot somewhere in her intestines threatened to manifest itself into gastrointestinal unpleasantness.

When the theater opened at last, she was one of the first inside. It filled up with an eclectic crowd. Pretty young women in stylish tartan slickers, old men in their best suits, their wives in pressed shirtwaists.

She took a look at the program. Simon Oliver, there was his name right there.

A young hellion squeezed his way along the narrow row of seats, ticket in hand. He plopped into the seat beside her. "Evening," he said, nodding. "Got in a bit of wet out there, did you?" He motioned to her damp hair.

She could feel herself turning red. "I guess I did. It was hard to tell if it was raining or not."

He grinned. A wide, pleasant face with lots of freckles, peroxide white hair with sandy brown roots. Short leather jacket and heavy buckled boots. Was this a real, genuine London punk? "American, right? Been with us for long?"

"I just arrived yesterday."

"What part of the US are you from, then?" he asked.

She was tempted to lie. Detroit, Miami, Boston, Wichita. "Los Angeles," she said.

"Hollywood, eh?" He grinned and looked beyond her to the empty seat on her other side. "You on your own, then?"

She should make up a boyfriend, husband, an older brother in the lobby, anyone. "Yeah."

"Ah." He examined her. She felt small and soggy under his stare. "Just taking in a bit of theater, right?"

"Just that," she said.

"I hear the play's good," he said. "You hear anything?"

"No. Just that it's good," she said. He was looking at her expectantly, so she elaborated. "I read something about it in the newspaper and thought it sounded interesting."

"Ah," he said. He nodded, and somehow she had the feeling he knew she was lying.

A middle-aged couple made their way down the row. They looked at their tickets in consternation. A whispered conversation, then the husband tapped on the young man's shoulder. "Excuse me."

He glanced over at them and grinned. "Is this you? Sorry." He turned back to Charlotte. "Suppose they'll be wanting their seats, then." He got to his feet and climbed over the chair in front of him to clear the row. "Nice chatting with you." He touched his hand to his forehead and started down the aisle toward his real seat several rows ahead.

So he'd just been trying to pick her up. Not the worst idea ever. Maybe a fling in London was what she needed to get this misery about Simon out of her system. It'd have to be a different Charlotte to do something like that, though. Maybe that was a pity.

Maybe she should watch the play. The curtain rose.

Impossible not to compare this to her own fragmented, still-born production of the same play. Her heart started thumping in advance of Simon's first entrance. She knew this script still, every line and every cue, so she was ready when he came onstage.

Simon. Beautiful Simon. He had the lead, of course, the dual role, nobleman and lower-class imposter. What was the name of the guy who'd had it in her production? Jeff? Was that it?

He was submerged in the character, no trace of his real self showing. If his face and voice hadn't been so familiar, and so dear, she wouldn't have recognized him. A spoiled young nobleman, murdered and replaced by his doppelganger, a butler on the make, he handled both roles with equal finesse. Simon was a gifted, trained actor, in a way she herself was not, no matter how much she'd learned from drama school and local theater. Strange and melancholy, this mix of jealousy and pride and loss.

The actress who played Annemarie was lovely. Had she been the girl in the photo with Simon? Charlotte thought she might be. According to the program, her name was Camille Caldwell. Camille was fine—Charlotte found it hard to be objective about her, but she couldn't grade her any higher than fine. Was she better than Charlotte in the role? Maybe, maybe not. She was fine, but it was difficult to pay attention to anyone but Simon.

She cried at the end, unexpectedly. She tried her best to hide it, because no one around her seemed to be crying and she felt awkward and unseemly in a sea of stiff upper lips. When Simon came out for the curtain call, she thought her wrists would be paralyzed from clapping.

Everyone gathered their belongings and streamed toward the exits. Well. That was it, then. She had gone to London, she'd seen Simon, and now she was devastated. She wiped her face on the damp sleeve of her coat and kept her head down as she joined the surge.

A hand on her wrist, irritating and, in light of recent events, frightening. She yanked it away and turned.

Her young punk friend had come up behind her. "You going backstage?" he asked.

She stared at him, confused for a moment. "I don't know. Can we?" Was it obvious she'd been crying? Probably, yeah, but he'd assume it was because of the play, which it was, and that she was one of those hyper-emotional Americans, which she was.

"It can't hurt to try, can it? All they can do is throw us out."

She paused. They were blocking the aisle, and they were getting dirty looks.

"No. I need to get back to my hotel," she said. She couldn't see Simon. She'd look crazy, even if she managed to convince him she hadn't come to England for the sole purpose of tracking him down, which, of course, was exactly what she'd done. He was in his element here, something extraordinary and rarified, whereas she was a product of Los Angeles, dull and interchangeable. The chasm between them would destroy her.

Also, he probably didn't want to see her. She shouldn't want to see him, either. That she did was her problem, and something she should probably get over, preferably without making a fool of herself any more than she already had.

"Come on. Just for a second." He tugged on her coat sleeve.

The physical contact pissed her off. "No. I'm sorry. No," she said, and yanked her arm away.

She turned and headed toward the exit before he could protest. He wouldn't come after her. She'd be lost in the crowd, and then she'd be out of the theater, and then she'd be alone.

It was dark and pouring outside. Crap.

The tube station was six blocks away. No distance at all during the day, but right now it seemed insurmountable. She got her umbrella out of her purse—still damp, and it had made the contents of her purse damp as well—unfolded it, and started walking.

Wait. This wasn't right. The station should be here, shouldn't it? This was where she'd arrived earlier this evening, four blocks over, two blocks up from the theater.

Or had she gone five blocks instead, and now she needed to double back? Nothing looked familiar—she would have remembered that pub, surely, or the Pizza Hut (*Pizza Hut?*) on the corner.

She'd managed to get lost in six blocks. Impressive. Not a crisis situation, obviously; she had to be in the right general area. Just a matter of doubling back and figuring out where she'd gone wrong. It'd be easier if it weren't dark and rainy, but she'd straighten herself out.

Back a block, then two. . . No. She'd strayed off course somewhere, and now she was making it worse. Was her sense of direction that bad? She was on a residential street now, and that was no good. Better to get back to the shops and work her way back to the theater if she could. Then she could take out her map and puzzle it out from there.

Ah. A school, dark and empty. She remembered seeing this building before. Good. Familiar territory. It looked like an elementary school from the construction paper drawings taped to the windows of a classroom. Probably didn't call them elementary schools here. Grammar school? Was that it? A dark stone building, somehow creepy and cozy at once. Might be a couple centuries old. That was the amazing thing about London: Things were old, in a way nothing in California or Idaho was old. Her elementary school had been built in the early seventies, a low, flat, beige building with pasteboard tiles on the ceilings.

A dog barked, very close. She looked around, but she was alone on the street.

Another bark. She glanced down. The windows on the ground floor of the school had high wells around them, maybe five feet deep, iron railings at the top to keep the students from climbing into them. They probably climbed in them anyway; she would have wanted to, back when she was in school.

There was a dog at the bottom of the well. A terrier, it looked like. Soggy and miserable, standing in a puddle, trapped. Poor guy.

The classroom windows could be opened from the inside, which would be the easiest way of freeing the dog, but the school was closed and empty. Probably no one would come to open it until morning, which wouldn't do the dog much good.

She looked about. No, she was still by herself.

She couldn't leave the dog trapped. If she climbed down there, she'd be able to hoist it to safety, then she could grab the bars and pull herself up. What with the splint on her thumb, her left hand wasn't all it could be, but she could manage this.

She'd be trespassing, but she could do it quickly and no one would see her. Plus, she had an obvious mission here—rescuing a small, furry, helpless, adorable animal—and she probably didn't seem much like the criminal type anyway. She folded her umbrella and laid it on the ground.

She climbed over the low fence. The dog stopped yapping and stared up at her, blinking into the rain. She crouched down and hopped into the well, several paces away from the dog.

Ugh. She'd thought her shoes—heeled loafers, practical enough for walking about, useless in a London rain—were already as wet as they could get. She'd been wrong. She landed in four inches of water and mud.

The dog yapped at her. She crouched down.

"Are you going to let me pick you up?" she asked. "I'm going to have to do that if I'm going to get you out of here."

He kept barking. Splendid. She extended a hand. He shimmied away from her.

"Oh, come on!" she said. It was cold and wet, and she was in a London gutter. She stepped forward and grabbed the dog, hoping he wouldn't bite.

He was too surprised to bark. Then he wagged its tail. He burrowed against her and pressed his soggy head against the front of her coat.

"Okay, sweetie. Okay." It felt good, this sudden rush of unadulterated affection. Reminded her how love-starved she'd been lately. Maybe she should have just adopted a puppy. Maybe that's all she needed. Would have been cheaper than this jaunt to London. "Here you go."

She lifted him over her head and released him on the ledge surrounding the well. He wriggled through the bars and ran off, yipping. She could hear him retreating until his barks faded into the night.

Well, he was on his own. She'd done her part. Now to get out of here.

She grabbed on to the lowest part of the railing, using just her right hand and the four fingers of her left. The railing was too slick and her hands were too numb to get a good grip. It was painful to try.

Damn it, what could she do? No sense in panicking; she wasn't in any trouble. She took off her coat, her soggy, sopping coat, and tossed it up over the bars, keeping hold of one sleeve.

There. Now she just had to reach the other sleeve. . . She stood on tiptoes and groped up for it.

Oh. That was a problem. Her abdomen and shoulder sent out prickly needles of pain. She'd forgotten about her stitches.

No alternative, she had to get out of here. She grabbed onto both arms of the coat with both hands and pulled up, intending to walk herself up the wall.

Up one step, two. . . If she did this right, she'd be able to grab the railing and swing her legs up above the top of the well, and from there she'd be home free.

Her hands felt like they were tearing, cold wet flesh on wet wool. It hurt too much. She had to let go.

She couldn't get her legs down off the wall fast enough. She fell back onto her ass in the mud.

A spasm through her torso, from tailbone to shoulder. God, that hurt. Did she break something? Was she paralyzed, even? No— mild injuries in cold weather always felt worse than they were. She stayed where she was for a long moment, assessing her condition, before she dared to move.

She got to her feet. Her shoulder hurt, and she thought she might've torn some skin from her hands, and she'd probably have a nice bruise on her tailbone, but nothing was broken. Her stitches weren't pulled, though they sent her sharp reminders she was a fool for getting herself into this situation.

Somebody would have to help her out. It was humiliating, the idea of yelling for help, but the alternative involved spending the night here.

"Help!" she called. Her voice sounded feeble in the rain. "I'm stuck down here. Is there anybody around?"

No response. She tried again, louder. "Help!"

"Hello? Is there somebody there?" A young male voice. From the sidewalk, maybe. Her heart leapt.

"I'm in the window well. Over here!" she called.

A fair head popped over the side, looking down at her. "Good God, it's you."

It was her punk friend from the theater. He looked astonished, eyes wide, then he broke into a grin. He turned. "Simon, it's Charlotte!"

There were too many things in that sentence she couldn't process.

Simon, in the rain, stared down at her. "Charlotte? What are you doing here?"

In London, or in the window well? "There was a dog trapped down here. I got him out, but now I can't climb up."

"Here." Her punk lay belly-first down on the wet sidewalk and extended his arms through the bars. "Grab my hands. We'll pull you up."

"I can't," she said. "I have stitches in my shoulder."

He stared down at her, uncomprehending. Then he nodded and got to his feet.

"Coming down," he said. He climbed over the bars and hopped down in one smooth motion. He beamed at her. "Hello, again."

He squatted down, linking his fingers together and offering his hands as a makeshift stepstool. "Will you be able to do this? Where are your stitches?"

"Right shoulder and my stomach," she said.

He looked up. "Grab her left arm only, right, Simon?"

Simon nodded, looking confused and worried and totally incompetent. She'd missed that look.

She stepped onto the punk's clasped hands, ashamed of her muddy shoes, and let him give her a boost. She reached up and took hold of the bars. Her hands were too cold and numb to get a good grasp, but that was okay, because the punk supported her from below, and now Simon had a hold of her arm.

She stepped up to the rim of the well and, with Simon's guidance, climbed over the low railing. She was coatless and freezing. She shuddered in a sudden gust of rain-wet wind. Simon, well-intentioned but never demonstrative, hesitated, then folded her in his arms.

He wasn't warm—his coat was heavy and wet, and she couldn't feel any of his body heat through it—but just the sensation of his arms around her helped.

"Are you all right?" he asked, his mouth next to her ear.

She didn't trust herself to speak, so she just nodded.

The young punk swung himself up out of the gutter with an ease that made her feel incompetent and inadequate. He stared at the two of them, bemused. He should be included in this—they hadn't even been introduced, and he'd been hugely instrumental in her rescue. More, he had some kind of important link to Simon, and therefore he had and important link to her, but in order to introduce herself, she'd have to let go of Simon.

## CHAPTER THIRTY-FIVE

SHE STARTED CRYING. It shocked Simon. He pulled back. "Charlotte?" he asked.

She shook her head. "Sorry. I'm fine."

The young punk ambled over. "Told you it was her," he said to Simon. "Didn't believe me, did you?"

"Charlotte, this is Alex. Alex, Charlotte."

"Oh, yeah, we've met," Alex said. "Hello, Charlotte."

"Hi." Alex. A name on Simon's cell phone, his flatmate, a part of his life she knew little about. "Thanks for getting me out of there."

"No worries." Alex made a disapproving noise at her appearance. "You came out here without a coat?"

"No, it's over there." She glanced at where it was draped over the iron bars. Better to leave it where it was, soaked and ruined.

Simon picked it up. He grimaced at the sodden material, then shrugged off his own coat. "Here," he said.

"I can't take your coat," she said.

"You can. You must. You're freezing half to death," he said. He draped it around her shoulders. She slipped her arms into the sleeves. He looked at her. "What are you doing here? Did you come to see me?"

She shook her head. "I don't know. I think so, but not really."

"Clears it right up." Alex looked up at the sky. "Do you suppose we can do this inside?"

"Our flat's not far from here. Do you want to come with us? You can dry off there," Simon said.

It sounded like the best possible idea, since she wasn't sure she could make it back to her hotel before she froze to death. Simon, coatless, slid an arm around her shoulders, carrying her soggy coat in his free hand.

They turned the corner, and there was the theater, marquee still lit up. She was never going to find her way around London, ever.

A moment's wait, and Simon bundled her into the backseat of a shiny black taxicab and climbed in after her, Alex on her other side. It was warm and secure, snuggled between them, and it was almost a disappointment when the driver pulled up in front of a small two-story building. She couldn't see much of it in the dark and the rain.

Simon hustled her up a flight of stairs and unlocked the door at the top. He fumbled around for the light switch, movements hampered by his grip on her hand. "Here we are," he said.

It was cute. Small: a living room, an attached kitchen. A short hall at the back. An unused fireplace, a small blue sofa, mismatched arm chairs. Framed theater posters on the wall. Productions he'd admired, or productions he'd been in? They might be Alex's, too—was Alex an actor as well?

She slipped off her wet loafers and left them beside the door. Simon hung up her soaked coat, then helped her out of his. "Let's get you into a hot bath, eh?" he said.

The fulfillment of every possible wish. "If I could. That would be great," she said.

He nodded at the splint on her thumb. "What happened to your hand?"

"Oh. Broke my thumb," she said. She shrugged. "It's almost healed."

He looked at her for a moment. "You said something about stitches?" he asked.

"Yeah. Don't worry about it, it's nothing bad. It's fine."

He looked worried anyway, but said nothing. She let him lead her down the hall to the bathroom. Huge old raised tub with peeling paint, a tile floor in need of patching, threadbare towels on the rack. "I should warn you, the hot water supply is not all it could be. The robe behind the door is mine if you want to use that."

"Okay. Thanks, Simon."

He wanted to say more, it was written on his face, but he leaned forward and gave her a kiss on the top of her wet hair instead and left her alone.

She undressed and examined her stitches. Her wounds looked red against her clammy white skin, but they weren't bleeding or oozing. If she stayed out of gutters from here on out, they'd be fine.

The water couldn't get hot enough for her needs, and after a few inches, it ran tepid. She washed quickly, then toweled off and tied the heavy blue robe from the back of the door around herself. She hung her wet clothes over the shower curtain rod to dry.

She came back out into the living room. Simon sat on the floor in front of the unlit fireplace, his long legs drawn up close to his body. He looked up at her. "Better, then?"

"Much." She sat down on the sofa and pulled the bathrobe tighter around her, aware of her bare legs and dripping hair. Simon glanced over at her and smiled, but didn't say anything.

Alex emerged from the kitchen, bearing a cup of tea in a chipped mug. He set it down on the end table beside her. "Here you go. Warm you through."

"Thank you." She picked it up, cupping both hands around it for the heat, then took a sip. Hot and strong and sweet. She went to set the mug down, then paused.

The end table was decorated with her face. Jin's face, to be exact, a full-color photo from *Queen of Angels*. She looked closer.

The entire surface of the table was decoupaged with newspaper clippings from the film. Magazine articles, too, maybe some articles printed off the internet, all covered with layers of glossy lacquer until they looked yellowed and aged and the surface was smooth and shiny. She looked up at Alex and Simon.

Simon looked embarrassed. "It was Alex's idea," he said.

"Reviews of *Queen of Angels*. Simon was collecting them, God only knows why. I thought we should do something useful with them."

The reviews. Those terrible, crippling reviews. "Is this healthy?" she asked.

"I don't imagine so, no," Simon said, but he was smiling.

"It's brilliant," Alex said. "Converting that trash into a thing of beauty and a joy forever." He shrugged, pleased with himself. "And it was the only way to keep Simon from obsessing about them. Not that I blame him, really. Christ, they were harsh."

Alex sat down in an armchair and crossed his legs. He'd taken his heavy boots off. His socks were fuzzy and striped. "You shouldn't have been reading them anyway," he said to Simon. "Should know better than that. It can't help you."

Simon just shrugged, then turned to Charlotte. "Alex and I were thinking of going in search of our dinner. Are you up to going out?"

"There's an Indian place not far from here," Alex said.

She didn't want to go back out into the cold, wet night. Her clothes were still wet, her shoes would be miserable. But Simon hadn't had dinner yet, Alex either, and her unscheduled visit was throwing their routine into a tizzy. "I'd be up for it. Sure."

Alex and Simon looked relieved, and she knew she'd said the right thing. She took a long, restorative swig of tea and got to her feet. "I suppose I'd have to get dressed, right?"

"If you must stand on formality," Alex said.

Simon stood up. "Are your clothes still wet? I might have something you can wear."

She padded down the hall in her bare feet after him. Simon's bedroom looked like it belonged to a college kid. Mattress on the floor, a dresser piled high with unfolded socks, stacks of plays on the bookshelf. Open closet door with most of his clothes, his expensive, tasteful, designer wardrobe, off the hangers in a pile on the floor.

Simon was sloppy. Huh. How come she didn't know that about him? His hotel room had always been immaculate. Of course he'd had housekeeping service there.

He flushed. "Sorry. Excuse the mess, please," he said. "I didn't realize you'd be here. Obviously."

He rooted through the pile of clothes and handed her a black cashmere sweater, socks, and a pair of his jeans. "These will swim on you, but I've got a belt if you need it."

"Thank you," she said. She took the clothes from him. He hesitated.

"I'm glad you came," he said at last. "It's good seeing you." He smiled and nodded once and backed out of the room.

She retrieved her underthings from the bathroom. The thin nylon had almost dried already. The sweater was thick and soft. The jeans were an okay fit; Simon, with his narrow hips and tiny waist, wasn't that much larger than she was. Embarrassing. The loaned socks were cashmere, or a cashmere blend, and were toasty warm; sticking them inside her clammy loafers seemed almost a criminal offense. Simon loaned her a slicker, something vinyl and sturdy, and they were off.

It stopped raining. They walked to the Tube station. She tried to keep track of streets, just in case she got separated from them, but it was too hard to concentrate on where they were going and pay attention to Alex and Simon's lively chatter at the same time.

The Tube. Watching Simon in the station, on his home turf, slipping his ticket through the turnstile, shepherding her through before him. His motions quick and confident, his manner easygoing, none of the hesitation he showed in Los Angeles or during their trip to New York. He was a different person here, stronger and more real and yet distant. Thinking too much about it made her feel melancholy.

The train arrived. They got on. She nestled in between them on one of the benches, sleepy and exhausted and lost in her thoughts. Too much effort to pay attention to where they were going; she eventually decided to trust her guides not to lead her astray.

The restaurant was located in a neighborhood called Primrose Hill. The hostess was tall and beautiful, long dark hair and an amethyst-colored sari. She knew Alex and Simon on sight and presented her flawless cheek to receive kisses. Soon they were settled into a corner booth with glasses of a very good red wine and platters of hot spiced foods. Lentils and spinach, flat bread, spiced chunks of pumpkin, chickpeas and cauliflower. The wine and food restored her to life and made her sleepier all at once.

"So why are you here, Charlotte?" Alex asked. He winked. "Are you stalking Simon?"

"Alex. . ." Simon glared at him.

She smiled, lazy from the wine. "Stalking is such an ugly word," she said. "I heard you were doing a play and I thought I'd see you. I'm glad I did. You were wonderful."

"Thank you." Simon smiled. "I talked with Ted last month. He said you were in Harris Holt's new film?"

Had Simon asked after her, or had Ted volunteered the information on his own? She finished her wine. Alex refilled her glass without asking. Good. There was a second bottle already on the table, and it would be most welcome. "Well, I was. I was fired halfway through the shoot. They wrote my character out of the script."

"That wasn't very nice of them," Simon said.

"I didn't think so, no." She shrugged. "Things happen. It's fine. I thought I'd better get out of Los Angeles for a while to clear my head. So. . . here I am."

Simon's brows drew together. "What's this about stitches?"

"Oh." She took a bite of the spinach to give herself time to get her answer together. Spicy and warm and seasoned with things she couldn't begin to figure out. How come spinach couldn't always taste this good? "Yeah. It's nothing much."

She thought Simon and Alex might have exchanged glances, but she was looking at her plate so she couldn't be sure. Time to move onto safer ground. She looked up. "So how do you know each other?"

"Drama school," Alex said. "Hit it off, roomed together to save expenses, been living together ever since."

"We've been in, what, seven plays together since graduation?" Simon said.

"Eight, if you count that workshop for the RSC, though that wasn't a full-scale production. Just felt like one."

She didn't think she'd been in eight plays total since graduation. "How many plays have you done, altogether?" she asked them.

Simon shrugged. "Maybe thirty? Three a year since graduation, just about? Some years are better than others. Alex has done more than I have."

"That year you were doing *House of Medici* you barely did anything outside of that," Alex said. "That kept you busy. And then of course this last year, while you were faffing about in Hollywood. . ." He rolled his eyes.

Thirty plays. Yeesh. No wonder Simon was so much better than she was. If she stopped and thought about it, all her underproductive years of crummy day jobs would really start to depress her.

"I keep telling Alex he should move to Hollywood and try his luck there," Simon said. "I think they'd love him."

"And it's worked out so well for you." Alex said it lightly, but there was a bit of acid behind it.

Simon tilted his head to the side, considering. "I'm going to go back," he said. "After the play ends its run. Should be only another month. My American agent said he's received a lot of inquiries about me since *Queen of Angels* opened."

Alex didn't say anything, but what he thought about that was clear on his face.

Later on, after the second bottle was empty and Simon had excused himself to visit the loo, she found herself alone with Alex. "I take it you don't think Simon moving back to Los Angeles is a good idea," she said.

Alex considered. "Don't know. Don't know. His last splash in the pond seems to have really done a job on him." He looked at her. "I thought it was you at first. I thought you'd screwed him over somehow. I was all prepared to hate you. Then I saw you at the theater, and you looked so miserable, and you were planning on leaving without ever seeing him, and I figured you were probably all right."

"I don't really know what happened to him," she said. "He just left. I know he was unhappy, but he didn't say why, and he didn't talk about it." She shrugged. "So he left. The next thing I heard, he was in London."

"Yeah. Communication's not really his forte," Alex said. "Yours either, I'm guessing. Between the two of you, you should probably try to find some way around that. If he's going back there, I want him to have someone he can trust. Otherwise he's just going to let the little stuff eat at him."

"What's eating at me?" Simon asked, sliding back into his seat beside her.

"What makes you think we were talking about you? Self-centered much?" Alex settled back in the booth. "I was just telling Charlotte here that you two might want to consider talking to each other before scampering off to other countries. And you've got to stop reading your reviews. And develop a thicker skin while you're at it."

Simon rolled his eyes. "I won't read reviews anymore, I promise. But I don't want to develop a thicker skin." He picked up his glass of wine, those pretty eyes suddenly very focused. "I don't ever want to get to the state where someone telling me I suck doesn't affect me."

Charlotte thought about that. There was something there, something Simon wasn't capable of putting into words very well, that might be the germ of something important. Maybe something about his acting process, how he was capable of turning out those amazing performances. She thought back to him at the Getty, staring at the paintings, unaware of anything else. He narrowed in so much on things, focused on and obsessed about them, and maybe that was the key to his brilliance.

It made him a crappy boyfriend, though. Maybe that was the tradeoff.

"You're a bit of a flake, Simon. Anyone ever tell you that?" Alex said.

"You, all the time." Simon smiled.

She examined him. This Simon was a stranger in some ways, but one she felt a great deal of exasperated affection toward. Not the giddy rush of emotions she'd felt when they'd first met, but something gentler, yet durable.

Maybe she'd had too much wine and was feeling too beneficent and expansive. Maybe it was past time she found her way across London back to her hotel. She set down her glass.

"It's late," she said. "I should get back to my hotel."

Simon and Alex exchanged glances. "How long are you here?" Simon asked.

"Just until Sunday." Two more days.

Another glance. She thought Alex nodded, barely perceptible.

"You can stay with us," Simon said. "We've got the space. It's not fancy, but we can save you the hotel cost, at least."

"I couldn't," she said. "Thank you, but I don't want to inconvenience you."

"No inconvenience," Alex said. "Simon's got the play in the evenings, but it's not as though either of us have day jobs. We could show you around."

She paused, aware every fiber of her being wanted to take them up on their offer. There was nothing but genuine good feeling in their faces.

"We'll go to your hotel with you and pick up your bags," Simon said. He got to his feet.

It was something about that, how Simon was treating it as though the decision had already been made, that settled her mind. "Okay. Thank you."

Simon grinned, genuinely pleased, and she felt warmth flood over her.

Simon's room smelled like him, like lemon and thyme and all kinds of good things. It reminded her of the nights spent in his hotel room, the nights he slept over at her apartment, and that made her a little wistful, because Charlotte was in his bedroom and he was asleep on the couch in the living room.

She sat up, wide awake, the impact of being in a strange room, strange city, strange country flooding over her. The rain had returned sometime during the night and pounded at the window. The room was chilly, though she was warm under the cocoon of blankets. Simon, on the couch, couldn't be as comfortable.

She got to her feet. Opened the door silently. Alex's bedroom door was closed, the light off. Good.

She padded barefoot out to the living room, feet cold on the wood floor.

The living room was empty. Simon had made a big show of taking his blanket and pillow out to the sofa, but they weren't there now. Neither was Simon.

She stood in the middle of the dark room for a long moment, then looked at Alex's closed bedroom door.

She sat down on the sofa and thought.

Charlotte liked Camille right away. Maybe she shouldn't like Camille so much, because she had a sneaky hunch Camille was Simon's new girlfriend, even if no one—not Simon, not Camille, not Alex—had said anything definitive about it. The four of them were at a pub, post-performance. Camille's face was clean and shiny, scrubbed of all her stage makeup. Charlotte was drinking ale, because she thought she should, considering the setting, and her third pint sat on a coaster—pub mat—in front of her.

Camille drank red wine. They were at a rickety wood table by themselves while Alex and Simon stood at the bar across the room, talking to a cluster of guys they both seemed to know. Charlotte glanced over at them. Their heads were close together, shoulders shaking with laughter at something someone had said. Simon looked happy, if somewhat blurry, having a fine night out with his mates. While his ex-girlfriend entertained herself with his new girlfriend. Which wasn't at all awkward, not one bit.

Seeing Camille in person, she could forgive the message board girls for mistaking her for Charlotte in the photos of her strolling about London with Simon. Camille was a small-featured blonde with a slight build. Simon clearly had a type. She wore a large belted oatmeal-colored sweater with a shawl collar and bell sleeves.

Shoulder-length honeysuckle hair pulled back in a thin leather headband. She had pale blue eyes, thin lips, and a nice smile. She was being determinedly kind and friendly to Charlotte. Charlotte was doing the same.

Camille smiled at her. Bright and welcoming. "You're an actress too, aren't you? I believe that's what Simon told me."

"Yes. I was in that film with him. Just a small part."

Camille smiled and nodded. "Did you come here to see him?"

This was an important question, disguised behind an air of practiced English nonchalance. She considered and then decided to go for honesty over polite fiction. Maybe ale made her honest. Maybe that was its secret power. "Yeah, I did."

Camille smiled again and didn't say anything. Another swig of that truth-bringing ale, and Charlotte was ready to ask questions. "Are you with him now? I mean, are you and Simon a couple?"

"I think so." Camille blushed, as though she was embarrassed she couldn't offer up a more definitive answer. "We haven't talked about it much, but ever since the play started. . ." She glanced over at the bar, at Simon and Alex. She cleared her throat. "Were you with him? Back in Los Angeles?"

"Yes. At least, I thought so." Charlotte exhaled. "Simon's a great guy. I'm sure you know that."

Part of her wanted to leave it at that. Part of her wanted to avoid any appearance of being petty or vindictive, now that Simon had moved on. Part of her felt petty and vindictive. And part of her wished someone had been around to tell her what she was going to tell Camille. Would she have listened, or would she have been too smitten with Simon to care? "I don't know if it will matter to you, or if it should matter, but he just. . . kind of left me. He didn't really say anything about it. He kind of broke up with me over the phone, I guess, but not really. And then he left the country before I could ask him about it. So I guess I came here to find out why." She shrugged. "I don't think I'd get an answer, even if I sat him down and asked him directly. Which I don't think I'm going to do. I don't think it matters much anymore. But. . . I thought you should know."

Camille stared at her. It was impossible to tell what she was thinking. Her little speech probably hadn't been terribly coherent. She nodded once and twirled her glass by the stem. She looked over at the bar. "Are he and Alex involved, do you know? Together, I mean?"

Charlotte felt a small surge of something inside her, relief maybe, that someone else had guessed this. "Yeah. Maybe. I don't know for sure. He hasn't said anything about it."

Camille nodded. "Seems like something he might have mentioned while you were together."

"It certainly does. Seems like something he might have mentioned to you, too." She picked up her pint glass and, on a whim, clinked it against Camille's glass. A little ale sloshed out the top. Hand-eye coordination wasn't all it could be. Maybe she was getting drunk. Maybe that explained why she felt warm and happy and melancholy all at once.

Simon glanced over at their table. Charlotte caught his eye. He looked somewhat uncomfortable at seeing them together. Well, good. Maybe he had reason to be uncomfortable.

She was feeling kindly, though, so she raised her pint glass at him in a salute. He smiled at her, the faint worry leaving his face.

Her heart fluttered, just a little. Not as much as it used to, but still, there it was. Would there ever come a day when the sight of Simon wouldn't unhinge her, just a little?

She smiled back at him and mentally said goodbye.

## CHAPTER THIRTY-SIX

ANGIE'S NEW OFFICES were in a suite on a high floor in one of the historic old Art Deco buildings in the mid-Wilshire area. As far as Charlotte knew, there weren't any other production companies in the area. Maybe Angie would start a trend.

Charlotte pushed open the door with the edge of the cardboard tray, careful not to dislodge the coffee cups. "Success," she said.

"Hallelujah. I'm ready for a break." Angie stepped down off the stepladder and replaced the roller brush in the paint tray. The walls, drab white this morning, were now the color of cherry pie filling. It looked good, bright and glossy and cheerful. A plastic drop cloth was draped over entire floor, covering the conference table in the middle of the room. The windows were cranked open, letting out the paint fumes and letting in the breeze. A bright blue sky and fluffy white clouds framed the steeple of the Korean church across the street.

Charlotte set the coffees and the paper bag down on the table. "That one's yours. Two cream, two sugars," she said.

"Thanks, hon. You shouldn't have to fetch coffee."

She shrugged. "It wasn't going to fetch itself." She opened up the bag. "Roast beef and grilled vegetables on French rolls. I thought they looked good. You eat meat, right?"

"I surely do. Sounds fantastic."

The chairs hadn't been moved in yet, so they sat on the conference table, on a clean area of the drop cloth. Angie wore a tank top and cutoffs. Her shoulders looked broad and powerful. Her right bicep was smeared with red paint. She glanced around the room and took a bite of her sandwich.

"If we finish this today, it'll be dry by Monday. The movers will be bringing in the furniture and the copier then, and I'd just as soon have everything ready to go."

"It looks great. It's a good space," Charlotte said. "You should have plenty of room."

Angie nodded. "So you know how I said I wanted to talk to you about this project I'm developing?"

Charlotte nodded and waited. As nice as it was to see Angie, this was what she was really here for. Angie probably figured she wasn't donating her Saturday to painting her new offices just out of generosity.

"There's a script I'm really excited about. I'll have to email you a copy. Two girls—women, I guess, but girls from my perspective—sent it to me when I was still with the studio. First thing they've ever written, and it's great. Drama, women's issues, great character piece. The kind of film that just doesn't get made much anymore. It got lost in development there, and now the option has expired, so I might have a chance to push it through." She peeled back the plastic lid of her coffee and took a drink. "Anyway, there's a small part in there—supporting, but a lot more screen time than you had in *Angels*—that I think might be great for you. You'd be playing a welfare mom in Kansas City with a meth habit. Something you can really sink your teeth into."

It sounded vaguely awful, and a lot less fun than playing a killer robot, but until she saw the script, she wouldn't pass judgment. "Sounds great."

"I'm still lining up financing, and we're a ways away from this becoming a reality. Plenty of time for it all to go egg-shaped, but. . ." Angie shrugged. "I'm optimistic."

"Okay, cool. Keep me posted. Thanks for thinking of me."

"Thanks for being such a dream to work with on *Angels*. Made all of our lives just a little bit easier. I'd hire you again any day."

That wasn't quite the same as being hired for her once-in-a-lifetime talent or blazing charisma, but she appreciated the sentiment anyway. "Can I ask, why'd the studio fire you? It seemed odd, since the film did pretty well."

Angie considered. "I don't know. Maybe because I annoyed some people. Maybe because our second-week box office dropped sixty percent. Maybe just as simple as that. Doesn't really matter, since it wasn't anything I could control. It was time for me to go off on my own, anyway. Why'd Harris Holt fire you?"

"I don't know. I don't think he liked me very much."

Angie glanced over at her. "You're not obsessing about it, are you?"

"Only sometimes." She chewed her sandwich. It had soft herbed cheese on it, and the roll was pleasantly crusty. "Do you think there's such a thing as star quality?"

Angie thought for a moment. "No. I really don't. I think there's talent, and there's instinct, and sex appeal, and good PR people, and maybe if you have all these things in the right proportions, someone's going to call it star quality. Are you wondering about yourself?"

Charlotte shrugged. "Not really. Thinking more about Simon, I guess. Not even that, really. Just something I've been curious about in general."

"Simon." Angie took a drink of her coffee. "If I thought there was such a thing as star quality, I'd say that Simon has it in abundance. And I'd say most of our audience for *Angels* would disagree with me on that. As our leading man, he turned out to be a bit of a dud." She considered. "Talented guy, though. Beautiful, too. Maybe he just needed a different project to help him catch the fancy of the viewing public."

Charlotte paused. "Did you tell Simon to ask me out?" she asked. "Do you know if he was ever really interested in me?"

"Oh, hon, I don't know. I would assume so. I planted the idea that you were interested in him in his head. The rest he did on his own. Was it a bad thing? I thought you two were cute together."

Charlotte shook her head. "We had a good time. We're friends. Or friendly, at least. He's coming out here next month."

"To visit, or to stay?"

"I don't think he knows," Charlotte said. "He wants to give it another shot. Hollywood, I mean."

Angie shook her head. "Good luck with that. Hell of an industry. Hell of a town."

Charlotte looked out the window, out at the buildings lining Wilshire. "I like it, though. Most of the time."

"Yeah, me too. Most of the time. A day like today, with good food and good company, would be one of those times." Angie raised her coffee cup at her. "You're a good person, Charlotte Dent. With or without Simon, with or without acting jobs, doesn't make a difference. You'll come out all right. It's who you are."

The words were meaningless, or pretty close to it, and yet hearing them still made her feel better. Funny how that worked.

Rick and Ted had picked out the place. It was a jazz club on Pico. Small, one room with brick walls and a low red-painted ceiling. Red velvet drapes giving the illusion of privacy around the booths at the back. They were seated at a rickety wood table, picking at baskets of onion rings and fried crawfish. The guys drank whiskey and soda; she'd already endured a round of mockery for her champagne cocktail, but it seemed like a champagne kind of evening.

A chanteuse warbled something in the spotlight on the tiny stage. She wasn't very good, but she was lovely, with huge eyes and a great deal of cleavage, and that made up for a lot.

"How long have you two known each other?" Charlotte asked Ted and Rick.

Rick shrugged. "Forever, I suppose. We went to the same elementary school in Inglewood."

"Always wanted to be in the film industry," Ted said. "I was the creative one, Rick wanted to do the business side of things. Always thought we'd get together and take over the world that way."

"Or at least make a whole bunch of movies we wanted to see," Rick said. Ted grinned and clinked his glass against Rick's.

"Speaking of, you gotta start finding some work for our girl Charlotte there. She hasn't worked since that Holt thing went south."

"Yes. Thank you for reminding me of that, Ted," she said.

Ted shrugged. "It was kind of a crummy role for you, anyway. Rick should have talked them into letting you play Lana. There's a part you could've done wonders with." He settled back in his chair. "Friend of mine at the studio saw a rough cut last week with a bunch of the suits. Buzz on Paragon's performance is really strong. They've pushed back the release until next fall, just so they'll be better positioned for Oscar nominations."

"God help us all," Charlotte said.

Ted grinned. "Jealous?"

"Surprisingly little, actually." She considered telling Ted about the puddle of urine Paragon had left in her car, then thought better of it.

"Charlotte doesn't need to be jealous. Charlotte can act the socks off of some pop singer." Rick raised his glass at her in a quick salute. "Don't worry about Charlotte. She's going to have the world at her feet."

"I should do a sequel," Ted said dreamily. "*Queen of Angels 2*. Get the whole gang back together again. That was fun."

"You'd have a hard time getting me for it. I smashed into a million pieces in the first one, remember?"

"We'll bring you back. Fanboys hate me enough for the changes I made from the source already, we'll make a few more. Jin gets superglued back together, it'll work. I'm going to start working on this right away." He looked determined, but Charlotte knew this was one of the hundreds of leads that would never go anywhere. Ah, well. Maybe Angie's script would go somewhere, or maybe it wouldn't. Out of the hundreds or thousands of possibilities out there, one would go somewhere, sometime, and then she'd work again.

"Hey, either of you know any good acting classes?" she asked. "I'm specifically looking for ones that don't suck."

"If you're going to put those kinds of restrictions on it, no," Ted said.

Rick considered. "I know a few, maybe. I'll ask around. Not a bad idea. You looking to get your name out there?"

"I'm looking to get better. Maybe I'll do some kind of graduate program."

Rick shrugged. "Get your MFA, that's two years of your life when you could be working pretty much gone. You sure you'd want to do that?"

"I just want to make sure I know what I'm doing. I don't know. It's a thought." She looked at her watch. "I should get going."

Rick snorted. "Plenty of time. You only have to arrive at the airport two hours before international flights if you're catching one, not meeting one."

"I know. But there might be traffic. I don't want to leave Simon hanging around Customs." She got to her feet and gathered her purse.

"All right. Give Simon my best," Ted said. He motioned for her to lean down and gave her a quick kiss on the cheek. Rick got her other side.

"Are you and Simon back together?" Rick asked.

"No," she said.

"You going to get back together?"

"Seems very unlikely." She shrugged. "Never say never, I guess. But. . . it's probably fair to say never."

"If you don't mind me saying so, I hope you make it work. You two are real cute together. And you look happy right now."

"I'm happy. It'll be good to see him. We're friends. Or we could be, at some point."

She left the club. It was a warm winter night, muggy after the air-conditioned club. The city looked pretty, though, with tall palms silhouetted against a violet sky. Even the dingy storefronts along Pico looked better at night, when she couldn't see the peeling paint and barred windows. There was a band of orange against the horizon, caused by the city lights mingling with the smog; it was unnatural, but kind of pretty. Winds from the east brought the smell of jasmine, undercut with sour milk.

She had plenty of time to get to the airport. She'd drive south through the fields of oil wells surrounding La Cienega, windows down. She'd retrieve Simon from LAX before he had a chance to get lost and bewildered, then they'd go for a late dinner somewhere, or maybe she'd drop him straight off at his hotel if he was feeling discombobulated and fatigued from transcontinental travel. And then they'd take it from there. Tomorrow morning she had an audition for a hand lotion commercial, and Simon had a lunch appointment with his agent, but the afternoon would be all theirs.

And then. . . there was no use planning beyond that. She'd see what happened when it arrived.

## ACKNOWLEDGMENTS

MY AUNT ELSBETH Monnett painted the amazing cover portrait of my beautiful cousin Katie Heaslet; they both have my gratitude for their kind permission to use it. Thanks are also due to Morgan Dodge and Dan Liebke for their encouragement, and to my parents, now gone and sorely missed, for loving me and loving *Charlotte*. As always, my biggest thanks are reserved for my sister, Ingrid Richter, for sacrificing her time and energy these past few years to give me a greater opportunity to write up a storm. It's long past time for me to return the favor.

## ABOUT THE AUTHOR

A GRADUATE OF the screenwriting program at the University of Southern California's film school, Morgan Richter has worked in production on several TV shows, including *Talk Soup* and *America's Funniest Home Videos*, and has contributed pop culture reviews and essays to websites such as TVgasm and Forces of Geek, as well as to her own site, Preppies of the Apocalypse. She is the owner of Luft Books, an independent publishing company, and the author of *Bias Cut*, *Charlotte Dent*, *Lonely Satellite*, *Preppies of the Apocalypse*, *Demon City*, and *Wrong City*. *Bias Cut* won a silver medal at the 2013 Independent Publisher Book Awards and was a 2012 semi-finalist for the Amazon Breakthrough Novel Award (ABNA). *Charlotte Dent* was a 2008 ABNA semi-finalist; *Lonely Satellite* was a 2014 ABNA quarter-finalist. Born and raised in Spokane, Washington, she currently lives in New York City.

www.ingramcontent.com/pod-product-compliance
Lightning Source LLC
Chambersburg PA
CBHW032144190626
46814CB00005BA/1824